WEAPONFORGER

BY D.A. GODWIN

Guardian's Prophecy
Book One: Eyes of the Blind
Book Two: Hunter's Moon
Book Three: Weaponforger

WEAPONFORGER

GUARDIAN'S PROPHECY: BOOK THREE

By

D.A. Godwin

For Kay,
who said yes

www.dagodwin.com

FIRST EDITION

Edited by Marissa van Uden
Cover and Interior Art by David Godwin

ISBN 978-1-7328617-5-6

CONTENTS

CONTENTS

The Kingdom of Actondel

The Wildlands

Westholm

Ironwood

Evermen's Forge

Kirchmont

Verone

Ronse   Viaden   Anovin

Ceringion Reginum

Tirtdon

Fallhaven

Wiermist

Saxalm

Orthonia

Kenzing

Bexville

Durbris

Jonrin

Sandenmill

Bendin

Haltsford   Glint   Braunton   Calvia

Merrywood

Actondel

Small Sea

Ildalarial

Gyland   Kendenhall

Harlma   Iscar

Terent   Duraco

Lisiria

Locksall

Rexford

Orcaster

Briggenwell

Tornton

Adair

Shirath

Namarin

Merallin

Sereburn

Lightpoint

Dwarf Clans

Rossian Sea

Highfall

Chapter One

Resurgence

The wizard made his way down the stone stairs, spiraling ever deeper into the inky darkness. Only the soft pad of his footsteps disturbed the silence, just as the torch in his hand provided the only flicker of light. The need for such a base form of illumination was unfortunate, but it would, ironically, attract less notice than any use of magic. The consequences if he were to be discovered this night were best not considered.

The constant circling of the stairwell left him dizzy by the time it came to an abrupt end, depositing him in the middle of a long corridor that faded into curtains of darkness in either direction. After a furtive glance over his shoulder, he turned left. The air this far underground was cool and surprisingly dry, but it did nothing to prevent the beads of perspiration that began to form on his brow. Heavy iron doors without windows broke the smoothly chiseled, colorless walls of the hallway at regular intervals, their recessed entrances gaping like mouths ready to swallow whole any passerby who came too close. Wealth, power, and mystery lay hidden behind each, locked away by methods both magical and mundane.

Tonight, however, their wonderous contents held no allure.

After two hundred and thirty-seven carefully measured steps he came to a stop before a doorway that looked exactly like all the others he had passed. With caution he approached and placed a delicate finger into the thin groove between door and wall, careful to avoid any contact with the handle. The protections here were said to be impenetrable, and he believed it, but even the best locks were useless on a door already open. This one remained the slightest bit ajar, exactly as he had left it.

His pulse quickened as he wiggled the tip of his finger in as far as it would go and, with a silent prayer to Myrastus, the Keeper of Magics, gave a gentle tug.

The heavy door resisted such a feeble effort, but it moved just enough for him to work another finger in and gain more leverage. He repeated this pattern several times, carefully working in more fingers until the seal cracked with a silent puff of air.

A shiver of triumph ran up his spine as the door swung noiselessly open. Once across the threshold he pulled the door almost closed behind him. Though his torchlight failed to reveal the entire room, he already knew every detail of what awaited.

He edged his way around the circular chamber, keeping his body close against the wall as he lit the twenty-one torches secured evenly about its circumference. In the final, empty sconce he set his own torch, and turned to survey his work.

Spread across the floor before him lay a series of five narrow, concentric rings surrounding the center of the chamber, each painstakingly rendered from a different powdered substance specific to the purpose it served. Between the smooth lines ran an intricate series of arcane symbols written in the same powder as the ring that contained them. Twenty-one unlit candles surrounded the outer edge, precisely offset with the torches in the wall. Together the inscriptions and rings formed a summoning circle capable of containing even the strongest of creatures.

The wizard smiled as he looked upon it: the culmination of years of study and unwavering perseverance.

Though his time was limited, he reviewed the alignment and shape of each symbol meticulously. He expected no errors—everything had been inspected by a ranking Summoner—but any flaw could be catastrophic. Summoning was an unforgiving art.

Both room and circle had been prepared for his use the following day when he was to stand for the first of three trials that, once completed, would see him in command of a demonic servant of his own. Tonight, however, was about neither title nor servant; it was about knowledge. Knowledge that would further accelerate his already rapid rise within the most dominant order of wizards on the continent: the Conclave of Imaretii.

He allowed himself a moment to reflect on his purpose.

Nearly three years prior, shortly after his confirmation to full membership within the organization, he had been ordered to clean a room in the north tower. A menial task better suited for servants or apprentices, he believed it either a deliberate slight or a punishment for some unknown transgression. He had rebelled at the assignment, but his protests had fallen on deaf ears. The mess was an experiment gone awry, he was told, and the aftereffects would serve as a cautionary lesson on the limits of power. This was plausible, given which master's tower had been damaged, yet once inside he quickly grew suspicious of that explanation. The damage he beheld was extensive and bore the marks of an intentional rampage rather than an accident. Even more curious were the signs that other restorative efforts were already taking place.

The scrap of paper he discovered had been a revelation. Left on an emptied shelf, as if meant to be found, it contained a single word written in a hasty hand. An unusual word—a name—but one unlike that of any civilized tongue he had studied. So strange a moniker in that context could only belong to a demon, and its placement amidst the destruction could not be explained away by coincidence. Such names, critical to the summoning process, were among the most closely guarded secrets in the Conclave and unheard of for one of his rank to possess.

He could tell no one what he suspected, however, so he had memorized and then burned the scrap to ensure no evidence of its existence remained. Then he had waited, confirming his suspicion through countless hours of research, biding his time until he was strong enough to take command of such a creature.

Which was now.

With a wave of his hand he lit the candles at precisely the same instant—an important factor in establishing the protective ward's strength. The flames swayed in unison, and he allowed them to steady before aligning himself just outside the outermost ring of the circle.

He began the incantation in a low, steady voice. The spell of summoning was short but the words complicated, and the rise and fall of every syllable was precisely timed. The final sound to pass his lips was the name he had discovered on that scrap of paper: *Mataasrhu.*

Time stretched uncomfortably long into the silence, to the

point he began to doubt his accuracy in the casting. Then a mote of intense darkness manifested in the center of the circle. It was silent and without substance, yet occupied a physical presence that far outweighed its size. Tendrils of purple-black smoke stretched and pulled, tearing the air apart and distorting the fabric of reality as they expanded to form a swirling void.

His concern mounted as the mists billowed and twisted, pressing outward until they filled the innermost circle and obscured the looming shadow that approached from within. Large arms solidified, attached to a massive chest. Hooved legs the size of tree trunks took shape, followed by wings contorted to fit within the confines of the room. The entirety of its skin was a dark brownish-red, and a mantle of thick, dark fur covered its shoulders and wrapped its waist like a loincloth. The wings curled back and tucked themselves together behind the creature, revealing a squarish head set with eyes that burned red beneath a ridged brow knit together in a deep furrow.

The wizard could scarcely believe what he had accomplished. Before him stood a greater demon, a creature of near myth that would confer enormous prestige to the one who controlled it. Caution overrode exhilaration, and he quickly squashed any sense of pride. Maintaining control would be matter of focus and willpower, and in this aspect of his studies he had excelled.

"Greetings, mighty Mataasrhu," he said, using a tone appropriate for a valued inferior.

Mataasrhu ignored him and surveyed the chamber, his eyes taking note of everything in it.

"I thank you for coming this evening," the wizard continued. "Though you may fear that I have called you into servitude, such is not my intent."

Mataasrhu snorted in disdain and glared at him with an almost tangible malevolence.

The wizard chose to disregard the look. He could already feel the creature pressing against the wards that contained it, testing. Best to get on with it.

"Tonight, I desire from you only knowledge. Knowledge of whose failure resulted in the destruction wrought upon the north tower three years ago. I bid you reveal to me the events of that night."

The demon could not speak, of course, but there were spells that would allow a mental image to be shared between the creature and himself. It was a simple incantation, one that he mouthed now almost without thought.

In answer, the demon's hand shot towards him, crashing into the invisible boundary of the circle and sending angry red sparks streaking about the inside of the dome that enclosed it.

The wizard winced as his mind absorbed the blow, erasing the glowing cracks that had appeared in the air between them. It had nearly gotten through.

"You are summoned and bound," he commanded. "You must answer!"

Mataasrhu's lips curled, baring teeth as large as daggers.

"My friend does not wish to speak to you."

The wizard jumped in surprise at the soft voice that seemed to come from behind the demon.

From the swirling mists at the creature's back, a second, smaller figure emerged and slid to the side, stopping just inside the boundary of the circle's protection. It looked like a man, though he was wrapped in snug garments stitched from unfamiliar hides, and his face was hidden deep within a cowl. A sword and knife were belted around his waist, but his stance was relaxed and his hands made no move towards his weapons.

The wizard licked his lips nervously.

"You are not summoned," he stated with all the force he could muster. "You may not come."

"May I not?" the stranger asked in a manner that was terrifyingly conversational. "Then I'll intrude no further."

As smooth as a cat stalking its prey, the man stretched one leg outside the rings inscribed on the floor, taking care not to disturb any of the symbols.

The wizard sucked in his breath as a cold bead of sweat trickled down his neck. "You cannot leave the circle."

"*He* cannot leave the circle," the man corrected from where he stood straddling the protective rings. His shadowed head turned back to the demon, who regarded him silently. "Which hardly seems fair."

The wizard stood frozen in horror as the stranger pulled his back foot from within the circle, slowly dragging a line through the markings with his toe.

"No! You'll kill us all!" He sought to conjure an attack, but his mind stumbled and the words would not come fast enough.

The torches and candles were snuffed the instant the final circle was broken, plunging the room into absolute darkness. The last thing the wizard saw was the malicious grin spreading beneath the demon's burning red eyes.

He died so fast there was not even time to scream.

Mataasrhu savored the lingering traces of power that drifted like embers from the wizard's broken corpse. It had been far too long since he had tasted one of the despised Imaretii, and though this one had been small the sensation remained quite satisfying.

There was nothing else that pleased him about the situation, however. He was hunched over and uncomfortable, squeezed into a space more suited for a smaller being. He knew where he was, and knew as well that this chamber had not been prepared for him, which meant the wizard had not anticipated his size—probably one of their cursed students.

He shuffled around to face the stranger, who had yet to move. Though it remained pitch black in the chamber, neither needed light to see the other.

"You swore that you told no one!" Mataasrhu hissed in deep tones that could be felt as much as heard.

"And so I did not," the man replied, his voice laced with its usual smug humor. "Perhaps he divined your name through some mystic vision."

"He was pitiful and inept," Mataasrhu countered with a contemptuous snort. "No, it was provided to him."

Mataasrhu had somehow been outsmarted but could not fathom how it had been accomplished. There would have been signs of any contact, and he would have been made aware of any messages that were sent, but there had been nothing. The mystery made him angrier than being summoned to begin with, as he now felt trapped more surely than if the wizard's feeble prison was still in place.

"What now for us, then?" he asked spitefully. "Shall we wreak havoc upon this miserable place once more?"

"I have more pressing needs at the moment. Though I've

enjoyed our time together, I believe we have our own paths to walk." The man's dark eyes met Mataasrhu's in a penetrating stare. "We owe each other nothing."

Mataasrhu scowled. This would set his plans back significantly, but he could see no alternative. Here, he was no longer in control.

"Hunt well, then, Veluntrhu," he said sullenly, sliding back into the mists that still swirled in the middle of the circle. "We shall meet again, you and I."

The man bowed as Mataasrhu faded away but never dropped his gaze from the mists as they collapsed inwards. When they had winked from existence, he turned his attention to the wizard's body, or at least what was left of it.

"'Never summon from an untrusted source,'" he quoted with a mocking shake of his head.

He produced a small flame in the palm of his hand, then sent it spinning about the chamber to relight the candles and torches. Next he worked to restore the symbols in the circle. When he was satisfied that things were exactly the way they needed to be, he walked from the room, closing the door fully behind him.

"Now to find her."

Chapter Two

A Journey Resumed

Fendrick rested a meaty hand on the anvil, taking one last look around the forge that had served as home and workshop for many years longer than expected. He had created so many things on that anvil, coaxing iron and steel into forms both practical and appealing. Most were mundane, a few exceptional, and one… that one had been special.

It was quiet this early in the morning, the street outside devoid of the frenetic bustle of activity that would greet the new day. He tugged at his shirt, resisting the urge to remove it and set himself to work. His tools were all packed away, or at least the ones he was not leaving behind.

He took a poker in hand and absently stirred the banked coals. If it were only possessions he was walking away from, it would not bother him so much. But this forge like the one before it had served their purpose: he had been left alone for almost thirty years. No one thought twice about a dwarf owning a smithy, any more than they cared about elves frolicking in the woods.

"Don't worry, Master Fendrick, it's in good hands," Doran

said as he returned with an armful of the day's work. "I'll do right by all you've taught me."

Fendrick put away his sour expression and turned to the other smith. Doran was a serious-looking man with big shoulders and a bigger commitment to his craft. His beard would never be as impressive as Fendrick's, but it was respectable enough.

"I know you will, lad," Fendrick said with a sigh. It was unfair to consider Doran his apprentice anymore—the man had worked for and with him for over fifteen years—but he supposed he would never be able shake the concept. Doran was close to thirty and as capable a blacksmith as any human could hope to be, but everyone was a child to Fendrick. "It's hard to leave, no matter the reason. Still haven't finished all the work."

"Do we ever?"

"I suppose you'll be raising the anvil up at last?"

Doran chuckled. "I might, just to save my back from bending over that far."

"Well, before you go making changes, don't forget about that hole in the second chimney I've never fixed. And the bellows is near to needing replaced. Surena knows I'm going, of course, and she'll continue to…"

Fendrick chose to ignore the bemused smile that crept onto Doran's face as his list of instructions grew longer.

"…a watch on Luggan. That thief'll try to rob you blind with his iron prices."

The sound of someone politely clearing their throat caused both of them to turn. A youthful acolyte in the habit of Amalthee was standing in the open doorway.

Fendrick frowned. "And put a door on that blasted hole in the wall that everyone keeps walking through."

Doran laughed and extended his hand. "Best of luck to you."

Fendrick shook it, knowing that luck would be the last thing he would need.

Thoroughly unhappy, he faced the acolyte, who bowed.

"Good morning, Master Hammerstrike."

Fendrick hated being called that. "I can find my way there, and the appointed time hasn't passed. Did Nathan think I'd get lost along the way?"

"Our Patriarch instructed me to offer any assistance you might need."

"Good. Take this and make yourself useful." Fendrick shoved the lightest of the three sacks of equipment he was bringing into the boy's arms. The unprepared acolyte struggled to stay upright beneath the bag that weighed nearly as much as he did.

"What's your name?" Fendrick asked as he shouldered two other bags that were heavier still.

"Talley," the acolyte grunted, leaning against a wall for support.

"Well, Talley, let's move along. We'll go straight up the hill so it's a shorter walk."

Talley managed a terrified squeak as he teetered his way out the door behind Fendrick.

There were more or less two ways to reach the abbey of Amalthee, located at the top of the hill near the physical and political center of the city of Kirchmont: a long, gentle climb through an array of zig-zag thoroughfares or a more direct path that would take them up a series of steep stairs and side streets. Fendrick had elected the latter. He should have left earlier rather than dawdle around the forge, but some goodbyes did not need to be rushed.

His frown deepened. Setting the forge right was not the only reason for his delay, and he knew it. He pressed a hand against his side, feeling his most precious possession tucked firmly beneath his vest, and fought against the lump that formed suddenly in his throat. The trouble with making special things is that people remembered you had done it, and eventually they came back asking for something more.

"Come on, Talley," he said gruffly to take his mind off it. "We don't want to keep the good Father waiting. There's a lad. Keep your head up and breathe deep."

The buildings grew in size, crowding ever closer as they made their way up the hill, and the streets became more neatly kept despite the increasing traffic. It took more time than it should have, but they finally reached the market square that lay outside the abbey walls.

The large, open plaza bustled with all its usual activity. Merchants hawked their wares with boisterous enthusiasm from stalls around the edges and carts scattered throughout the middle. Costumed fools juggled or sang for anyone in the crowds who would give them attention. The expanse swirled with color and motion, mocking the thick, grey clouds which hovered low in the sky. Several people who knew him called out in greeting, and he answered with a wave or friendly word as he walked past. None of the well-wishers would be here when he returned—if he returned at all—but that was no reason to spoil their day.

A short stone wall set with columns at regular intervals marked the edge of the abbey compound. Only a single gate permitted access to the inside where long, rectangular buildings four-stories tall sat aside a towering cathedral that soared high above the surrounding city. The arched gateway was guarded by more than just statues of the Lady of Knowledge now. Men in chain hauberks flanked either side of the entryway. The heads of their polearms were polished to a ceremonial shine and the blue sashes they wore over their mail coats were equally pristine, but Fendrick took note that the edges of the weapons were as sharp as any sword, and that both men stood alert, aware of everything happening around them.

Fendrick gave both statues and guards a suspicious glance as he and Talley passed between them. He paid little mind to the beautifully terraced gardens which lay beyond, instead focusing on the collection of grey-haired priests impatiently awaiting them beside a large fountain in the center of the courtyard.

It had been years since he had seen the abbot, but it was not hard to separate Nathan from the other men. In contrast to their plain brown robes, Nathan's were of a deep blue edged in gold thread at the wrists. A short shoulder-cloak of white was draped about him, perfectly framing the polished gold symbol of Amalthee secured around his neck by an equally weighty gold chain.

Nathan's cleanly shaven face looked disapprovingly down at Fendrick as the dwarf approached. He did a lot of looking down now, from what Fendrick had heard.

"We had hoped you would arrive earlier," Nathan said by way of greeting. "Though the days continue to lengthen, you have a long journey ahead, and the rains will slow your travel."

Fendrick motioned over his shoulder to where an exhausted Talley had dropped his bag and was being helped away by his fellow acolytes. "We had to make more stops than I'd expected."

"Acolytes of Amalthee are not pack animals," Nathan chastised.

"He said he was there to help."

"It was a courtesy. How do you expect to take all of this with you?"

"Buy another mule, you've got the money."

That drew unhappy mutterings from the other priests. The wealthy never appreciated suggestions on how they should spend their wealth, and wealthy priests appreciated it even less.

Nathan, however, remained unperturbed. "There are plenty of mules, as you specified. I might have considered horses more appropriate for the distance."

"Mules'll keep their footing better. Is everyone ready?"

"They await you in the stables. If you require assistance with…"

"Don't worry," Fendrick said as he hefted Talley's bag onto his shoulder aside the other two. "I've got it."

Chapter Three

Reunion

Shalindra brushed aside the strand of blond hair dangling in her vision and rubbed absently at the ache in her forehead, wishing she were somewhere more cheerful. The wooden seat she so uncomfortably occupied did nothing to change that attitude. It had been her cousin Edward's campaign chair during the war, and stood out as the most ornate furnishing in the large hall, whose high ceiling and lack of adornment on the stone walls lent a hollow echo to the conversation she should have been listening to. Even the long table on which she propped her elbow lacked the usual carvings and finish expected of a proper keep. Though it had to be past midday by now, only thin shafts of light from windows set high along the walls pierced the dimness, their narrow openings better suited to defense than an open view.

Her blue eyes sought an escape through those windows which her body was denied. The sun shone bright for the first time in months, and the skies were blessedly clear. Patches of snow clung stubbornly to the trio of peaks known as the Three Sisters, though the trees along their lower slopes already displayed hints of the lush greenness that spring would bring. She shivered in spite of the warmth from cheerful fires that burned inside the hearths set on either side of the hall.

Her headaches were becoming more frequent. At first, she had considered them merely a product of stress, which was never in short supply. Though winters always took longer to recede this high in the mountains, this one had lasted longer than any she could remember. The rains that followed came as heavy as they were early, leaving the soil too soft and wet for planting. It had been a struggle trying to keep everyone together, and alive.

As if frequent headaches were not bad enough, the nightmares had begun a week ago—incoherent images of unfamiliar roads and mountains mixed with pain and swirling darkness that woke her in a cold sweat. Many would fade as dreams must before the approaching dawn, while others lingered, haunting her throughout the day no matter what task she set her mind to.

From halfway down the table Enna noticed her discomfort and shot her a questioning look, her elvish eyes sparkling green even in the dim light. Enna noticed everything. Though the only elf in the room, her impossibly straight, pristinely white hair caused her to stand out more than her small stature and upswept ears. She wore the same white robes befitting a Sister of Eluria as Shalindra did, save that Enna's were sleeveless in the custom of her people despite the chill in the air.

The six other men and women seated around the table continued to debate some matter that almost certainly warranted far less discussion than it was taking. Two men were notably absent: her cousin, Edward, the dispossessed heir to the white tower of Tarrendale, was patrolling the southern end of the valley, and Birion, former knight and architect of Tiridon's defenses, who had abandoned his command rather than serve the victorious Ceringions, still abed as he recovered from the fever that had ravaged the village. Their absence left her isolated at one end of the table.

Sister Marie, the dark-haired and olive-skinned cleric of Eluria who had once safeguarded Shining Moon, the holy warhammer carried by Eluria's Guardians, was speaking again. The sultry tones of her accent held the attention of everyone in attendance, though she was doing nothing more than describe the progress that had been made on Eluria's temple. Shalindra's thoughts drifted once more, as she already knew what would be said. The new dormitory wing would be completed within the month, just in time for the annual influx of summer pilgrims. Elvish followers of the moon goddess, 'Elurithlia' in their tongue, had been making the dangerous trek to this valley for generations, but their numbers had dwindled to almost nothing while the goblins claimed the remote location for their own. Many of the current structures Shalindra's people now occupied had been built over goblin villages, which themselves had been raised atop the original elvish settlements.

Rolf was talking now, about some triviality that only a farmer would care to listen to. The soil here was rich and the fields ready for the plow when they arrived, but for Rolf there was always something wrong. Shalindra glanced at the empty seat to her right, wishing again that Edward was there to keep the farmer on track.

Jamerson, the grey-haired master architect, finally cut him off and began his own report. "Another vein of whiterock has been located…"

Such a discovery would be good for Eluria's temple, if Honarch could get the rockhurlers to cooperate. The wizard had proven a valuable source of knowledge, and as capable as any at defending their struggling colony, but his former ties to the Conclave of Imaretii were well known and— Something Jamerson said drew enough of a reaction that even Enna sat up and took notice.

"Forgive me, Master Jamerson," Shalindra interrupted. "What was that again?"

"The latest investigation into the mines suggest reserves of both gold and copper," he answered.

'The mines' was a polite way of naming the warren of goblin tunnels dug into the side of the mountain at the north end of the valley behind the towering waterfall at the feet of the Three Sisters. Though no longer home to the creatures, the tunnels were cramped and foul smelling, and it was difficult to get crews to work in them. More than one miner had entered and never returned, though whether they simply became lost or had some evil befall them, none could say.

"That would be good, yes?"

"It would, my lady, though I cannot speak to how soon it can be verified nor what efforts it might take to exploit."

"It could bring treasure seekers down on us from every corner," Fulke cautioned. "This discovery must be kept secret."

Jamerson waved away the suggestion from the former soldier. "Too many people already know, but who are they going to tell?"

"Food should be our priority," Rolf broke in. "It's been a wet season already, and we're behind on the planting. You cannot eat gold, and we've nowhere to spend it." It was, perhaps, the most astute observation Shalindra had ever heard him make.

"I find that sentiment reasonable," she said to cut off any

further arguing. "Master Jamerson, please catalog these discoveries as you are able, but construction and planting remain higher priorities than gold."

Vestus, Edward's purser, leaned his considerable girth forward. "Ah... if I may, Your Highness."

She wished again that everyone would stop using that form of address, but she had long since given up correcting them. Besides, if he felt a need to speak out of turn, it would not be good news. She motioned for him to continue.

"Construction requires workers, and workers not in the fields making food for their families require payment. Most of the coins we use are Kingdom in origin, and many are worn smooth from being passed hand to hand so frequently. At some point, we must give people more than just a promise of safety."

"He speaks truth," Fulke agreed before she could reply. "We all know your reluctance to strike new coins, but it must be done if we're to continue growing."

Shalindra felt a stab of pain in her temple, but whether it was from her headache or the topic of conversation she could not tell. She had been adamantly opposed to having coins stamped, given that those seated around her wished to do so using her own likeness. Being a monarch held little allure—she had not even wanted to be named head of this council—and it also seemed a final and irreversible severing of ties to the family and kingdom she had once known. But they were right, and her head hurt too much to argue the point again.

"Your council is wise, as always. I will leave it to Master Jamerson to determine how best to proceed, but with the planting season upon us, it cannot be..."

She winced in pain and clutched her temples as something dark coiled its way around her mind, squeezing hard enough to make her gasp. Her stomach knotted at the terrifyingly familiar sensation even as her hand sought her symbol of Eluria, and she fought to push the mental assault away. There were no black tentacles or looming mountains of darkness seeking to ensnare her as before, but there was also no mistaking the feeling. The last time she had felt such a thing was when they had been pursued by a demon.

"Are you well, Sister?" Marie asked.

Shalindra put the past out of her mind. Whatever was searching for her now was strong. She could almost feel its approach.

"My dear?" Marie asked again.

Shalindra shook her head. "It knows I am here. Can you not feel it?"

"I feel nothing out of the ordinary," Marie said cautiously. "Our island is warded against—"

Shalindra gave a small cry as the pressure clamped down on her with an almost physical strength. She screwed her eyes shut and staggered to her feet. It knew exactly where she was, in spite of all the protections on this place.

So strong. How is it getting so deep in my mind?

It's outside the room.

Had Enna said that? The elf was already out of her seat and moving towards the door, Eluria's symbol clenched in her delicate hand.

A shouted command came from outside, followed by the sounds of a scuffle that ended abruptly as something heavy thudded against the door.

Ignoring the shocked looks from those seated at the table, Shalindra unlimbered Shining Moon from her belt and rushed to place herself squarely between table and entrance. The sacred hammer came alive in her left hand, sending a comforting warmth surging up her arm and banishing the pressure from her mind.

A swirl of mist, black with tinges of deep purples and reds, manifested at waist height just inside the door. There was an explosion of frantic motion behind her as the councilors scrambled away from it.

"Eluria protect us," Marie said as she came to stand with them.

What emerged was not the expected beast with claws and horns come to kill them. Instead, a man with dark hair shot from the mist and landed squarely, his sword rattling loose in its scabbard as he came to an abrupt halt before the three women. He relaxed as he straightened, and Shalindra's breath caught in her throat when his dark eyes met hers.

Tormjere held his hands up in mock surrender. "I was hoping for a warmer greeting."

He looked the same, but different. His clothes were layered in the elvish pattern of green cloth and tanned leathers he preferred, but all of it appeared new. The intensity of his gaze was precisely as she remembered, as was the short beard around his mouth.

Yet his shoulders where stockier and there was an unfamiliar resistance as she attempted to look into him. If, indeed, it even was him. She regarded him suspiciously and did not lower her weapon.

"Not even a hello?" Tormjere asked, sounding uncharacteristically tired. He affected a nonchalant pose, which allowed his hand to discreetly brush across his sword hilt, seating it fully.

"Who is this?" Rolf cried. "Guards! Guards!"

Marie silenced him with a disapproving look that would have made Sister Kayala proud, had the old cleric been there to see it.

"After three years, we began to wonder if you would ever return," Enna said with an unusual amount of vehemence.

Shalindra felt a ripple of surprise slide across Tormjere's mind, strong enough to disrupt whatever barrier existed between them. The emotion evaporated like smoke on the breeze, but the mental link she shared with him remained tenuously attached.

Is it really you?

I hope so.

Shalindra took a step closer. Reversing her grip, she extended Shining Moon towards him. Both Maria and Enna tensed, but she had to be certain. Apart from herself, he was the only one who could lay a hand on Eluria's weapon without suffering harm.

He reached for it, never taking his eyes from hers. As his fingers wrapped around the shaft, whatever fog lay between them seemed to lift, and her mind touched his in a way that had been missing from her life for far too long.

"Satisfied?" he asked.

I am overjoyed to see you again, but your manner of entry will require some explanation.

Probably. I'm glad you're both safe.

Enna allowed her silver disc of Eluria to slip back to its place around her neck and crossed her arms, frowning at him.

"You should keep this," Tormjere said to Shalindra, releasing his grip on the hammer. "I doubt I'm the only one coming to visit."

As if to punctuate his statement, the door behind him burst open. Armed men rushed in, led by a bedraggled Birion clad in nothing but a nightshirt.

Seeing the pair together and without any visible threat, he straightened and lowered his sword.

"You're late," he said to Tormjere by way of greeting.

Tormjere raised an eyebrow. "And *you're* not wearing any pants."

The knight's state of dress was scandalously indecent, and rarely was he seen in such a disheveled state. It was all Shalindra could do to keep her eyes from his muscular, hairy legs.

Birion smoothed his moustache, then bowed to her with all the dignity of a knight on parade. "By your leave, Your Highness."

Shalindra dipped her head with as much gravity as she could muster, careful to keep any hint of a smile from her face.

Chapter Four

A Fireside Gathering

Tormjere stared into the fire, watching the flames dance above the crackling wood. The warmth it provided was comforting, but the coolness of the room was far more enjoyable. He had already seen a lifetime's fill of hot places.

They were assembled in the same hall where he had originally found them, which seemed to occupy almost the entirety of the first floor of the castle. The table had been moved against the wall after the evening meal, and chairs arranged before the hearth. The food had been as delicious as anticipated, but his stomach had judged it less than fulfilling, just like everything else he had eaten. The conversation, never something he enjoyed participating in, had mercifully avoided him beyond general inquiries which he deflected with equally vague replies. Most of the twenty or so people in attendance barely remembered him. Either out of respect or distrust, those who did had kept their questions bottled inside.

He glanced out the same window Shalindra had viewed earlier, wondering if his haste had been warranted. The clouds outside were now brushed in the pinks and reds of the fading sun, and the valley lay in shadow. He had never thought to return here, much less to find a town growing where before there had been only wilderness and goblins. When he had been forced to flee last time with the Book of Amalthee, his life and the lives of Treven and Honarch had hung in the balance. Four years later…

Had it really been so long?

The sound of Birion's muffled coughing drew his attention back to the other occupants of the room. The knight, who sat wrapped in heavy garments close to the fire, thanked Enna as she handed him a cup of warm broth. Shalindra appeared not to notice any of it from where she sat, as lost in thought as Tormjere had been.

"Why here?" he asked of no one in particular.

The directness of the question seemed to catch them off guard. Enna's green eyes betrayed annoyance at his query, as much as everyone else's silence indicated their reluctance to revisit the past.

It was Birion who answered. "The last time we saw you, we were fleeing into the mountains, trying to outrun the small army of Ceringions that had designs on our lives. There was no further pursuit from them after you… disappeared."

They all know of the demon. Edward sent scouts back to find you.

Birion coughed again. "From there, we turned south and made for Evermen's Forge. The town could not support our numbers, so we occupied a neighboring valley and waited to see what would happen in the Kingdom. We lost perhaps a third of those with us as they snuck back into the Kingdom to return to their homes. Those of us who remained tried making new ones. That lasted only a few months." He took another drink before resuming the tale. "Food became scarce. It was too late in the year to plant crops, and there was nowhere near enough arriving from Kirchmont. A few enterprising merchants brought what they could, and charged us a steep price for their troubles, but once the snows hit, they stopped coming."

We were also running out of ways to pay them.

"Troubles with the residents of the Forge began to boil over, as they did not appreciate such a large group nearby. Nor, it seemed, did the lord of Kirchmont. There were rumors that come spring, he would send troops to evict us. Honarch had spoken of this valley, though its significance escapes me now. We hoped it was far enough away that they would leave us alone, so we packed up and made our way here, to Newlmir."

There were other reasons, which I will tell you later.

"Newlmir?" Tormjere asked.

Birion glanced at Enna but her lips remained firmly pressed together, and after a short silence Shalindra stirred from her thoughts to answer.

"It is a combination of the elvish name for this valley, Maetholmir, which translates as 'Mystic Home,' and our desire for a new beginning."

"What about the goblins?" Tormjere asked. "There was a pair of settlements close to the falls and at least one other not far west of this island."

"The lake that surrounds us provided protection," Birion said, "and while there are still a fair number of the creatures scattered about, we've largely driven them off. Edward currently leads a company to the south to push them further away. Honarch coerced the rockhurlers into helping, somehow," he added with a frown.

Tormjere raised an eyebrow, but before he could inquire

further, Shalindra gave him a warning shake of her head.

"That's his tower at the other end of this island?" he asked instead. "I assumed it was the Imaretii's doing—it's a similar style."

Is that why you came charging in? You thought me a captive?

There wasn't anything friendly about this valley the last time I was here, and you were longing for escape.

"It is his," Birion confirmed. "He's likely there now, doing whatever it is that wizards do rather than honest work."

"And where have *you* been?" Enna challenged, finally meeting his eyes.

"It's a longer story than yours," Tormjere said as he stifled a yawn, "but I'll leave it for tomorrow, if you don't mind. I was in Evermen's Forge a couple of nights ago, and I'm about to fall asleep."

"You made it here from the Forge in two *days?*" Birion asked incredulously.

Tormjere shrugged. "I was in a hurry."

How long has it been since you slept?

Too long.

I have never seen you so tired. I have as many questions as they do, but they can wait.

Shalindra stood, signaling an end the gathering. "I am certain we can find you a bed."

Birion agreed. "We've more than a few empty houses nearby, unfortunately."

You've lost that many?

It was a difficult winter, and a difficult summer before that.

"Any roof over my head will do," Tormjere said. "I'm not picky."

Birion muffled another cough. "I can show him, then I'm for bed as well. By your leave?"

Shalindra nodded.

You're staying here in the keep?

At the temple, but only during the night. My duties keep me active in the village or here, where I will not be a distraction to Marie's work. Sleep tonight, and we will speak more in the morning.

Tormjere felt Enna's eyes upon him as he followed Birion from the room, but she made no further comment.

The evening was pleasant, and the moon bright despite the clouds in the night sky, but Birion had not even made in down the outer steps into the small bailey before he began coughing in the damp air. "Cursed sickness. Didn't touch a bite of food for two days."

"Eluria's clerics have never been good with illnesses," Tormjere said, keeping his pace slow as they crossed to the gatehouse.

"That they are not, though they're the only reason any of us are still alive at this point."

Birion returned the salute of the soldiers on watch as the pair passed beneath the gate tower and continued along the road. There was a smattering of dwellings close to the castle, but most were clustered a short distance away. The immense falls at the base of the Three Sisters could not be seen through the darkened trees, but nothing could fully mask the distant rumble. Tormjere had paid little attention to the waterfall this time, but the river it spawned flowed through the valley to feed the lake which surrounded them.

Birion coughed again. "We need one of Amalthee's priests, or even a mediturgeon, but there is little to entice them here."

"Didn't we have a mediturgeon with us after Tiridon?"

"We did, but he was one of those who returned to the Kingdom rather than risk the unknown. It's certainly been hard enough, but it's had its share of rewards as well." He walked in silence for a moment before continuing. "I did not wish to say anything more in front of Shalindra as it upsets her, but you're aware of what has transpired in Actondel since we left?"

"I've heard almost nothing, actually."

Birion's gave him a quizzical look. "We expected the bulk of the Ceringion army to return home after the war, but they did not. They were used to drive the goblins out of the western territories near Fallhaven and Jonrin, or to solidify control of their newly seized holdings in the east and south. We've heard of a number of small wars as this lord or that resisted the changes. It seemed safest for us, and for Shalindra in particular, to stay as far away as possible. Most of us could have snuck back in and made a new life, but not her. She would have been hunted mercilessly, by her enemies as well as her family. She is aware of this, and I believe she carries some guilt over our decisions, though she does not deserve it. We followed her because we believe in her, not out of pity."

"Does her father still rule?"

"As best we know. We see only a handful of travelers each year, and while there are plenty of elves, they care little for what happens in the Kingdom, unless it involves some trespass upon their lands. Here we are."

They came to a stop beside a small wooden hut of hewn logs with a thatched roof in need of repair. The building was no more than a few paces to a side, with a short door that Tormjere had to stoop to pass through.

The interior was dark, but he could see that it was largely

empty even before Birion lit a candle.

"It's a bit damp," Birion said, "but nothing a fire won't solve. I'll have some wood sent over to see you through the night, but after that you'll have to cut your own."

"I can manage, thank you."

Birion extended his hand. "It's good to see you safe again."

"It's good to be safe," Tormjere said, shaking it. "Go get some rest."

Chapter Five

Unravelling

The temple of Eluria was the second largest structure on the island, dominating the small collection of houses and farms that made up the village at the northern tip of the island. The rising sun shimmered against the quartz accents inset in its curving whiterock walls, lending an added brilliance to the building. Gardens were being cultivated around its entire circumference, though only a few of the plots were filled in. Behind the temple proper was a nearly complete two-story building of post and beam construction which butted up against the evergreens.

Tormjere waited just outside the stacked stone cairns that marked the edge of the temple grounds, watching the early morning activity. A handful of fishermen had pushed their boats into the cold waters of the lake at sunrise, and not long afterwards the early risers shook off the morning chill to work their small farms, tend to livestock, or generally just go about their day. A dog barked as it was chased by a trio of children too young for chores. In spite of the normality of it all, Tormjere kept a sharp watch.

It was near midmorning when Shalindra and Enna at last

emerged. Shalindra approached with a smile, but Enna refused to acknowledge him and continued down the road towards the castle.

She doesn't like me now?

She distrusts your potential influence on me, which is different.

"The temple looks different than the ones I've seen," he said, keeping the mood light. "But I like the roundness of it."

"Enna designed it. It was not our first priority, given so many other concerns, but the stonemasons were eager to apply themselves to something, and the rockhurlers dislike quartz and whiterock. Did you sleep?"

"A little," he replied, falling into step beside her as she followed the same direction Enna had taken.

"I will assume, then, that you investigated the entire island last night."

"Most of it," he answered with a grin. "The bridge is impressive."

The road they followed, more of a wide trail really, ran along the eastern edge of the island from the village and past a long, low causeway with arched footings that linked the island to the shore. The road continued from there to the castle, which stood only a short distance beyond, where its battlements commanded an unobstructed view of the crossing. Though not much larger than the gatehouses guarding the outer walls in larger cities like Tiridon, the keep was enough to give pause to any seeking to force their way onto the island.

"The original bridge was of wood," Shalindra said. "When we first arrived we camped at the shore, but after discovering that goblins are terrified of deep water, we quickly moved onto the island for safety. While it met our need for protection, the island's soil is too rocky for any significant plantings, so we put our efforts towards pacifying the lands nearby. Honarch was instrumental in the defenses, and in many other ways. He can be truly fearsome when he must, which sometimes frightens people already suspicious of those who employ magic. No one has forgotten why we were forced to come here."

"Is that why his tower is so far removed?"

"He claimed it was for the peace and quiet, but few were sorry to see him keep his distance."

Tormjere cast an annoyed glance back at the village. "He deserves better."

"I have kept him on the council despite their protests, though he rarely participates. I wish I could offer him more, but we have many other problems and the arrangement seems to suit everyone, for now. Between the winters, and the goblins, and the sickness, we have had a challenging time, but I will assume that our trials were no more difficult than yours."

"I'd imagine building a castle so quickly was the bigger challenge."

"It is a hollow shell," she admitted, allowing him to steer the conversation away once more. "Once you exit the central keep, there is little but grass inside the walls, but, by Her blessing, we have seen little in the way of conflict."

"You still carry Shining Moon everywhere."

Her response was preempted as the dog he had been watching earlier came running past, then circled around to Shalindra with its tail wagging.

"Hello, Max," she greeted the animal with a smile. "Are you in need of being rescued again, or have you managed to escape this time?"

The dog continued wagging and sniffed at Tormjere. He gave it a good scratch behind the ears, thankful that friendly animals still existed. Squeals of excitement sounded as the trio of children came running with as much speed as their short legs could muster. Max bounded off just fast enough to avoid the small hands that grasped at him, but not so fast as to fully elude the laughing children.

"There are still things worth protecting." Shalindra smiled as she watched them play, but her eyes were troubled. "Eluria placed Her weapon with me for a purpose. Enna and I have pondered this mystery many times, but I still do not understand why. Am I to be Her Guardian, or is that role destined for another? This valley was home to elves who worshipped Her long before we arrived, and Enna is convinced that there are answers to be found here."

"But you haven't found them, have you? Is this working, then? Living out here in the woods away from everything?"

Her blue eyes searched his. "You give voice to my doubts as easily as ever. We have been left alone, and with what these people faced during the war that is, perhaps, the best we could ask for. While our time here has been anything but peaceful, at least we are no longer fighting each other. Argus actually retired, and runs our only inn onshore."

Tormjere grinned. "Though it's hard to imagine him out of the fighting, that seems a perfect thing for him to do."

She came to a stop as they drew near the castle. "This meeting is certain to bore you, and I need the councilors that you frightened half to death yesterday to focus on our business instead of pestering you with questions."

"I'll wait outside until you're done."

"You should go speak to Honarch. He dislikes such formal gatherings as much as you do, and I am certain that he will be eager to see you again."

"There are still plenty of unfriendly things roaming the woods. Aren't you worried about that?"

"Goblins may cause problems in the farms, but they have never set foot on this island. Birion and Edward constantly patrol the valley, and Marie established wards that will supply warning against more dangerous creatures. We have remained safe the entire time we have been here."

He had gotten in easily enough, but he kept that thought to himself, as it would only beget further questions. Still, he had not come this far to leave her protected by nothing but flimsy walls. Before he could voice another protest, she cut him off gently.

"I have been in hundreds of these meetings with little damage to anything other than my sanity. I will be fine."

Tormjere could produce no further argument. As she said, there was little threat, and he was confident that he could return to her in an instant now that he knew where she was.

As Shalindra entered the castle, he went in search of Honarch's tower. Not that it would be difficult to find. He had taken the measure of the island the night before, though he had explored only a portion in detail. Beyond the castle lay only a thin footpath leading through the trees, and he fell into an easy stride that would cover the distance quickly.

The roughly triangular island was a bit over three miles long and half as wide in the middle, with the village end forming a point aimed at the waterfall that spilled from the feet of the Three Sisters.

From there, the landmass widened as it moved south, eventually attaining a width near to its length. Today a steady breeze roughed the lake and pushed a blanket of clouds across the sky, but on his prior visit the waters had remained calm enough to reflect the sky. He had been given little time to appreciate its natural beauty as they fought to wrest control of the Book of Amalthee from the goblins, whose villages lay a few hours' walk upriver at the north end of the valley. Those memories were less unpleasant than his more recent ones, but he did not care to relive any of them.

He put the past out of his mind and concentrated on the fragrance of the trees and the sounds of birds singing.

Honarch's tower was located at the southern extent of the island, perched on the edge of a solid shelf that fell some twenty or thirty feet as it split the upper and lower lakes. It stood as far from the town as possible while still remaining on the island, rising high enough above the trees to be plainly visible from anywhere within the valley.

The octagonal spire was of a stone so smooth it seemed carved from a single piece of slate. An outer wall of the same material and shape ringed its base, tall enough to keep anything from wandering in or over without deliberate effort. Tormjere passed through the open gate into a sheltered courtyard and found only one small door in the tower, made of stout oak and aligned perfectly north.

Tormjere thumped his fist against the door and waited. After a short pause, the portal opened silently. He stepped into the dimly lit interior, and the door swung closed behind him of its own accord.

A series of small windows provided a feeble illumination that was quickly swallowed by a room whose ceiling and floor were of the same smooth, dark stone as the walls. The chamber was devoid of furnishings, and the fireplace cold. Steps curved upward around the wall to his left, disappearing into the upper floors. Hurried footsteps descended those stairs, and moments later Honarch came rushing down in a swish of reddish robes, his bearded face split into a wide grin.

"Tormjere!" he exclaimed, clapping him on the shoulders. "What happened to you?"

"It's a long story, but I'm glad to be back."

"I'm sure. Sorry to have kept you waiting. I usually have warning when anyone comes to visit, and I need to get an apprentice to let people in. Come on upstairs where it's more cheerful. I hardly ever use this room."

Honarch led him to the second level, which contained a kitchen with a small table and chairs and a trio of more permissive windows. "Something to drink?"

"What do you have?"

Honarch winced. "Just water, I'm afraid. I hear that Cogan over on the shore brews a good ale, but I don't do much entertaining so I rarely keep any here."

"Water sounds good, actually."

"How are you?" Honarch asked as he poured two mugs.

"Fine. Why wouldn't I be?" Tormjere answered more defensively that he should have, judging from the appraising look he received.

"Well, you disposed of a demon and somehow managed to bring the army that was chasing us to a standstill, and then you vanished. I doubt you've been idling the time away, but I won't pry. Yet. When did you get here?"

"Yesterday afternoon."

"I'm sorry I missed you then. I sometimes join the evening meals, but I was deep in my research. Did you see everything we've built on your way in?"

"Only in passing. It's different than what I remember."

"That's an understatement. Fewer goblins, more food, and... well, you remember. It's almost civilized now. Shalindra or Birion would be the best ones to show you around. I tend to stay here most days, which suits everyone just fine, I believe."

"So what do you do?" Tormjere asked.

"Study, experiment. If there's any trouble, I assist with defending, but that's becoming less frequent. It's a lot quieter now than when we first arrived."

"I'm definitely eager to hear how this all came about, but why did you bring everyone all the way out here? There are countless valleys closer to the Forge with everything you needed: water, game, trees."

"Other residents," Honarch added. "You remember the ogres, and wolves, and wyverns and whatnot we encountered on that adventure with Treven? And even with all that we faced we were still lucky. I think the only reason we didn't have to fight more often is that we were such a small group and never stayed in one place long enough to be found. This time there were hundreds of us, and our passing did not go unnoticed. We were attacked by something different almost every day. Wyverns are prevalent in far more of these mountains than you might expect and are highly territorial. This was honestly the safest place we stopped."

"Even with all the goblins living here?"

"I... might have taken care of them already, on an earlier visit."

Tormjere raised an eyebrow.

"One village was destroyed and the other all but abandoned when we arrived, but that's definitely a tale for another time. Come. I want to show you something up in my study, at the top of the tower."

He led the way further up the steps that continued to spiral around the outer wall of the tower, passing a landing with a door to the interior at regular intervals that marked each level.

Honarch paused at one of the landings. "It's a lot of steps, I know."

"What is it with wizards and towers, anyway?" Tormjere asked. "Just have a need to gaze down on everyone?"

Honarch threw him a black look and resumed the climb. "It has to do with the contamination of energies. When you're working, you want to guard against any type of interference. There are some rather cumbersome spells that can mitigate the effects, but the easiest thing to do is remove yourself from unintended influences."

"You have to get away from everything?"

"Exactly. For best results, you can either go as far up or as far down as possible." He shrugged. "Up has a nicer view."

Having experienced what the opposite direction had to offer, Tormjere could not disagree. They eventually reached a landing that had to be near the top of the tower and entered a room which occupied the entire floor. The furnishings were sparse but functional and the walls largely bare, save one which contained an ornate bookshelf half filled with books. That caught Tormjere's eye immediately, as more than one of those books were edged with a faint hue, reminding him of the library in the abbey of Amalthee in Kirchmont.

"Where did you get the books?"

"Felzig. Well, indirectly." Honarch crossed to the shelves and selected a small, leather-bound tome. The surface had once been tooled in an intricate pattern but was now smoothed by constant use. Tormjere recognized it instantly.

"Felzig's spellbook?"

"One of them," Honarch answered. "I'll never understand why laymen assume that each wizard has only one, as if everything we know could reside in a single work."

He handed it to Tormjere.

"That was one of three he carried with us when we left Kirchmont. There's a rather complicated incantation in the back that will bring this entire shelf and its contents to the caster."

"Interesting."

"Astounding. Felzig, for all his flaws—"

"Like wanting to murder us…"

"…was exceptional at his craft. I've heard of similar retrievals of smaller objects but nothing on this scale."

Tormjere returned the spellbook to the shelf as Honarch went to the desk and rifled through several drawers. "Speaking of Felzig… Ah, here it is." He tossed a dohedron to Tormjere. Each jewel embedded in the golden surface of the multifaceted, apple-sized device twinkled with a faint light as his fingers brushed across it.

"You killed another wizard?"

"Of course not," Honarch huffed indignantly. "You're the one who likes chopping people up with your sword. I made it."

"Where did you get the gems?"

"From the ones my former master so kindly left us. You still have any of yours?"

"Somewhere." The pouch with Tormjere's share was still buried under a rock in Kenzing, if no one had found it. The memory of his home and family was unexpectedly strong and jarring, and he quickly suppressed it.

"What's wrong?"

"Nothing. I'll bet making that took some time."

"The instructions were in one of the books I retrieved. I had to teach myself all manner of spells related to gem crafting and metalworking, and it took me almost six months, plus another to work out a code that was usable." He produced a folded sheet of paper with a series of colored dots beside different words and letters. "Here's what I came up with. Most of it works with these three stones, which can all be reached with one finger."

"Your handwriting needs some work," Tormjere observed.

"Penmanship was never my passion. My studies would go much faster if I had an apprentice or at least a scribe I could trust with dictation."

Tormjere started to return the device, but Honarch held up a hand. "Keep it for now. I need to see how well it works, but I'm short on volunteers offering to help."

"I get the feeling you aren't the most liked person here."

Honarch's expression soured. "No matter what I have or haven't done, or what I try to do now, people are still distrustful. I don't blame them, really. For all they know, I'm still part of the Conclave."

"The Conclave did their best to kill us, and if you can drive off wyverns and clear goblin villages singlehandedly, you're beyond anyone's control."

"Well, I don't know that I could do all that, but I've achieved a lot." His smile returned. "I may be Felzig's equal now, though more likeable, I would hope. But there is no end to what can be learned. Should I live a hundred lives, I doubt I would ever tire of discovering new things."

Tormjere glanced back at the bookshelves. "I can add to your collection, I think."

Honarch looked interested. "How?"

With a mischievous grin of his own, Tormjere reached inside his tunic and withdrew a small, nondescript bag.

Honarch looked at it for a moment, then his eyes grew wide. "Is that what I think it is?"

Tormjere stuck his arm into the sack far enough that it should have come bursting through the bottom. When he pulled it back out, there were two books in his hand.

"Where did you get that?" Honarch asked.

"Someone left it lying on a table."

"And the books were in it?"

Tormjere avoided the question and withdrew two more. "I picked these up at the same time. They just looked interesting."

"You certainly have a knack for grabbing important things, don't you?" Honarch said, so eager to view their contents that he was attempting to skim through two of the books at the same time. "You've some talent for magic; are you certain you don't want to keep them?"

"I've gotten all I care to from them."

The answer seemed unsatisfactory to Honarch. "Well, I'm glad you've been able to study, but if you ever want something to read you're free to try any of the works I have. Did you ever master anything more than the small flame?"

"I've picked up a thing or two, but nothing like what you can do, I'm sure. What's happening here in the valley?" Tormjere asked, changing the subject. "I understand your reasons for coming this far, but has everyone been content to hide rather than finish what we started?"

Honarch gave him a curious look. "There was no going back and saving the Kingdom, if that's what you mean. I don't know exactly what transpired between Shalindra and the king, nor do I wish to, but no one who followed her over the mountains has a place in his realm now. Their homes were seized in the best of cases, burned in the worse." He shrugged. "At this point it hardly matters. People have become used to living here, for all its hardships."

Tormjere moved to a window and looked across the valley. It was an idyllic town they had created, and likely a predictable life, but the wilderness that surrounded it was far from tamed. He wondered if Kenzing had been as raw as this when his grandfather first settled there. "Have you seen any demons?"

"None," Honarch answered. "They disappeared the same time you did. Were you expecting anything different?"

Tormjere was thankful he was looking away, as the relief he felt almost certainly reached his face. He was not too late. "Of course not."

Honarch set the new books on the shelf, and joined Tormjere in looking out the window. "So, what are you planning on doing now that you're here?"

"Whatever I need to." Tormjere winced uncomfortably and

put a hand to his forehead.

"Are you ok?"

"Just hungry, I think. I should probably head back."

* * *

Enna watched Shalindra rub her temples as the last of the councilors filed from the room.

"Another headache?" she asked. Shalindra seemed to be having them more frequently with every passing day. "You push yourself too hard, of late."

Shalindra waved aside her concern but looked tired as she stood. "I feel the need for some air. Would you walk with me?"

"Of course."

They left the castle and turned in the general direction of Elurithlia's temple, but Shalindra said nothing and seemed to have no specific destination in mind.

"Why are we here?" Shalindra asked suddenly.

"That is a very broad question."

Shalindra's forehead wrinkled in thought. "Not in a philosophical sense, but here, in this valley."

"Because it is our home," Enna answered, stating the obvious even as she braced herself for where this was headed.

"That is not the reason we came here. This place means something."

"You know that answer as well as I. Elurithlia's presence is palpable, waxing and waning with the seasons. It was a group decision to come here and see what we might discover."

Frustration began to creep into Shalindra's voice. "But we have not yet achieved the peace and prosperity we prayed for, nor have we found any sign of Her will."

Enna dreaded this conversation, one which they had endlessly debated but never resolved. Though she felt Shalindra's frustration just as keenly, she was certain that what both of them needed lay within this valley. She had also looked for signs of whatever that might be, but discovered nothing of what once made this valley the second most holy nexus of Elurithlia's might. They just needed more time.

"It is more than just the problems with the planting and the mines that are troubling you, isn't it?" Enna prompted.

"I have been thinking again about what it means to be Her Guardian. I cannot believe that so precious an artifact as Shining Moon was given to me so that I might safeguard a village in the middle of the woods."

She was returning to the unanswerable question that had driven countless discussions over the years. Despite all of their prayers, Enna remained no closer to an answer than Shalindra was.

"If I am truly Her Guardian then it must be for a reason. I feel as if I have been hiding from my duty more so than from the Ceringions and my father."

"No one would accuse you of cowardice," Enna protested. "You have a responsibility to these people who followed you here. That is not something which can be set aside for personal fulfilment. When Elurithlia is ready, She will give you a sign."

"What if She already has, and we are simply unaware of what we saw?"

She was becoming far more agitated about this topic that usual, and Enna could easily guess at the cause.

"Are you sure this isn't because he came back?"

Shalindra seemed to wrestle with the question. "That is

possible, but I feel it is something more. We have huddled in the shadow of the Three Sisters for years, simply surviving. I begin to doubt that I will find answers here."

Enna cast her gaze towards the sharp peaks of the mountains to the north, equally conflicted. Regardless of the cause of Shalindra's sudden shift in attitude, she was correct. The mountains were a sacred symbol to those who worshiped the moon, wrapped tightly into the oldest lore of their faith. From somewhere in or near this valley they could invoke *Alta Amalia*, the sacred ceremony which would allow the person performing it to speak directly with their goddess. It was that promise of divine communion which had called her people here ages ago. Because of that, Enna had been only too willing to follow Honarch's suggestion to come here, eager for any excuse to stand in Her presence. Yet the valley had provided less than what either of them had prayed for. Enna knew of only one other place where they might find others capable of giving them direction, but to go there could well be more dangerous than returning to the Kingdom, if for vastly different reasons.

"Thank you for listening," Shalindra said. "There is little we can do until the planting is complete, regardless. I will seek Her wisdom tonight and pray that She may guide my decisions."

"Do not worry," Enna said in parting. "Her patience and Her love know no bounds. Elurithlia will provide us with clarity when we are ready."

"You are correct, as always with these matters," Shalindra said. "I should take comfort in what we have accomplished, rather than dwell on what we have not."

"Do not let these endless clouds or the arguments of the

council dampen your spirits. Set both aside for a time and seek Her wisdom. The sanctuary will be empty for hours, and no one will disturb you."

Enna came to a stop and allowed Shalindra her peace. Shalindra smiled her thanks at the gesture, but from the way she continued walking with her head down, such thoughts were a heavy weight upon her.

Enna watched her go. She would have to find some way to help, but was at a complete loss for what else to try. Motion in the corner of her eye caused her to turn, and she spied Tormjere returning from the direction of Honarch's tower.

She fixed him with a narrow gaze and waited for him to approach. His brow was furrowed in thought and his eyes were so dark that she could almost see herself reflected in them, which somehow annoyed her even further.

"You don't look happy to see me," he said by way of greeting.

"You don't look happy to be here."

"I'm trying to put my unhappiness behind me. It isn't always easy."

"So it's just behind you then? No explanation, no apologies?"

"What should I be sorry for?"

"Some sign of remorse would be a good place to start." She seethed with barely contained anger. "Maybe sorry for not coming back? Sorry for not helping? Or perhaps sorry for not letting anyone know you were alive?"

Rather than allow him the satisfaction of a response, she turned and stormed away.

Tormjere did not follow. The past could not be changed, even if it needed to be, and their attention had to be on what was coming. He squeezed his hand into a fist to keep it from shaking and tried to ignore the emptiness that twisted restlessly in his stomach.

Chapter Six

Deepening Night

Tormjere crouched silently on a rock, waiting. Morning mists lent the trees around him a faded and ghostly appearance, and left his cheeks damp as they drifted lazily past. The forest had just returned to its usual quiet when he felt Shalindra touch his mind.

What are you doing?

He looked up through the branches above him to the soggy overcast that had dominated the sky every day since his arrival.

Exploring. It's nice to be beneath the trees again.

Were you so far removed from them?

Too far. Too long.

Then I am thankful you are back where you belong. Have you seen the size of the rabbits here?

Yes. They're even larger than the mountain hares I tried to trap when I was younger.

He tired of staring at the uniformly grey clouds and shifted his gaze to the nearby ridgeline.

I do not recognize where you are.

I'm probably farther south than you normally come.

Edward is at that end of the valley, somewhere.

I know. I saw their camp last night.

You did go far. Be careful. More than just goblins inhabit the lower valley. The north, closer to the falls, would be—

I remember what that part was like.

His stomach twisted around itself insistently, but he ignored its protests.

Are you well?

I'm just hungry.

I envy your freedom to wander, as my duties dictate my movements once more. Do not be gone all day or you will miss the evening meal again.

I won't.

Only when her attention shifted away did he look down at the freshly strangled deer still clenched in his hands. Confident that she would not see it, he tore a steaming chunk of flesh from the carcass and consumed it eagerly, hoping that it would help, but knowing that it would not.

* * *

Edward's patrol, twenty men strong on horseback, returned to the island the next day just as a light rain began to fall. Tormjere went with Shalindra as she hurried from the keep to greet them, more out of habit than from any need.

Upon catching sight of them Edward turned and said something to the closest rider. With a salute, the soldier led the column on towards the stables, and Edward wheeled about and trotted towards Shalindra.

"My lady," Edward said, dismounting. "Ranger, we thought you dead."

"I'm pleased to prove you wrong," Tormjere replied.

"What did you discover?" Shalindra asked.

Edward removed his helm and wiped the water from his face. "Clawfoot's tribe had as bad a winter as we did. Their fields are a mess and the fruits are late blooming, so they were more irritable than normal."

"Are all of our men accounted for?"

Edward shook his head sadly. "They are not, my lady. We were ambushed three times. Alexi and Habernath were lost."

As if to punctuate his statement, a wail sounded from the crowd. They turned to see Marie comforting a distraught woman as the soldier who had delivered the news stood stoically beside her.

"We will see that she is taken care of," Shalindra said.

It seemed a needless loss when at least three accomplished healers were present in the town.

You don't send any clerics with the patrols?

I have offered, but Birion and Edward always refuse. Only Enna, Marie, and I are experienced enough to not be a burden. The few others we have are not made for a life outside the temple.

"There are some minor injuries, as well," Edward added. "If we could impose upon you to set them straight."

"I will tend to them at once, as you are no doubt eager to escape the weather."

"After a week, a few moments more are no trouble, but I thank you. I will see to the horses and meet you inside."

Tormjere's stomach churned uncomfortably.

You are always hungry.

Unfortunately.

Go to the kitchen and get something.

Tormjere did not argue. As she had reminded him almost every day since his arrival, there was little danger here. He made his way to the rear of the keep where a small stone cookhouse was set against the wall. The fire was out and there was no sign of movement. He slipped inside and pulled the door shut. Satisfied that he was alone, he cast about for any meat he could find.

He had just pulled down a leg of mutton when he heard the small click of a latch being opened. He spun towards the door, tossing the mutton away. The door opened with a bang, revealing a young woman with a rolling pin held threateningly before her. She relaxed as soon as she saw him.

"Oh, it's you, my lord," she said, lowering her makeshift weapon. "If you're hungry enough it can't wait for the meal then have a seat, and I'll fix you something proper."

Tormjere sat on a stool beside the table as directed. "You look familiar."

She blushed. "Corolin, my lord. From the keep at Tiridon. We've a fair stock of cheese, and I made the bread fresh just yesterday, but we won't be having much meat until they slaughter the next pig, my lord."

His hands clenched beneath the table, but he kept a smile on his face. "Cheese and bread are fine, and I'm not a lord, just Tormjere."

"You're kind to say that, my lord."

"You weren't with us when we left the city."

"No, my lord. When our knights rode out after you, rumor was that they were never coming back. Well, Lord Poloni was in a foul mood about it, and Lady Dirensi even fouler. She'd looked at me sideways more than once since I'd hurt myself on Lady

Shalindra's weapon, and I knew there'd be suffering if I stayed. But where was I to go?"

She looked at Tormjere, but the question seemed rhetorical as she proceeded to answer it herself.

"I had to follow Lady Shalindra, of course. She made my hand better, and did it so that foul Lady Dirensi wouldn't find out and punish me again. So I slipped out when the temples were being burned, but Lady Shalindra was hard to find. Some said she'd gone north, others said south. I was in Kirchmont, living in one of those shelters run by the monks of Toush and begging for my food when I heard she'd set roots near the Forge. It scared me more than a little to go over the mountains, what with all the stories I'd heard, but I was alone and at wits end and didn't care to fall into anything disreputable. One of the monks set me up as a cook with a merchant making the trip out here."

"I'm glad you made it safely," Tormjere said, hoping to forestall a detailed accounting of her entire journey.

"I think Lady Shalindra's glad you're back, as well, my lord. I can tell. She's as kind a ruler as I've ever heard tell of, but I've not seen her so happy since I came here."

She set a plate with cheese and thick slices of bread before him. "There we are. Is there anything else I can do for you, my lord?"

"This is plenty, thank you."

"Then I'll be seeing myself back to the other work. Just leave the plate there on the table when you're done and I'll clean it later."

Tormjere chewed on a piece of bread as she departed. He knew Shalindra was unhappy. No matter how her blue eyes sparkled it was there, just below the surface. Even the cook saw it, but none of those closest to her could see because none of them looked. She couldn't stay here forever. Eventually, she would have to accept that, whether the world came to her or she returned to it. Either way, he would be ready.

He finished clearing his plate. Unfulfilled, he cast about for the mutton, finding it wedged behind a sack of potatoes. With a sigh he retrieved it and hung it back where belonged.

It would not help either.

Chapter Seven

The Problem with Secrets

Shalindra awoke with a start, grasping desperately for Shining Moon in a vain attempt to defend herself, but there was nothing except the sounds of her own rapid breathing to break the silence of her small room.

Another dream.

Two weeks had passed since Tormjere's reappearance, but the normalcy she longed for had not returned with him. Her headaches continued to be a distraction, and the nightmares were becoming more vivid and much worse.

From the faint moonlight piercing the almost-drawn curtains, she knew it to be well past midnight. She set the hammer back on the bedside table with a sigh. Her dreams had not been this troubled since... since the first time she and Tormjere had been forced to run from demons. Were the creatures seeking her again? She waited for the familiar touch of Tormjere's mind to reassure her, as he always had. Eventually, she settled back into the pillows. The absence of his thoughts worried her more than any nighttime terror. Where was he?

She closed her eyes and sought to place him, but there was nothing—not even a flicker of his presence. That caused a stab of panic, and she forced herself to take a deep breath. He was harder to read now, though whether it was due to his long absence or some other factor, she did not know. She had always been able to gain a sense of where he was from what he was seeing, but since his return that connection had been intermittent.

Sometimes, when he was close, it was almost as it had been before. His thoughts and hers mingled to the point that it was often difficult to tell whose they were. At other times, he might as well be… wherever he had gone.

Enna and the others thought that he was avoiding their questions because he was hiding something, and though such sentiments had yet to turn to accusations, they were increasingly more vocal. Even she, who wanted to give him every benefit of the doubt, was finding it difficult to ignore the mystery of his past. His silence on the matter was likely an attempt to protect them from something rather than to obscure some terrible secret, but whispers had begun to follow him everywhere he went.

She wrapped an evening robe around herself and hurried from her room, padding silently from the temple and towards the house Tormjere had been given. Marie would have a fit if she saw her walking about in this condition, but Shalindra felt an urgency that pushed her caution aside.

Upon reaching his house she raised a hand to knock, then paused. What if she was being foolish, and he was sound asleep? She disregarded the thought almost as soon as she had it. Rather than turn away she tried the door handle, and was surprised to find it unlocked. Without thinking, she opened the door and slipped inside.

The small room was dark. The bed in the corner lay empty, and the fireplace cold.

He had to be close, but why was she having so much trouble finding him? A vague sensation of pine needles and rocks at her back was all that came to her, but it was enough to give her direction. She stepped back into the night and moved cautiously into the darkened forest behind the house. Something scurried away from her path, and an owl hooted its mistrust of her presence in its domain. She crept forward as her eyes adjusted to the dim light.

When she finally came upon him, her heart sank.

Tormjere was huddled against a tree, as motionless as the rock he sat upon. Though she could make out the dark shadow of his outline, he seemed wrapped in a veil that obscured and distorted everything about him. As she took a step closer, his eyes snapped open and he tensed as if he were a wild animal suddenly denied its only avenue of escape.

She froze, frightened by the lack of recognition in his eyes.

Tormjere?

He blinked, and whatever barrier enveloped him dissipated as quickly as melting snow. Gently, she let her thoughts brush against his before he could seal them away. Torment and pain tumbled through his mind like water across stones. Just as in her dream. But no ordinary nightmare would send him running into the woods.

She took another cautious step forward and knelt in front of him. "You dream this each night?"

"I live this each night."

"You are free from such evil here."

"Not forever. They will find you, and they will find me. They never stopped looking."

"We have made no secret of our location."

"They've been preoccupied, and so you've been safe."

"And what did this safety cost?"

His jaw tightened. "A fair bargain."

Shalindra felt hollow inside. "What has happened to you?"

"I'm the same person I was."

"And yet, I think you are something more. I can feel the changes in you, no matter how much you try to shield me from them."

"But you don't know if it's for the better."

She sat back on her heels. He was close to telling her. She could feel those memories welling inside him, demanding release. But he shied away at the last moment, his mind still aswirl with thoughts that he struggled to keep from her.

Rather than pursue them, she let her mind guide him to happier memories. The stories of an old sailor. The joy of a dog's greeting. Sunrise over the mountains.

Many were the times that he had watched over her as she battled her own demons. Tonight, she would do no less for him.

* * *

Enna was less than pleased when she finally found them emerging from the woods the following morning. There was already enough talk about the two of them going around the village, and this would not help at all. She leveled a frosty glare at Tormjere, certain that the situation was his fault.

Shalindra gave her an understanding smile. "I am going to put clothes on now, Enna. Do not fret."

59

"We were worried when you missed the morning prayer," Enna responded. 'Worried' did not accurately reflect the general level of panic, given that Shining Moon had been left abandoned in her room while Shalindra was nowhere to be found, but it was the most tactful term she could use.

She hurried them along to the temple as quickly as possible, hoping that no one would notice their nominal ruler traipsing about in her nightclothes. When they finally arrived Shalindra entered the building, but Enna came to a stop so that Tormjere would have no excuse to follow her inside.

He slouched against one of the columns and fixed his eyes on her, but she purposefully ignored the invitation to converse. He seemed amused by that, which did nothing to help her mood.

"So she hasn't been blessed as the Guardian yet?" he eventually asked.

"No."

She turned her back to him and faced the Three Sisters, praying that Shalindra finished before she decided to ask Elurithlia for the strength to harm him somehow.

"Why not?"

She breathed in and out several times. What was taking Shalindra so long? "The armor remains in Ildalarial."

"And you can't go get it?"

Enna spun to face him. "Had you been here, you would know that tensions are high along the border between Ildalarial and Actondel. We do not want to wander into another war."

He looked like he was going to ask something else, but she did not allow him the opportunity. "Regardless, we have been so busy surviving that there has been little time for such thoughts of leaving."

With that, she returned her attention to the mountains. Shalindra finally emerged from the temple, properly attired in the white robes of Elurithlia, although Enna would never understand why humans liked covering their arms all the time. Some silent communication seemed to pass between Shalindra and Tormjere, then he shrugged as if none of it mattered.

Together, they began their morning trek towards the castle.

"I promised you a better answer to why we came here," Shalindra said to Tormjere. It was true that she had, but it was oddly timed and Enna felt she was joining a conversation already in progress.

"It was not simply to escape the Ceringions. Honarch had mentioned this valley in passing, even before we sought it as a place to call home. It was far away and mysterious, but once Enna had given me a proper understanding of the significance of the Three Sisters, I took it as a sign. We initially planned on coming here ourselves, just a handful of us, but with the problems the first settlement was having, almost everyone wanted to follow."

She was glossing over their struggles at Evermen's Forge. Enna remembered that time all too well, mostly as being cold, wet, and afraid. She had hoped to finally escape the senseless war that had disrupted Shining Moon's journey to Ildalarial, but the refugees who had followed Shalindra had very nearly come to blows with the inhabitants of Evermen's Forge. When Shalindra's intentions were revealed, most had refused to abandon her, and Shalindra, in turn, had felt responsible for their continued safety. Both Shalindra and Shining Moon belonged in Ildalarial, but as time passed, the urgency for such a journey faded to the point that Enna could not

61

even convince herself of the proper opportunity to attempt it.

"I knew there was a reason—some purpose for us here—the moment I saw the Three Sisters," Shalindra said. "There is something special about this place. I have sought to understand what it could be and have prayed to Eluria every day hoping for some revelation, but to no avail."

"I gathered the mountains were important since they're inscribed on your symbols," Tormjere said, "but what's special about them?"

Shalindra looked at Enna, and so she begrudgingly obliged. "The mountains are the manifestation of the women who lifted Elurithlia to Her place in the heavens. Their depiction on the base of our symbols is a reminder of their sacrifice and devotion."

"Interesting history, but it doesn't explain what you could gain from them today."

His observations were as infuriating as they were sound, but she clenched her teeth and answered anyway. "The mountains stand where the sisters lifted Elurithlia back to Her place in the sky, and it is said that their peaks can still be observed holding the moon aloft at special times, if you know where and when to observe them. They allow—"

Tormjere's pace slowed so abruptly that she almost ran into him. Her sharp words of annoyance died on her lips as a look of dismay flashed in his eyes. It was gone so quickly that she was unsure if it was real or only imagined.

Shalindra stopped as well and turned to him in surprise. "You have seen the alignment? You know where the site of the ceremony is?"

Enna stood speechless as he slowly nodded.

"And it is close? Somewhere in the valley?"

The sweep of his arm encompassed the northern end of the valley. "It's up there. I can show you today, if you want."

He seemed less than eager for some reason, but Shalindra turned towards the bridge without hesitation.

"But… the council meeting," Enna protested.

"For this they can wait," Shalindra answered. "Enna, if it is true…"

"It's a long walk," Tormjere warned, "but we should be able to reach it and return before dark."

"Then we should be off."

At risk of being left behind, Enna hurried to follow. She was not about to let the two of them wander off alone again.

He led them across the causeway and off the island, then followed the edge of the lake to where the river emptied into it. Enna wondered if he would stop there, but instead they continued up the river. Not long after, Tormjere made a sudden turn east onto the road running between the two villages, as though he had been unaware of or even forgotten its presence. This they followed all the way to Rumbleton, the perplexingly named collection of houses built atop the former goblin village near the base of the falls. It was a ramshackle assortment of dwellings that reminded her of Evermen's Forge, and not in a good way. Only those who worked the mines lived here, and were it not for the bridge there was little reason to visit.

Tormjere made for that bridge, which was nothing more than a series of ropes strung across the river above burnt pilings where something more solid once stood.

They had been waling for hours now, and she lamented not

suggesting that they take horses, which would have gotten them here much more quickly. Enna's mouth watered at the smell of fresh bread emanating from an outdoor oven, but neither Shalindra nor Tormjere seemed inclined to stop. Indeed, he ignored the village completely and barely slowed as he set foot on the bridge, despite how much it wobbled. With the three of them on it, it sagged almost enough to touch the raging waters near the middle.

Once across, they pressed through the burned and abandoned remnants of the goblin village, and for once Enna was thankful for the rapid pace. There was something unsettling about an abandoned town, and it had left her with an eerie feeling the few times she had been near. She would have happily broken their silence just to stave off such unpleasant thoughts, but between the competing roars of both falls and river, even a simple conversation would have entailed yelling at each other to be heard.

Only a short distance past the ruins, they reached a broken, weed-infested door in the base of the mountain. Another turn pointed them towards the valley wall, and they started to climb the steepening slope. There was neither path nor markings, but Tormjere clearly knew where he was leading them. They changed direction once more at an overgrown hole that resembled a large animal burrow large enough Enna would have been able to wriggle through. Soon their feet found their way onto a game trail, which continued steadily upwards. She began to grow nervous, for while this end of the valley was reasonably tame, the lands beyond were not.

Tormjere forged upwards now with such purposeful strides that Enna nearly broke into a jog to keep up. Shalindra was forced to quicken her pace as well, but made no effort to alter their speed.

At the end of the long climb the terrain leveled sharply, then began to descend as they crossed over the ridge. She briefly wondered if he meant to continue all the way down the other side. Instead, he stopped so unexpectedly that she assumed he had become lost and needed to regain his bearings.

"Here," was all he said.

They were standing in a small rocky area clear of trees, allowing an unobstructed view in nearly every direction. Before them rose the Three Sisters, their majestic peaks lost in the thick clouds. To the west, beyond the wooded foothills, endless plains of grass faded into the grey gloom of approaching rain. Enna shivered as a cool breeze carried mist past them and over the exposed ridge. Looking back down into the valley, she could see the lake and island far in the distance—far enough that she doubted they would make it back before sunset.

"Do you feel Her presence, Enna?" Shalindra asked in hushed tones. She was breathing heavily, though whether from the climb or her emotions Enna could not tell.

Enna did not feel anything special, but Shalindra clearly did. She set aside her thoughts of weather and distance, and took Elurithlia's symbol in her hand. Closing her eyes, she sought Her divine presence.

There was something. It was faint, but subtle tones of warmth stirred in the air around her. Such sensations were common throughout this valley, however, and if this was indeed the site where the ceremony of Alta Amalia was to be performed, the moon was not in the proper alignment or phase to confirm his claim.

Shalindra circled the area deliberately, then knelt facing the peaks. "It feels right, somehow."

She believed. Enna wanted to, for Shalindra's sake if no other, but they had experienced so many failures. She looked down at the silver disk of Elurithlia she held in her hand. Three mountains were depicted in the lower edge, and the dome of a pearl represented the moon above them. Her eyes returned to the skies just as the clouds thinned, bringing the mountain tops once more into view. She raised her symbol, and her breath caught in her throat as the three peaks on it came into alignment with those of the mountains before her. The clue she had so desperately sought had been under her nose the entire time.

Shalindra saw her, and aligned her symbol with the peaks as well. "It cannot be coincidence. This is the place, and we need only discover the time. I will come here the day of every full moon if I must, until…"

"The first full moon after midsummer's festival," Tormjere said with a certainty that refuted any thought of argument.

Enna almost screamed at the unfairness of it all. There was no explanation, no circumstance, which could justify his knowledge of either the location or the time. Her fists clenched as she spun to face him, but the angry denial died on her lips. Tormjere was not paying attention to either of them, or the mountains. He was staring at a stone flat enough to have been set there as a bench, and his hand trembled at his side.

Before she could question him, he turned away, his words uncharacteristically somber. "We should head back if you want to reach the island before sundown."

Shalindra rose reluctantly. "Would that midsummer was tonight, yet this revelation has come to us just in time. The new moon is almost here, and then we are but two weeks away from the festival."

It was certainly a sign from Elurithlia for them to have found it so close to time, no matter the source of the revelation. Enna could not deny it, even had she wished to. But as they followed Tormjere back into the valley, she could not help but question why it had taken so long, or why she had not been the one to find it.

Chapter Eight

Breaking Point

The door to Tormjere's cottage opened just as Enna raised her hand to knock.

"Good morning," he said.

Caught off guard, she froze, then pushed past him and waited for him to close the door.

"How did you know?" she demanded.

"Know what?"

"Do not play games with me. How did you know where to see Elurithlia atop the Three Sisters?"

"I saw it the last time we were here. Would you like to sit down?"

"No. Explain why you were there at just the right time, on just the right day."

He winced at what was obviously an unpleasant memory. "Maybe I'm just lucky. It certainly wasn't where we intended to be that night. And you never really told me what was so special about it."

"When the full moon sits in alignment atop the tallest peak our

68

Mistress is at Her strongest. The one who stands aligned with Her would celebrate Her greatness and be given what guidance they seek. It is known as Alta Amalia: the Moon's Wisdom. Shalindra could learn what she is to accomplish as Guardian."

"Shouldn't she go see the Manalathlia for that? I'm sure there's a shrine or statues or someplace there where she can figure it out better than here."

Enna stared at him. He had never been there either, and somehow he still knew. Enraged to the point that coherent words would not come, she struck his shoulder with her fist.

"What was that for?"

In answer, she hit him again, and what she lacked in strength she made up for with emotion. Then she was hitting him over and over.

"Stop knowing things!" she shouted.

"What's wrong with knowing things?" he protested as he backed away, wisely placing the small table between them.

"You helped retrieve Amalthee's Book. You guided Shalindra to Shining Moon and were at her side when it was presented to her. Now you reveal the exact time and location where Elurithlia can be seen resting atop the Three Sisters, a sacred place that has been sought unsuccessfully for thousands of years. Why?"

"Maybe I just pay attention?"

"I almost died searching for it! Do you think I've just been sitting here waiting for you to come back and tell me where it was? No one knows what you do. No one should know. The wisest scholars cannot answer the questions you so casually reveal!"

"I'm pretty sure they're smarter than me, whoever they are. I can't know everything."

"Whose conundrum established the tenants of our pacifism?" she challenged.

"Ah… Glimeralis?"

With an inarticulate sound of rage, Enna grabbed the closest pot and sent it whizzing at his head.

"What?" he asked, ducking. "You were supposed to pick something I don't know."

"You know everything! Which type of tree is safest to shelter beneath in a storm?"

"Everyone knows that."

"No, they don't! Name my closest childhood friend."

"How am I supposed to—"

"Name her!" Enna shrieked, seizing a mug from above the fireplace.

"Trilaria?"

That name struck her like ice water in the heat of summer, and the cup slipped from her numb fingers. She squeezed her eyes shut, but the images of that terrible day were burned into her mind forever. The noise and chaos of the battle. Her decision to remain behind as the other elves climbed the hill with the Kingdom knights. Trilaria's scream as her body was torn open by the claws of a demon.

The day before Tormjere and Shalindra had walked into her life.

"What happened wasn't your fault," he said, taking a step towards her. "You can't—"

"I could have." Enna clenched Elurithlia's symbol tightly in her hand, then turned away to hide her tears. "But you are right, as always."

Her tortured green eyes made fleeting contact with his, then she pushed her way out the door and was gone.

Tormjere began to follow but doubled over as his stomach spasmed. His breath hissed through clenched teeth and he gripped the table for support, squeezing it tightly enough to snap a corner off. He pushed himself upright as the pain subsided, but by the time he stepped outside, Enna was nowhere to be seen.

What is wrong?

Nothing. I just didn't sleep well.

Enna is a mess. What happened?

I accidentally reopened an old wound.

We are all growing restless, no matter how much we pretend otherwise.

Tormjere turned towards the keep, certain that Enna had gone that way. Restless was not the word he would have chosen—something deeper than his accidental knowledge of where elvish ceremonies were to be held was eating at her. Maybe she knew that staying here would resolve nothing, no matter what religious significance was to be found. His thoughts were interrupted by a shout.

"Ho, Tormjere!" Birion called, waving him over to where Edward was drilling several squads of soldiers in the cleared space outside the castle walls.

Tormjere hesitated, more eager to find Enna than talk about soldiering.

Go. They need your help, and I will speak to Enna.

Tormjere suppressed a sigh as he turned towards the men.

"Heading somewhere specific?" Birion asked, setting aside his practice sword. He was sweating beneath a double gambeson, and reached for a waterskin offered by a squire.

"Not particularly," Tormjere lied.

"Good. We're aware that, sooner or later, we'll face another demon, or if not one of them then something equally large and dangerous."

"Ogres, wyverns, and who knows what else inhabit these mountains," Edward added as he joined them. "We can't always rely on magic, so we need to find other ways to effectively deal with such creatures."

"A horse charge remains our best option," Birion said, "but it's unlikely we will have the opportunity to meet anything in the open field as we did at Tiridon. Considering this, we've made several attempts to redesign our spears."

Tormjere felt a sudden upwelling of strong emotion from Shalindra, unrelated to himself, and glanced anxiously towards the keep.

"Are we keeping you from more pressing business?" Birion asked. "The castle walls will remain standing without you leaning against them all day."

I am fine. They need your expertise, and you need something to do.

Tormjere capitulated, returning his attention to the former knight. "Are those the spears?"

Edward hefted one from the ground and handed it to Tormjere. "It's a beast, and inconvenient on horseback."

Tormjere took it in one hand and judged its weight and balance. It was thicker than a typical spear—almost a lance, really—and the point was little more than a squared spike the length of his forearm.

"It should work better against a thicker hide," he said, "if you can put enough force behind it."

"That's what we're attempting to sort out," Birion said, pointing to where one of the squads was taking turns using wooden versions of the spear on a target typically employed for jousting practice.

"The quintain is fine for tournaments, but it doesn't move or fight back," Tormjere pointed out. "You've both seen how fast a demon can move."

Birion gave him an appraising look. "Do you have another suggestion? You know better than any of us how demons fight."

"So does Shalindra."

"She's tried before," Edward said. "But she uses magic or the power of the gods or whatever you call what she does. No demon we have seen has employed either weapon or magic against us. You understand how to physically attack them. Besides, everyone was terrified of hurting her." It went unsaid that no one was likely to have such reservations about Tormjere.

Birion offered him an oversized shield. "Perhaps you could take a turn offering them a more mobile target. I've done my best, but you're faster. Unless you're afraid they'll knock you around too much."

Tormjere rolled his eyes but accepted the shield anyway and moved to a clear spot. Edward called a squad over to explain the plan, and they faced off against Tormjere with shields and practice spears.

"Wedge!" Edward shouted.

The three soldiers in front dropped their spears and locked shields together, while the remainder of the squad fell in behind them and leveled their weapons at him.

"Advance!"

Though it was only a game, Tormjere's shield instantly came up, and he slid to the side to force them to alter their path. The squad pivoted smartly but struggled to bring the heavy spears to bear. He leapt at the opening, using his shield to force his way into their side and shoulder half of them to the ground with a shove.

Edward shared a surprised glance with Birion. "Tighten up and hold in the middle!"

The soldiers tried again, with the same results. More than one rose from the soggy ground with a groan or muttered curse.

Tormjere found himself enjoying the exercise and backed away once more. "Plant the shafts against the ground next time and see if that helps."

They did it better that time, and he almost came to a stop as he pressed the shield against them, but the soggy ground gave way and their line began to collapse once again.

Tormjere was about to congratulate them on getting killed a little slower when the wooden point of a spear skidded past his shield and struck him hard in the temple, snapping his head around. His reaction was instinctive: his hand latched onto the spear like a vise, and he slung both the weapon and the hapless soldier still holding it across the field. He swung his shield edge-first like a scythe, cutting across the spears leveled at him in a shower of splintered wood. The soldier before him barely had time to raise his shield in defense before Tormjere drove his fist into it, smashing the man to the ground.

People were shouting, but he did not care. He kicked the next man to the ground and slashed his hand towards the now unprotected throat, but his arm came to a sudden stop in a shower of silver sparks.

Stop.

He pivoted and swung at another soldier, striking the sparkling barrier hard enough that a stab of pain jolted through his mind.

You must stop, they are your friends.

Tormjere spun. Shalindra stood just outside the castle gate, her symbol of Eluria radiating a silver glow as she held it before her. Her blue eyes locked on his, piercing the darkness that clouded the edges of his vision.

Tormjere let the tension drain from his body, and Shalindra lowered her symbol. Enna came rushing out beside her, and gasped when she saw the carnage at his back.

Without a word, he stalked past them both and disappeared into the forest.

* * *

Tormjere stood alone by the shore, watching the water lap gently against the rocks. Neither the water nor the distant, pleasing rumble of the falls did anything to soothe his mind. Cautious footsteps betrayed Shalindra's approach.

"At least I didn't kill anyone," he said without turning.

"No, but you could have." She came to stand beside him. "Why?"

"I haven't been around friends in a while."

"Who is it then that has surrounded you these past weeks?"

He did not answer, because he had spent his time avoiding most of them.

"This cannot continue. You must tell me what happened to you."

"It wasn't pleasant," he replied, still avoiding her gaze, "and it can't be changed. I would spare you the unhappiness of knowing."

She brought his eyes to hers. "We have known unhappiness together from the very day you rescued me. Life has been anything but kind to me in the years since then. I was betrayed by those I trusted most, been hunted and beaten, faced horrors I could never have imagined, and lost the family I held dear. Had I to walk the same path again, there is no one else I would have by my side. Allow me to share your pain, as you have shared so much of mine."

He did not turn away. She saw neither regret nor remorse in his eyes, but, somehow, he had never appeared so vulnerable. That was more terrifying to her than any enemy they had faced, but she refused to yield to her fears.

Do not judge me too harshly.

In response, she allowed her mind to brush tenderly against his. The wall that kept his past from her melted ever so slightly, and together they sank into memory.

Chapter Nine

Nowhere to Run

Tormjere stood silently on the rocky ridge, watching the Ceringions push their way up the side of the mountain towards him. There had not been a trail for Edward and Birion's men to follow, but hundreds of feet had trampled leaves and broken branches to the point that a blind man could have followed them up the mountain. Behind him, the last of the survivors who had fled Tiridon following Actondel's capitulation struggled down the opposite side. The treacherous terrain and steep descent had forced them to walk single file and had sent more than one horse plummeting to its death. The front of the column, led by Edward and Shalindra, was now at the bottom of the valley some two miles below. The tail of the column was only a quarter of the way down and would likely not finish their descent before dark.

They had no option but to press onward and hope the Ceringions tired of the chase. There were too many people to simply disappear into the woods and too few to stand their ground against what was coming.

The front of the Ceringion line came to a stop a hundred yards below Tormjere's vantage point. Their trailbreakers had probably seen him—he wasn't making any effort to hide.

They're getting close.

There is a small river in the bottom of the valley. Edward is taking us to that outcropping on the far side. He thinks we will all fit.

I see it. It's a good choice, but only defensible from two sides. We need to move faster.

The ridge on the far side of this valley looks lower than what we have already crossed over. If we can regroup near the river tonight, then make it over the next ridge tomorrow, we might—

A familiar sensation carried to him like a flash of heat from a fire, interrupting their thoughts. Tormjere's attention shifted back to the Ceringions. He still couldn't see anything through the trees, but that feeling was unmistakable.

Demon.

Here? I cannot get to you before it does. You must flee.

It will catch our tail if I do, and then we'll be fighting it uphill.

He cast about for anything that might give him some advantage, but there was nothing about the terrain that would help against a creature that size. There might be a way for him to distract it or to gain control of…

He froze. Could it be that simple? Honarch had said that a summoning talisman and a name were all that was required to control a demon. He had no magical necklace, but there had to be a wizard nearby who did. As for the name…

I know what you intend, and it frightens me. Should it not work…

If it does, we'll gain the time we need.

Trees snapped and toppled as the demon forced its way towards him at an unhurried pace, yet one that left the Ceringions around it running to keep up. It was difficult to get a clear view through the branches, but this creature was easily the equal of the largest demon they had faced. Those bits of the dull, reddish skin he could see were heavily muscled, and the rumble of its steps could be felt through the stone.

If you were to lead it down here, we might be able to—

There isn't time. Just keep them moving.

He stepped into the middle of the pass and waited.

Demons were not the mindless creatures everyone assumed them to be. Whether the visions he had seen were memories from the demons he had killed or simply dreams, he knew that they could talk. He had also seen their cunning and travelled through a portal wrought by their magic—one that had taken him instantly from one end of the battlefield to the other. That required intelligence, and intelligent beings did not enjoy forced servitude.

He rested a hand on his sword, hoping that the name he had been given belonged to this creature. If either demon or Ceringions made it past him, there would be no escape for anyone below. It was so desperate an idea that it could not fairly be called a gamble, but it was all he had left.

Moments later the first Ceringions arrived and began warily encircling him. Tormjere ignored them as the distraction they were. His indifference to their actions gave them far more caution than if he had brandished his sword, and many glanced nervously about as if expecting some trick or ambush. He continued waiting until the demon broke through the trees.

This one was man-shaped yet nearly the size of the wolf creature they had faced atop the walls at Tiridon, towering over the soldiers. A thick, squarish head sat atop massive shoulders, and its chest was broad and deep. Coarse brown hair wrapped its waist like a loincloth, while legs as thick as a horse's girth ended in dark hooves. It paused to evaluate the pass, then took a step towards him with a sneer.

"Greetings, Mataasrhu," Tormjere said with a half bow.

The Ceringions stopped and looked at each other in astonishment, then burst out in laughter, unaware of the creature's shocked reaction behind them.

An elegantly armored soldier with a plume in his helm strode to the front. "If you believe this creature can speak, it explains why you're foolish enough to think a mountain would stop us." He raised his sword. "For the amusement you have given me, I shall offer you one chance to surrender."

The soldiers crowded eagerly closer. The demon's massive hands clenched into fists, and it glared at Tormjere with hatred as it took a step closer.

Tormjere kept his eyes locked on the creature. "It must be difficult having to obey two masters."

Mataasrhu's advance paused once more.

"Between this wizard who treats you like a slave and the other demon who forced you to—"

"Enough!" Mataasrhu commanded, his deep voice echoing in the deathly quiet that settled over the pass. He stepped closer, ignoring the Ceringion soldiers as they scrambled aside. "I do not know how you came to this knowledge, but it is forbidden to speak of it."

"What do I have to fear by speaking truth?"

"Your abilities are feeble. Do you think to contest against the one who binds me?" He bent down, close enough that Tormjere could feel his breath. "Do you think," he said slowly, biting off each word, "you can control me?"

It was all Tormjere could do to keep from drawing his sword. "Why would I want to do that?"

"There is no reason but to disrupt my master's influence over me," the demon said with a contemptuous toss of its head. "And you are making a poor attempt."

Mataasrhu was correct in that observation, and Tormjere's mind churned as he sought any solution that did not involve fighting everyone around him. Perhaps he could divert the creature's attention.

Tormjere waved at the still speechless Ceringion soldiers. "You know that your friends here will lose, as have all the others. They have no power."

"They have already heard too much and will spread that knowledge to those with greater talent."

Tormjere's lip curled into a humorless grin. "You could prevent that easily enough."

The Ceringions, still uncertain as to what was happening, began to back away as Mataasrhu's gaze shifted to them. Those at the back turned to flee, but there was no escape. The demon's claws tore men in two, and his immense hooves stomped and ground others messily into the stone. Mataasrhu was thorough.

Once satisfied that there was no one left alive, Mataasrhu stalked back to Tormjere.

"You toy with forces you cannot comprehend, and doing so has delayed your fate by only a little. Where is your shield maiden?"

"Oh, cooking, cleaning, whatever it is women do."

Mataasrhu snorted dismissively, sending a blast of hot,

sulfurous air towards Tormjere. "You are attempting to stall."

"I'm attempting to achieve a favorable outcome for us both. Why speak to me if you did not want the same?"

"What I want matters little. What you want matters not at all." Mataasrhu took a step closer.

"We both want to be free of the one who has imprisoned you."

"An arrogant presumption on your part, but…" Mataasrhu paused. "He is aware that something is amiss, and approaches with haste."

"Then time is short." Tormjere drew his sword. "Help me kill him, and I will free you to return to your home."

The demon's voice dropped to a hiss. "I am forbidden to move against him, as you are aware."

"Why? Others of your kind have."

It was a half-truth mixed with an assumption, as he had observed only one demon even remotely contest its master's control, but Mataasrhu reared back in anger and surprise.

"Just take care of any soldiers he brings with him," Tormjere said, wondering what part of his statement had caused such a strong reaction. "I will kill the wizard for you."

A calculating look came over the demon's face, followed by a satisfied nod of his head. That left Tormjere unsure as to which of them was being used the most by the other.

"It is bargained," Mataasrhu whispered.

The thud of boots running up the side of the mountain heralded the arrival of more soldiers. Their commander shouted an order, and they came to an abrupt halt as they looked upon the carnage surrounding Mataasrhu. Another command sent them fanning out to block the narrow pass, unknowingly leaving their backs to Tormjere.

A dark-robed wizard pushed his way forward, and his eyes narrowed as they focused on the demon.

"What happened here?" the wizard demanded.

Mataasrhu shook his head sullenly.

"You will show me," the wizard said forcefully, mouthing an incantation as he took hold of the cage-like pendant that dangled from around his neck.

Mataasrhu did not wait for the wizard to finish. As promised, the demon sprang at the unsuspecting soldiers. The Ceringions were as woefully unprepared to face his wrath as their dead comrades, and fared no better.

The wizard, however, was not taken by surprise. As the unprepared soldiers were savaged by the demon he raised a hand, and energies pulsed on his fingertips. With a flick he sent them lancing into Mataasrhu. The demon flinched, but did not slow his attack, grabbing two soldiers and smashing them together.

Tormjere rushed from his hiding place as the wizard drew back for another strike. Too late, the magician realized the danger, and whatever defense he might have conjured was cut short by Tormjere's sword slicing across his back.

Tormjere snatched the necklace from the sorcerer even as he lay gurgling his final breaths. The sight of it filled him with satisfaction. More than just killing an enemy, the man's death had stolen away a demon.

Mataasrhu disposed of the final soldier and rushed towards him, then stopped short, his chest expanding as he drew a deep breath. Tormjere let his perception shift and saw the demon absorb the lingering flickers of power that rose from the dying wizard. It was a discovery that was both surprising and somehow familiar. He had little time to wonder at it, as he stood alone with the demon once more.

"It was bargained. Give it to me," Mataasrhu demanded.

Tormjere looked at the pendant in his hand. It was a victory, but what he needed was a way to strike at the Conclave directly. To hurt them enough that they would be left alone. "I have a question."

"How dare you renege!" Mataasrhu bellowed. "You are a liar and a coward, and I will roast your bones on a spit for eons!"

Tormjere sighed to mask his relief that the creature did not immediately carry through on his threats. "I am none of those things, and if you would cease frothing at the mouth for a moment and listen—"

"You may not bargain again with one unfulfilled! Give it to me, or I shall end you regardless of the consequences!"

"I do not offer you another bargain!" Tormjere shouted, holding out the necklace. "I offer you a choice. If you have indeed satisfied your thirst for vengeance then you may have this now. You will depart in freedom, as we agreed."

Mataasrhu grasped for it, then stopped. "Or?"

"Take me to the Conclave, and we shall both have revenge for what has been done to us."

"The cursed wizards are everywhere. You may as well ask to be taken to the stars."

"Then to their seat of power."

Mataasrhu's fists clenched. He began to speak, then held his tongue as an altogether too satisfied look came over his face.

Tormjere considered that the demon was giving in far too

quickly to his demands, but he was beyond the point their course could be altered. He felt Shalindra's awareness press into his mind, forcing her way past the blocks he had erected.

Do not!

There's no other way. Trust Honarch. I'll find you.

"Very well," Mataasrhu agreed. "I shall take you to where they are strongest." He gestured, and a swirling void of blackish mist appeared beside him. "Know that your fate is not my concern. I will have what is promised, and in exchange—"

Tormjere dashed into the mists before the demon could finish.

Mataasrhu threw back his head and sent a bellow of rage echoing through the mountains. Tormjere did not slow, sprinting through the darkened, mist-wrapped tunnel towards the light in front of him. He emerged ready for anything, but found himself alone in a circular room without windows.

Bookshelves lined the walls, and tables covered with glass bottles and other assorted implements. The floor surrounding him was inscribed with symbols and circles, but the candles about the circumference were unlit.

Mataasrhu shuffled from the mists beside him, hunched over to keep from banging his head even though the ceiling was more than double a normal height.

"Where are we?" Tormjere asked.

"The tower of my former master," Mataasrhu replied as he held his clawed fingers uncomfortably close to Tormjere's face.

Tormjere dropped the necklace into the demon's palm, unwilling to push his luck and further. Mataasrhu squeezed his powerful hand around it, shattering the device. Tendrils of black mist leaked from between his fingers and shrieked angrily as they shot throughout the room before dissipating.

"For that favor, you have earned my temporary benevolence," Mataasrhu said. "What do you now intend?"

Tormjere grinned without humor. "I'm going to make a mess. Enjoy taking your vengeance."

Mataasrhu's grin was unsettling in how closely it matched his own. The demon gathered his legs beneath him, then thrust himself upwards. The ceiling exploded in a cloud of dust and shattered stone as he forced his way through the hole. There were cries of terror from above.

Tormjere ran from the room. His desired direction had been up as well, but he considered it ill-advised to follow a vengeful demon. With a muttered curse he rushed down the stairs.

If he was in a tower, it must have been massive, for the steps that wound around its circumference were easily three paces across and curved gently. He flew down them two at a time, searching for the wizards that should be here. He tried the first door but found it locked tight, as was the next. Tormjere was preparing to force his way inside when a pair of wizards came hustling up the stairs. They stopped when they saw him, and one raised a threatening hand that crackled and swirled with fire.

"Demon!" Tormjere shouted in what he hoped was wild-eyed panic. "Demon on the loose!"

The wizard lowered his hand and looked at him as if he was deranged. "Calm yourself, and remember the protocol. Now stand aside and allow us to deal with it."

Tormjere flattened himself against the wall as the wizards hurried past. His sword took them both from behind before they had gone two steps.

He turned to leave, then stopped and allowed his vision to shift. Flickers of energy rose from the bodies, just as they had with the demons he had slain. He hesitated, unsure if it was wise to consume such powers from his own species, then took the gamble and drew the embers towards himself. They proved as uncomfortable to swallow as those of any demon he had taken, but rather than burn in his stomach they set his head throbbing with equal intensity. The tower shuddered under some mighty impact from above, reminding him that he had to hurry. He shook his head clear before continuing down the stairs.

He managed only a short distance further before encountering a wall of shimmering energy blocking his way from floor to ceiling. Beyond the distorted field the stairwell was crammed full of armed men. Spying the blood on his naked blade, they shouted demands and beat helplessly against the barrier.

With that direction blocked, Tormjere turned and charged back up the steps, jumping over the bodies of the two wizards. An explosion rocked the tower, then another. Somewhere above him Mataasrhu roared in pain.

He was running out of time and had accomplished nothing beyond the death of two wizards. If there was to be any opportunity to salvage this insane gambit, he would have to create it himself. He put his shoulder to the next locked door he encountered and forced his way through into a room filled with row upon row of bookshelves.

He immediately dove to the side as a bolt of energy sizzled past to explode against the wall behind him, sending chunks of masonry flying. Before he could regain his feet, a glowing serpent came slithering around the end of a bookshelf and launched itself at him.

The impact bowled him over, but he caught it by the neck with its fangs only a finger's span from his face. It coiled tight around his arm and began to squeeze.

He drew his sword across its neck, and it dissolved into greenish smoke. Without rising, Tormjere kicked the closest bookshelf hard with both legs, sending it and the dozens of books upon it crashing over onto the next. Somewhere in the deafening racket of collapsing bookshelves came a sharp cry of pain, and Tormjere hurdled the fallen shelves to find a wizard pinned to the floor.

His sword cleaved the wizard's head off before the man could muster a defense, and Tormjere absorbed his energies without hesitation this time.

Seeing no other exit, he turned for the door, but the sight of all the books was simply too much of a temptation. He grabbed the first sack he could find and shoved a pair of books into it. Surprisingly, the bag did not feel any heavier or appear larger. There was no time for amazement. He stuffed a few more books into it, then stowed it inside his shirt and hurried back up the steps. None of this was working as he had envisioned it. He needed to find a way out.

The next door he arrived at was breached with a well-placed kick, and he charged in with sword at the ready. This room was uninhabited, however, and dominated by a long table littered with papers and alchemical devices.

Seeking to cause what damage he could Tormjere upended the table, shattering the vials and releasing their contents on the floor. One flashed with a puff of smoke, and another released an acrid odor so strong it made his eyes water. He spied a door which opened onto a balcony and went through it quickly, gasping for air.

The warm, salty breeze and bright sunlight allowed his head to clear, but he could only look about in dismay. This tower was immense, one of several in some type of citadel set high on a hill. The skyline of the seaport city below was dotted with dozens of similar, if much smaller, towers. A leap from the balcony would be unquestionably fatal, and unless he sprouted wings he could never hope to jump the distance to the next closest tower. He was trapped.

Mataasrhu might offer his only way out, but Tormjere no longer had a bargaining chip and any help was certain to cost him more than he wished to pay. Taking a deep breath, he plunged back into the room, tore a scrap of paper from a book, and, after locating a quill, hastily scrawled Mataasrhu's name on it. He swept a shelf clean and left the scrap there. It might give him a little advantage or none at all, but if names conveyed some power over the creatures, it was all he had left.

A shattering noise like a cabinet's worth of dishes hitting the floor all at once carried up the stairs, and he suspected that the magical barrier below had been breached. Choosing not to wait and find out, he ran back up the stairs to the room they had first appeared in. Once inside he bolted the door shut.

Mataasrhu was descending through the hole he had torn in the ceiling, his skin burned and torn in dozens of places. "Too many come now, and I shall depart. Enjoy what is left of your life."

"But we made such a pair," Tormjere said. "Care to help a friend out on your way?"

Mataasrhu grinned cruelly, almost as if he had expected this turn of events. "Now it is I that shall offer you a bargain," the demon said as the purple-black mist began to swirl next to him. "Your salvation for your servitude. I will keep you alive, and you will kill those that I wish dead. And you shall give my name to no one."

An explosion shook the door, stretching the wooden planks apart and sending multicolored light streaming into the room.

"Time is short," Mataasrhu sneered.

"I will kill those *demons* you tell me to, and any others I so choose, until our return to this world." It was not much of a concession, but it was all he could think of.

"It is bargained," Mataasrhu agreed.

Tormjere bowed his head mockingly and stepped near the demon. Dark mists enveloped them both, and the world plunged into darkness.

Chapter Ten
Fallout

Shalindra's eyes snapped open as Tormjere pulled away. A wave of vertigo swept over her as she sought to reconcile the pleasant scene at the edge of the lake with the chaos of the one she had just witnessed. Of all the horrible fates she had feared for him, none came close to the reality of what he had faced.

"You did not need to do that."

His voice was insistent and filled with purpose. "I had to hurt them enough that they would leave you alone. I took away their sense of safety, and it seems to have worked."

"I would never have asked so much of you, no matter the price we would have paid. Never."

"I certainly would have preferred a different outcome. But I don't regret it. There are times when the only choice is to walk the path before you."

Shalindra shuddered. She wanted desperately to know what he had endured while under the control of the demon, but hints of those torments had revealed there was more pain than he would admit even to himself. She had seen enough, for now.

She tilted her face towards the Three Sisters and sought strength from their enduring solidness. "There were nights when I would have dreams, much as I did when you first rescued me, but they were different, less focused. I prayed they were yours, though it defies all logic. It was almost a relief each time they came because I knew, somehow, that you were still alive. If only your thoughts could have reached me more clearly."

"What difference would it have made? What could you have done other than suffer with me?"

"I do not know." She returned her eyes to his. "But I would have tried. And if my efforts had failed then I would have tried again, and then again once more. I would have continued until something worked, no matter how long it took. Your negotiation in the pass was opaque to me. I never knew the exact bargain you struck with the creature, as I never knew where it was taking you. All I could do was pray that Eluria would watch over you and see you returned safely."

"I doubt She could have done anything. The demon's world had different moons and only one god."

Shalindra tried to wrap her thoughts around such a concept but struggled to imagine a place so different from their own. "Will you tell them now?"

"If they know I've spent years living with a demon, half the village will be calling for my head, if they aren't already. And they would be right."

"It will not come to that. I think you underestimate them."

He shrugged. "It hardly matters what I think. They're almost here."

Shalindra looked back the way she had come to see Enna,

Birion, and Edward approaching with caution.

"We wished to ensure all was well, my lady," Birion said, watching Tormjere warily.

"I believe that it is," Shalindra replied.

Tormjere said nothing, but heads turned to him expectantly.

They are your friends. You owe them some explanation.

"As you recall, we fled into the mountains after being turned away from Kirchmont and Westholm. When the Ceringions sent another demon we were strung out with no hope of holding the pass, but I tricked it into betraying its master. We killed both the wizard and those soldiers with him. Hoping to distract them from further notions of pursuit, I then travelled with the demon to the citadel of the Imaretii, where we destroyed who and what we could. My only avenue of escape was to follow the demon back to his own realm."

Enna's hands flew to her mouth, but not fast enough to hide the desperate denial on her lips.

"I managed to free myself a short time ago and made my way here."

Shalindra held her breath as she awaited their reactions, but his recounting was greeted with stunned silence. Birion attempted to keep his face impassive as he stroked his moustache. Edward's jaw tightened, but there was sympathy in his eyes. It was only the slightest of comforts that they had not expected such a tale either, but they had not known him as she did, and she should have done more.

Edward finally freed his tongue. "How did you bargain with it? Not a one of the creatures that we faced ever made a sound like anything but the beasts that they are. And why not tell us?"

She heard frustration work its way into Tormjere's voice. "Demons, which we thought unintelligent monsters, not only speak but have a structured society and are adept at magic. And they've hidden those facts from the most powerful wizards on this world for generations."

Birion shook his head. "Most would consider you a raving lunatic for saying such things."

"And this demon that held you just let you go?" Edward asked, clearly struggling to comprehend it all.

"He had no choice," Tormjere replied.

"Then why didn't you leave sooner?"

"Because I had no choice."

Edward's brow furrowed. "You speak in riddles when there is little cause to do so."

Tormjere's eyes narrowed, and Shalindra quickly stepped between them. "This revelation is troubling on many levels, but it poses no immediate threat that we are aware of. Today has been difficult for all of us, and I think there is much that we must now consider."

Birion began to speak, but Shalindra cut him off. "Enna and I will attend to matters at the castle." She turned back to Tormjere. "You should discuss what you know of the demons' capabilities with Honarch."

Sending me away?

He can best determine how this might affect our dealings with the demons in the future, and you need to talk to someone who can understand what you know.

And after that?

Find me, and I will listen to what you feel.

94

***

The pounding on his door startled Honarch out of his thoughts. He would have to check his alarm spells again, because none of them had alerted him to anyone's arrival. He hurried down the steps and opened the door to find Tormjere standing outside.

"Oh, it's you. Come in. Shouldn't you be with Shalindra?"

"She sent me here to settle things down."

"What happened?" Honarch asked as he closed the door.

"I may have almost killed a bunch of our soldiers."

"That seems... unfortunate. Should I be worried?"

Tormjere made no effort to hide his frustration, though it was likely with himself more than anyone else. "No, but no one wants me around."

"And I'm to keep an eye on you? Trap you in a cage of mystic energies or something?"

"I think that was the intent."

Honarch was not surprised. They always sent their problems to him, after all. The clerics were kind enough, and Shalindra was as generous as she could be, but no one else bothered him unless they needed something done. Tormjere was likely treated the same. Commoners never trusted those with power, regardless of what good they accomplished.

"Consider yourself trapped, then. Why don't you come up to my study? I find the height helps my thinking."

Tormjere lapsed into silence as they climbed the steps, wearing a look Honarch recognized far too well. Whatever he had done was obviously serious, and no one was ever harder on Tormjere than he was on himself.

Once in the room, he waved Tormjere to a chair before

occupying his usual seat by the window.

"I take it this is somehow related to the mystery of where you've been all this time."

"More or less. I bargained with the demon, travelled with it to Tythir, wrecked one of the Conclave's towers, and then escaped by following him to his own realm."

Honarch was thankful he was sitting down. "And I thought my adventures were noteworthy. I'll admit that I'm full of questions."

"Everyone seems to be. I'm not sure why it matters now. I didn't show up bringing hordes of demons into the valley. The past is behind us."

Honarch tried to hide his concern. Something had changed in the youth that had saved him from this same valley years before, and he doubted that change was for the better.

Still, the problem had come to a head, and it could be solved like any other. No matter what was eating him Tormjere had never been one to talk about himself, even when he needed to, so Honarch elected to take a purely academic approach and see what he could coax out.

"The demon realm, as you called it, is most commonly named *Urtratu* in the texts. I believe the word derives from an elvish term. I'm not sure if it is truly a realm or a different plane of existence, but either construct serves for our discussion."

"They call it 'the world,' just like we do."

"Interesting. There are few authoritative works on the subject, and those that do exist are kept locked away. The knowledge of where demons come from is tightly controlled."

"It wasn't much of a secret when they kept showing up everywhere we went. You know how many times they tried to kill her."

Honarch stood and began pacing. "This is true. Something must have changed during the war for them to sanction such overt use. There have been no sightings or verifiable reports since then that I am aware of."

Tormjere rested a hand on his sword hilt and repositioned it more comfortably, but the motion failed to hide the fact that his hand was shaking. Honarch decided to shift the conversation away from the fighting and tried to keep the worry from his voice.

"I'll assume that dealing with the Ceringions pursuing us was accomplished with the usual application of force, so let's set that aside. How did you bargain with a demon?"

"The same way I would with any merchant: I offered him something he wanted in exchange for what I wanted."

"That implies the ability to communicate, unless you figured out the requisite spell."

"Demons can talk."

"There have been theories about that," Honarch said, "and as I do not consider you to be infirm, I choose to believe you. However, it would be only slightly less disturbing had you come bearing news that cows could speak."

"Cows talk to each other all the time."

He chuckled, hoping to lighten the mood. "Point taken, but they don't speak to us. How did you discover it?"

"I just guessed. Something you mentioned once about them having names came to me, so I gambled that having one would allow me to control it."

"Wait, where did you get the name?" Honarch asked. "They're never written down. It violates the directive."

Tormjere looked out the window. "This one was."

Sensing his friend's unease, Honarch did not press for more. He had yet to see a demon, but he had heard plenty of descriptions and it took little imagination to conclude that the deal reached was unpleasant. The particulars could be sorted out later, when Tormjere was less on edge. "Where did you go from the pass, once this agreement was reached?"

"A tower in the Conclave's citadel."

"Tythir," Honarch said in amazement. "That's hundreds of miles away. Which tower?"

"I was too busy to ask."

"I'm sure. I inquire only because... Well, it doesn't matter. And you fled from there to their world?"

"That was our bargain."

Honarch suppressed a shudder. "I cannot imagine that was pleasant."

Tormjere put a hand to his forehead. "Life is unpleasant, at times."

There was neither defeatism nor self-pity in that statement, just an unvarnished appraisal. Honarch sighed inwardly, wondering how much longer Tormjere would remain in Newlmir, and if his leaving would be by choice. It was doubtful that this would end any other way. He himself was tolerated only because of his occasional usefulness, and the times when he had journeyed from the valley he had not been missed. The thought filled him with sadness.

"There's been enough sorrow for everyone these past few years," he said, almost to himself. "And all of us have changed."

"I'm still me."

Honarch placed a hand on his friend's shoulder, hoping that it was so. Either way, when Tormjere did leave, he would not go alone.

* * *

The dented shield landed on the table with a clatter, startling Shalindra from her thoughts. The center was caved in on itself, and blood stained the straps on the back.

When she looked up she was confronted by Birion and Edward's grim expressions. She silently prayed for strength, steeling herself for what was certain to be an unpleasant conversation.

"What is this?"

"This," Birion said, "is the shield that he put his fist through."

"Today's incident was unfortunate, but the situation—"

"Your Highness, a lance at full charge would not do this much damage. He is not the same as he was when he left us."

"None of us are."

"We can appreciate what he has done," Edward said. "I cannot imagine what he has been through, living among demons, but we must recognize the risk he poses. Had you not been there to stop him…"

"He is the most trustworthy man I know, and he has always been loyal to us."

"He has always been loyal to *you*," Edward corrected, "and what is best for you might not be best for the rest of us."

Conversation paused as the door opened and Enna entered the room. She took one look at the serious faces and stood quietly to the side so as not to interrupt further.

"Tormjere is not our enemy," Shalindra reiterated, "no matter

99

where he went or what he did."

Birion looked pained. "Neither of us are suggesting that he is, at least not by choice."

"If you are leading up to something, please just say it."

"I respect his prowess, Your Highness. He is, without question, the most capable fighter I have ever seen." Birion pointed to the mangled shield. "But no man can do this. Were I to force myself against steel with such vigor, I would be begging for your aid to repair my crippled arm."

Shalindra put a hand to her aching forehead, wishing that prayers were enough to banish the headaches. "I understand your concerns, and they are valid. Tormjere did what he thought best to save us from the Ceringions and the Conclave. We owe him our lives, yet he has asked for neither reward nor thanks."

"In that, at least, he has my respect," Birion said. "How do you intend to deal with this situation?"

"I do not know. But I will do everything in my power to see him through this, and I would ask that you do the same."

The men exchanged less than enthusiastic glances, then bowed and exited the room, leaving her to ponder the damaged shield in silence. When the door had closed behind them, Enna approached.

"Those that were injured will recover, with Elurithlia's blessings."

"May Her light keep them safe. Enna, what am I to do about this?"

Enna shook her head, sending ripples up and down her white hair. "It cannot be swept aside. Word has already spread through the village."

"Had I only paid more attention…" Shalindra sat and put her

head in her hands. "I feel I have ignored him when he needs me the most. He seemed so normal. How could I have not recognized the turmoil inside him?"

"There is no way you could you have foreseen this," Enna said. "If he has become isolated, then all of us must share some part of the blame. No one has been willing to press him for explanations."

"Myself least of all. Having him back is like having the use of both arms again. No one knows me so completely. It was almost as it was when we travelled together, before meeting you or the demons. Everything was simple then, no matter how unpleasant. We had only to survive, and I knew that so long as we were together, we would."

"And now?"

Shalindra hung her head. "Neither of us needs the other in the ways we once did. There is nothing for him to protect me from on this island, and I cannot heal wounds he does not receive."

Enna seemed equally helpless. "It could be that the scars he bears are much deeper than we can see, and require an even greater level of care in their restoration."

She was almost certainly correct, but Shalindra remained at a loss for how to resolve it. "Could you ask Argus to help counter the rumors he hears? It is an injustice that they have driven Honarch away to his tower with their mistrust, and I will not allow that to happen again. Not to him. Not after what he sacrificed to keep us alive."

"Of course."

She took a deep breath and let it out slowly. "I will be along shortly, I just… need a moment."

Enna looked like she might say something more, but did not.

"Yes, Sister."

When Enna was gone, Shalindra rose and walked in aimless circles about the room. The castle was beginning to feel more like a prison than a palace, and the ridges of the valley a fence denying her freedom. She had not been outside that boundary since… since she had arrived here. What had she been thinking all that time? Had she made the correct decisions? Certainly, no one thought she was doing the right thing now. It should not bother her so much, but it did.

It's because they're right.

Why is it that you can block your thoughts from mine, but I cannot?

You don't try very hard.

It is not you they fear, it is the unknown. If you would tell me what happened to you there, I could alleviate their concerns.

It won't change anything, and might only make it worse.

What could you have possibly done that would make us think less of you?

His silence was her only answer.

* * *

Enna collapsed to the ground. The sand was sharp against her skin, more like shards of rock than dry silt. Her eyes burned from the acrid air and dust driven against her by unending gusts of wind. Forcing herself to her knees, her shaking hands brought a blackened, gooey mass to her lips. She took a second bite and then a third, each one squirming in her stomach as if it were still alive.

Eventually, her body rebelled, sending most of what she had swallowed back out onto the sand.

"Do you find such delicacies unacceptable?"

She recognized the deep voice that came from behind her but could see nothing but the sand between her fingers. Something lashed across her back, and she jerked in pain but refused to cry out. Everything blurred, and she fought to bring it back in focus.

"Get up," the voice commanded. "Get up and eat or I will leave you to be eaten."

She rose once more, though every fiber in her being protested the action. The corpse lay open at her feet, though she struggled to remember how it had died or even what it had been. She gripped a piece of the still-warm flesh and tore it free. Raising it defiantly to her lips she…

…bolted awake, gasping for air. Her room was dark and quiet, save for her panting breaths. Though by herself, she was certain she was not alone. On her chest, Elurithlia's symbol radiated an insistent warmth. She wiped the damp hair from her face with a trembling hand. That one had been so real.

She had experienced such nightmares before. The first had come while they were outside Evermen's Forge, the second not long after arriving in the valley. Then nothing for over a year. There was no pattern to them, and she could never remember enough of what she had dreamed to consider it worth mentioning. But this one…

She whispered a prayer to Elurithlia and lay back on the pillow, searching for happier thoughts to counter the nightmare. It was only a dream, she told herself, but no matter how tightly she closed her eyes, sleep continued to elude her, and her mind returned to the same frightening images again and again. She had to know where they came from, and there was only one person she could ask.

She bit her lip indecisively, then threw on her clothes and tiptoed from her room.

Shalindra's door was closed, as was Marie's. Enna padded silently down the hall and out of the temple. As she hurried through the gardens, it occurred to her that she had chastised Shalindra for doing this exact sort of thing not long ago, but the irony was not enough to change her mind.

The night was dark and the stars lost behind the clouds that seemed to have established a permanent home above their heads. Little stirred other than the occasional night creature and the soothing roar of water pouring over the falls. With haste she made her way to Tormjere's cottage, praying that he was there and not at Honarch's tower. She paused at the doorway, but the door swung open before she could knock. Again.

"A little late for a visit, isn't it?" Tormjere asked.

"I... Yes, it is," she said, suddenly feeling foolish. "I apologize for waking you."

"I wasn't asleep," he said, stepping back to allow her in.

He turned and lit a candle, though she noticed in a distracted sort of way that the flame sprang to life without a spark. It could have been a trick of the light, but his face seemed pale.

"I... had a nightmare," Enna said. "One that I hoped you might... I was somewhere hot... a desert, maybe, and there was someone forcing me to... eat something. It was dark and foul, and... I don't know if it was dead or not, but I put it in my mouth and ..." She trailed off. He seemed almost not to be listening, like he was somewhere else.

"Tormjere?"

He stared through her like she did not exist. His hands shook, and he clenched them at his side. Though no fire was lit and the room was cool, he was sweating.

She reached for him, but he jerked away.

"Don't."

He doubled over with his hands clutching his stomach, his face contorted in pain.

Driven by the fear twisting its way up her spine, her words came out as more of a demand than she would have wished. "Tell me what is happening to you."

"You should leave."

"Just breathe," Enna implored, placing a hand on his shoulder. "It was your dream I saw, wasn't it? I don't care how it happened. Wherever you were, you're no longer there. You're here, with me in the valley. Tormjere, focus on me. I want to understand."

"Do you?" he snapped, uncoiling like a striking snake. He seized her by the arms, pinning them against her sides as he lifted her from the ground. "You have a dream and suddenly you want to understand everything I went through? You think you can comprehend what it's like, or what I could do?"

"Let go," she pleaded.

"I know what you taste like. I know why demons who haven't set foot on this world in eons still speak of your kind. If I wanted it, no one here could stop me."

"What are you talking about?" Enna gasped, struggling impotently in his vise-like grip. His normally calm eyes were a terrifying maelstrom that reflected the red of the flickering candlelight. Darkness seemed to gather around them, swirling ever more tightly as the room faded from view. "Mistress, help me," she whimpered.

Blue light flashed across his eyes, pure and cold, quenching the fires that burned in them. He seemed to teeter, then took a ragged breath, as if collecting himself. The wild look did not leave him, but he jerked away and she tumbled to the floor.

His arms trembled as he wrapped them about his stomach once more.

She took a step away from him in shock, rubbing her arms where his hands had been.

"Enna…"

She spun and fled into the night.

Chapter Eleven

Approaching Dawn

Enna made her way up the darkened trail, her small feet leaving no trace of her passage on the damp ground. The trees around her stood like silent sentinels silhouetted by the pre-dawn light that sprinkled through the sparse clouds above. Her path was steep, but she had walked it so many times that her legs covered the distance easily. She needed peace. Needed somewhere to think. Everything was wrong—Tormjere, the settlement they were building, the missing pilgrims from Ildalarial, the lack of any message from her mother. It felt as if the world were teetering on its edge, uncertain if it would right itself or tumble into chaos.

Her destination was a rocky bluff that capped a sheer cliff on the eastern edge of the valley. She had discovered it not long after they had arrived but told no one of its location. Shalindra undoubtedly knew of it but had never inquired or followed her here. She respected Enna's need for solitude, understanding so much that never needed to be said. Everyone else just assumed she needed to wander in the woods. Her private refuge was a beautiful, solitary place where she could pray in the way of her people, rejoicing in the sun's return and thanking Elurithlia for Her protection through the night.

Except that this morning it was occupied.

Tormjere stood on the edge of the bluff, facing the pending dawn. For a moment, she thought him unaware of her presence.

"It's a beautiful view," he said without turning.

She hesitated, then continued forward to stand beside him. She had seen that look before, and it reminded her that he was at least in some ways the same person he had been: always more critical of his own flaws than his most vehement detractor.

"Enna..."

"Don't. I know who you are, even if you sometimes forget."

His jaw tightened as he continued wrestling with his thoughts, staring into the distance as if he could pierce the mists shrouding the mountains and reveal what lay in the darkness cast by their shadows. There was a hint of resignation in his voice when he at last spoke. "You're here to pray, and I'm interrupting."

He was, and she did not want him here despite her charitable statement. Her arms still ached from where his hands had painfully gripped them just hours ago, but she recognized that it was a different desire that had led him here this morning. "I hold no claim over these woods. You are welcome to stay, if it pleases you."

She pushed further thoughts of conversation from her mind. The dawn would not wait, and Elurithlia deserved the honors She was due. Enna knelt in the place she always did.

She began facing west, away from the dawn. The barest sliver of the moon was low on the horizon, having almost completed Her watch over the night. Enna cleared her mind. She rarely spoke the words aloud, but today she felt it appropriate. They escaped her lips without conscious effort as her mind drifted somewhere else, seeking the calming strength of her goddess.

Behind her, the sun broke the crest of the mountains, turning the mists to fire and throwing brilliant oranges and reds across the clouds.

Completing the verse, she turned to face east without opening her eyes. The sun's first rays bathed her face in warmth. The world slipped away as she began to sing softly. The heat of her devotion mixed with that of the sun, penetrating deep into her soul and easing the burdens she carried. It was in this moment of quiet reflection that so many things could become clear, and Her true desires could be determined.

Today, her thoughts turned to the man who stood beside her. It was what she needed to confront, no matter how much she sought to deny it. It was with no small amount of guilt that she realized her initial anger towards him could have pushed him further away. What she had seen last night was not who he was.

Guide me, Elurithlia. Show me the way in your glory that I may return him to the man he should be.

Her direction now confirmed, she opened her eyes with a touch of regret. It was only then that she noticed the looped end of a golden chain dangling from Tormjere's clenched fist. It was odd, as she had never known him to possess any form of jewelry.

"That was much nicer in your language," he said.

"I suppose you've learned to speak elvish now, as well?"

This time, the smile almost made it to his eyes. "Just bits and pieces."

"It was the first prayer I ever learned, and one that never fails to bring me comfort."

She rose half in front of him, perilously close to the cliff.

"Mind the edge," he cautioned.

Her eyes searched his for the chaos she had witnessed, but today they held only the dark calmness that she had always been able to rely upon. "I do not believe that you would let me fall."

"You trust me more than you should."

"Perhaps my fault was in not trusting you enough. Why did you come here today?"

In answer, he took her gently by the shoulders and turned her—not east towards the sun as she had expected but angled to the south. There was nothing different about the mountains in that direction, but he gave every indication that he was looking *at* something.

A stiff breeze could have sent her plummeting to her death, but his hands remained protectively on her arms. The chain he held was surprisingly warm as it brushed against her skin, but it struck her as a private thing and she dared not look at it. The sunrise before her was beautiful, casting warm light across the mountains and causing the mists that shrouded the valleys to practically glow. A pair of wyverns took flight in the distance, their silhouettes soaring ever higher in the slowly warming air. No matter how long she lived, she would never tire of such sights.

"Close your eyes and tell me what you feel."

That was an odd thing to ask and tested the trust she had just spoken of, but she did as he requested. "The warmth of the sun lopsided on my cheeks. The coolness of the air. A hint of a breeze." *The touch of your fingers on my skin.* "There is nothing else."

She opened her eyes and turned within his arms to face him. "The gift of divination faded from our race ages ago, if that was what you hoped for."

He stepped back, guiding her away from the precipice. "There are some who still can."

"True, but it is an isolated talent, rarely found outside our wilder kin."

"Who follow Lithandris."

Why did it sound like it pained him to say it? "Did you study the history of elves in those books you read? Or perhaps theology?"

When he did not respond, she continued. "The god of the forest is known for his keen senses, and in rare cases his followers inherit that gift. But you already knew that, didn't you? What did you want me to feel?"

He did not answer immediately, but his hand tightened around whatever was at the end of the golden chain.

"They're bringing it back."

His tone implied a poor decision on someone's part, but she was at a loss for what it might mean. Whatever realization he had come to seemed to spur him to action, however, and he turned towards the trail that had brought her here.

"Tormjere?"

He paused and glanced back at her over his shoulder.

"You are welcome to join me here whenever you wish. You may find it as ideal a place to seek answers from the gods as I do."

"And when the gods don't listen?"

It hurt her heart to hear the bitterness in those words, but her answer was as absolute a promise as she had ever made. "I will."

Chapter Twelve

Returning Purpose

Tormjere watched the column of men and mules wind its way into Newlmir two days later. The procession carried no banners, but the dozen or so priests in the habit of Amalthee left little doubt as to their affiliation. Edward rode at the van with two squads of his best men, though judging from the size of those behind him the escort was more ceremonial than determent. He counted at least fifty armed guards, plus an equal number of teamsters and retainers. Most of the guards were common men-at-arms, but those who walked closest to the priests were handsomely accoutered in mail coats with polished helms, and carried both halberd and sword. Their tabards were blue trimmed in brown and gold, and were topped with a sash of blue.

The entire complement was such that they should have remained undisturbed, but judging from the relief on many of the faces Tormjere doubted that it had been an entirely peaceful journey. The visitors were enough to swell the population of the village, which had spent the past two days scrambling to prepare for the unexpected visit. Most everyone in the valley had turned out to watch their arrival, regardless of whether they gave their devotions to the goddess of wisdom and gold.

Shalindra and Enna stood awaiting them alongside the entire council in what passed for the town common area: a clear field located at the shoreward foot of the causeway. The two-story inn Argus had established was off to one side, squeezed between several other buildings which formed a semi-circular perimeter.

Tormjere observed the proceedings with Honarch from a short distance away, thankful that he held no formal rank and was under no obligation to participate. Honarch should have been with the council, but no one objected to his absence. The villagers gave them both plenty of space, which was irksome but hardly unexpected. His stomach moved suddenly of its own accord, and he shifted his feet in an attempt to settle it.

What is wrong? You are so anxious that you are beginning to make me *nervous.*

I should've just gone with Edward to meet him, and done without the ceremony.

But you did not, and now we must respect the formalities.

Edward rendered a proper salute as he reached the field. Half the formation of horsemen behind him continued across the bridge towards the stables while the rest peeled off and came to attention behind the waiting dignitaries.

An equally serious-looking commander of the blue-tabarded soldiers called the visiting procession to a halt, and the priests, most of whom were sitting atop mules, began to dismount and assemble by rank. Mixed in among the weary movements of grey-haired elders and eager acolytes was a sandy haired young man in simple brown robes.

He was the one you rescued? He looks so young.

There was truth to that. Age had yet to lay its fingers on the Legitarso of Amalthee, and Treven's ever-youthful features and open countenance belied both his years and the power he now commanded.

"You were right," Honarch whispered beside him. "But I can't believe he's actually here. The route from Kirchmont is no more safe than the last time we walked it."

Tormjere kept his thoughts to himself. He had no ready answer for why they had come here—a fact he had considered pointing out to Enna—but he could not shake a nagging feeling that the timing of this visit was less coincidental than it might appear.

An acolyte hurried to help Treven from his mule, then offered his arm and lead him forward. Each priest bowed respectfully as he passed, save an older priest who fell into step in front of him.

Treven's robes were the same brown they had always been but were of a finer cut and material than before, and a small, gold symbol of Amalthee's open Book hung from a matching chain around his neck, as it did on the other priests. But it was the battered haversack slung across a shoulder that drew Tormjere's attention. Standing in stark contrast to the other finery, it radiated a familiar warmth that Tormjere could feel like the sun on a cool day.

The crowd edged closer to the priests as everyone tried to get a good look. Treven's cheerful expression lent him an air of approachability, like a good friend come to visit, and his eyes were… cloudy. Not quite the milky white that Father Gelid's had been, but their once youthful sparkle was now misted and grey.

The three came to a stop before the waiting dignitaries, with the acolyte whispering a description of the scene in Treven's ear.

"Welcome to Newlmir," Shalindra said with a polite bow. "I am Shalindra, Sister of Eluria and head of our council. On behalf of all who reside here, it is my pleasure to receive such distinguished visitors."

The priest in front of Treven returned the bow. "It is in the name of Amalthee that we thank you. Father Treven, Legitarso of Amalthee and Reader of Her Word, is pleased to receive your greeting."

The corner of Treven's mouth turned up in amusement. "And he is also pleased to speak for himself, when protocol and Father Ignatius allow it."

The senior priest cast his eyes heavenward at the interruption but stepped to the side as Treven was guided closer to Shalindra.

"I pray that our presence will cause no disruption to your efforts to sow your fields," Treven said. "We have come so that I may fulfil a vow I made years ago, that others of my order could see this place firsthand and understand what was sacrificed to bring Her Book home."

"Visitors are never a disruption," Shalindra replied. "Anything that we may do to make your stay more comfortable, we shall. I am afraid that our inn is incapable of providing for your entire number, but Sister Marie is pleased to offer accommodations at Eluria's temple as best she is able."

Treven turned his head towards where Tormjere and Honarch stood at the back of the crowd. "Friends should never stand on formality."

"We tend towards the informal here," she said, "but if I may present my fellow councilors?"

Introductions of each group's worthies were made by Shalindra and Father Ignatius, and with that the formalities were concluded. Edward took charge of finding places around the village for the teamsters and hired swords, and the gathering began to slowly disperse.

Honarch nudged Tormjere, and the two of them drifted closer as the councilors and priests mingled, though the guards saw to it that everyone kept a respectable distance from Treven and Shalindra as they conversed.

"We are weary from our journey," Treven said to her, "but if you would allow me a moment with some old acquaintances?"

He looked towards Tormjere and Honarch and waved them forward. The pair made their way through the crowd, both well aware of the guards' eyes upon them.

Honarch bowed. "It is good to see you again. I hope your journey here was less eventful than our last."

"It had its own share of challenges," Treven said with a grin. "But some things remained the same. No matter how hard I tried, I still managed to place my bedroll atop every root in the forest. It was most uncomfortable."

Honarch chuckled. "I'm sorry I did not return sooner. We'll have to continue our conversation once you are settled."

"Indeed we will. There is much to catch up on." Treven turned to Tormjere, though his eyes remained unfocused. "Still so quiet at formal gatherings?"

"I didn't have anything to add," Tormjere replied.

"I somehow doubt that, but we will see. How have you been?"

The question was delivered with casual innocence, but it felt like Treven's cloudy eyes were looking right through him.

Tormjere found himself wanting to give a straightforward answer, but this was neither the time nor place.

"Busy."

"As are many who spend their time helping others these days, often to their own detriment. But, as everyone now seems to be waiting on me, let us proceed to this beautiful island. I fear I must impose upon your guidance, however." He placed a hand on Tormjere's arm.

It was difficult to tell who was more surprised: Treven's acolyte, his fellow priests, or the villagers that still clustered around them. Tormjere ignored their shocked expressions and led Treven towards the bridge. So caught off guard were the others that they almost had to scramble as they fell into line behind the pair.

I see that he enjoys causing a stir.

Only when there's a reason to.

Tormjere described the castle and island for him as they walked, much as Treven had himself done for Father Gelid years before. It was difficult to tell if Treven was completely or partially blind, but the level of detail he provided must have been correct as Treven offered no objection.

"I remember how beautiful this valley looked, and I am relieved that it is being put to a more peaceful use now," Treven said as they set foot on the island and turned towards the temple. "There is a degree of overlap in the teachings of Eluria and Amalthee when it comes to the restorative arts, and though our approaches differ in the execution, the relationship of the two faiths has always been cordial."

"How is life as an oracle?" Tormjere asked now that they had less of an audience.

117

"People who come seeking fortunes and foretellings rarely receive the answer they wish for, and often they leave more unhappy than if they had never asked." Treven's voice turned so serious that he almost sounded like a different person. "Answering questions about the weather or personal fortunes is not why Amalthee allows me to read Her Book. I conduct my own studies, and through Her wisdom I have discovered knowledge once thought lost. She has shown me wonderous things that can be achieved through effort and application by the correct craftsmen, concepts and ideals that might revolutionize our world and shake empires. And, most importantly,…" Treven gave a sideways glance over his shoulder at Father Ignatius, then leaned close and whispered conspiratorially to Tormjere. "…I know everything about bears now."

For a moment, his face held its familiar look of wonder. Treven's grin was infectious, and Tormjere felt as if a pressure had been released from around him and he could breathe again. A lump formed in his throat, and he found himself chuckling, then laughing. Without any regard for formality he wrapped Treven in a hug.

"Thank you," was all he could say.

Though Father Ignatius looked askance at this complete breach of protocol, Treven hugged him back. "You are welcome, my friend."

What is so amusing about bears?

* * *

It took the remainder of the day for the visitors to settle in. In some ways, it was a blessing that the elvish pilgrims had not appeared this year, as the space they would normally have occupied could be completely given over to the priests. Their guards had been packed into the soldiers' barracks until it overflowed, and a few of them still ended up in tents outside.

Many of the priests retired to their rooms almost immediately, but Treven was eager to 'see' more of the island and resumed walking with Tormjere after only the briefest respite. Treven's acolyte, a youth named Talley, was given the time to rest, but Father Ignatius saw to it that no matter who he was with a pair of guards followed a discrete distance behind.

It was not long before their conversation turned to Tormjere's past, and he filled Treven in on what had happened since they had last met, including his forced visit to the demon realm.

"I cannot put into words how terrified I am that you endured such hardships," Treven said when he was finished, "but I know what you are capable of when the rest of us need saving. You have questioned this decision, haven't you?"

"A little. Should I have simply let the demon go, or tried harder to stay with them, rather than consigning myself to his service?"

"Whether by accident or design, you have always made the right decisions, even when they were not in your own best interest. Your actions served to keep those around you safe, and still you dwell on things that cannot be changed."

Treven reached into the haversack at his side, and when his hand reappeared it held a sheathed dagger. The leather was scuffed and slightly oversized for the blade it contained, and the handle scratched and worn. "I used this to save Father Gelid's life, even though it had very nearly ended your own."

"It's funny how weapons work," Tormjere observed.

"Indeed. Whenever I am frustrated by some problem or at my

119

inability to understand Amalthee's words, I use this dagger to remind myself of what can be accomplished when we try. Yet, in spite of how we grow, in some ways we never change."

"Some changes are more apparent than others," Tormjere said.

"A delightfully oblique reference to my eyesight, though you seem far less surprised than I might have expected."

"The cause isn't difficult to determine, and it doesn't affect who you are."

Treven smiled. The same calm, assured smile that Gelid always had. "Amalthee's Book does not require the blind to read it, but our eyes are ill suited to comprehending Her holy script, and so, over time, they will be altered. The more accustomed to Her words our eyes become, the less suited to our own vision."

"It certainly explains the requirement to already be blind."

"Amalthee is a compassionate goddess. Sight is our primary sense, and She would never ask Her followers to sacrifice something so essential."

"Except you."

"True, but it is a small price to pay. I know so much more than I ever could have hoped to learn. Such knowledge is not given lightly, and so I must assume that it will be worth the sacrifice."

"It seems a steep price."

"Is it? How much would you give for what you cherish? How much have you given already?"

Tormjere avoided that answer, but another thought struck him. "So She did choose Gelid."

"I believe so. Though I was with him when he was tested, I have little doubt that he was the one evaluated favorably. Yet when we finally reached the Book, his health, as you know, was failing."

"And there was no one else there but you."

"There is always someone else, no matter how special we are in our own minds."

There was certainly truth to that, though Tormjere could have pointed out that 'someone else' was often not around when they were needed. Nevertheless, it was good to talk to him again, though he doubted that Treven had come all this way just to make him feel better.

"When are you going to see Gelid?"

"The day after tomorrow, I think. Our weeks on the trail proved taxing for some of my older companions, and I wish them to be well enough for the experience."

Tormjere had been reluctant to visit the eastern ridge, but if he had to return to the site where Gelid was buried, at least it would be with friends who could understand.

* * *

Enna could scarcely believe it, but they had somehow managed to cram four tables into the main hall, three of which had been hastily constructed just the day before. Calling the eating arrangements 'cramped' would have been like referring to the Three Sisters as 'tall hills.' It was undoubtedly below the standards that the visiting priests of Amalthee were accustomed to, but the Legitarso, who insisted on being called Treven, was gracious with his comments and humble with his requests.

Shalindra and Tormjere sat with Treven and Father Ignatius, and the remainder of Newlmir's councilors and a few senior priests had squeezed into the table. Though she could have demanded a place at the same table, Enna had given up her seat so Honarch could be with them as well. It had seemed the best way to stem the arguments and maneuverings of who sat where, and the wizard deserved to be there as much as anyone.

Tormjere had brought his sword and knife to the table as always, a fact that caused the guards no small amount of consternation. It was an unnecessary concern, as he would likely be quicker to Treven's defense than they could ever hope to be. No matter what was being said or how much he laughed—which was a relief to see—his eyes darted about like a hawk's. The only other time he behaved like that was when he was with Shalindra. It left her curious as to what had transpired between him and the Legitarso to forge an equally tight bond.

The Legitarso, whom she had learned was the only one who could read Amalthee's sacred book, was indeed an interesting person. He looked less a man and more a boy, but there were lines on his face that did not belong on one so young, and his calm observations rivalled the profoundness of the most learned of sages. The battered haversack he carried was so out of place that she could only assume it possessed some sentimental value.

In truth, she could only guess at the reasons. Amalthee was a minor but respected goddess among the elves, and, as with their elvish counterparts, Enna found most of these priests polite if a bit stuffy. The priest sitting across from her, one Father Tonnoli, was a middle-aged man with thinning hair and an interest in breads that bordered on obsession. By the time plates had been set before them, she was already wondering why Elurithlia had supplied him as a dinner companion. Maria was at the other end of her table, currently instructing a pair of raptly attentive acolytes on the far more interesting subject of restoration. Enna repressed a sigh as Tonnoli slathered a piece of bread with butter and launched into a dissertation on the merits of the leavening process. Though it was improper, she hoped that Honarch appreciated this sacrifice she was making.

After dinner, the extra tables were cleared and stacked to the side, and the remaining table moved close to the fire. Perhaps responding to some request Enna was unaware of, Shalindra politely shooed away most of the councilors by assigning them to important sounding work.

Father Tonnoli took his leave of Enna as well, but not before promising to complete his dissertation at a later date.

Soon the room had emptied, leaving only Birion, Edward, Honarch, Treven and Father Ignatius chatting around the table with her and Shalindra. Even the acolyte who normally guided the blind priest around had been dismissed.

Tormjere leaned against a nearby wall, making clear his desire to not participate.

It was Treven who brought an end to the small talk. "I would like to thank you all for your hospitality, and for an excellent meal."

"As we thank you for your visit," Shalindra replied. "We have seen fewer than our usual number of pilgrims this year, and we always enjoy any contact with the larger world."

Father Ignatius looked intrigued. "Could the weather be a factor? Every cloud in the sky seemed determined to rain upon us these past weeks, and the entire Kingdom has seen little of the sun since last fall."

Shalindra looked to Enna, as she did whenever the subject turned to the elves. "It is possible, but, like you, my people are willing to endure much for their faith."

"All who visit this valley seem destined to endure something,"

Treven observed.

"You have been here before, then?" Birion asked. She considered than he should have already known the answer, but then he had never paid much attention to Honarch and might not have believed him anyway.

"Indeed. A wizard stole the Book of Amalthee, our most precious artifact, and it ended up here. I shall not bore you with the details, save to say that the only three members who survived the expedition to retrieve it are now in this room. At the time, it seemed a simple theft of questionable motive, but events since then have cast that evaluation into doubt."

Enna looked at Tormjere, but his face was typically impassive. Honarch had never spoken of what happened here either, other than in the most general terms. Whatever had transpired, it had left a mark on all three men.

"Wizards always meddle where they aren't welcome," Edward agreed, then nodded apologetically to Honarch. "Present company excluded, of course."

Honarch indicated that he took no offense. "It is an open secret that my former mentors exerted tremendous influence, even when they chose not to reveal their involvement."

"Who is involved," Treven said, "is often more important than the actual event. We learned later that the Conclave of Imaretii was likely instrumental in the decision to steal the Book, though proof of that involvement has been elusive enough that there was little action we could take."

"The culprits left no trace?"

"The signs are always there. We simply need to listen to them and act accordingly."

It could have been Enna's imagination, but his words seemed to carry a larger meaning, and she saw Shalindra shift in her chair.

"But why?" Edward asked. "Their involvement with the Ceringions was easy enough to understand."

"Why, indeed? Amalthee has always sought to share knowledge, not hoard it, and so their desire to deny us the Book remains a mystery."

"Are there any magicians who are not members of the Conclave?" Enna asked. She actually knew very little about magic in the human kingdoms.

Honarch leaned forward. "Very few in this part of the world. They are the strongest guild in both Actondel and Ceringion, and there is little magic that escapes their notice."

"We have wizards in Ildalarial," Enna pointed out. "They do not belong to such a group."

"They focus on different disciplines," Honarch said. "It wasn't my field of study, so I remain ignorant of what interactions take place. For us, magic is not common outside of the larger cities."

Treven nodded. "Our dialog with Ildalarial has also been more limited than perhaps they should be, though for entirely different reasons. As for the Imaretii: members of the Conclave often studied in our libraries, and priests of our order would, at time, visit theirs. Of late, however, that exchange has become more one-sided."

"A curious set of circumstances," Shalindra observed.

"Yes," Treven agreed. "Members of the Conclave tried to keep us from reading the Book of Amalthee, and wizards of that same group later employed demons in a way that effectively prevented your weapon's return to the elves. Curious, indeed."

Edward shook his head. He had resisted the idea that Shalindra was specifically targeted by the creatures for as long as Enna had known him, and the years without further problems had reinforced that position. "What of the demons that attacked cities where we were not?"

"I have followed reports of other sightings to their logical conclusions, but they proved to be only rumors."

Shalindra glanced at Edward. "We suspected as much, though we were told otherwise."

Though Shalindra no longer debated the point with her cousin, Enna held no reservations about the demons' intent. "That they followed us everywhere is not in dispute. But we never discovered how, or for what ultimate purpose."

"I, too, was interested in their pattern of movement," Treven said. "On those points, Amalthee remains vague. I believe that She has tried to tell me, but not in ways that I understand. In either case, it is likely to be a truth that we were never meant to discover."

Enna could not contain her curiosity. The implication that he had a more direct method of communication with his goddess could provide insights into their own desire to speak with Elurithlia. "Why wouldn't She just tell you outright?"

Treven smiled with the calm assurance of a man who had already pondered such questions. "I have often asked myself that same thing, and I will answer you with a query of my own: if you were asked a question for which you knew the answer, why would you choose not to respond?"

"Because I did not trust the person asking it," Enna answered.

"Possible, though I will assume, for my own sake, that is not the case here."

The discussion was interrupted as Rolf stepped into the room.

The farmer hurried to Shalindra and whispered frantically in her ear. Enna suppressed a smile, wondering which part of the sky was about to fall upon them this time.

Shalindra discreetly rolled her eyes at Enna as she stood. The rest of the group rose with her. "I apologize, but there are some matters that I must attend to."

"The hour grows late," Treven said, "and we should likewise retire, though I have enjoyed our conversation immensely. Do not delay on my account. I fear I move more slowly now and will enjoy the walk to our lodgings at a more leisurely pace."

"Thank you again," Shalindra said with a bow. "And if there is anything we can do to make your stay more comfortable, please let me know."

Tormjere did not move as Edward and Birion followed her from the room with polite partings. Enna hung back as well, hoping to ask the blind priest another question about his method of communion with Amalthee. She was surprised when Father Ignatius closed the door, leaving only the four of them still in the room.

Treven rose and walked closer to Tormjere, his fingers tracing their way along the edge of the table. Enna suddenly felt as if she were intruding on a private matter, but Father Ignatius was aware of her continued presence and to excuse herself would have risked an awkward interruption.

"You were quiet," Treven said.

Tormjere shrugged. "They were asking you enough already."

"'A wise man knows when to talk and when it is best to listen.' But you know of an answer to the question they only hinted at, don't you?"

"Amalthee doesn't know."

Treven grinned. "Or She knows, and does not think me ready for such knowledge. Indulging our every curiosity is not why our gods exist."

"So why do they exist?"

"One of the great theological questions that has been debated since we first discovered that gods share our world. Even the origins of those we are aware of remains shrouded in mystery. There are some, however, whose genesis was recorded." Treven's sightless eyes turned to look directly at where Enna stood.

Enna stiffened in surprise, certain that she had been forgotten and unnerved at the ease with which he knew where she was.

"But there are others," Treven continued, "who can tell that story far better than I, and with more accuracy."

"It's not in Her Book?" Tormjere asked.

"Not that I have yet seen. You are welcome to look for yourself."

Tormjere's eyes returned to the table where Treven had been sitting, as if he were debating the wisdom of Treven's offer. Enna could see nothing, but there was a reluctance to Tormjere's movements as he walked towards it.

Father Ignatius opened his mouth to protest but fell silent at Treven's raised hand.

Tormjere's arm swept across the empty air above the table, as if he were opening a book and turning the pages. Father Ignatius' face had turned a splotchy red, and he looked ready to throw himself bodily at Tormjere for what he must surely have regarded as a violation of Amalthee's most holy relic.

Treven's soft voice was filled with curiosity. "What do you see, when you look at Her?"

Tormjere did not lift his eyes, and there was an uncharacteristic note of resignation in his voice. "The outline is edged in gold, and shimmers like sunlight on water. The pages are invisible and more smooth than any paper I've ever touched."

"What did you see," Treven said, his voice calm even as it took on a surprising intensity, "when She spoke to you?"

Tormjere closed the invisible Book. "She gave me a name—a full year before I would need it."

Treven seemed unfazed by his answer, but Enna could scarcely believe what she was hearing. He was capable of reading from a holy relic which no one else could even see, *and* he could wield Shining Moon?

Father Ignatius appeared as dumbstruck as she no doubt did, which was the only thing that kept her from believing that she had misunderstood some part of the conversation.

Treven's words were as carefully considered as ever. "I find that remarkable, on multiple levels. Through Her words, I have learned lore long forgotten, witnessed places which no longer exist, been shown the past and even the almost present. But She has never favored me with a glimpse of the future, and I know of no occasion in our history when anyone other than the Legitarso has been able read from Her Book."

"The why is obvious," Tormjere said. "Clearly, She wanted me to defeat the demon, and thus for Shalindra to escape."

"That explanation would fit, but there could be many other reasons of equal or greater validity. Perhaps you were intended to convey the name to someone else or employ it in a different manner, or perhaps it was simply a reward for your considerable efforts on my behalf."

"Regardless of what was intended, was it required to make our escape? Could it have been accomplished in a better way?"

Treven chuckled. "Still you dwell overlong on things that cannot be changed."

"The past is a book that has already been written," Tormjere finished for him with a sigh.

Treven returned the invisible tome to its place in his ever-present haversack. "It is probable that our understanding of these circumstances remains less than it should be. You have given me much to consider, but I believe it a good time to retire while Father Ignatius can still restrain himself. Do not fear the choices you made. If She chose to bestow this gift on you, it can only be because you were worthy. We will speak more."

Father Ignatius offered his arm, and the priests made their way out of the room. Tormjere stood in thought for a moment, then followed them without looking at Enna.

She should have said something to him. Far from resolving his inner conflicts, the conversation seemed to have only deepened his pain. She hurried to catch up to him.

"I believe I owe you an apology," she said.

Tormjere came to a stop and raised an eyebrow. "I thought you wanted one from me."

"I do, but it does not absolve me of responsibility for my own behavior, and I fear I may have been hasty in my judgement. I offered to listen when you needed it, but I cannot expect you to trust me to do that if I hold you under an unjust obligation."

Tormjere seemed to accept that, but rather than reciprocate he directed her attention to the Three Sisters, barely visible against the backdrop of stars in the sky. "Tell me how Eluria was born."

Before tonight, such a request would have resulted in an abbreviated answer, but Treven had called out her knowledge of the event specifically and must have done so for some purpose.

"Elurithlia was born in the heavens as a small, dim child fixed into the night sky. Yet people rejoiced in Her appearance and She grew rapidly as the ranks of Her faithful swelled. Most welcomed this new beacon of hope, but there were others among the gods who were jealous of Her rapid rise to prominence. Zarua, god of the night, was angered by the light She brought to his domain, and He cast Her from the heavens. Elurithlia's mother, Iniach, the Earth, caught Her as She fell, and in Her rage at what had been done flung mountains of rock and fire into the sky.

"Though Her subjects cried out for the return of Her brilliance, no one dared to risk Iniach's wrath by seeking Elurithlia where She had fallen. None, that is, save for a trio of sisters recently driven from their village for witchcraft. Desperate for food, they followed Her light, hoping to find a means with which to sustain themselves. Though they discovered no bounty in the wasteland that enveloped Her, they were drawn ever deeper, and there they found Elurithlia, beautiful and pure amidst the destruction.

"She calmed their fears and provided them succor, and spoke to them of Her need to return to the realm of Her birth. Thus it was that three sisters—Kyliria, Draylia, and Hylalia—agreed to aid Elurithlia so that She might fulfil Her purpose and resume Her nightly vigil.

"This task they considered for days, gathering all the strength possible so that they might be worthy of the attempt. On the first day, Kyliria, the oldest, wrought a staircase of gems that stretched

131

to the heavens, but it collapsed beneath Elurithlia's weight as She attempted to mount them. On the second, Draylia bent all her powers to the task, creating a rope of unimaginable length which she attached to the sky, but still it was not long enough to ensure Elurithlia's return. And on the third, Hylalia called into being a mystic horse with wings to carry Elurithlia aloft. It soared far beyond the clouds, but it, too, was bound to this mortal world, and ultimately failed to lift Her high enough.

"Upon the fourth day the sisters realized that, though each was powerful in their arts, individually they could not hope to succeed, and so they combined their talents. With the eldest standing atop her sisters' shoulders, and with the blessings of Iniach, they raised the earth itself until it touched the sky. Elurithlia ascended to the top of the highest peak and stepped into the heavens once more.

"The sisters remain standing to this day, honoring their vow to keep our Mistress raised to the heavens for all time. It is in their honor that we name ourselves Sisters and strive to uphold their ideals and devotions."

"Horses don't have wings," Tormjere pointed out.

"And yet there they stand," Enna said, pointing at the mountains. "Different from the rest, sharp and pointed and tall where those around them are worn and low."

"But how was She actually created?"

"I do not know, nor do I wish to. That would be… rude. I haven't asked you where you came from."

"I'll assume it's the same way everyone is born, but I'm not sure that—"

Enna stamped her foot. "Ask Her yourself then! Perhaps She will smite some sense into you when She answers."

Tormjere suppressed a grin as she stormed off.

You have a singular ability to infuriate her.

I suppose I do.

She was trying to help.

She did.

Chapter Thirteen

Gelid's Rest

The deep tones of Amalthee's chants emerged from the morning mists, blending with Eluria's uplifted voices to produce a soothing melody as clerics of both faiths performed their morning devotions.

Tormjere waited outside Eluria's temple, watching as Father Ignatius lead his service from the gardens while Treven observed the equivalent ceremony taking place inside the temple. The priest's words invoked the history and majesty of his faith, reminding those who listened of what had been sacrificed to gift Amalthee's wisdom to the people of the world.

It was a stirring oration, but Tormjere remembered only too well what sacrifices had been made for Her Book, and he was more interested in whether the ever-present clouds rolling above their heads would continue to withhold their precipitation for the entire day.

"I see they've picked up a few converts," Honarch observed as the service came to a close and the priests began to shuffle towards them.

Tormjere nodded silently in agreement, using his response as an excuse to turn his head and evaluate the forty-odd men who would escort them. Half wore the blue sash of Treven's personal guard while the rest were composed of Birion's most experienced. Horses had been offered but were politely declined. The priests intended to walk their pilgrimage as Treven had done before, and so their protectors would as well. Only a handful of mules would be used for those priests who could not manage the hike.

Tormjere chuckled to himself at that. The three of them had been exhausted and beaten, moments away from being killed by goblins, and would have gladly accepted a mule or horse or any other method of transportation that would have sped their flight to Kirchmont. Father Ignatius' version of their escape sounded much better.

He returned his attention to the temple as Treven emerged, his hand resting on Shalindra's arm as they chatted pleasantly. It was somehow appropriate to see the two people who carried the most powerful artifacts of their respective goddesses standing together. Shalindra caught his eye and smiled.

Treven cares for you greatly.

Talking about me, were you?

Only in passing. He is the wisest man I have ever met.

Treven's acolyte took over and escorted him to his mule, which he mounted without assistance. Tormjere and Honarch joined him. Shalindra allowed the friends their space, falling back to speak with Father Ignatius as the column began to move.

The mood was cheerful and expectant, in spite of the gloomy weather. They followed the road from the village as it wound generally eastward. Honarch spoke with Treven as they walked. Their conversation, as always, encompassed any number of interesting topics from the nature of magic to the hibernation patterns of bears. Tormjere said little, instead keeping his attention focused on the woods around them. If not for the number of people with them, they could well have been on their way back to Evermen's Forge after retrieving the Book.

They passed up and out of the valley via a series of switchbacks before descending down the other side. Upon reaching the base of the mountain they stopped at a rocky clearing. It was just as empty now as the night when he had come struggling into it with Father Gelid on his back, hoping to find their supplies and additional guards waiting. The only difference now was a seldom used but definitely man-made path leading up towards the rocky outcropping.

An expectant hush fell over the priests as they crowded close to the trail, and the mood turned suddenly somber.

Treven dismounted and adjusted his haversack. "Tormjere, if I could impose upon you once more?"

The barest of tremors ran through Treven's hand as he rested it on Tormjere's arm, and the priest's whispered words carried to his ears alone. "Do not allow me to falter."

Tormjere indicated that Honarch should lead, and the trio started up the path. There was a general shuffling as the group began to move behind them, but Father Ignatius laid a gentle hand on Talley's shoulder to keep him from following. At that signal, the other priests came to a halt as well, leaving the three men to walk alone into the trees.

The trail was narrow and hard, climbing sharply upwards. After only a short distance, they reached the tiny alcove where they had huddled to escape the bitter wind on the night of their escape.

Treven said nothing as they passed, but his grip on Tormjere's arm tightened as if he was somehow aware of it.

They had gone but a few steps further when the ground began to shift beneath their feet. A jumble of stones rose unexpectedly from the beside the trail, like a small avalanche travelling the wrong direction, assembling themselves into a bulky, oversized humanoid shape with a stout chest and over-long arms, head and shoulders taller than the three men.

"Rockhurlers?" Treven asked.

"Yes," Tormjere answered. The creature's manner was unthreatening, but he kept a watchful eye on it all the same.

"That's Grokka," Honarch said. "I think. It's hard to tell them apart, and he doesn't usually leave the valley. Let me see what he wants." He began to mouth the incantation that would allow him to speak in the grating language they used, but was interrupted when another of the creatures rose on the opposite side of the trail.

The two rockhurlers faced each other with a scraping of stones, extending their arms as they leaned inward to form an arch across the trail.

Honarch looked over his shoulder at Tormjere. "They've never done that before."

"What?" Treven asked.

Tormjere supplied a quick explanation.

"Fascinating."

Honarch continued between them, and Tormjere followed with Treven. The rockhurlers remained as still as the mountain while the men passed beneath them. No sooner had they emerged than another pair rose beyond the first and assumed a similar position.

Tormjere glanced up at the ledge high above, and found dozens of rockhurlers now stood there. He caught Honarch's eye and motioned with his head towards the line of rockhurlers.

By Her light, look behind you.

Tormjere did. All around them, on every ridge and patch of stone, hundreds of rockhurlers stood facing them like silent sentinels.

"So many," Honarch whispered in awe. "I thought there were only a handful scattered about."

Treven put Tormjere's thoughts into words: "Perhaps the sacrifice he made left a mark on a broader audience than we could have imagined."

They continued solemnly until they at last stood before the solid outcropping of stone that stretched high above them. Treven released Tormjere's arm, and after a few halting steps he knelt at the base of the rock. He withdrew the Book from his haversack and set it on the ground before him, as he had done when using its power to create the tomb where they had laid Gelid. This time, however, he left it closed as he bent his head in prayer.

Tormjere struggled with his own memories in silence. Gelid had been more kind and encouraging to him than he sometimes deserved. He would always wonder if there was something else he could have done, some way in which he could have steered the eventual outcome to a more positive result. None of the other solutions he had considered were satisfactory, and Gelid's tomb offered no answers either.

When Treven at last raised his head, his voice was thick with emotion.

"It seems like yesterday."

"It is not something we can ever forget," Honarch agreed.

Treven retrieved the Book and rose to his feet. "I would not be who I am today without his tutelage, and without you both, I would not be here at all. I find myself unable to convey just how much that means."

Tormjere placed a hand on his shoulder. "Sometimes words are simply insufficient for what needs to be said."

A smile brightened Treven's face. "I count myself the most fortunate man in the world to have your friendship. Though I see the two of you much less than I might wish, it is the time I cherish the most. I could remain here all day, but there are others who must experience this as well. We should allow them their time."

Tormjere touched his hand to the stone in farewell before taking Treven's arm once more and leading him back down the path.

* * *

Shalindra had done her best to keep out of Tormjere's thoughts once he had reached the sacred site, for it was a private place for the three men. They were quiet as they came back down the path, but Treven's smile had returned. The waiting priests began to file forward two at a time to visit the rock wall that Tormjere had named Gelid's Rest. They lingered for a shorter time, but many were visibly moved when they reappeared, and some openly wept.

Treven and Honarch sat beside each other, quietly reminiscing about their shared experiences. Tormjere sat with them for a time, but she felt his growing restlessness and was not surprised when he moved away so as not to disturb them. The rawness of his emotions, the burning desire for justice that was as yet unfulfilled, seeped into her thoughts. Sooner or later, the Conclave would be made to answer for all the evils it had done.

"And how do you intend to accomplish that?" she asked as she joined him.

"He deserved a better fate," Tormjere said, avoiding a direct answer. The lack of words hardly mattered. The obligation he had placed upon himself bubbled just beneath the surface of his thoughts, and his desire to see Gelid and Treven to safety was as easy to understand as if she had made the promise herself.

"That is not in dispute. From all accounts he was every bit as remarkable as Treven and would have done just as much good. Yet he continues to give hope and meaning long after his passing, and has touched lives he never knew existed. Is that not enough?"

Tormjere seemed to have no answer to that. And no matter how many times he tried, she doubted he ever would.

When the last of the priests had completed their visits, Treven led the assemblage in a brief prayer. As with his private conversations, the young priest had a gift for keeping his words simple and plain yet infused with depth and meaning far beyond their simple phrasing. His prayer left the group more rejuvenated than somber, and Shalindra saw no sign of sadness as they began the journey back to the village. The sun at last broke through the clouds, casting streaks of afternoon light across the valley floor.

Tormjere took his station a few protective paces in front of Treven and Honarch, exactly as he had earlier in the day. She could easily imagine it had been that way when the three men fled years ago. There was always someone he needed to protect.

She quickened her pace to join them.

"That was a beautiful prayer you offered," she said to Treven.

"Thank you. I do not possess the gift of oration that Father

Ignatius enjoys, so it is something I constantly work on."

Honarch grinned. "There's always something to make better, isn't there? It's been wonderful having you here, but I know it won't last forever. How long until you must leave?"

"Likely a week or two," Treven answered. "Father Bentoni seeks a suitable location to establish Amalthee's church, if you would allow it."

The council would have to officially approve of such construction, of course. Vestus had been given authority for parceling out the available land, but Shalindra would ensure that the new church received a favorable location. The benefits of having a solid link to one of the most powerful organizations in Kirchmont would be immeasurable, and Treven deserved no less.

"We would be honored," Shalindra replied. "Her knowledge is well respected and will be a blessing to us all."

"Then we will stay long enough to see the foundation set and bless its construction."

"You will be here for our midsummer's festival, then," Shalindra said.

Treven practically glowed with excitement at that observation. "I always have duties to attend to during that time, but as our contingent is minor, such obligations should be handled quickly. Father Ignatius might even allow me to partake of the festivities." The last was said just loud enough to be sure the older priest heard him, but Ignatius just shook his head disapprovingly.

Shalindra chuckled with Honarch, wondering how much fun the reserved priests would actually allow themselves to have. Her amusement faded as she caught sight of the Three Sisters, their stoic peaks reminding her that she had her own pilgrimage to make soon. She could only pray that hers would be as successful as the one they had just completed.

Chapter Fourteen
Summer Solstice

Midsummer's day marked the time when the endless cycle of day and night was shifted most in favor of the sun, and therefore contained the shortest night of the year. It was an event observed by nearly every pantheon with celebrations, prayers, and offerings. No one could say when such celebrations had originated; it was simply something that was done.

Followers of Hototo, the Laughing Farmer, often crowned their hair with wreaths of flowers as they danced and leapt over fires. Priests of Amalthee, whose year began with the winter solstice, would set aside rank and privilege and offer their knowledge and restorative arts for free. Ruling lords would pardon minor offenses and host feasts and games open to all in their domain. Two years prior, Birion had even reported seeing festive activity from the goblin tribe at the south end of the valley, though it was difficult to imagine the combative creatures celebrating anything other than a victory.

For the Sisters of Eluria, the solstice also marked the date on which their goddess was given to the world. It was not only the first day of the lunar year but also the time Her power was at its peak.

The day had taken on an additional meaning for the inhabitants of Newlmir, for it was on a midsummer's eve just a few years earlier that they had first beheld the valley that became the end of an arduous flight. There had been no celebration that year, only the simplest of ceremonies when Shalindra had stood before them and proclaimed that, finally, they were home.

This year, a stiff breeze finally forced away the rain that had threatened for days, leaving the sky more blue than grey for the first time in weeks. The sunshine brought with it a wet summer heat, but there were few who objected. Many took it as a sign that the fields would dry out and the crops begin to grow at their usual rate.

The presence of the visiting priests was taken as an excuse to expand the usual events. Simple but colorful banners were hung throughout the village. A small platform had been thrown together in the commons, where a pair of minstrels now sat tuning their instruments. A bonfire was stacked and prepared in the middle of the field, ready to be lit that evening by the boys who had reached their manhood during the past year.

Tormjere wandered aimlessly through the preparations as Shalindra and Enna were performing their morning devotions in the temple. The priests of Amalthee were similarly engaged, leaving him little to do. He made his way across the bridge and through the village, evaluating the area for potential dangers for no other reason than to allow his mind to focus on something. Few of the villagers paid him any mind, but at least those who did no longer did so with distrust. The shift could have come from the calming influence of Amalthee's priests, or from the simple passage of time.

Regardless, he was happy to be ignored.

As he approached the inn, a barrel-chested man with a thick beard reaching halfway to his belt emerged from within, straining as he hefted a long table on his shoulder. His beard and hair were now shot with streaks of grey, but Argus was easy to recognize. The former soldier had been Edward's second in command during the war, and Tormjere could never forget his aid as Shalindra fled her father's court.

"How's life running a tavern?" Tormjere asked as he walked over.

"Tormjere!" Argus exclaimed. He set the table down and came around it to shake his hand. "I heard you were back, but this place keeps me busy sunup to sundown. Can't complain, though, as no one's tried to kill me in at least a year."

"A definite improvement," Tormjere chuckled.

"Since you're still carting around that sword of yours, I'll assume you've not gained any such sense of self-preservation."

"Not yet. I'm surprised Edward let you go."

"He didn't want to, but I'd had my fill of soldiering, and walking up and down all those mountains to get here took a toll on the knees. Always wanted to try my hand at running an inn, and as there was no competition it seemed as good a time as any to give it a go."

"Every town needs one," Tormjere agreed. "I'm glad you've found a more relaxing occupation."

"Still have to thump someone on the head every now and again, but it's peaceable enough."

"Argus!" a woman's voice yelled from inside. "Stop yapping and help me with this stew!"

Tormjere raised an eyebrow.

"Shut up," Argus replied with a mock glare. "One of these days, you'll get yourself a woman and settle down, too. Come back this afternoon once I've got food out."

"I will," Tormjere promised with a laugh.

Argus hustled back inside, muttering something about missing deliveries, but he walked with a noticeable limp.

He took a spear through his side during a raid on the village. I barely reached him in time.

I should've stayed with you.

And changed what? You cannot protect everyone.

* * *

There was no official initiation to the festivities, with smaller groups beginning here and there until some critical mass was achieved. By the time the council arrived, a good portion of the crowd had already been engaged in revelry for some time. Practically everyone in the valley was in attendance, including those who lived beneath the falls in Rumbleton, though a few unlucky soldiers patrolled the surrounding woods to ensure that there were no surprises.

Tormjere caught up with Honarch, and as neither of them were required to do anything, they secured a quiet place in the shade of Argus' inn from which they could watch and sample his ale.

The local dignitaries made their way onto the platform and Edward rang a handbell to call the gathering to order, or at least attract the attention of those still interested in giving it.

"Welcome to the Midsummer Festival!" Shalindra called out. "On behalf of my fellow councilors, I would like to again welcome

146

our esteemed guests and declare the festival open to one and all. As we are blessed to be without any serious crimes in need of pardoning, it is the decision of the council to forgive all debts owed to us."

The proclamation was met with a rousing cheer from the crowd, drowning out whatever she said next.

"Helps that the priests are here," Argus said as he joined them. "They've brought enough gold with them to solve many a problem, and they're spending it on every service we can provide."

"Money is something they're never short on," Honarch agreed.

"It's odd how they outnumber our clerics this year, but it's good to see their getting along without any religious fighting. We usually have a few dozen elves hosting their own party off in the woods on this day."

"Still no idea why they aren't here?" Honarch asked.

"You're the one on the council, in case you're forgetting."

Honarch tried to look chagrined, but failed.

Argus shook his head. "We've heard naught beyond what you likely have. The swordsmen the priests brought with them are full of talk about fighting between Ildalarial and the Kingdom, but that's a conflict that ebbs and flows over the years."

"It's certainly nothing new," Tormjere agreed.

"I'd be more worried about the Kingdom tearing itself apart, but that's their business now and not mine."

"Well, I'm glad Treven and his friends don't drink," Honarch commented. "This is good ale you serve. Perhaps we should spend more time in this establishment."

Argus barked a laugh. "Your coin's welcome, but I remember what happened the last time I saw the two of you in a tavern. Don't be thinking of stirring up trouble in mine or I'll thump you like anyone else."

"I was eating in peace," Honarch pointed out. "He started it."

Tormjere made no effort to appear innocent, and they both laughed and promised they would cause him no more trouble than he deserved.

Shalindra's speech was concluding, to the relief of nearly everyone. It was a confident smile she displayed as she led the officiants from the platform, but Tormjere saw her eyes linger on the Three Sisters yet again.

"That's my cue to get back to work," Argus said. "Enjoy yourselves, and if you see a dwarf walking around, remind him my beard's better than his!"

The musicians occupied the stage, and the air soon filled with song. Villagers mingled in groups large and small, enjoying tables filled with food and drink. The workmen and guards who had accompanied the priests of Amalthee mixed with the residents easily, though the priests themselves were more reserved. Treven, however, clapped his hands to the music and appeared to be having a good time of it, despite Ignatius' whispered comments that likely concerned the dignity of his position.

Tormjere chuckled at the thought. Treven had probably been stuck in the abbey ever since returning with the Book and had not been able to have any fun. Tormjere had not either, now that he thought about it, not since… the summer before his brother left to join the monks of Toush. He hoped Eljorn's path had been smoother than his own.

Honarch cursed under his breath and turned away from the crowd. "I think Rolf spotted me. Do me a favor and claim I'm not here. He'll probably ask me to make his crops grow faster."

"Can you?"

"Do I look like a field hand?" Honarch shot back as he ducked inside the inn.

The farmer appeared moments later, searching about, but when his quarry failed to appear, he turned his attention to Tormjere. "Have you seen the wizard?"

The way he said it grated on Tormjere's nerves, and he took another drink before answering.

"His name is Honarch."

Rolf seemed unsure of which way to take that and cleared his throat nervously. "Yes, of course. Well, I'll just keep looking."

Tormjere shook his head as the man walked away. The music changed again, and people began to dance. Enna's flowing white hair caught his attention as she bounced and twirled to the merry tune. He caught his foot tapping along to the music as he watched her, and let himself relax just a little.

As if it had been waiting to seize the opportunity, his stomach twisted uncomfortably of its own accord. He pushed away from the wall in an attempt to ignore it as he headed towards the shaded awning Shalindra and Treven were standing beneath. Being near them allowed him to suppress his urges better than anything else he had tried.

Hungry still, with all this food for the taking?

It's not what I need.

Then you must learn to no longer need it. The only demons here are the ones you carry with you.

As the music ended, Enna swirled breathlessly to a stop beside him and took him by the arm, her green eyes sparkling mischievously.

"Put away that sour face. Come, and be with your friends," she said, making a show of dragging him towards Shalindra.

He resisted her efforts, as he was already headed in that direction and needed no help, but Shalindra's obvious amusement at his predicament was enough to cause him to relent and play along.

"I have always enjoyed the unrestrained elvish perspective on festivities," Treven commented as they arrived. Tormjere was hardly surprised that Treven knew he was approaching, but eventually he was going to ask him how, like Father Gelid, he knew so much about the world he could not see.

"You mentioned having few elvish visitors," Shalindra said, "but have you been able to spend time with them?"

"Unfortunately, I have not. A few have petitioned me in Kirchmont, but that journey can be as difficult for them as coming here was for me, though for different reasons. Tormjere was the only one of our group to meet an elf last time."

"They must have been from Silvalaria," Enna said. "Their nation lies only a few day's ride south, between us and my home of Ildalarial."

"That close? Have you been able to establish amicable relations with them?"

"Indirectly," Shalindra answered. "We have reasonably cordial relations, as we do not compete for any resources and both have a common enemy in the goblin tribes. Most of our pilgrims actually come all the way from Ildalarial."

Treven tapped his chin. "The ones who were to stay in the magnificent accommodations we now occupy? The weather could certainly play a part. I've heard that the southern parts of the Kingdom have seen so much rain that flooding has become a significant problem, and that on top of record snowfalls this past winter."

The mention of snow sent Shalindra's eyes once more to the white-capped peaks of the Three Sisters.

They aren't going anywhere.

She tossed an annoyed glance at Tormjere and tried to return her attentions to the festivities, but the worry never left her eyes.

"You're beginning to look almost as unhappy as he does," Enna told her. "Honestly, I should have you both thrown in the lake."

Treven chuckled. "I believe that would be the highlight of the day, and it might even begin a new tradition."

They all shared a laugh as Shalindra blushed. "I have been given every reason to be happy this year, but there is always something to worry about. I did not mean to cloud this day."

"Fear not," Treven said with a smile. "Those who care about us the most overlook our failings the quickest, as Father Ignatius will hopefully ignore my intent to sample your innkeeper's ale. I hear that it's excellent. If you'll excuse me?"

Treven placed his hand on his acolyte's arm, and bowed his head as he excused himself.

Shalindra answered him with a smile of her own, and both women bowed.

"He is so good at putting my mind at ease," she said when he had gone. But you both know the source of my concerns. The full moon arrives in only a few days and I cannot stop thinking about what I will attempt."

"You still have not told anyone?" Enna asked.

"No. Birion will ride with us to Rumbleton, and Marie knows that we will be gone overnight."

"It's just another day," Tormjere said, though not believing it any more than she did. For everyone else it would be, but for her, it could well be the most important day of her entire life.

"I feel as if I should be preparing somehow, but formality has never been a hallmark of my relationship with Eluria. She will see me as I am, and I can only pray that is good enough."

Chapter Fifteen

In Her Light

The next two days passed like an eternity, each one crawling slower than the last as the moon waxed slowly towards fullness. Yet the morning of their departure arrived with terrifying swiftness, and it was all Shalindra could do to maintain an air of normalcy for those around her.

She left the temple with Enna after the morning prayer, as she always did, but today Tormjere and Birion awaited them with horses and a squad of soldiers. After the briefest of greetings, they rode for Rumbleton under the pretext of inspecting the road and rotating the guard. There were many reasons Shalindra had elected to keep her attempt secret, but the biggest was simply the odds of failure. She and Enna had seen enough of those already.

They reached the town quickly and without incident, and Birion sent the men to their posts before conferring with her.

"Do you remain committed to this course of action, my lady?" he asked, his voice raised just enough to be heard over the roar of the falls. "Given recent events…"

"I know your concerns, but we will be in no danger."

The knight bit off any further protest. "When do you plan to return?"

"I expect by midday tomorrow."

"I will stable your horses then. If you have not returned by midday, we will come looking for you. I wish you success, whatever your endeavor may be."

He left them with a salute.

Shalindra took a deep breath and nodded to Tormjere, who shouldered a small pack and led them across the rope bridge once more.

I'm still surprised he's letting you go.

He was adamant in voicing his displeasure with the idea, but I am no longer a princess to be kept under guard.

They followed the same path as before, though this time Tormjere kept a more comfortable pace. The day was clear and bright, and the summer sun shone down on the valley with all its strength. The air grew thick and oppressive as they left behind the cool mists of the river, until even the shade of the trees was not enough to offer relief from the humid heat.

The butterflies in her stomach grew more restless with every step as they climbed higher out of the valley. Not a word was spoken. Tormjere stalked a few paces ahead, alert for danger, and with footsteps as smooth as they were quiet. Enna trailed an equal distance behind her, her quiet presence as supportive as ever. Neither of them could help her with the question she had wrestled with for days: what would it feel like to speak to a god?

She ducked beneath a branch and stepped over a rock, wondering as she did so if she would be able to navigate the conversation with Eluria so easily. Would it even be a conversation?

She repressed a sigh. No matter how she approached the subject, she was always left with more questions than she started with.

They arrived atop the ridgeline by midafternoon but stopped short of the clearing. With nothing to do until the moon joined them, they made themselves comfortable and waited. They had brought enough food for several days, but Shalindra ate little, unable to contain her nervousness as the afternoon dragged into evening.

Would this ceremony even work, or would it be yet another false hope? If it did succeed, what would she ask Eluria? There were dozens of questions that readily came to mind, but each seemed trivial upon examination. Despite memorizing everything that Enna had been able to remember from her own lessons years ago, Shalindra had little sense of what level of piety was expected of her. Though she was terrified to admit it, she did not even know what she needed to do. She had been so eager for this day to arrive, but now that it was here she was terrified of what the evening would hold.

The moon peeked above the horizon just before sunset, full and round. Tormjere was propped against a tree with his eyes closed, but she doubted he was asleep. Enna sat in prayer, much as she had since their arrival, but Shalindra could do little more than stare at the moon's beauty and gauge its trajectory as it arced slowly across the sky. As the hours drifted away, its path drew ever closer to the peaks of the mountains.

When the moon neared the peaks of the Three Sisters, Enna rose. "It is time. Remember to take your place at the moment Elurithlia rests atop the first of the Sisters. Do not allow your thoughts or your gaze to wander from Her light as She climbs atop the tallest peak. When She stands at the pinnacle, with one foot in our world and the other in Hers, you will receive all that She may give."

Shalindra took a deep breath and tried to slow her pounding heart. "Will you walk with me? Should I falter…"

Enna shook her head. "Only one may seek Her. You were meant for this."

Shalindra could not speak, certain that if she opened her mouth, her fear would come pouring out and she would flee down the side of the mountain. She squeezed Enna's hand in thanks, then walked the final steps to the clearing alone.

The stone ground was empty, as it had been when she had seen it last, and yet this time it was different: it was as if the rock itself was aware of her and waited expectantly. A soft warmth stirred within her symbol, dispelling her doubts and soothing her emotions. Shalindra was barely aware of her steps as she crossed the small clearing and sank to her knees. Though her eyes remained glued to the moon, her body sought a specific alignment with the heavens.

The air was clear and cool against her skin. Only a handful of small clouds floated by, their rumpled edges rimmed in silver light. Thousands of stars gave life to the blackness of the sky above, causing the full moon to appear as the center of an immense eye looking down upon her.

She had never felt so small and alone in her life.

Shalindra laid Shining Moon across the stone in front of her and watched the moon as it watched her, each patiently waiting on the other. After long moments it rolled slowly atop the tallest of the Three Sisters, matching exactly its placement and perspective on the symbol clutched in her hands.

The sky paused expectantly.

She took a breath, and the world seemed to breathe with her.

Her consciousness ebbed and flowed with the rise and fall of her chest. The moon's light was all she knew, its edges blurring as its whiteness and purity consumed everything around her—the trees, the mountains, even the sound of the waterfall—each faded one after the other into that light. It wrapped her in a cloak of majesty and radiance that was both warm and comforting, and she became lost in its glow.

She drifted without substance.

How long she could not ascertain, for time was a concept oddly without meaning. Everything was white, but it was a whiteness with taste and texture, brightness and shadow, and filled with coolness and warmth. She possessed neither past nor future but was aware of the significance of them both.

Another breath.

She became conscious of Enna, praying for her success as passionately as she had prayed for anything in her life. Tormjere stood silently beside her, ever watchful.

The howl of a wolf reverberated like a prayer inside her, its primal urge as easily understood as any speech of man or elf. A moth turned to her for guidance as it fluttered aloft on soft wings.

Another breath.

A woman whispered a devotion from within the temple at Fallhaven. Another in Kirchmont begged for forgiveness of her indiscretions, while still another in Merallin prayed for an end to the constant deluge of rain. Prayers of gratitude swept like a wave across the world, racing with the dawn and giving shape and grain to the entirety of what existed.

The multitude of voices grew, melding into a single tone that came to her as a steady hum, a tangible sound with rhythm and wrinkle, nuance and structure, and with a pulse that she could feel as if the world itself had a heartbeat.

It was a thing she could sample and taste, which she could see distinctly but read with her ears more than her eyes. As she sought to examine it shapes began to form in the whiteness around her, each solidifying like an ethereal haze of smoke resembling the creature from whence it originated. Though she had no form, she moved among them. One flared like a beacon above the rest, a call she recognized as a frantic plea for aid, and she felt herself compelled towards it.

The whiteness around her evaporated, and a new scene came into focus in shades of white outlined in silver. She beheld an old woman kneeling over a man, his body pierced and broken by a fallen tree. The woman's words were lost in the wind and rain of the storm that buffeted her body, but they blazed like a torch that illuminated every injury. Filled with compassion, she let herself flow through the woman, and a life was spared.

Another breath.

Her perceptions shifted once more, nudged in a new direction by an unseen hand. Time and distance changed at equal rates, though by how much she could not judge. She heard calls for mercy and salvation like trumpets in the stillness of the night. Seeking the source of the lamentations she cast herself towards it, descending into skies above a home with which she was intimately familiar yet had never visited.

Forests lay ablaze in every direction, the hellish devastation wrought by the flames undiluted by the whiteness in which they were depicted. Once joyous voices now cried out in terror, only to be consumed and scattered like ashes upon the wind. Creatures of death stalked through the smoldering fields, tearing down anything and anyone that stood in their path. So mindless were the cries, so primal in their execution, that they sparkled in their brevity like falling stars, and the images they painted were so ephemeral that she could gain little sense of what was happening or why. There was no salvation to be offered, no balm capable of soothing the rending of their souls. In the end, they left only the flickering embers of their passing.

Another voice called out, this one rising strong and clear above the carnage. She willed herself towards it, suffusing her strength into the caller, and the scene came into focus. Other figures hovered near an elvish woman who stood tall in their midst. A circle they had formed, and at their backs stood a gleaming suit of silver armor, the unworn metal their final charge in a world bereft of hope. One by one, the defenders winked from her sight like expired candles. The vision collapsed inwards with each loss, its boundaries slipping to empty whiteness until at the last there was only one who remained unbowed. A shadowed presence swept towards the woman and took shape. It was a thing of nightmares, rising above her with a twisted and hideous visage that was all too familiar.

The face of a demon.

Empty whiteness swept the image away. She recoiled from that outcome, filled with a desire to change what had happened.

Another breath.

Time flowed like water running up a hill to meet the spring

from whence it issued. The forests stood again as they had for millennia, and the moon lit the darkness with its full glory. She wished to understand more of their purpose, to know not only their dreams and fears but their lives and purpose, to see *them*. But she was not a bird who could fly above to gaze down upon the lands around, nor was she gifted with eyes that could see in the light of the sun.

She sifted through the cacophony of voices, culling from them the ones that were relevant to what she needed so desperately to know. One she beheld, as a woman placed her hands on the shoulder of a man fallen from his horse. She brought herself to the woman and found herself surrounded by thousands of soldiers preparing for war. Another call came and was followed, this to another woman who asked only for protection from the sorcerer whose lair towered above her city. She flew towards another call, which passed from the lips of a young girl clutching at her mother's hand, wishing she were anywhere other than cleaning the pots that the warriors in the camp heaped on them by the dozens.

And from these vignettes, a larger understanding grew. The death and destruction she had witnessed had not yet occurred, though it was poised to, and there remained time to prevent it.

Something brushed against her, as soft as a feather yet carrying the majesty of a mountain. It smelled like a star and tasted like the notes of a harp, filling her with hope and desire and with a joy so pure and perfect that it banished her fears to the point that she forgot even the concept of such an emotion.

But the contact was fleeting, and her awareness shrank at an ever-increasing rate as color and sound leaked once more into her senses. There was sorrow in that separation, but she knew it was not an end; it was only her beginning.

Shalindra blinked.

The moon shone bright in the sky above, a hair's breadth beyond its alignment with the tallest of the Three Sisters. She wanted to remain there, in that feeling, forever, but knew she could not. She retrieved Shining Moon as she stood, holding the weapon before her with both hands.

I know what must be done Mistress Eluria, and I will not fail you.

With a last, longing glance towards the moon, she hurried back to where Enna and Tormjere waited.

Enna jumped to her feet in surprise.

Shalindra wanted to share what she had seen, to allow them to experience even a portion of the joy she had experienced. But as she opened her mouth to speak, she realized that no sound she could make could ever convey the passion that she had felt, no words could relay the wonders she had seen, or the final, fleeting contact that had altered her very being in ways she did not yet realize. Overcome by the unexpected surge of emotions, she collapsed to her knees and wept.

Enna rushed to her and held her close. Unable to speak, Shalindra surrendered to the exaltations in her mind, and as the moon rolled from above the last of the Three Sisters, she laid her head in Enna's lap, and slept.

* * *

Shalindra awoke the next morning, refreshed. The air was cool and damp against her cheeks and the sky clear. She pushed the blanket covering her aside and sat up, finding herself on the bench-like rock in the clearing. She separated pine needles from her hair as she stretched, for the stone had been covered in piles of the soft material before she had been placed on it. Enna lay asleep nearby, huddled beneath her cloak.

Tormjere leaned against a tree, watching them both.

Do you ever sleep?

Bad things find you when you sleep. Enna tried hard to stay awake, but she didn't make it to the dawn.

Did you see Her last night, as I did?

No. As Enna said, that was for you alone.

Would that you had experienced such joy with me.

Enna's eyes flickered open, then she bolted upright when she saw Shalindra awake.

"Eluria spoke to me," Shalindra confirmed Enna's unasked question. "But it was unlike any conversation I have ever had or can even describe. I will not pretend to understand all that I was shown, but this I know: I must travel to Ildalarial, and seek the Guardian's armor."

"When?"

"Before it is too late."

Chapter Sixteen

That Which Was Lost

Edward and Vestus flagged them down as they rode across the causeway onto the island. Though she dearly wished to return to Eluria's temple and continue to sort out what she had been shown, Shalindra turned her horse in their direction.

"We saw your approach," Edward said as they dismounted and passed the reins to waiting soldiers. "Did you discover anything in Rumbleton that requires our attention?"

"There was a small matter that we may discuss later," Shalindra replied.

Enna shot Tormjere a look at the understatement, but said nothing as she hurried towards the temple.

"I can see that there is a more pressing topic to attend to first," Shalindra said. "What is the trouble, master purser?"

"Forgive me, Your Highness," Vestus said with a small bow, "but our last merchant to Silvalaria is overdue by more than a week. Given that we have also seen no sign of the elves who usually visit, the council feels that someone must be sent to investigate."

Edward bobbed his head. "I feel we should, as well. The elves may be absent due to their own affairs, but Crosby is not the kind of man to dawdle when he has goods for sale."

"Normally I would agree," Birion said, "but with one patrol already out, I am loath to commit a full complement to another with so many visitors in the valley."

"Treven is trustworthy," Tormjere said quickly.

"The priests may be," Edward admitted, "but their hired swords not as much. We've had a few altercations with the watch, here and there, but nothing worth making a stink over. There's little enough to entertain them here, and I think most are more eager to return to Kirchmont than they let on."

"I am also reluctant to leave ourselves so lightly defended," Shalindra agreed, "though I would trust the Legitarso with anything. Can we send a smaller group?"

"We could," Birion answered, "though they would be ineffective should they encounter anything. You remember what happened last year when we tried to shrink the patrols."

"I'll go," Tormjere volunteered.

Are you certain?

I need something to do, and it's ground we'll cover on the way to Ildalarial.

You have done very well since Treven's arrival, which makes me happier than you know. But Enna and I cannot go with you, and after what happened with the soldiers…

I'll be fine as long as no one pokes me with a stick.

Shalindra almost said no. The emotions of the previous night were still raw and her passions inflamed, and she wanted to depart as soon as possible. Birion caught her eye and gave her a curt nod. Despite his reservations he had honored her request and had made attempts to draw Tormjere from his shell. Clearly, he saw this as another such opportunity.

She relented. "I think that would be beneficial, for all involved. Enna and I will need a few days to prepare."

"I'll join you and bring a few from Sam's squad," Birion said, exchanging a questioning glance with Edward, who indicated his agreement with the decision. "We'll leave at first light tomorrow."

"I'll be ready," Tormjere said.

Vestus bowed again. "Thank you, Your Highness. If you'll excuse me?"

Shalindra returned his bow.

"He has cause for concern," Birion said when Vestus had left. "We've needed to do more in the south for some time."

"We have," Shalindra agreed, "and we may put our efforts in that direction sooner than we had planned. If you gentlemen will join me for a moment, I have news to discuss."

"I've heard it," Tormjere said, "and I wanted to speak to Honarch before I leave."

"I believe he's wandering with the priests," Edward offered.

Tormjere gave him a quick nod of thanks and headed towards the village.

Join me at the temple when you are done.

I will.

It took him little time to find Honarch and Treven as they walked at a leisurely pace along the road, followed by his acolyte and a pair of guards.

"Ho, Tormjere," Honarch called, interrupting their conversation. "I was wondering where you'd run off to."

"Here and there, as usual," he replied. "What problem are you two solving today?"

"Actually, we were discussing architecture," Treven said. "I had not realized that rockhurlers aided in the construction of some of the buildings here."

Tormjere looked at Honarch for confirmation.

"I guess we never got around to talking about that. I went looking for them when we arrived, to try and avoid any confrontations with the village. It took some effort, but one or two were willing to help in exchange for some concessions."

"Is that how your tower was built?" Tormjere asked. "I thought they hated water."

"They do, and it was a miracle that I could get one of them onto the island. They regard it as sort of a holy place, though I'm using our words to poorly describe their outlook on things. Their aid really saved us that first year."

"Those who help us the most often arrive from unexpected directions," Treven said.

"None were more unexpected than this. They really don't like goblins, so having a mutual enemy helped."

"How far south do they travel?" Tormjere asked.

"I don't know for certain. Why?"

"We've a merchant long overdue, and we're taking a patrol to find them."

"You say that like you're leaving," Honarch observed.

"I'm going with them," he confirmed. "It's where I'm needed."

Treven smiled at the reference.

"Well, take the dohedron," Honarch said. "We'll see how well it works at distance."

"I will." Then to Treven, he asked, "How's the new church

coming along?"

"Well, thank you. We had to adjust our plans to fit within the available space, which is what we were debating when you joined us."

Tormjere looked to the mainland. "Why not build it on shore where there's plenty of room and more people?"

Treven chuckled. "Father Bentoni has a fascination for islands and was most eager to construct it here. The land was also in less demand than across the water, so the price was more equitable."

"Even knowing that something the size of the abbey in Kirchmont will never fit on this island?"

"I think a more modest structure will suit our purposes for the foreseeable future. Would you like to see it?"

"Sure."

"We just visited the site," Honarch said, "and I need to check on one of my experiments, which is hopefully not bubbling onto the floor right now, so I'll leave you two."

He bade them both a good day with a wave.

Treven did an about face and steered Tormjere back towards the northern point of the island.

"You seem to have achieved some level of peace with your decisions since we last spoke," Treven observed as they walked.

Tormjere glanced at the temple of Eluria as they passed it, and shrugged. "It isn't worth stewing over. I have more important things to worry about now."

"I'm glad to hear that. We can never escape our past, just as we should never feel bound by its influence."

"I find it difficult to ignore the benefits of those influences at times. It seems to be what I'm good at."

"How we employ the tools and weapons we possess, whether given or obtained, is entirely our choice to make."

Treven was correct, and Tormjere was certainly not about to debate the point, but the world was never quite so simple. He shook his head. "Every weapon has its purpose."

"Indeed. As you are well aware of my own limited experience with swords, I think I know of another who can give far better counsel on such matters, though he is as skilled as you at avoiding attention."

"I don't avoid it," Tormjere protested. "I just don't see a benefit most days."

Treven came to a stop facing the new church, which lay a polite distance away from Eluria's temple. The stone foundation had sprung from the ground overnight, and now a small army of workmen were processing felled trees into walls and beams. The ring of a smith's hammer came from a temporary forge situated beneath a slanted roof.

"I believe you have met our blacksmith," Treven said.

Tormjere looked more closely at the shirtless dwarf as he tapped the glowing head of a nail into shape and dropped it atop a pile of similar pieces with mechanical precision.

"Fendrick?"

The smith paused, then turned and gave them both an unkind look. "You were expecting perhaps some nymph from the lakes of Elessia come to shower you with affection?"

"Do I have a choice?"

Fendrick just frowned at him before confronting Treven. "Just couldn't wait, could you?"

"Those who find reason to delay often miss their best

opportunity. I should probably check on Father Ignatius, so I will leave you to your conversation." He beckoned the waiting acolyte closer, though the lad eyed Fendrick with obvious trepidation as he took hold of Treven's arm. "Good day."

"Priests," Fendrick muttered the moment Treven was out of earshot. "Always sticking their nose in where it doesn't belong and claiming divine right to do so."

"Treven's a good man," Tormjere countered.

"Never said he wasn't."

Fendrick pulled a rod of metal from the forge and set to tapping the glowing end into a point.

"I suppose I should thank you again for the sword," Tormjere said.

Fendrick grunted something unintelligible and stubbornly kept working.

"Not once have I sharpened it." Tormjere pressed. "I've killed men and goblins in numbers I can't count, chopped through mail like it was butter, cut through hide thick enough to blunt a spear, and the edge is as keen as the day you gave it to me."

Fendrick flattened the head of the nail with one blow and cast it aside. "You knew it was special when I was making it. How?"

Tormjere shrugged. "It just looked like you were putting extra effort into it. I don't know how. It just seemed... different."

"Different is an understatement, but I'm sure you've figured that out by now."

"I've figured out a lot of things, but if you've been here with Treven all this time, why didn't you want to talk to me? Were you afraid of the questions I'd ask?"

Fendrick set his hammer aside and turned to face him. "No,

169

lad. I was afraid of the answers I'd have to give you. Did you ever wonder why you were given something so special?"

"You said it was because you sold enough of those extra swords."

Fendrick cleared his throat. "Did turn a good profit off that. Look, when his high-and-mightiness Father Nathan brought me the lump of metal you saw me working, he didn't tell me where he'd gotten it or why he needed it made into a sword. He only said that no one was supposed to know that their abbey was behind it. It made sense, given their cultivated image as kindly custodians of knowledge, but I figured out later that it was meant for you, or whoever Nathan got to go on his little quest."

"So why are you telling me now?"

"First, because you're here and Nathan isn't. Second…" His hand went to a pouch on his belt. "…because a swordsman needs to have a thorough understanding of what his weapon's capable of."

That was not what he was originally going to say, but Tormjere let it slide. "Apart from the edge, what's special about it?"

"You ever have any flashes of inspiration you weren't expecting?"

"I follow my instincts all the time."

"Well, they're obviously sharper than your head, or you'd have noticed that your mind is clearer when the sword's with you."

Tormjere raised an eyebrow. "I thought I was just good."

Fendrick turned his eyes heavenward. "Hyrim, what am I to do with this bag of sand?"

"I'm not sure how I would have ever noticed. Other than the few weeks I was home, I haven't taken it off since you gave it to me."

"Well, accept that it is."

Tormjere crossed his arms, tired of accepting anything. "Fine. I'm not good; I'm just lucky to have a magic sword."

"It doesn't give you a brain if you don't already have one!" Fendrick roared, loud enough that everyone nearby paused and looked their way.

"So what am I supposed to do with it?"

Fendrick threw up his hands. "How should I know? Go and ask the priest, and come back once you've figured out the difference between a blessing and an enchantment."

"I'm going on patrol tomorrow."

"Then come back after that," Fendrick huffed as he returned to his work. "There'll be time enough to sort you out then."

Chapter Seventeen

Encounter in the Woods

Tormjere rode with Birion from Newlmir the next morning, accompanied by a trio of soldiers. Jax was short and stocky, while Samuel was tall and lanky. Diran was the youngest member of the patrol but near to Tormjere's own age, and seemed as competent as the rest. All the soldiers wore mail coats and sat their horses comfortably. Each kept their spears, the new, heavier sort, from becoming entangled in branches with casual ease.

The road from Newlmir generally followed the river from the lake all the way to the southern end of the valley, where the flowing waters had carved a wide gap in the mountains. He could have travelled the distance in a day had he been in a hurry, but Birion preferred a more measured speed. Going somewhere became slower the more people you brought along.

It is no longer the two of us against the world.

It was much easier when it was.

Tormjere chafed at the overly cautious pace, and after half a day of nothing but watching the trees go by, he looked for a way to hurry them along.

"I haven't seen anywhere to make a wrong turn yet," he said. "It seems more likely that whatever befell them happened outside the valley."

"Getting lost within sight of the Three Sisters is improbable," Birion agreed, "but these forests have other inhabitants and the road is not always uncontested."

They had not seen any of those other inhabitants either, nor had any such creatures bothered Tormjere on his wanderings. The remainder of the day passed without incident or sign of the missing merchant, and they stopped for the night far too early.

Tormjere doubted he would be able to sleep and so chose not to even try, though he allowed himself brief periods of rest when others took their turn standing watch. He envied their deep slumbers, but he still could not bring himself to relax so completely. His body was beginning to protest the effects of being awake so long, and his stomach twisted with an unpleasant reminder of what it would take for him to continue ignoring such needs.

They were moving again by the time the sun crested the ridge of the valley the next morning, speaking less and watching the woods more closely the further south they travelled. A goblin foraging party was spotted on the far side of the river near midday, and they came across the fresh footprints of an ogre stamped in the soggy ground, but there was not a wagon track or hoofprint to be found.

They forded the river at a broad, shallow crossing, after which the road began to fade to more of a grassy path. Birion called a halt not long after, and they made another early camp near the exit of the valley. Jax shot a wild pig with his bow, and Diran drew the task of butchering the animal. It was while everyone was helpfully telling Diran exactly how he was going about his task the wrong way that something shot through the underbrush with a rustle of leaves and a thump that sounded like an impact against a tree. The soldiers turned in the direction of the sound, hands seeking nearby weapons.

"It's a pair of mountain hares fighting," Tormjere said without moving. He had been half paying attention to the battle raging behind him, because rabbit fights were always amusing with all their hopping and paw waving, no matter how large the protagonists happened to be.

His proclamation was greeted with some skepticism, but moments later they heard distinctively high-pitched rabbit growls as the combatants chased each other past the camp and away.

The entertainment gone, Tormjere pulled the dohedron from a pocket, taking care to avoid touching the jewels. He tapped the green gem once. It sparkled briefly at his touch, then went dark. After a lengthy delay, the same gem pulsed twice in answer.

Tormjere recalled most the code Honarch had established and with a series of taps on different stones he attempted to convey that they had reached the bottom of the valley but had yet to see any sign of the missing merchant.

The reply came more quickly this time, as the lights pulsed in a sequence he interpreted as 'All is well here.'

He returned the dohedron to a pocket. It was good to know that it worked across such distances, but they would have to work out a less cumbersome way to convey information. Tedious or not, he could only imagine the advantage that would be conferred by having even a handful of the devices.

What, exactly, did you intend by 'at nothing of valley end?'

That's what I said? His codes are difficult to remember.

So I gathered. Nevertheless, Honarch is overjoyed at your successful use of the device. He has gone to tell Treven about it.

Our way's easier.

Do you ever wonder why, or how?

No, but I still think it's your fault.

Her exasperation was clear even without words, and he chuckled as he settled back against a tree.

Diran was now turning several choice cuts of meat on the spit, and the fat from the pig sizzled as it dripped into the flames, emitting a pleasant aroma. Tormjere squeezed his hands together, wondering if meat alone would be enough this time. His conversations with Treven had served as a soothing balm which tempered the angry churns of his stomach, but Treven was not there and he could only suppress his body's desires for so long.

"Relax," Birion said from where he sat on a nearby rock. "There's nothing more dangerous than us in the valley now."

Tormjere could barely remember what relaxing felt like, but he forced a smile to his face. "Scared everything away, have you?"

"One good look at us was all it took," Samuel declared, puffing out his chest with mock bravado.

Diran snickered as he turned the meat. "Because he's the only one uglier than the goblins."

"They ran away howling the first time they saw him," Jax confirmed solemnly.

Their comments earned them black looks from Samuel, though Tormjere had to admit that the man's rough face was not one to make the ladies swoon.

"Best we can figure," Birion interjected, "is that between the goblins and rockhurlers, there's little reason for anything else to be here. Add in a well-trained contingent such as our own, and anything thinking to make this their home never stood a chance once we arrived."

No one would ever accuse Birion of bragging, but the others swelled in pride at the implied compliment.

Diran began cutting slices of meat and distributing them. When he came to Tormjere, he opened his mouth to say something, then closed it just as quickly.

Samuel noticed and elbowed him a few times, and after a mumbled argument finally egged him on enough to speak.

"So, what's it like?" Diran asked Tormjere.

"What's what like?"

"Where the demons live. You went there, didn't you?"

Tormjere eyed Birion, but the knight gave a small shrug as if to say he had not been the one to tell them. He considered any number of answers but settled for the simplest. "I did, unfortunately."

"And? What's it like?"

"Miserable."

"Fair enough," Diran said when he failed to elaborate. "All of us took the field against the demons at Tiridon, so we know they aren't the best company. What do they do when they aren't here trying to kill us?"

"Do they have farms and forests?" Samuel asked, jumping in.

"Not in the manner we're accustomed to," Tormjere said, though his stomach rumbled longingly at the thought of one of their 'farms.' He felt Shalindra's attention shift back to him, just as

176

curious as the men around him.

"Cities then?" Diran guessed.

Tormjere shook his head. "It's mostly like packs of wolves running around, fighting each other."

"Makes some sense," Birion said between mouthfuls, "but if there aren't farms or merchants, what did you eat? Were there pigs?"

Tormjere just shook his head.

"Cattle?" Jax asked.

"Cheese?" Diran chimed in.

Samuel answered for him. "Can't make cheese without milk."

"There could be goats," Diran said defensively.

"Mutton?" Samuel asked, getting into it.

Tormjere answered each with a shake of the head.

"Maybe they eat grass, like a horse."

Tormjere ran a hand over his face. "There isn't any grass either, just sand and rock."

Birion threw up his hands. "Gods, man, don't make them guess all night. What do demons eat?"

The answer was both complex and nuanced in ways that his present audience would never understand. "Each other."

That put a damper on the growing merriment, and the group settled into an uneasy silence.

Is that what drives this unnatural hunger inside you?

I had to eat something, and you get used to it eventually.

"Well, that tears it," Birion said in mock dismay as he tossed a bag towards Tormjere. "You'll be wanting all the cakes then."

The group erupted in laughter. Tormjere withdrew a piece of the sweetbread, nodding his thanks to Birion before taking a bite.

It did taste good, but it did nothing to help.

* * *

Tormjere stopped at the ridge. Something felt… odd in the narrow valley in front of him, like an unpleasant smell on the wind. The horse's impatience made it difficult to get a good sense of it, so he dismounted and tossed the reins to Birion. He let his senses extend through the woods, enjoying the texture and grain of the forest, even as he sought what was wrong with it.

How are you doing that?

I don't know. I just can.

That feels… incredible. It is little wonder why you love the woods so much.

But there's something that doesn't belong.

Show me.

He guided Shalindra's mind towards what could only be described as a lingering odor, or perhaps a sour aftertaste on the forest.

"What is it?" Birion asked when the silence had stretched too long.

"Demon," Tormjere answered. "Or at least traces of one."

"How can you tell? We have seen nothing that would indicate their presence since we abandoned the Kingdom."

"It's distinctive. How often do you send patrols outside the valley?"

"Almost never. We don't have the manpower. From here to the borders of Silvalaria, the land is untamed."

Tormjere looked up at him. "We should find out where it went."

"We're here for our missing merchant, not a trophy hunt."

"What if the two are related to one another? We can split up and I'll track the demon alone if you'd prefer."

Birion stroked his moustache as he weighed their options. "We are too small a group to be separating. If you feel it worth going, we go together." He leaned in close and lowered his voice. "We may carry the heavier spears, but we are too few in number to be testing them just yet. I will allow one day, and then we continue towards the elves."

I agree with him. We will be leaving soon, and I need you both here with me. Be careful.

"Fair enough," Tormjere said. "I'll stay on foot and move ahead. It's easier to find the trail if I'm not riding."

Birion whispered orders to Diran behind him, which were passed silently down the line, then motioned Tormjere to continue.

The mood turned serious as Tormjere led them down from the ridge and away from the trail they had been following. The woods around them remained light and airy, but clumps of vegetation combined with the uneven nature of the terrain to keep the visibility short. He relied on his other senses to keep them headed in the proper direction.

It was not long before he came across unmistakable signs of a large creature's passing. He knelt to inspect the ground. Mixed in among the trampled vegetation and hoof prints as big as his head were the tracks of men. It was difficult to judge the number, but if there was a demon then one set most certainly belonged to a wizard.

He signaled back to Birion, then followed as the trail of footsteps curved back east towards the road. Almost immediately,

Tormjere became aware that they were not alone. He could not see them, but two other people were moving on a course that would intersect theirs. He made a slight change in direction and felt them shift to follow. Whoever it was made no sound as they drew steadily closer.

Tormjere held up a hand, and the team stopped behind him. Birion dismounted and crept beside him.

"Is it close?" Birion asked, hand tight on his spear.

"No, there's someone else. Stay here, and draw no weapons." He walked a short distance ahead and waited, his attention focused on a tree which concealed someone.

Moments later, an elf not much taller than Enna stepped from behind it and fixed the men with a suspicious stare. His snug garments of green and brown, which were layered in a pattern similar to Tormjere's own, blended seamlessly into the forest.

"You are valley-men?" the elf asked without preamble.

"Yes. I'm Tormjere, and behind me is Birion."

The elf's eyes lingered on Tormjere's deer-hooved knife before responding. "I am named Orodell, of Silvalaria. Why are you outside of your valley, if that is indeed from whence you came?"

Birion surrendered his spear to Jax in a politically astute move and came to stand beside Tormjere. "We are looking for a missing merchant named Crosby. He should have returned to Newlmir a week ago."

"How many animals?"

"Twelve," Birion answered. "With eight men."

Orodell considered, then motioned behind him. Another elf appeared and returned an arrow to his quiver as he came trotting forward. Orodell's gaze softened. "They were killed not long after passing from our borders."

"Goblins?" Birion asked, his face hard.

"It did not appear so."

"Urtrifornu?" Tormjere asked, using the elvish word for demons.

Orodell shifted uncomfortably. "We have not seen such creatures in an age. They are practically legend, though we have heard the rumors in the east. Whatever is was that attacked your friends was large, and there was more than one. I will show you where they fell."

The elves moved with speed to rejoin a trail. Tormjere ran with them, happy to have an excuse to remain on the ground.

"I am glad to see that at least some humans avoid riding their animals everywhere," Orodell said.

"I prefer to be on foot, especially in the trees," Tormjere said. "Horses are useful but noisy, and they smell."

Both elves chuckled.

Once back upon the road, they turned south and increased their pace, jogging fast enough that the horses had to trot to keep up.

The unmistakable smell of death greeted them even before they came upon the gruesome remains of the merchant train. The horses had been stripped to the bones and their cargo scattered, while the mangled corpses of the men lay as they had fallen. They had tried to mount a defense, but the effort proved to be futile.

Birion swore, then dismounted. Tormjere said nothing as he inspected the damage. Orodell was correct that there had been two, judging from the trampled underbrush.

Demons?

Yes.

Why would they attack the caravan?

To hurt us, or simply because they were hungry. Either way, it was an easy target.

You said they ate each other.

They can subsist on lesser beings as well. It's just less satisfying.

"Their tracks are here," Orodell pointed, "and return in generally the same direction as the ones you were following."

Tormjere looked at the indicated prints. One was a cloven hoof shape and the other resembled a large bear's prints, but each was spaced as if its owner had walked upright.

"Two demons," he confirmed to Orodell. "The one which disappeared likely took a mist gate when it was dismissed. Did you find any human footprints nearby?"

"Only those made by your friends. Why?"

"We found human prints mixed with those hoof-like ones. There are always wizards nearby, one for each demon. They control the creatures by means of a pendant worn about the neck."

Orodell shook his head. "Our lore does not speak of anyone controlling them, though such tales are used to frighten children."

"If only they remained as nighttime stories," Birion said before turning to Tormjere. "I had hoped never to see such creatures again, but I find no fault with your assessment."

"We can't wait for them to show up in Newlmir. We have to find them first."

"I am willing to seek their location," Birion said, "but what do you intend to do against them?"

Tormjere did not have time to answer as Orodell spoke once more: "I am sorry for your men, especially given their proximity to our borders. We will continue our search for these creatures."

"Care to join us?" Tormjere asked.

Orodell hesitated, and his eyes flicked down to Tormjere's knife once more. "These woods are vast, and we lost their tracks once. If they can move about without leaving a trace how do you intend on finding them?"

"They leave a different type of impression. When you've been around them long enough, it's easy to spot."

Orodell gave him a curious glance but made no comment.

"How far did you follow them?" Tormjere asked.

"Only as far as that ridge," Orodell said, pointing. "The tracks disappeared there, and we broke off our search when we heard your horses."

Tormjere looked at Birion, who considered once more before speaking to Orodell. "These are your woods more than ours. We will follow your lead, but I wish to avoid conflict."

"As do I. Very well, let us see where these creatures went."

The elves took them west once more, paralleling the tracks they had been following earlier. The trail was not difficult to follow, as the demons had left a string of broken branches and crushed rocks in addition to their massive footprints. The creatures had not plowed through the forest indiscriminately, but neither had they put forth the effort to disguise their passing.

As Orodell had said, both sets of tracks disappeared suddenly. Tormjere stopped to survey their surroundings. The terrain became more uneven in the direction they were facing, and the trees grew thick—not the easiest for that type of demon to navigate. They must have taken a mist gate, but to where? A quick search revealed no signs of anyone else. Goats and bears, as he labelled them, were two of the more common demons, but neither were capable of conjuring a gate.

"It's likely they were dispelled by their wizards," Tormjere said, "though the timing is odd."

Orodell nodded. "If their conjuring was undone, it would leave us unable to follow. We will check the area once more to be sure, but we must make haste in reporting what we've found."

Tormjere was about to wish them safe travels when he felt a burning itch crawl across the back his neck. It was a warning he recognized all too well.

Both Orodell and Birion picked up on his stance, but he raised a cautionary hand before either could voice a question.

"They're close," he whispered. "And they're aware of our presence."

With silent hand signals, Birion sent the men scurrying. The horses were quickly tethered and weapons readied.

They crouched low and waited in silence, each aware of the unnatural stillness that had settled over the forest. It was broken by a rustling of leaves, and the trees not far downslope them shook as might a branch brushed against by a passing traveler.

Orodell's sudden intake of breath revealed his shock as a goat-headed demon covered in grey fur lumbered into view. It paused, its gaze sweeping side to side as it searched. A moment later a second demon raised itself beside the first. This one was also covered in fur, but it was dark and mangy, and its face bore a canine resemblance.

"I never thought to see such creatures in my lifetime," Orodell whispered.

"We should retreat before we're spotted," Birion said.

"Why?" Tormjere asked, drawing his sword as he rose. "There are only two."

"What are you doing?" Birion demanded.

"See that lake, and the clearing beside it?" Tormjere asked, ignoring the question as he pointed to a small body of water that lay along the demon's line of travel. "Move the men to the edge of the trees,"

"Are you mad?" Orodell hissed.

Tormjere did not answer. They could join him or not, but he would see that neither demon would escape to kill again. His legs carried him down the hill at a sprint, ensuring he reached the clearing first. His hands trembled as he took position in the middle of the sunlit glade, but not from fear.

Why are you so eager for this?

They aren't going to leave on their own.

But against two of them? Think of the men with you.

I don't need them.

I do not know if I can aid you from so far, but I will do what I can.

The goat-demon's slotted eyes caught sight of Tormjere the instant it emerged from the trees. It took an eager step towards him, then stopped just as abruptly. The sound that issued from its mouth could have been a grunt, or even a wet cough, but it was closer to a word than any animal should have been capable of uttering. "Veluntrhu!"

Tormjere remained motionless, savoring the unmistakable edge of fear in that name. The dog-headed demon gave a warning growl as it burst into the clearing, but also stopped and regarded him warily. It should have been strange to see a dog with the arms and legs of a bear, but he cared less about the odd assemblage of body parts and more for what weaknesses it betrayed.

The weaker of the two—likely the goat since it walked in front—would make the first move. This pair had some sense of self-preservation, as they crouched and stepped apart from each other without showing their hand. Tormjere continued waiting for one of them to order the other forth.

That command came in the form of a deep rumble from behind both creatures, and a third, larger demon came into view. Where the others bore some resemblance to animals this one lumbered like a grotesquely fat man, though its face looked like no man who had ever lived. Its nose was flattened and long, and sat between sharp cheekbones that splayed outwards, giving its head the appearance of a shield that had been embossed with some horrible visage.

The sudden appearance was alarming, but Tormjere forced himself to remain still. The thing had to be an overlord, and maybe even close to attaining wings. As best he knew nothing of that size had ever been bound to wizards. How, then, had it arrived here? Both question and demon were problems he would have to face, but not just yet. It would attack last.

With an angry toss of its misformed head, the most powerful demon spurred the lesser ones to action. Fearsome howls and cries echoed through the forest as they charged.

Tormjere sidestepped the grasping hands of the goat, and his blade bit deep into one of its arms. The creature shrieked in pain, but before it could react Tormjere had sliced it across the back of its leg, and it staggered to the side.

The dog was already upon him, but he had taken the measure

of such creatures before, and its snapping jaws found only empty air. It was quick enough to avoid his blade, and both demons retreated out of reach as Tormjere circled, careful not to put his back to the larger demon. He would die before ever showing such weakness.

I am trying to help you, but it is difficult to focus. Are you closing me out again?

The two demons attacked together with animal savagery, a mass of snarling teeth and claws. Tormjere sprang forward to meet them, catching both off guard. He struck the goat a devastating blow across its nose, then ducked beneath the swipe of the dog's claws and slid his hand along its back. Where his fingers touched, fire sprang up in the coarse fur. The smell of burning hair filled the air as the dog twisted about in panic.

Undaunted by the black blood oozing from its wounded face, the goat struck at him again. Tormjere feinted, but the creature jerked away before he could capitalize.

The dog had already snuffed the flames, and Tormjere cursed the wet ground that had aided it. It staggered to its feet, now only a minor threat, and were the greater demon not present Tormjere would simply have allowed both creatures to thrash about until they lost the strength to defend itself. He needed to end it quickly, and so he forced his shoulder against it and sent it stumbling towards where Birion's men were finally arriving.

"Finish it!"

Birion shouted a charge, and the men rushed forward to meet it. Its reflexes dulled by pain, the demon was unable to avoid them, and the sharpened points of their spears penetrated its hide as elvish arrows struck about its head and shoulders.

The goat was taken by surprise by their entry into the battle, and wavered between this new threat and Tormjere. It took a step back.

Tormjere came in low, faster than the wounded creature could react, and cut deep into its oddly jointed leg. The demon bellowed and dropped to one knee. Tormjere thrust his sword up through its chin and out the top of its head, and the demon's lifeless bulk collapsed atop him. He shoved the thing aside and inhaled deeply, feasting on the flickering embers that floated up from the demon as it expired.

It had been too long.

Birion's men had the dog demon pinned to the ground, taking turns as three held it in place while the fourth rammed his spear into any weak spot. Its cries were the terrified sounds of a creature unable to stave off its own death, and the men did not need his help.

Tormjere stalked towards the waiting overlord. It cast a disdainful glance at the lesser demons and heaved its ponderous bulk into motion. Tormjere was not fooled by the display of sluggishness, and so was not taken by surprise when it sprang at him. Its attack came twice as fast as the others, with both massive fists flying at him like boulders in an avalanche. Unable to close with it, Tormjere could do nothing but try to avoid the flailing arms. The trees around the clearing were like a fence that hemmed them in. It was so much easier on the open plains of their world.

His foot caught a log and he pretended to stumble. The demon set a fist crashing into the ground where he should have fallen. Tormjere was left off balance by the ruse, but took a risky swipe. His blade met flesh, but the cut was ineffective and left him exposed. The demon's backhanded blow caught him square in his side, lifting him off his feet and sending him rolling across the clearing.

Rather than pursue, the demon ripped a sturdy oak from the earth and flung the entire tree at him. It sailed through the air, leaves rustling as if in a gale. Tormjere threw his arms over his head and braced for the impact, but a silvery nimbus snapped in front of him at the last moment, and the timber cracked as it smashed against Shalindra's barrier.

By Eluria's light, I can reach you.

The demon's eyes widened, then it grinned in sudden triumph. Black mists began to swirl around it, and it sank into the darkness with a mocking tip of its distorted head.

Tormjere hurdled the tree and sprinted towards it, determined to prevent its escape.

Do not leave me again.

He skidded to a stop, half inside the shrinking mists, then took a reluctant step back as the gate closed before him. She was right. It would do little good to have finally escaped only to throw himself back.

The scent of the dead demons overcame that of burned hair and torn earth, dampening any sense of disappointment. He had to hurry.

Rushing to the goat's corpse, he plunged both hands into an open wound and tore away a meaty chunk of flesh. Black blood splattered to the ground as he shoved it into his mouth, wolfing down bite after bite. Familiar strength surged through him, squirming its way into every extent of his body and dispelling any weariness.

Footsteps approached from the other side of the corpse, and he brought his sword up defensively, but instead of another demon come to contest the kill there was only Birion.

Tormjere blinked and everything came back into focus. The chirping of birds and the stirring of a gentle breeze confirmed that he was no longer in their world.

Is this how you survived? Is it what you became?

Orodell stood with Jax and the other men, all of them staring at him in disbelief.

Birion looked down at Tormjere with a disconcerting mixture of pity and sadness. Then he took a piece of demon flesh and raised it towards his lips. Tormjere tried to blurt out a warning but no sound made it past what he had forced into his own mouth.

Birion took a large bite, his eyes shining in defiance as he chewed deliberately. Almost immediately, his face took on a pained expression, and his cheeks bulged before turning purple and then green. His chewing slowed and his hand started to shake, but his eyes never left Tormjere as he forced himself to swallow.

The knight stood there for a moment, apparently determined to hold it down by force of will, then staggered to the side and retched. Wild hoots of laughter erupted from the men as their commander fell to his knees and emptied his stomach in front of them.

Tormjere would have chuckled as well, but the memory of the first time he had been forced to eat it left him more sympathetic than amused. He swallowed what was left in his mouth and went to help.

"Gods preserve us!" Birion gasped. "How can you eat that filth?"

He collapsed back onto all fours as another bout of vomiting hit him. When it seemed there was nothing left to come up, Tormjere lifted Birion to his feet and half dragged him to the edge of the lake. "Splash some on your face and try to get the taste out."

Birion groaned and bent halfway over when another wave of sickness hit him, and he collapsed unceremoniously into the water with a splash. Another cheer went up behind them.

Tormjere was attempting to pull him to his feet once more when rough hands seized him from behind. He tensed, ready to strike.

"You're going in, too!" Jax yelled in his ear.

"By the hells, you stink worse than he does!" Samuel added to more cheering.

Tormjere half-heartedly fought it before allowing himself to be tossed into the water beside Birion. This time, he came up laughing.

* * *

They stayed awake late that evening, sharing a fire with the elves. There were few things that brought soldiers together like victory, and though all were exhausted, no one felt tired enough to sleep just yet. Birion was regaling Orodell with tales of prior battles against the demons, and Orodell was comparing them to his own exploits. Both men, thankfully, made little mention of the events at the end of the battle, though likely for different reasons.

The crackle of the small fire was a pleasant sound, but Tormjere sought answers from the flames rather than warmth. Three demons should mean three wizards, but they had seen no sign of them. He had done his best to locate them, but even his senses had found nothing. The wizards had proven the one constant in everything they had been through, and their absence was disturbing. There had to be some truth to this thread that he was missing, but it continued to elude him.

I agree it makes little sense, given what we saw during the war.

Wizards should have guards as well, enough that we should've seen some sign by now. They've never been that far away.

It is one of several mysteries before us. How did you learn to defeat them so easily?

I fought, and I read the books I stole from the wizards. Sometimes I would get to eat.

That is all you have done for three years?

At least I'm good at it now.

You are good at a great number of things. There was never a need to hide it.

It's in the past, and I don't need anyone's pity.

Tormjere turned his attention to the more pleasant conversation going on around him. He should have used the dohedron to tell Honarch what had happened, but as Shalindra already knew, it seemed a waste of effort.

"We saw a drop in goblin attacks during your conflict in the Kingdom," Orodell was saying, "but they are on the rise once more, and the road to Ildalarial remains dangerous."

"Would Ildalarial not help keep the way clear?" Birion asked.

Orodell's expression clouded. "We have warred with our southern neighbors at times, and the relationship remains strained. Stone and structure are their choices now. They turned their backs on our heritage long ago and grow more human-like with every generation, though I mean no offense."

Birion indicated that he took none. "I would hope that a

common foe would inspire them to action."

Samuel came rushing into the camp and addressed Birion. "Sir? There's a light to the west."

"Douse that," Birion commanded, pointing to their own campfire.

Jax and Diran rushed to smother the flames. Tormjere sprang to his feet, following Samuel's pointed finger to where a tiny flicker of firelight could be seen.

"Good eyes," Birion commended him.

"I'm going to check," Tormjere said.

"We will accompany you," Orodell said, already shouldering his bow.

Tormjere and the elves slipped into the night before anyone could object, moving swiftly up and down the wooded hills towards the source of the light.

They slowed to a crawl as they drew within sight of the camp, occupied by at least a half-dozen men. Tormjere pointed to where the lone sentry stood apart from the rest, and Orodell nodded. As the elves circled away from him, Tormjere crept closer to where two men were seated away from the fire, conversing in low tones.

"...will complain if you request another name," the swordsman was saying.

The other man with him was largely hidden in shadow and Tormjere could see few details, but his robed silhouette was identification enough. "If Verelli doesn't like it, let him come wander these cursed woods himself."

"Our instructions were to monitor, not wander. Allowing it to roam was a risk."

"The illusion of freedom kept it content, and content creatures are easier to control."

"You should have been more cautious, even here."

"Cautious of what? People make claims of all manner of creatures in these woods, and few are believed even by their own friends."

"What if it was the elves? We could have tipped our hand."

"I don't care who or what it was. We cannot complete the directive with a handful of men. I must obtain another."

The wizard stood, and the swordsman echoed his movement, both unknowingly turning their backs to Tormjere as they rose.

"And I appreciate your advice, even when I choose to ignore it. It should be nearing dawn in Tythir." The wizard reached into a pocket and withdrew a jeweled dohedron. "I will make the request now, while—"

Tormjere's blade took the swordsman's head off with a single swipe, and his fist slammed into the side of the wizard's face before the startled man could react. The wizard crumpled to the ground. The soft twang of a pair of bows was followed by a muffled gasp, indicating that the sentry had been dealt with.

Tormjere paused only long enough to ensure the wizard was unconscious, then drew his knife and dispatched the sleeping men. He was already binding the wizard's hands when the elves joined him.

"Care with his mouth," Orodell warned, "lest he curse us with his foul tongue."

Tormjere cut a strip from the wizard's robes to use as a gag and tied it tightly around the unconscious man's head.

"We should take him to friend Birion," Orodell said. "When he awakes we shall discover his purpose."

Tormjere made a quick search through the bodies, looking for anything of value. From the wizard, he took a pair of books, a ring, and the small cage pendant used to summon demons, the interior of which swirled with dark mists as if it were alive. The swordsmen had little he could take beyond their coins.

Tormjere tossed the unconscious wizard over his shoulder, and they returned to their own camp.

"Are you certain he's still alive?" Birion asked as they arrived, inspecting the wizard's swollen face.

Tormjere eased the wizard against a tree and tied him to it. "He twitched once or twice on the way over, so I'd assume so."

"Well, he won't be awake for a while, and perhaps not until morning. I want a full half-watch tonight."

The men groaned as loud as they dared. A half-watch meant that half their number would be awake and alert at any given time, they would rotate out every hour, and no one would get enough sleep.

Tormjere handed the recovered coins to Birion. "They've a decent number of weapons as well, but we couldn't bring it all back."

"We'll check it in the morning," Birion said, "assuming no further complications."

Tormjere made himself comfortable atop a large rock, determined to ensure there would be none.

By the time the wizard awoke well after dawn, his jaw and the side of his clean-shaven face had turned an ugly purple. His mood was just as foul, and his eyes flashed dangerously as the gag was pulled loose.

"Your name," Birion demanded.

The wizard glowered at them beneath bushy eyebrows. "I shall assume you wish to know it so you may notify the Conclave of your actions and beg our forgiveness."

"That remains to be seen, but your recent actions do not aid your cause."

"What was your purpose in our woods?" Orodell demanded.

"My business here is none of your concern, elf."

Birion's tone remained even. "Then perhaps you could explain why demons are preying on travelers."

"I don't know anything about demons."

Tormjere balled his fists.

Do not hit him, please.

He's lying.

Eventually he will say something of worth.

Tormjere dangled the demon necklace in his face. "We are well aware of the purpose of this device, and so are you. You should answer the questions while there is still a reason to keep you alive."

"Am I not allowed to provide for my own defense?" the wizard said, sulking. "Your cutthroats are not the only dangerous thing in these woods."

Biron crossed his arms. "Three demons seem excessive, even for this wilderness."

The wizard's answering laugh was thick with scorn. "Had I three demons at my command, I would raze your town and wipe away even the faintest memory of you. You are no more than a lucky thief, sulking in the shadows of the civilized world. I know where you're from. Do you think that pathetic little settlement you've created could stand against anyone? The only thing that's kept you alive has been the inconvenience of killing you."

Orodell leapt upon the admission. "If not for them, then you are here to cause trouble for us."

"Think what you will. It will not change any of your fates." The wizard lapsed into a stubborn silence.

"I think he has nothing else to say," Tormjere said, drawing his knife.

Birion raised a cautionary hand. "He does not need to be tortured."

The wizard's smile grew smug, a look of satisfaction that was erased as Tormjere's blade sliced across his throat. Tormjere allowed his vision to shift and inhaled the embers that floated up from the wizard's body. The tingling sensation that raced through his head was far more satisfying than Birion's angry visage.

"Why did you feel that necessary?" the knight demanded.

"He told us enough."

"We could have—"

"Done what?" Tormjere demanded, as he wiped his blade on the wizard's robe. "Asked him nicely to leave? Bargained with him to allow us our peace? Remind me how well that worked at Tiridon, or Kirchmont, or as we fled into the mountains."

Birion seemed as unsettled by his words as those around him, but refused to relent. "He could have remained useful. Until today there has been nothing—"

"Because they've been too busy to care about you." Tormjere stood to face him. "The only thing that has ever given them pause is when we've killed their demons or killed them, and I will continue doing both until they leave us alone."

"And if they never do?" Birion asked, his expression hard. "You are becoming the very thing you claim to fight against."

"Do not lecture me on the ideals afforded you by the luxuries of this world. In theirs, ideals die faster than the weak."

Both men stood toe to toe, eyes locked together, neither willing to back down.

Orodell's words broke the tense silence. "It has ever been the misfortune of those who shield us from demons to suffer, even in their victories. I must inform our Calontier of what we've learned, but I thank you both for your efforts in bringing this truth to light." He placed a hand on Birion's shoulder. "I will see that your merchant's goods are salvaged and returned to you, along with their remains."

"We thank you for that," Birion said.

Orodell turned to Tormjere and bowed. "May Lithandris continue to favor you, Velantriar."

Chapter Eighteen

Unexpected Answers

Enna stood by Shalindra's side as the patrol rode across the bridge towards them. There was no mistaking how unsettled she was, but it seemed more a sadness about what could no longer be changed than any uncertainty for their safety. Why she was that way so soon after her triumph of Alta Amalia remained a mystery, but Enna was certain it had something to do with Tormjere.

Tormjere dismounted almost before his horse had stopped.

"We'll see it stabled," Birion said brusquely, his displeasure as evident as the sun in the sky and equally as hot.

Tormjere handed the reins to one of the other soldiers, who gave him a more respectful tip of his head. That was interesting.

"I'm going to take this to Honarch," Tormjere said, holding up a small sack.

Enna was surprised when Shalindra nodded. Surely she was eager to know what had transpired.

Birion made no effort to hide his annoyance at Tormjere's behavior, but he put his emotions in check as he bowed to them. "Your Highness, Sister Enna."

"What did you find?" Shalindra asked.

"Much that was unsettling. Crosby and his entire team were slain by demons. We tracked them with the help of two elves from Silvalaria and discovered three of the creatures. Two were disposed of and one fled."

"You fought three demons?" Enna asked when Shalindra offered no reaction.

"He did," Birion answered, with a glance in the direction Tormjere had gone. "We only cleaned up the scraps. The new spears were much more effective, but the creature was already weakened. There is more."

Shalindra's hands were tight at her side, but she made no motion to stop his recounting.

"The demons recognized Tormjere, and they were afraid of him."

"Three demons were afraid of *him*?" Enna asked incredulously. It was so far-fetched that she thought it a jest, but Shalindra's face was awash with emotions and Birion was clearly not in a mood for levity.

"It grows more disturbing," Birion continued, his tone softening at Shalindra's obvious distress. "One of them spoke when it saw him. I wondered if my ears had betrayed me, but both elves later confirmed it. It named him 'Veluntrhu.'"

Enna bit her tongue. That was not possible.

"That is a strange word," Shalindra offered, almost as if he was relaying information that was already known.

Birion seemed equally unsettled by her lack of reaction. "We spotted another camp that evening and found a wizard. He was taken captive, but before—"

"The details are unnecessary," Shalindra interrupted, her voice brittle. "I know how such situations will end."

"Forgive me, Your Highness. I should have done more to prevent it."

Shalindra managed a half-smile. "I know you did your best, in spite of your own feelings, and for those efforts on my behalf I thank you. I do not believe they were in vain."

"I am at a loss for what else he needs, but it is not us."

Shalindra looked towards the tower at the opposite end of the island. "I have done what I can to see that there are those who can provide him the solace we cannot. I pray that it is enough."

Birion bowed his head to her, then turned to Enna. "One of the elves called Tormjere something similar to what the demon named him, but I cannot recall the exact phrase."

Enna was certain that she knew the title the elf had used but prayed she was incorrect in her assumption. "Velantriar?"

"Yes, that was it. What does it mean?"

"There is no direct translation to your tongue. 'Protector' is valid, but in a more active sense. 'Hunter' may be closer to the actual intent." She opened her mouth to say more, then stopped. "If you will excuse me."

* * *

Tormjere rapped his knuckles on the door of Honarch's tower, and it was opened moments later by Treven's acolyte, Talley.

"Welcome," Talley said with a short bow. "Master Honarch asked that I let you in should you visit. He awaits you in the study upstairs."

"Thank you," Tormjere said, smiling in spite of his sour mood. Honarch had finally escaped the need to run down and back up his own stairs, if only once. Even better, it meant that Treven was here as well.

Tormjere made the climb quickly and entered Honarch's study through the open door.

"How was the patrol?" Honarch asked a little too casually, waving him towards an empty chair.

Tormjere frowned as he plopped into the seat. "That depends on who you ask."

Treven steepled his fingers. "Our opinions often color the facts before us, but I, too, am interested in what happened."

"You went silent with the dohedron after the first couple of nights. Did you find them?"

"I just forgot to use it. Things got busy."

"What's that?" Honarch asked, eyeing the bag in Tormjere's lap.

Tormjere handed it to him. "Some gifts you may find valuable."

Honarch accepted it and peeked inside. With a small sound of surprise he withdrew the demon necklace and held it aloft for inspection. The darkness trapped inside the pendant swirled angrily, and a chill settled over the room. The gentle warmth emanating from Treven's haversack flared in response, and the blind priest sat straighter and placed his hand upon the Book inside.

Honarch must have felt something as well, for he quickly retrieved a small metal box and pushed the necklace into it. A hasty incantation sealed the container, but did little to diminish the animosity of the device inside.

Treven was as serious as Tormjere had ever seen him. He

settled back into his chair, but did not remove his hold on Amalthee's Book. "That was unexpected."

"I believe you should start at the beginning," Honarch said as he took his seat once more.

Tormjere did, recounting all that had happened, though he omitted his consuming of the demon's energies. Even with his closest of friends, there were things he did not want to discuss.

When he was finished, Treven shook his head sadly. "I am sorry that your efforts to bring the merchant home were not successful and more sorry still that you faced such creatures once more."

Honarch began to pace. "I don't understand why members of my former order continue down this path, but I wish I had gone with you. I cannot believe they have all given themselves to some evil purpose. Had I the opportunity to speak with the wizard, I might have persuaded him to be more cooperative."

"Might or might not," Tormjere said. "Even had you been there he would have tried to escape the entire time. Then we would have needed to build a dungeon capable of containing him. We would have fed him, tried logic and reason in an attempt to make him tell us what we wanted to know, and in the end we would have killed him anyway. I just saved everyone the trouble."

Honarch sighed. "I don't mean to question your judgement, given that they've tried to kill me almost as much as they have you, but I can see why Birion would be unhappy with that choice."

"He used words to that effect. Of all people I expected him to realize that our enemies are still fighting the war they started, regardless of whether we think it's over."

Treven leaned forward. "One-sided conflicts present a host of problems for those who do not wish to participate. Most notable of which may be the appearance of so many demons at one time. I find that troubling in many ways, beyond the immediate threat."

Honarch glanced at the box that now held the necklace. "It is, and I feel that we have only a murky picture of what we are up against."

"Their ability to enter our world has interested me since I learned of their appearance during the invasion," Treven added. "Amalthee remains unusually quiet on the subject, but it could be that I am simply asking the wrong questions."

Shalindra's mind brushed against Tormjere's thoughts. It was a comforting, gentle nudge that receded almost as soon as it began, but this time he held onto that touch and drew her awareness closer to his, unwilling to let go.

"What do you want to know?" he asked.

Honarch waved his hand, encompassing the entire world. "How are they organized? How do they live, and reproduce? Everything, really. Our knowledge of them is incredibly limited."

Maybe it was because he felt better after defeating the demons, or because of how settled his stomach was after consuming their flesh, or perhaps it was simply because it was his friends who wanted to learn, without passing judgement, but he accepted the cup of water Honarch offered and began to talk.

"Their world is scorched and burnt. It's hotter than ours, even though the skies are always covered by clouds. The days are longer, or at least it felt that way. Water…" he held up his cup, "…is difficult to find and isn't remotely clean. Nothing grows. It's just sand and rock and wind."

"I can scarcely imagine a place so desolate," Treven said, as

Honarch took quill in hand and began to write in an empty book. "Even the great Suhraswalo desert offers comfort, if one knows where to look."

"I've never seen a desert, but it lacked any cheer," Tormjere said. "The only satisfaction to be had was killing something before it killed you, so the demons organize themselves into clans for protection from one another."

"How do those clans work?" Honarch prompted.

"The word they use is *hapdrhu*. It's probably somewhere between clan and herd, but it doesn't line up with our way of life very well. It's less about loyalty and more a matter of agreed upon ownership by those above you. Lesser creatures might agree to serve a more powerful demon in exchange for protection. In return, they agree to share a portion of anything they kill."

"So they're all slaves?" Honarch asked.

"It's more a series of binding agreements, but nothing is written down. I don't even think they have a written language of any sort."

"That societal structure is not so different from a farmer paying land lease to their lord," Treven observed.

"To an extent. The easiest way out of any agreement is to kill the bargainer."

Treven shook his head sadly. "In that regard, we can be more similar than we might care to admit."

Honarch tapped the quill on his chin. "Are they of different sexes?"

"There's not really a difference as best I could tell."

"That begs the question of how demons are born."

Tormjere hesitated before answering, then plunged ahead.

"The process is… not pleasant. Effectively, they dig a large hole in the ground. Into that is placed various bits and parts of lesser demons, preferably from a rival clan. It's a huge vat of slime and offal, and the smell is, well, not good."

The others shuddered.

"Once critical mass has been achieved, the demons surround the sludge and tear bits of themselves and each other off and cast it into the mixture. From these seeds, new creatures emerge."

"They come out full grown?"

"No." Tormjere shook his head. "They feed on the goo and each other. They grow and fight until they achieve enough awareness to crawl from the pit. Beings known as *wharudrok* await them, acting as mother and protector. They shield them until the new demons are strong enough to survive on their own. No parent awaits them, only their masters. Some demons are assigned as herders and guards."

"What happens to the wharudrok?" Honarch asked, his lips stumbling over the unfamiliar word.

"The new demon eats it. They are like mother and egg wrapped together, a final shot of power to see their 'child' on their way."

"That is disturbing," Honarch said, repressing a shudder. "Though again we can see similarities to our own world. We know of spiders who eat their mate, for example, but it is unheard of in the higher species. I would not even want to imagine eating another of my own kind, even if I was a demon."

Tormjere new exactly what it felt and tasted like, but he was unwilling to share that, even with his friends.

Honarch finished transcribing his thoughts and sat back. "I'm curious about something you mentioned with the demons you and

Birion faced. You said only two attacked while the third watched? We have heard no accounts of such behavior."

"Demons have a hierarchy to their lives. Stronger demons will send the lesser ones to fight each other. It's a way of testing each other without always having to kill each other."

Treven folded his hands in his lap. "We can deduce many of their motivations simply by thinking through the information you have provided. They will have a different sense of self-worth, and less regard for others of their kind."

Tormjere nodded. "They hate or fear everyone, so that's not a bad description."

Treven's cloudy eyes met his, and Tormjere had the feeling he was being studied far more deeply than he found comfortable. "So, why do they fear you?"

Honarch's quill stopped moving, but he did not look up.

"I wasn't bound by their rules."

All three of them were waiting for him to elaborate, but he chose not to. Honarch closed the book he had been writing in, perhaps interpreting Tormjere's silence as a desire to end the discussion.

"I'm glad that you got that off your chest."

"It wasn't that much of a burden. It seems to be bothering everyone else more than me."

Honarch shook his head. "If that's your idea of a small burden, I would hate to see what you consider to be a large one."

Treven chuckled with them. "I would never have wished such trials upon you, yet there is a silver lining to what you have suffered through. Amalthee has blessed you with the ability to recall the most relevant of details, and you have revealed more in one conversation than we could have uncovered with a lifetime's worth of research."

Honarch nodded in agreement. "This is immensely valuable. I doubt that any text of the Conclave's contains a fraction of that knowledge. We can use this against them, should we encounter more."

"I'm sure we will."

"Shalindra informed me that you will be leaving soon," Treven said, changing the subject.

"I heard that as well," Honarch said. "Something related to her prophecy, I think?"

Tormjere nodded. "She should have left long ago. She's meant for more than this."

"All things happen in due course," Treven said, "even if we do not understand why."

"I'd like to go with you this time," Honarch said. "If you run into another demon you may need the help, and should we find a wizard I might be able to talk some sense into him. I'm honestly growing tired of sitting here in isolation all the time."

"I have no objections," Tormjere said, "but I'm sure others will."

"Thankfully, I've sworn no oaths of fealty and can go wherever I please."

"The time of our leaving draws close, as well," Treven said.

"So soon?" Tormjere asked, unable to hide his disappointment.

"Father Bentoni is well on his way to completing the church, and my fellow disciples long for a return to their routines. But I am most thankful that Amalthee allowed me the opportunity to revisit this valley, and I am doubly blessed that you were both here when I did." Treven stood and placed a hand on Tormjere's arm. "And I believe that I have accomplished all that was needed here."

Chapter Nineteen
Into the Wilderness

Though they had made every effort to downplay her leaving, the news spread rapidly throughout the small community. The council met repeatedly, arguing and debating their best course of action, until finally agreeing to accept Edward as the titular authority until her return. Tormjere found the tumult unnecessary, as having Edward assume Shalindra's role had been the plan all along. He had even heard talk at Argus' inn about whether everyone should pack up and follow her once more, but those suggestions fell on few sympathetic ears. As Honarch had said, people had grown used to living here.

The caravan was assembled and prayers offered by both orders, this time with an emphasis on safeguarding the travelers on the road ahead. Now all that remained was for Treven and Shalindra to give their parting advice to those remaining behind.

"You know," Honarch commented to Tormjere as they waited, "the last time I embarked on a trek into the wilderness with you, it turned into quite the adventure."

"This should be an easier journey, and I promise not to

antagonize any ogres this time."

Honarch chuckled.

From the front of the line, Shalindra signaled, and the caravan groaned into motion. Birion's knights, twenty strong and all handpicked, led the way. Behind them the priests were tucked safely between their own guards. Tormjere and Honarch fell into step alongside Treven's mule once more.

A small gathering had assembled in front of Argus' inn to see them off, but it was nowhere near the size that had greeted the priest's arrival. Tormjere searched the crowd for Fendrick, but the dwarf was not to be seen.

Were you expecting him to see you off?

No, but I'm surprised that he's staying.

You will have plenty of time to figure out why when we return.

Says the one who's so happy to be leaving.

I confess that I will enjoy the simplicity. I have been trying to reduce my duties for years, but could not when so many looked to me for answers. In Ildalarial, I will be neither princess nor savior, only a Sister of Eluria.

They were through the town and winding their way east through thick stands of trees in short order, following the same route they had taken to see Gelid's Rest. This part of the valley was generally safe, but the guards did not sit idle as they rode.

They achieved the edge of the valley without incident and paused at the ridgeline to take one last look back. The falls were flush with water as they tumbled from the base of the Three Sisters, and sunlight sparkled off the river and lake it fed into. On the island, the castle and temple were clearly visible, and he could just make out the foundation of Amalthee's new church.

Once over the ridge, the mountains muted the ever-present roar of the water that filled the valley, and the natural silence of the forest surrounded them as they descended into another lush valley.

There was safety in numbers, and so they continued with Treven's group at a steady but unhurried pace towards Kirchmont for as long as they could. Whether by divine providence or simple luck, or perhaps the imposing size of their number, they encountered no credible dangers.

On the afternoon of the third day, it was time to say goodbye. The caravan paused beside a stream, and those who had made acquaintances and established friendships during the visit bade their farewells.

"I wish we could follow you all the way," Tormjere said to Treven.

"As do I. But we should have little difficulty from here. The trail we follow remains visible, if not always straight."

"Ours seems to be neither, and there's sure to be something standing in the way."

Treven looked amused. "External dangers are always the easiest to detect, but we often remain blind to those we make for ourselves."

"You sound like Gelid," Tormjere said.

"I believe that is the highest compliment I have ever been given." Treven adjusted the haversack containing Amalthee's Book. "When you are finished with your business with the elves, come to Kirchmont. You may discover that where you ask your questions can be as important as whom you ask them of."

It was a tempting offer. Tormjere remembered the abbey as an interesting place with good food and an abundance of books. "I think I will do that."

Treven smiled. "When you are ready. Take care, my friend."

"I will. Be careful."

Tormjere swallowed a lump in his throat as he stood watching Treven's now smaller company depart. Had he the choice, he would have seen Treven safely to Kirchmont as he had done before, but the road to Ildalarial was even more of an unknown.

And likely fraught with our own dangers.

There's never a time when it isn't.

One of the soldiers rode forward and offered him a fresh mount. Tormjere gave the horse an unhappy look, which the animal reciprocated.

"We could ask for one of the clerics' mules, should you prefer," Birion noted.

"Mules, horses, what's the difference?" Tormjere replied. "I'd rather walk."

"Do as you will," Birion replied, "so long as you keep up."

Tormjere pulled himself up, muttering under his breath.

* * *

Shalindra ducked inadvertently as a trio of wyverns raced across the tops of the trees with a whoosh of air that sent leaves and branches raining down on everyone around her.

"I think they're mating," Honarch said. "The smaller one in the lead is a female. The two in pursuit are males."

"As long as they keep to each other," Birion said. "I'd not care to be the subject of their affections."

Where they stood offered a clear view of the sky, and so they watched as the larger males wheeled and banked sharply, each trying to injure the other even as they pursued the female.

"The wyverns weren't interested in us," Tormjere said as he rejoined them without warning, causing Enna to jump. "But I discovered someone who will be: thirty to forty men under no banner, and two wizards."

"Here?" Birion asked incredulously. "In the middle of nowhere?"

"We are between Ildalarial and Silvalaria," Enna snapped. "There are many 'somewheres' to be found here, if you know where to look."

Birion bowed his head in apology, though Shalindra was certain he had meant no offense. Enna seemed increasingly on edge, though for no reason she could name. Since parting ways with Treven they had travelled more south than west. Their route had taken them through uncivilized, though not unoccupied, forests and brought them to the southernmost reaches of the Aldantan Mountains. It had not been without its share of mishaps and trials, but it had also been no more trying than any journey through these woods.

Tormjere pointed west, across peaks and ridges which time had worn down to foothills. "They have scouts watching the road between the two nations, which should be in the next valley in that direction." He looked at Enna, who nodded a confirmation. "The hills to our east are uncomfortably steep for travel, so their camp occupies a natural funnel that anyone travelling up or down the road will pass through."

"That many men is consistent with a light raiding party," Birion said, "but the addition of the wizards is not. You are certain they camped under no colors?"

"Not so much as a single tabard. I doubt the Kingdom has

shifted to the wizard's cause, so it would be safe to guess they were Ceringion."

Shalindra fingered her symbol, mindful of the visions she had seen of demons killing the elves. "The other wizard you found was between us and Silvalaria, though you said the group was smaller. Perhaps it is the elves that occupy their attention and not us?"

Enna's worry was apparent. "Or they seek to keep my people isolated from one another."

"We have no one to ask," Birion observed with a sideways glance at Tormjere, "so we can only guess at this point. Regardless, we would do best to avoid them and tell the elves of their position."

"What if we were to capture one of them?" Shalindra asked.

Enna and Birion stared at her in surprise. Tormjere's eagerness at the suggestion flooded into her, but she pushed his desires aside. This needed to be done, but not as revenge for their continued animosity.

"My lady, are you certain?" Birion asked.

Enna's question came before the first could be answered. "Can we not go around, as Birion suggested?"

Tormjere dismissed that idea. "We would have to backtrack at least half a day. The horses can't handle the slopes near here."

"Under ordinary circumstances, I would choose that path," Shalindra said. "However, the situation we find ourselves in is anything but ordinary. At some point, we must cease allowing them to dictate our actions. Whether their target is us or the elves, they have the makings of a war party and must be dealt with. We need to know why they are here, and that means we must capture some of them alive."

"Our numbers do not match theirs," Birion pointed out,

stroking his moustache. "There is significant risk."

"I can take care of the wizards," Tormjere stated. "Once they're out of the way, we should be able to handle the rest easily."

Birion looked unconvinced. "And if they summon demons as well?"

"Then it's no more than two that I can likely defeat by myself. We've got two clerics and a wizard of our own, plus the new spears if needed."

"Also, not every wizard is capable of summoning," Honarch reminded them. "It's actually fairly rare among practitioners."

Enna gave him a disbelieving look. "All the ones we run into can, and do."

Honarch conceded her point.

"It is your decision, as always, Your Highness," Birion said. "If you wish it done, it will be so."

Shalindra looked at each of their faces in turn. "I do," she said, certain that this was the right decision. "I will leave the timing and planning in your capable hands."

"Then we will camp here and hope night finds us before anything else does."

* * *

Tormjere crept through the darkness towards the end of the Ceringion camp, where two small tents lay concealed in the bushes. Nothing moved except the handful of guards around the perimeter.

Are you certain we should not be closer to you?

Not yet. Wait until I've dealt with the sentries on this side.

Shalindra, Enna, and Honarch trailed not far behind him, ready to aid in the capture of a wizard, while Birion led his men towards the opposite end of the camp. A handful of archers had been positioned near the middle, where they could harass the Ceringions and cover any retreat, if needed.

He slipped up behind the half-asleep guard, inching his way closer. When the guard shifted position and looked away, Tormjere pounced, clamping a hand over the man's mouth and wrenching his head around with the other. No sooner had he eased the lifeless body to the ground than a raucous screeching split the night. Shouts sounded immediately from the camp as the Ceringions bolted awake.

Tormjere drew his sword with a curse and charged towards them.

What was that?

Some kind of alarm.

It is too soon. Birion cannot be in position yet.

We can't wait.

The Ceringions were bleary-eyed but competent, already gaining their weapons and organizing into a defensive posture. A twisting mass of magical fire signaled Honarch's entry into the conflict, arcing like a comet through the night to explode in their midst. Men and trees were set alight, lending a hellish glow to the battlefield.

The air tingled as crackling energies shot from the camp in response, coming to a spectacular stop somewhere in the woods as they slammed into Enna's silvery-blue shield. Close on its heels flew a trio of glowing orbs, which spun about themselves as they sliced through the air. They cut through the trees like a scythe to wheat, causing them to topple haphazardly.

The sharp ring of steel joined the shouting as Birion's men

charged into the camp. The Ceringions were collapsing inwards in an attempt to defend themselves and regain control.

We have to get to the wizards.

Tormjere cut down a pair of men before him and drove forward with single-minded purpose. One of the robed wizards saw his approach and shouted orders, which sent a group of men rushing to block his path. Tormjere dealt with them quickly, but the delay was enough.

The wizard's hand was clenched around the pendant hanging from his neck, and a swirling black mist had already taken shape before him. There was little Tormjere could do but watch as a segmented demon skittered out like a centipede on long, spikey legs. The flattened oval of its head searched back and forth for a target as its large mandibles gnashing eagerly.

Can you turn this one against its master?

There's no reasoning with the insects. They're just mean.

Arrows from Birion's archers came whistling towards the creature. The second wizard waved a hand dismissively, and the missiles halted their flight. With a flick of his wrist, he reversed their course and sent them streaking back towards the archers. Screams in the night said that at least some had found their mark.

Tormjere feinted to keep the demon's attention on him, then dove to the side and grabbed the body of a fallen Ceringion. He hurled the body towards the wizard, hoping to distract him enough to break his hold on the demon.

The wizard's hand shot forward, and the body stopped in midair, dangling like a macabre marionette before falling once more to the ground. Tormjere raced towards the wizard, but the demon flung itself between them. Tormjere dodged away as its mandibles clacked against Shalindra's shield.

The wizard gestured again as he incanted, and the ground beneath Tormjere's feet liquified to a soft mud, sucking him down. The demon slid sideways to Tormjere's undefended back, then reared back in sudden pain as Shalindra announced her presence by bringing Shining Moon crunching into its carapace.

I will occupy it. Get the wizard.

Immersed nearly to the waist, Tormjere summoned a trio of flames in his hand and sent then corkscrewing towards the mage. Surprised by the magical attack the man twisted away, barely deflecting the flaming darts. Tormjere jerked himself free of the ground before it solidified around him. With a leap, he was at the wizard before he could recover, and his blade cut him open from shoulder to thigh.

The demon paused its attack against Shalindra, mandibles grinding together as it swiveled its faceted eyes towards the dying wizard. Tormjere fixed it with his own stare as he absorbed the fleeting embers of strength from the dying wizard. It was an act of dominance familiar to every demon, one that even such a lesser creature understood.

The remaining wizard's eyes darted from Tormjere to the demon and back, seemingly unsure of which was the more dangerous threat. The creature snapped at them both as it retreated, no longer interested in continuing the fight. That seemed to make up the wizard's mind, as he threw his hands in the air and yelled above the melee.

"We surrender!"

He had to shout it several times before the handful of Ceringions surrounding him disengaged, then reluctantly threw down their weapons.

The demon clearly had other designs and turned to flee.

"Stop it!" Shalindra shouted.

Tormjere sprinted to cut off its retreat. It made a half-hearted attack, then pivoted with unnatural speed and rushed away again. Soldiers of both sides scattered as it trampled through the camp, only to have its path blocked once more by Honarch and Enna. Tormjere and Shalindra closed in, and it hissed and snapped at them as they encircled it.

Magical energy struck it, and Shining Moon accelerated into its side even as Tormjere's sword severed a leg. The doomed creature thrashed about, unable to defend itself from every direction at once. With a violent lurch it sprang towards Enna, desperate for escape. Silver and silvery-blue shields wrapped her in armor, but the demon's leap carried it beyond her instead of atop, and it scurried from them as quickly as it could. The four rushed to catch it, but it no longer sought escape. Its mandibles seized the necklace still looped around the dead wizard's neck. The caged darkness spun within, and a swirling void of dark mists began to manifest.

Tormjere vaulted onto the creature's back and cleaved his sword through its head. The demon's limbs spasmed before it collapsed and lay still.

The portal it had created began to diminish then surged outward as a blast of heat and wind erupted from its twisting depths, bending trees and forcing everyone away as it expanded at an alarming rate.

A massive being of shadow and nightmare emerged from the roiling cloud of ash and mist. Its skin was of crumbled stone and as dark as a moonless night. Black mists seeped from every crevasse and wrinkle like incense from a brazier. Segmented horns twisted from a skull lit by eyes that glowed an angry orange. It was power incarnate, and the very air about it burned foul with the malignance of its intent.

Dark wings unfolded as it drew itself up to its full height and stared down at them, displaying in its clenched fist a serrated, double-curved blade made from the bones of some massive creature.

Men of every allegiance stood rooted in place, staring at it slack jawed and seemingly incapable of willing themselves to flee from the horror before them. With a casual flick, the tip of the demon's sword skewered the wizard like a piece of meat at the table. It drew a deep breath, shriveling the wizard's body as he died with a tortured scream that spurred the frozen soldiers to action. Their terrified flight ended as the massive sword sliced through them like a scythe.

"Eluria preserve us," Shalindra whispered.

The demon's wicked glare fell upon her, and its voice carried such scorn that it mocked not only her plea but everything she had ever held dear. "Take care when bringing the gods into your conflict, shield maiden."

How does it know me?

They all know who we are.

"Birion!" Tormjere shouted. "Get them out of here!"

"Veluntrhu," the demon hissed, beckoning Tormjere forward. "Come. Meet your fate willingly, and I shall offer you the oblivion you so desperately seek." Baring its teeth in anticipation, it advanced towards them without awaiting a reply.

Enna swung her symbol down with a shout. A blast of divine force streaked towards the demon, but the mists around it solidified and deflected the blow. The creature's bone sword shot towards her only to be turned aside at the last instant by Shalindra's silvery shield.

Tormjere dove in, drawing a hiss of misty blood as his sword cut across the demon's leg. The creature jabbed at him with the sharpened point of its sword's pommel, nearly impaling him as it had the wizard. Tormjere's desperate leap to the side took him straight into the creature's tail just as it snapped towards him. Of course it would have a tail. He took the blow full in the face and was sent tumbling across the ground.

The demon flapped its mighty wings, buffeting them with dirt and sticks as it rose from the ground. It dove at them with a roar, driving its sword at Shalindra. Her defense held and the blade was deflected, but she cried out in pain at the effort. Tormjere rushed to attack the moment its feet touched the ground.

Honarch was incanting, and golden circlets of arcane symbols sprang into place around the demon's wrists, forcing its arms apart. Before Tormjere could capitalize on the opening, the demon strained forward, snapping its bonds.

"Do not seek to contain me, wizard!" it shouted, and its hand shot towards Honarch, sending blackened tendrils of sharply pointed mist streaking towards him. They disintegrated to vapor once more as they impacted Enna's silvery-blue shield, but the effort left her staggering, and she dropped to one knee with a whimper.

The creature lifted itself from the ground once more. Black mists flecked with fire and ash swirled like a cyclone around it, expanding outward and blinding them to its position.

Though his vision was blocked, Tormjere could still feel its presence.

From above and left.

Shalindra's shield snapped into place just in time. Tormjere saw and felt the demon's passing, and he lashed out with little effect.

Honarch gestured, and the swords of the fallen Ceringions came spinning up from the ground. They flew straight into the maelstrom, a twisting ball of sharpened metal. A roar of pain sounded from within, and as the demon reappeared they saw the membranes of its wings shredded.

A piece of the swirling black mist solidified in the demon's hand, which it hurled like a javelin towards Honarch. Again, the wizard was saved by Enna's shield, though she reeled under the impact.

"Bind it!" Enna shouted to Shalindra.

Shalindra had never attempted such a feat on something so large but knew what Enna spoke of. She manifested her shield, willing it to grow in brightness and intensity until it formed a cone enveloping the demon. Bands of silvery-blue energy wove themselves through her barrier as Enna lent her strength to the effort.

The demon forced itself against it but was driven to its knees by the torrent of energy pinning its arms to its side. The stony ridges of its brow creased as its body bent with tremendous effort. With a sudden jerk, the demon reversed its grip on its sword, and the spiked hilt shot towards her. Shalindra saw it coming, but there was no way for her to respond.

Tormjere slammed into her, knocking her to the side as he occupied her place. The sharpened hilt of the demon's blade pierced his stomach and came out his back.

Tormjere!

The pain hit him with such shock that his body was simply incapable of processing it, and in that briefest moment of lucidity, he brought his sword slashing down on the creature's wrist with everything he had, lodging the steel in the stony skin.

Follow my blade.

With a flash of silver, Shalindra hammered Shining Moon onto it, driving his sword like a guillotine through the demon's wrist.

The creature roared in agony and jerked away as its severed hand dropped to the ground, dragging sword and Tormjere with it. The demon clenched its jaw as its stony skin began to stretch and meld over the wound.

Tormjere pushed himself off the spike. His vision blurred and dimmed as he willed his perception to shift, searching for the small embers of power leaking from the demon's severed stump. He drew them to himself, tearing them from the still-living creature as it had done to the wizard, using the energy to close the gaping hole in his stomach.

The demon recoiled from him in surprise, covering the wound with its good hand as it turned away.

Tormjere staggered to his feet, still clutching his stomach and hoping it had been enough.

Eluria help me, your insides are a mess. Hold still. Tormjere, please.

With jerky steps, Tormjere advanced towards the crouching demon. It sprang at him in a savage frenzy nearly too fast to follow.

Silver and silvery-blue sparks lit the night as both women struggled to keep him alive.

"He's too close," Honarch yelled. "I can't risk attacking!"

"Do it anyway!" Enna screamed at him.

Honarch's swirling ball of fire exploded against the creature's head, showering Tormjere with globs of flame that singed his arms. No longer capable of avoiding the demon's blows, he trusted in Shalindra and Enna to defend him as he struck the creature again and again.

Then Shalindra was beside him. Shining Moon accelerated towards the demon where it cracked its skin like a chisel against stone. Tormjere slashed across the wounded stump of its arm as it stumbled. Another blast of magical fire slammed into it from behind. Shalindra hammered it solidly in the chest, and the demon doubled over and collapsed sideways. Tormjere plunged his sword through its face, piercing its eye and travelling so deep into the massive skull that half his forearm went in with it. Planting his foot against its chest, he tore his arm, blade and all, from the side of the demon's head.

The demon sagged to the ground with a heavy thud. It reached feebly for them with its once mighty arm, but Tormjere batted it aside. The horrific wound in its face gushed a vile substance upon the earth, and its voice rasped like a message from the grave.

"Our mistress has seen the prophecy you have not, Veluntrhu. Your death will signal our release, and all you know will be ours. When at last your soul is cast into the void, I shall be waiting for you."

Tormjere's sword descended, extinguished the flame in its burning eyes forever, but he did not stop. He hacked another piece from its face. Then another.

It is dead.

It's not dead enough.

Tormjere sank to his knees, his sword slipping from fingers to numb to hold it. His head spun as the last of his strength melted from his limbs. With effort, he forced his vision to shift. The embers that flew from the demon blazed with life unlike anything he had ever known, and like a glutton at a feast he gorged upon them. He drew them into himself until he could contain no more and the overwhelming abundance of energy leaked from his pores. The world tilted of its own accord, and had he not been on his knees he surely would have collapsed.

Nearby, Shalindra staggered against a tree as her stomach burned and twisted, sending bile to scorch her throat. Enna rushed to keep her upright.

"I am fine," she gasped, though her knees were as mud and her vision swam.

Does it always feel that way?

No. You get used to it, and that one was exceptional.

Tormjere waited, allowing the dizziness to pass as his body recovered.

His strength now restored, he pried open the stony outer skin before plunging his still shaking hands into the dense flesh beneath. He devoured a chunk of the steaming, black meat with gusto, relishing the squirming burn that flowed through his body.

Do you still need it so badly?

It will sustain me for days, and I will grow stronger.

At what cost?

I get to keep living.

Tormjere became aware of the soldiers who were rejoining them, but he ignored their looks of horror. "In their world, a fresh kill like this would attract every demon for miles. They would gather like vultures, with the strongest taking what they wished and the rest of us feeding on scraps."

Honarch took a deep breath as he wiped a smattering of blood from his face. "You ate this every day?"

"Maybe one day in ten." Tormjere stood and offered a piece to Birion, who declined in an impolite manner. "You don't feel hungry for a long time after eating it."

Enna wrinkled her nose. "Please tell me you are not going to bring any of it with us. The stench is already an affront to my senses."

"It turns putrid the moment it goes cold, and no form of preservation will keep it from making you sick."

"I think I'm going to be sick watching you eat it," Honarch said.

"Our men?" Shalindra asked Birion.

"We lost almost half, my lady. The remaining injuries are survivable, but your attention would be appreciated."

"They will have it immediately."

Birion gazed at the grisly scene around them. "Any of our enemies still living when the demon appeared have likely expired or fled. I doubt we will find any answers."

Shalindra looked back at the dead demon and shook her head. "You are correct. Tonight has given us only more questions." She whispered a prayer, and a soft light appeared at the end of a branch nearby. Enna did the same as Birion's men began their search.

The wounded hobbled or were carried to Shalindra, while the

soldiers combed through the remains of the Ceringion camp, looking for survivors.

Tormjere let his senses extend through the woods, his stomach now pleasantly full. Between the raw power of the demon and Shalindra's efforts, he felt no ill effects from the battle. The pain he never forgot, and so he shoved it into the past where it belonged and turned to what came next. He cleaned his blade and joined Honarch in inspecting the wizard who had summoned the first demon.

"Anyone you knew?" he asked.

Honarch shook his head. "Mercifully not, though I wish it had not come to this. I cannot understand what rationale drives the Conclave's thinking."

"Clearly there's something they wish to gain."

"Almost certainly, but what? They supported Ceringion during the war, yet Actondel is not yet fully pacified. There's nothing out here but the elves, who are of little threat to anyone."

"Maybe there's something we don't know."

"I just can't see any purpose to it," Honarch repeated as they moved to the second wizard. "Ugh, I hate searching dead people. No summoning pendant."

"That's a welcome first."

"He did enough damage without it. I'd not be here without Enna." He made a satisfied sound as he plucked a dohedron from one of the wizard's pouches. "I'll keep a watch on this and see if I can piece together any messages that come through, but without the—"

An anguished cry caused them both to turn as Enna crumpled to her knees at the edge of a small wash. Shalindra reached her just before they did.

The depression Enna stared at had been filled in a hasty manner with fresh earth. Bushes and rocks protruded through the dirt, but light reflected off the half-visible edge of a silver symbol matching those worn by both women.

Tormjere slid into the wash and brushed aside a layer of dirt from atop the pile to reveal the remains of first one and then another elvish woman draped in the sleeveless white robes of Eluria. Enna sobbed helplessly as Shalindra put her arms around her.

We must bury them properly.
They won't know the difference.
Not for their sake, for Enna's.

* * *

Tormjere sat and placed his back against a tree, as quiet as everyone else around him.

In total, they had reburied almost forty elvish bodies, all but a handful in white robes. Enna had collected their symbols and said the appropriate prayers for them, then withdrawn into herself. The Ceringion bodies and their own dead had been piled into a makeshift pyre, which Honarch had burned with magic. When it was done, they packed up what they could and resumed their trek without enthusiasm. The camp they now occupied was only a few miles south, but it could have been fifty for all the weariness they felt.

Conversation happened in fits and starts and lacked any of the usual joy that follows a victory. He could not blame them. Their world had been altered by the previous night's battle, and many struggled to reconcile the event with the natural order with which they were familiar. No one could deny the intelligence of the demon they had faced, but as Shalindra had said, they were left with far more questions than answers.

Birion was the first to broach the subject. "Never did I think to see such creatures speak, but this time there was no denying it. Why do they hate you so fiercely, Tormjere? Did you kill that many of them?"

"A few," he replied, still staring at the fire. "But not enough to warrant this."

"The last demon wasn't summoned by either wizard," Honarch pointed out, "and it spoke of a prophecy centered around your death."

"Prophecies abound," Tormjere said, "and we would all live happier lives without them."

"I would be the last to disagree," Shalindra said, cutting off Enna's defensive response, "but Honarch is correct regarding its means of arrival. Can demons travel to our world at will, without the command of a mage?"

Honarch spread his hands. "I don't think so, but I also don't know enough to defend that opinion. It would seem logical that we would see far more of them if they had unfettered access to our world."

Shalindra looked at Tormjere, but he shook his head as well. "Before today, I had seen nothing to indicate that they were capable."

He let the group's continued debate fade into the background as he sought his own answers. Wings, weapons, and magic. Not once had he faced a demon with all three. That would make it... he could not remember the rank, but it was far above what should have appeared here. And he had not been strong enough to defeat it. It had taken all four of them, and their success was by the slimmest of margins. That made it even more imperative that Shalindra attain the Guardian's armor and whatever went with it. Hopefully, that would be enough.

He saw Honarch excuse himself and move a short distance away, pulling out a book that had been taken from the dead wizards. Tormjere gave him a moment to get settled, then went to join him.

"Find anything good?" he asked.

"Not yet, but maybe you should take a look through as well."

"Magic is your providence."

"Indeed? The corkscrew was a nice touch on the flame spikes by the way. Just how much did you learn from those books you gave me?"

"Enough to stay alive. I can't do the larger explosions like you can."

"But you can create a portal, just as they did. And without the talisman that makes it possible."

Tormjere chuckled. "I thought everyone had forgotten that little trick. It's not an uncommon talent for demons, and it was something my life depended on more than once. But there are limits, even for them. I can only make them to cross short distances that I can already see. It's difficult to control, and there can… unpleasant side effects when done wrong."

"I'll stick to the more conventional methods of travel then," Honarch said with a wave towards the horses. Tormjere caught a glint of metal on one of his fingers that had not been there earlier. "New ring?"

231

Honarch nodded and held up hand. "It's a talisman against blades and physical attacks. Our enemy no longer had a use for it."

"Didn't help him much."

"Hopefully, it will prove more effective against lesser mortals," Honarch said with a wry grin.

Tormjere rolled his eyes. "I'm as mortal as you are, unfortunately."

"You do a good impression of someone who isn't." He fingered the ring thoughtfully. "How did you do it?"

"Do what?"

"Get to that wizard so easily. I saw the protections he had in place. It should have provided at least some resistance to your attack."

Soft footsteps approached, and Tormjere looked up to see Enna standing above him.

"I wish to ask a question of you," she said.

When he made no move to stand she added, "Alone, if you do not mind."

Tormjere left Honarch without an answer and followed Enna a few steps into the woods where they would not be overheard.

"You should be dead."

"I'm rather happy that I'm not."

She placed her hand against his stomach, as if she could feel through the hastily stitched hole in his tunic where the demon's sword hilt had impaled him. "It is because you healed yourself, didn't you?"

"Yes."

"How?"

He gently pulled away. "You really don't want to know."

"I do, because it is not possible. For you to have found how it could be done…"

"I didn't discover anything you don't already know. You told me once before: a vessel of water cannot be poured into itself."

"This is a universal truism, though there are ways for one being to augment another. But if that was not the case, where did you get…" Her eyes widened in horror as realization dawned on her. "You took something from the demon, didn't you? When you cut off its hand?"

"What I could. It wasn't much, but it was enough to keep me alive until Shalindra could heal me."

"Can you steal life from the living now?" She shuddered, and her voice dropped to a whisper. "I remember what that feels like, and it is a terrible thing to inflict upon another being."

"Not from the living," Tormjere reassured her. "It only works with the dying."

"The demon was still alive."

"Its hand wasn't. The stump of its arm wasn't. But none of this is what you wished to ask me."

"I remember what you said about… about how elves taste to demons." Enna drew her arms about herself, and shivered. "Do you… Do you think for those we found… Were they…?"

"No. Their deaths were horrible, but they were not consumed by a demon."

She bit her lip and let her eyes thank him the way her voice could not.

I mourn the loss of my Sisters, but my heart breaks for her tonight. We'll reach Ildalarial soon, and she will find the peace she needs.

Chapter Twenty

Friends in the Forest

They followed the road for another day, taking them along a south-westerly curve around and through the hills and valleys of the lower Aldantan Mountains. The thoroughfare was wide and the ground packed firm, and it often made detours around particularly large trees or changed course to follow the flow of a river. Enna had travelled this road between Ildalarial and Silvalaria only once, and while her memory of that visit to their northern neighbors was clouded by her youthful perceptions she did not recall the road being so desolate.

They paused atop a small rise, and she made a sweeping motion with her arm to encompass all the lands before them. "The forests of Ildalarial." Though a simple statement, it filled her with joy to realize how close she was to her home. "From here, it is but half a day to our northernmost town."

"Is this road always so empty?" Shalindra asked, echoing her own thoughts. "I would have expected to see someone on it by now."

"So would I. Ildalarial and Silvalaria lack the constant

mingling that your kingdoms enjoy, but it is unusual to see the road completely barren." They had surely passed dozens of tiny villages and homesteads, each situated away from the road as was customary, but as no one had come to greet them it would have been inappropriate to seek them out.

"Given our size, I doubt our passing has gone unnoticed," Tormjere said. "I'm going to have a look ahead."

"I will accompany you," Enna offered quickly. "Anyone we encounter may be more hospitable should they see another elf." Tormjere was unquestionably the best scout they had but, regardless of his intentions, he did not always have the patience required for diplomacy. Few humans arrived from this direction, and her people were generally suspicious of uninvited guests.

It was no surprise to her when he dismounted to proceed on foot, and she slid from her horse as well, hoping that her doubts had not been overly apparent.

"We will follow at a slower pace," Shalindra said, "so there is no misunderstanding as to our purpose. Try not to get too far ahead."

Thank Elurithlia, Shalindra always understood, and was equally cognizant of the rumored tensions between Ildalarial and the Kingdom of Actondel. Should so large a party of armed men approach, they could well be greeted by arrows instead of words.

Tormjere motioned her forward with a half-smile as if he knew every thought that had just run through her mind. He probably did, somehow, which only made it more infuriating. Still, he never used his knowledge for his own gain, unlike others that she knew.

She shook her head, annoyed now at herself. *Others.* Her mother, she meant. The most powerful and highest-ranking Sister of Elurithlia's devotees.

Enna kept quiet as they walked, letting Tormjere watch the woods as she struggled with the turmoil that admission released within her. Her mother was devout in her faith, even fanatical on some topics, and such fervor could make her unpredictable. Enna had no idea how she would react to Shalindra when they finally reached her.

Tormjere held up a hand. "I think we've found them."

Enna stopped beside him. "I don't see anything, but our Woodswardens are unlikely to announce their presence."

They waited only a short time before an elf in the usual greens and browns stepped onto the road and approached cautiously.

"Revered Sister, are you well?"

The question was delivered in elvish, and his tone and the way his hand rested on the long knife at his belt indicated that he wished to know if she was here of her own free will or as a captive.

"I am well and relieved to return home once more," she answered in the common tongue. "We have no cause to fear those who accompany me."

He relaxed, but his hand did not leave his knife nor did he move from their path. "As you have arrived at the head of a hostile complement, caution is warranted."

"Caution, perhaps, but there is no reason to be unwelcoming."

"I stand here alone," the Woodswarden countered. "Surely that is not unwelcoming."

Tormjere glanced pointedly at the woods behind the elf. "That's a lot of alone standing behind you."

Enna could see no one else, but he was likely correct. The elf appeared surprised and perhaps impressed. "Indeed." He turned back to Enna. "I am Woodswarden Gilbran. May I know your intent, Revered Sister?"

"I am escorting my friends to our capital of Eitholmir, where we will seek an audience with the Manalathlia of Elurithlia."

Gilbran looked as if he had swallowed something unpleasant. "The human kingdoms make war with us again. You have chosen an inopportune time to bring even one human warrior into our home, much less the numbers that follow you."

"Such times are the cause for our visit," Enna replied. "Not every human is our enemy."

"That is not for me to decide."

"You have our word," Tormjere interjected, "that we are not here to cause problems."

"Your word, unfortunately, is not enough to justify our trust." Gilbran's eyes flicked across the deer-hooved knife that Tormjere carried. "No matter what services you may have performed in the past."

Enna was disappointed but hardly surprised by Gilbran's reluctance. Though a knife such as Tormjere possessed represented a significant honor, it was not a key that could unlock every door. Fortunately, she had other options.

"I would ask your permission to address the Calontier," Enna said. "My friends act in Ildalarial's interests."

"Such is your right, Revered Sister. How many people do you intend to bring?"

"Myself, Tormjere who stands beside me, and another of my Sisters." To Tormjere, she said, "Birion and Honarch will need to remain behind with the soldiers."

"And what do you intend for those soldiers?" Gilbran pressed.

"We have travelled from the feet of the Three Sisters, and are eager to enjoy the comforts of civilization again. I would not leave them camped along the road where their intent may be mistaken."

Gilbran considered, then whistled a short pattern. More than a dozen similarly clad elves materialized behind him. "We will await them here, Revered Sister."

"I thank you," Enna said. She turned to fetch Shalindra and the others, but Tormjere stopped her.

"They're already on the way."

She questioned him with her glance but found only an amused look in his eyes that teased his knowing of something she did not. In the interests of aiding Shalindra's journey, Enna swallowed her retort and waited patiently. When the group arrived, Enna was relieved to see that they rode at a casual pace, and that all their spears had been stowed on the pack animals.

Shalindra and Birion dismounted and joined them. If Tormjere's knife had impressed Gilbran, Shining Moon seemed to leave him momentarily speechless. There were few in Ildalarial who had not been raised on tales of the Guardian's exploits, and there was not a single Sister who carried a weapon.

Gilbran glanced her way in surprise, then bowed deeply to Shalindra. "I was not aware you carried such a gift, Revered Sister, or my greeting would have been more welcoming."

Shalindra smiled in that way that caused her blue eyes to sparkle. "Your caution was entirely appropriate, Woodswarden Gilbran. It gladdens me more than you can know to see Ildalarial well defended. I am Sister Shalindra."

Gilbran indicated one of his companions. "Maris will show your men to a place of safety. We have a camp nearby where they may rest in comfort. If it pleases you, Revered Sisters, I will escort you to the Calontier immediately."

"We would be most thankful for that assistance," Shalindra replied.

As the rest of the company dismounted, Enna saw Tormjere pull Honarch aside for a hushed word. The wizard gave him a curt nod, but she could not hear anything said, and they did not linger in conversation.

"If you would follow me, Revered Sisters."

"This is my first time visiting Ildalarial," Shalindra said, falling into step beside him. "May I ask where we are going?"

Gilbran seemed more at ease now that Birion's soldiers had been left behind. "To our village, Revered Sister, known in your tongue as Rivermist."

"That is a delightful name. Is it far?"

"It is a comfortable distance, and we will arrive there soon."

Shalindra was understandably curious, and her friendly questions put Gilbran further at ease. Enna realized how tense she had been and willed herself to relax. She remembered her own shock when first seeing a human woman holding Shining Moon, and with another war looming she had every reason to fret over her people's reaction. Their reception in the capital would almost certainly be different than here on the border, but this first meeting boded well.

"I must apologize again for my welcome, friend Tormjere," Gilbran was saying, "or do you prefer 'Valtilaniar?'"

His use of the title jolted Enna from her musings and caused her normally sure feet to stumble. For his part, Tormjere seemed either unaware of its meaning or unimpressed by its attachment to him. He shrugged his indifference. "Both have their uses."

"I would imagine so."

"Can you tell me more of whom we will address?" Shalindra asked, adeptly steering the conversation to a neutral subject. "Do they fulfil a role such as a duke or baron?"

"No," Enna answered. "We are not ruled by single families as you are. Each city is overseen by a Calontier, what you might consider a council. Membership is achieved based on virtue and wisdom, but influenced heavily by local customs. Each calontier is led by the *Altalathlia*. She is usually but not always one of our Sisters."

"Those words are a mouthful," Shalindra remarked, "but it is not so dissimilar to how we govern in Newlmir."

Enna agreed. "The structure was established millennia ago, and tradition dictates our use of the old words. The position is most similar to the Sister Superior at your temples, though it is not always exclusive to our order."

"We have found it to be a superior form of governance," Gilbran added. "That results in fewer pointless conflicts."

There was no hard boundary to mark where the forest ended and the town began, but rather a gradual shift from a predominance of trees to that of buildings. The structures flowed in and around the oaks and elms, with the majority being made of wood. There was more stone than Enna expected, but it was primarily of stacked and rounded stones and rarely were the businesses and dwellings more than one-story high. The rounded shapes and curved lines were so much more pleasing than the hard angles of human cities.

The people in the streets took note of their passing, and more than one stopped with an odd look or to stare at Shalindra. She and Tormjere both stood out as the only humans in sight, but Enna was certain that Shining Moon was more the focus of their attention.

Gilbran stopped outside the council hall, a compact building of wood with a decoratively carved entrance. After a hushed conversation with the attendant inside, they were led through the building and into a circular glade ringed by towering trees.

Beneath the towering trees stood the five elves of the Calontier, all of whom had greying hair. The lack of seating was designed to prevent meetings from droning on, something Enna wished those in Newlmir would have adopted. It was mildly surprising that only two of the five wore the white robes of Elurithlia, and neither of them stood in the middle where the Altalathlia should. Regardless of affiliation, every member of the calontier shifted in surprise at the sight of Shalindra's weapon.

The attendant bowed to the assemblage. "Altalathlia, councilors. I present Revered Sisters Ennathalerial and Shalindra, who petition for passage to Eitholmir." He turned back to them. "Revered Sisters, before you stands the Calontier of Rivermist, presided over by Altalathlia Aquilindalia."

Aquilindalia regarded them coolly, evaluating everything about them. Rather than the white of Elurithlia, she was draped in a graceful dress of a light brown, and about her neck hung a golden chain with the symbol of the open Book of Amalthee.

"You come well-armed for simple travelers," she observed. "Given our current situation, there seems little wisdom in granting such a request, yet there are times when even a little wisdom may open doors. What do you seek?"

Enna stepped forward. "Sister Shalindra seeks council with the Manalathlia. It has been a difficult road through the wilderness to the north to reach our borders, and haste is in order."

"It is cause for rejoice that you bring Alta Suralia to us," one of the Sisters said. "Yet now is also a time of strife. The armies of Actondel threaten us with a war not of our choosing."

"The threat we seek to end may be greater still," Enna said, "but their ultimate cause could be one and the same. You are aware of what this could portend."

Aquilindalia's eyes studied Shalindra. "It is a possibility. Yet such threats have surrounded us for generations and we have endured. Is there a reason for your present haste beyond simple eagerness?"

"On the way here, we were attacked not only by men, but wizards and demons."

There were murmurs from the other elves, but they were silenced by the barest turn of Aquilindalia's head. "And?"

Enna fought to keep her emotions in check as she answered. "We were able to overcome them, but at their campsite we found dozens of bodies. It appeared that they had been preying on travelers along the road to Silvalaria, particularly those on pilgrimage to Maetholmir."

Enna was reluctant to provide details of the horror she had witnessed, but she could see the understanding in Aquilindalia's eyes. Indeed, all the councilors registered sorrow as the weight of her words sank in, and several uttered prayers.

"This is devastating news indeed."

"It is as we suspected, then," one of the male elves said grimly. "They seek to isolate us from the outside."

"Though not of your faith, I am well aware of the importance of that which you carry. In light of this, I believe that we should aid your journey."

Enna bowed her head. "We would welcome any assistance, thank you."

"Given current conditions, by boat would avoid the most conflicts."

"River Annyre is dangerous now," another councilor protested. "The Actondel armies watch its entire length, and we have barely..." He trailed off at a sharp glance from Aquilindalia.

"We cannot spare transportation for your entire complement, nor do we feel comfortable sending so many armed men, and a wizard, downriver."

Enna looked at Shalindra for guidance. There was no way they would gain passage for the entire troop, and while she was more than comfortable negotiating a resolution she had no power to command anyone beyond herself.

"Such a large escort will be unnecessary within the safety of your borders," Shalindra said diplomatically. "We would be best served with six of us, at a minimum."

"That number would require multiple boats, and no matter who was in them it would attract far more attention than you or I would be comfortable with."

"We three, then."

Tormjere shifted uncomfortably and was about to speak, but Shalindra stopped him with the barest shake of her head. From the way he continued looking at her, it seemed that the pair were again exchanging more than meaningful glances.

"It is decided then," Aquilindalia said. "We will see to your accommodations and sustenance, and bring your men here to rest with you. You will depart on the morrow."

It was a polite way of keeping so many humans off the streets, and out of the public eye. Shalindra no doubt recognized it for what it was, but remained gracious.

"We thank you for your generosity."

"You must be tired, and I thank you for indulging this meeting so soon," Aquilindalia said. "We have some additional business to attend to, but if the calontier will allow me a brief recess to accommodate your needs?"

The other members of the council bowed to her and departed, though more than a few eyes lingered on Shining Moon. When they were gone, Aquilindalia waved the attendant forward.

"Inish will show you to a place where you may rest, and will attend to your needs."

Enna relaxed. That had gone as well as could be expected, though the separation from Birion and Honarch was unfortunate. Aquilindalia approached for what Enna assumed was to be a more casual conversation. Such encounters often happened after a negotiation, but she was stunned when Aquilindalia spoke directly to Tormjere.

"If I might have a word, Valtilaniar?"

Tormjere inclined his head and followed her towards a narrow path that led from the clearing. Enna's eyes locked briefly on his, still trying to process what had happened.

For his part, Tormjere was as surprised as everyone else. Just once he would like to be omitted from all these intrigues that seemed so necessary to some people.

Be polite. She could still change her mind.

When am I ever not?

Aquilindalia led him to a smaller clearing which was also open to the sky, allowing the half-moon to peer down at them through a thin veil of clouds. Unlike the council clearing there were no walls, but the arrangement of the surrounding trees lent a feeling of intimacy.

"I realize that our names can be difficult for you. Here you may address me as Aquilin."

"Tormjere is fine for me."

"From your mannerisms, I will assume that formalities are no longer needed."

"I'm fine without them."

A small smile graced her delicate lips, but it evaporated just as quickly. "Know that it is through no act of kindness that I provide you aid." Aquilin paced slowly as she spoke. "Your people war with us, for no purpose other than their insatiable need for conquest."

Tormjere had no response to that and remained silent, waiting for her to get to the point.

Aquilin studied him curiously. "No angry denials? You do possess wisdom beyond your fellow men. I can see why he favors you. You are the one who saved our Legitarso and saw Her Book returned, yes?"

"Honarch and I escaped with him, but Treven was as responsible for our success as anyone."

"You are either humble, or the accounting that I have heard is incorrect."

Tormjere shrugged. "Ask Honarch if you don't believe me."

"Recent events have given us little reason to trust wizards."

"They've done us few favors, but some are worthy of it."

"Perhaps. I met the Legitarso once, after making a pilgrimage to Kirchmont. It was… difficult to reach the city."

"I can imagine. The Kingdom has mixed feelings towards elves."

"Yet we persevered. Strange are the paths we walk in life, and at times stranger still are those with whom we walk them. Even some within my own order were unable or unwilling to assist us, and so it fell to those who walk the Sixfold Path to aid our travel." Her glittering eyes studied his face, as if waiting for a reaction, but when there was none she continued. "When we arrived, the Legitarso was gracious in his welcome. I asked for his guidance, as do all who seek him out, but in answer he simply recalled his own journey to retrieve Her Book. I was confused by this at first, and feared that he was not the man I had hoped for him to be. As I learned of his trials and the eventual return of Her Book, however, I found inspiration in his words and lessons which I continue to apply to my own situation."

"He's good at that."

"It was not what I had asked to hear, but it was what I needed. I see it as a sign of Amalthee's wisdom that your journey should lead you here, where I may reciprocate some small part of the favors bestowed upon me. It could be that on your next visit, I will be more pleased to see Honarch, and I might have the opportunity to enjoy his company as I do yours. But now is not the time. I already risk much by speaking to you."

"Shalindra is here to find answers, not to cause trouble."

"And why are you here?"

"Because I said I would be."

Aquilin fell silent again, seeming to consider her words

carefully. "I would ask that you allow Gilbran and one other to accompany your horsemen when they travel to Silvalaria on their way north."

"Is that where they're going?" he asked.

"They cannot remain here, nor will they be allowed to continue south. There is little to be gained from travelling either east or west, and to return to their home in what was once Maetholmir will take them through our northern neighbors."

She is correct. There is nowhere else for them to go.

"I'm certain that Birion would appreciate their company," he said. "And your Woodswardens will reach Silvalaria safely."

Her eyes narrowed almost imperceptibly, signaling that he had guessed correctly. "As I said, our needs are in alignment. I would, however, offer you a word of caution. Though you travel with a distinguished Sister of Elurithlia, and another who carries with her a weapon just as powerful as Amalthee's Book, do not expect to be greeted with warmth or affection."

"Her arrival seldom is," Tormjere replied. "Thank you for you counsel."

"As I will thank you for your efforts. May Her wisdom be with you, and I pray that the change you are certain to bring will benefit us all."

* * *

It was early the next morning when two elves in the greens and browns, Pelan and Baylon, arrived to escort them to the river. Shalindra was thankful that Tormjere had woken her early, as the elves seemed eager to the point of impatience to begin the journey.

"Try not to forget the dohedron," Honarch reminded Tormjere, fighting back a yawn. "I'll look for your messages at sundown, at least until we determine how far apart they will work."

"I'll keep you updated as I can. I have no idea how long it will take to get there and return."

Shalindra placed a hand on Birion's arm. "Take care, and may Eluria watch over you."

"Thank you, Your Highness. We will await word that you are headed north once more, and will meet you where we may. I'll not sit idle while you walk all the way back by yourself."

"I hope it will only be a few weeks," Shalindra said to them both, then bent close where only Birion and Honarch would hear. "Safeguard the elves as you would me. I would have them know that not every human they encounter is worthy of distrust."

"As you wish it, my lady," Birion said with a salute. "We will be prepared to aid you in any way we can as soon as we have seen them to Silvalaria. Come, magician."

Pelan approached to a polite distance and bowed to Shalindra and Enna. "If you would follow me, Revered Sisters."

Tormjere shouldered his pack and fell in behind them, still unhappy about the decision.

I know you did not want to be separated from your friend, but it will not be for long.

Doesn't mean I have to like it.

There are a great many things which I dislike about this effort. I can only pray it will improve.

Unlike the wide and flat riverboats she and Tormjere had ridden before, the one waiting for them was more like an elegant canoe. The vessel was long and thin, and carved from a single tree. The surface had been polished to a rich golden shine, and though it appeared sturdy enough for utilitarian purposes, there was

248

artistry in its construction. Both ends curved upwards to an almost vertical point, which was carved in a similar motif as the houses.

Their escorts took station at the front and rear of the vessel, while Shalindra occupied the middle with Enna and Tormjere. A modest amount of provisions had been loaded, leaving it a tight but not uncomfortable fit. Pelan untied from the docks, and a solid shove sent them away from shore to where the current quickly took them.

Soon she would be in Eitholmir, in the place Eluria had wished her to be. Shalindra could only wonder what answers she would find when she arrived.

Chapter Twenty-One

Elvish Hospitality

Shalindra stepped onto the dock almost before their craft had ceased moving, eager to escape the cramped confines of the boat they had been stuck in for two days. She placed a hand on her symbol of Eluria and pressed it against her chest. She was finally here.

"I know the way," Enna said to Pelan as she disembarked. "Thank you for the speed of our arrival."

Both elves bowed. "It was our honor, Revered Sisters. May your journey achieve as smooth a resolution."

It won't.

Stop being so pessimistic.

Have you looked at Enna? She's as nervous as a doe before a wolf.

He was correct about that. Enna's face was almost as pale as her hair, and she constantly fidgeted with the end of her belt as she led them away from the river. Shalindra resolved to ask her about it, but quickly became swept up in the sights and sounds of the elvish capital.

Eitholmir was a city as active and vibrant as any in the

Kingdom, yet it was difficult to grasp its scale because of the trees. The buildings rising between them were tall and thin, some soaring to the same height as the tallest branches surrounding them. Wood and stone intertwined in pleasing patterns, and with a minimum of straight lines. Natural tones dominated, save for the brightly colored signs, banners, and ribbons which hung from every doorway and window. Troops of minstrels played melodic tunes at various places, each attracting a small crowd that danced and clapped to the music. It was more festive than any celebration she had ever seen, yet the people went about their day as if nothing unusual was occurring.

"Are we going straight to the temple?" Shalindra asked. She had given up on thinking she would recognize it, as nearly every building bore the symbol of Eluria somewhere upon it.

"Oh," Enna said, startled from her thoughts. She stood for a moment getting her bearings, then set off down one of the streets. "I thought we might get something to eat first. The meeting will likely take some time."

"Do you think we will we be able to see the Manalathlia this evening?"

"Her name is Elothlirial," Enna said, "though she prefers to be addressed by title no matter the setting. It might be possible to see her before the evening prayers, but once begun she will not make herself available until tomorrow."

Enna lapsed back into silence, and Shalindra left her to her thoughts. The winding streets were cool and shaded despite the summer heat, and speckled with sunlight as it filtered through the branches high above. There seemed as many squirrels, birds, and other woodland creatures as there were elves. Commerce moved apace with every appearance of normalcy, but there was a nervous undercurrent—an urgency—to many of the activities. More than a few of the people they saw cast suspicious glances their way, and others stopped to stare and whisper.

For all their joyous mannerisms, it reminds me of Tiridon during the siege.

You're right. It could be this border conflict is closer to outright war than we thought.

I pray it is not. My father was never eager for conquest.

Enna led them down a street with more buildings than trees, and then to a pleasant little shop with large windows. The sign affixed above the window was in elvish, but the smell of fresh breads drifting from the open door spoke to what lay inside. The interior of the shop was crowded with both people and tables piled high with baked goods, and further warmed by a pair of ovens in the back wall.

Enna picked a loaf from one table and cheese from another, then caught the baker's attention. The man eyed what was in her hands and gave her a respectful nod, then turned back to his other customers.

They exited through a different doorway and onto a shaded porch surrounded by manicured bushes which shielded it from the street. Cups had been stacked beside a fountain bubbling with cool, clear water. They each filled one and then found seats at a small, round table near the edge of the porch.

"We will not need to pay for this?" Shalindra asked as she accepted her portion.

Enna shook her head. "No. He will keep an accounting and petition the temple for reimbursement."

The smells were making her hungry, and Shalindra took an eager bite. The bread proved light and sweet, and the cheese was sharper than what she was accustomed to but nonetheless delicious.

"I cannot imagine such transactions taking place on nothing more than faith in the Kingdom, save perhaps for those who follow Toush," Shalindra observed.

"My people follow the gods, and Elurithlia in particular, with more reverence than yours. It is a complex relationship, one that is woven into the fabric of our society."

They finished their meal and returned to the street. People were moving up and down the road as would be expected, but as she followed Enna a group of elves who had been watching the bakery suddenly straightened and fell silent.

She felt Tormjere drift closer, walking protectively on her right hand and slightly behind. Shalindra risked a glance over her shoulder and saw the entire group trailing at a respectful distance behind them.

Why are they following us?

They aren't following us; they're following you.

Enna became aware of them as well, for she increased her pace, looking neither left nor right.

A young girl plucking apples from a cart stopped what she was doing and tugged at her mother's dress, pointing in Shalindra's direction. The woman began to say something in response, but her mouth dropped open as Shalindra walked past.

Enna rounded a corner onto a thoroughfare packed with people. She slowed, then took a sudden turn back the way they had come. The group that had been following them was caught off guard by the sudden change. The followers stepped aside, and

253

more than one bowed to Shalindra as she passed through them. Their actions added haste to Enna's already hurried steps, and Shalindra was almost at a jog to keep up. By the time they had reached their destination, there were several dozen elves in tow, and their numbers were growing.

Shalindra had expected the temple of Eluria to be constructed of white marble, but instead they were greeted by only a wall of trees so thick that it was impossible to see through. Piercing the greenery were two tall, arched tunnels formed by interwoven branches that looked as old as the world itself. Set a good twenty paces from each other, both were wide enough to have allowed four horses abreast. Centered high between the entryways was a large but tastefully sized symbol of Eluria. Its wooden surface was polished to a bright finish, but from the patterns in the grain she could not tell if it had been carved or simply grown in that shape.

She followed Enna into the nearest tunnel, the floor of which was of stones arranged in curving arcs and worn smooth by countless feet over centuries of use. Soft lights floated near the ceiling, each slowly pulsing in a pattern that was as random as it was deliberately soothing. Shalindra's heart beat fast as the bustle of the city faded behind them.

A woman in the sleeveless white robes of Eluria awaited them in an alcove halfway through, but before she could greet them her eyes grew wide.

"Alta Suralia!" She stammered something else in elvish, then turned and hurried through the tunnel without waiting for a response.

Shalindra understood none of the words but their meaning was clear, and they hurried after the woman.

The tunnel soon opened into a sunlit clearing of immense size, large enough to have contained the castle in Newlmir three or four times over. The space was empty save for a modest number of worshippers clustered together at the far side.

The Sister they were following took them directly through the center of the clearing, which drew the attention of those who were already there. Whether due to the speed of their approach or the crowd that pressed in eagerly behind her Shalindra could not tell.

The assemblage was facing a line of eleven Sisters of Eluria, all but one draped in elegantly sleeveless robes of white and displaying a silver symbol of their goddess more intricately detailed than any she had ever seen. There was no dais or stage, but the ground rose gently such that they stood above the floor of the clearing.

The woman in the center of those eleven Sisters stood out from all present in both dress and demeanor. Her robes were of a translucent white and silver with hints of green, and of such a delicate material that they seemed to float about her as she moved. The fine lines of her face matched Enna's so closely that the resemblance was impossible to miss, though she was older and her flowing hair was the palest of yellows. Her bearing could only be described as regal, but her eyes were as joyless as a statue's.

Her hand moved, and an expectant hush settled over the clearing.

The Sister who had brought them across the field was excused by another delicate motion, and she bowed and backed away, leaving the three of them to stand alone before the council.

Shalindra suddenly became aware of her own tattered appearance, with her robe worn thin in spots and stained with the dirt of the road at the hem.

The Manalathlia, for that is what she must have been, addressed Enna formally, her words as graceful as they were incomprehensible.

"I am pleased to return, mother," Enna replied in the common tongue. "It has been a difficult journey."

The woman regarded Shalindra and Tormjere coolly. "You have brought guests."

I've never heard 'guests' used so contemptuously.

"Yes. Manalathlia Elothlirial, may I present Sister Shalindra, bearer of Shining Moon, and Tormjere Valtilaniar."

A second ripple of surprise ran through the assembled priestesses and was echoed by the crowd behind them.

Why did she say that?

Elothlirial's brow creased in the same way Enna's did when she was annoyed.

"Auspicious names. It is even more auspicious to see Alta Suralia brought home. I must thank you for returning Elurithlia's sacred warhammer to us so that it may join Her other gifts."

"I have come seeking guidance, not bearing gifts," Shalindra replied, annoyed at being spoken down to.

"Do you then not follow our Mistress' prophecy?" Elothlirial said. "Did you fail to notice the blood moon that placed Her weapon on its journey to where it belongs? That is Her command, as we have always known. You would not seek to go against Her will, would you?"

"Her prophecy seems to have found me, and it is by Her direction that I have come to this place."

"Manalathlia," Enna interjected, "I fear that in our haste we are communicating this tale from the middle rather than the

256

beginning. Not only has Alta Suralia returned, but Sister Shalindra received Alta Amalia."

The declaration elicited excitement and even cries of joy from the crowd.

Such reactions were unsettling, and Shalindra glanced around uncertainly. Everyone here seemed to know and even expect these things that she had not imagined until they had happened, and she began to realize just how great her lack of understanding was.

You've lived what they've only dreamed about. Remember who you are, and don't let her intimidate you.

Elothlirial quieted the assemblage once more, though even she seemed affected by this proclamation. "To spurn Her word is to flirt with darkness."

Shalindra did not flinch from Elothlirial's imperious gaze. "I have faced darkness already, and I do not fear it. It is in darkness that Her light shines the brightest."

She was completely unprepared for the reaction those words would cause. Elothlirial drew back as if stung, as the others in the council looked among themselves with nervous glances. Even Enna turned to her in surprise.

Elothlirial recovered quickly. "It may be that you have, and yet words are easy to come by."

"Manalathlia," a woman in line with her spoke up, "it would seem that the test would put this issue to rest with a minimum of theatrics."

This drew nods from up and down the line of… Shalindra had no idea what the eleven Sisters should be called. They reminded her of the councilors from Rivermist, but no temple she had ever visited had any rank beyond Sister Superior. She would have to ask

257

Enna to explain it to her later.

"Yes. Those who would ascend must be judged."

"We have only just arrived," Enna protested. "Our journey has been anything but easy."

"No Guardian's journey is easy," Elothlirial proclaimed. "Nor should it be influenced. Follow."

Enna's face was a mixture of helplessness and terror, but after all that Shalindra had been through she feared no test of Eluria's.

The congregation erupted into excited talking all at once as Elothlirial and the Sisters Superior filed from the clearing and onto a narrow trail. The path wound its way through woods that were thick but not dark, leading them past only a single pair of intersecting trails before coming to an end at a small, oval clearing surrounded by a similarly thick wall of trees. In the center lay a curved pool of clear, still water, ringed with stones. A trio of rocks arranged like an oddly primitive alter rested in an alcove opposite where she had entered.

"Stand here," Elothlirial beckoned, directing Shalindra to a place beside the pool. She did so, noting that the edge stone at her feet was inscribed with a symbol matching the current phase of the moon: just a few days past half as it marched towards fullness.

Elothlirial moved around the pool as she spoke. "You stand now in the Glade of Atonement."

Reaching a place directly opposite Shalindra she halted, waiting for the nine other Sisters Superior to space themselves evenly around the pool. The last of the Sisters Superior approached her with a beautifully inlaid box, perfectly sized to hold the weapon.

"All who seek to ascend are judged by our Mistress. There is no risk to you beyond that of failure, but you must clear your mind and open it to Elurithlia," Elothlirial said. "To do this requires that Shining Moon be set aside, as its power will alter the results unfavorably."

Shalindra lifted the hammer from her belt and handed it back to Tormjere without ever taking her eyes from Elothlirial. The shock that travelled through the room as his hand wrapped around the hilt was almost tangible.

"How far away should it be taken?" she asked.

Elothlirial's eyes narrowed, but she waved the last Sister with the box away and swallowed whatever words had first come to mind. "To the side near the entryway is sufficient."

There was a moment's pause as the last Sister set the box aside and settled into her position, and when all were in alignment Elothlirial commanded Shalindra's attention once more. "Now, center your thoughts upon the task our Mistress has given you to perform. Focus on it to the exclusion of all else around you."

"I am ready."

Elothlirial's voice lifted, her chant filled with ritualistic inflections. The other elves delivered a unified response at specific intervals, their words intertwining to weave a prayer which was deliberate and purposeful in ways Shalindra's had never been.

Energy seeped into the glade, filling it with a humbling majesty that defied words and evoked memories of her night at the Three Sisters. Yet the sensation was different, and less comforting in its structure.

Shalindra felt Tormjere's awareness latch onto hers protectively as a hazy curtain obscured her view of everything around her.

Don't let her isolate you.

She closed her eyes and sought the vision she had been shown of Ildalarial in flames. Though indelibly etched into her memory, the scene fled as pressure squeezed against her from every direction.

I cannot focus. Something is trying to enter my mind.

She felt him fighting whatever was trying to interpose itself between her mind and his, and she pushed towards him with equal vigor. The more they sought to remain together, the more the discomfort grew, until it crossed the threshold into pain and left her teetering unsteadily.

Warmth flared in Shining Moon. She felt it through his hands, suffusing herself in his awareness and taking hold of his strength and desire, and turned it to her own.

Enough.

Silver light flashed, and the haze that enveloped her exploded outwards. Elothlirial rocked backwards, and more than one of the other Sisters stumbled to a knee. Whatever the woman had expected the rite to reveal, it had not been that. She looked at Shalindra with her mouth open and eyes wide as she struggled to regain her composure.

Shalindra felt tired and ill-used. She had come seeking answers but had been presented only with obstacles. This time she did not allow diplomacy to mask the displeasure in her voice. "I did not come here to play games, nor to bend my knee to your will. Eluria sent me here with a purpose, and I will see it fulfilled with or without your help."

She turned her back on them and strode from the glade, accepting Shining Moon from Tormjere on the way.

That went well.

Shalindra did not disagree, but as the trio marched back down the trail towards the large clearing they had first entered, she could not help but think she had just thrown away her best chance at finding the answer to who she was supposed to be.

Enna was on the verge of tears, but she ignored the crowd that pressed eagerly around them and directed her out through the tunnel and across the street to a long multistoried building.

Upon entering, they were greeted by an older elf woman in white robes. She was the plumpest elf Shalindra had ever seen, though she moved with a spryness that defied her age.

"Ennathalerial!" the woman exclaimed. "My dear, it has been too long."

"It is good to see you, too, Olya," Enna replied, her face briefly lit by a smile. "My friends and I require a place to stay."

Olya's penetrating gaze made Shalindra feel she was being evaluated more thoroughly than in the ceremony she had just come from, as if the woman were taking an inventory of every smudge and blemish marring her attire. Shining Moon did not escape her inspection, but she controlled her reaction to a momentary pause of surprise.

"I can see that they do," Olya said matter-of-factly. "When will she be presented?"

"We just came from the temple," Enna said sheepishly, before wilting beneath the scolding look she received.

"By Her Light, child, what were you thinking? She looks like she just fell down the side of a mountain." Olya made an unpleasant sound in her throat. "Well, nothing to do but set it straight. Come with me, Sister...?"

"Shalindra."

Olya paused in surprise and pursed her lips, then turned and directed a finger at Tormjere. "You may occupy the first room, there. Do not leave it unless escorted. She will be quite safe here, and I'll not have any scandals from you wandering about."

* * *

It was evening when the three of them reconvened in Tormjere's room. The chamber, like every other one in the building, was small, containing only a bed and nightstand in addition to a tiny window.

Enna sat on the bed with her head in her hands, dreading what awaited them tomorrow. She should have waited instead of rushing in, but the gathering crowds had driven her to throw aside caution. There was little her mother could have done to make the day any worse, and her stomach rebelled at the thought of what damage might have been inflicted.

She peeked through her fingers at Shalindra, who sat next to her on the bed, lost in thought. Her hair was now clean and her robes new. Shining Moon lay across her lap, and her blue eyes shone bright for no other reason than because they could. She was so strong and so beautiful. How could anyone deny that she was who was promised?

"Why did your mother react when I said Her light shines brightest in the dark?" Shalindra asked, running her hands up and down her bare arms in spite of the warmth of the room.

"It is the most recent component of the prophecy, given to us by the last Guardian. The words are considered suspect due to their method of delivery, and they have never been written down or shared with anyone not of our race, save the one who first spoke them to us."

"Why?"

"I do not know, and I question the explanations I have been given. It could be attributed to simple rivalry more than any legitimate reason."

"There is so much wisdom here of which I am unaware," Shalindra said with a sigh.

Enna continued to stew silently. She needed a quiet place to contemplate the dilemma she had put them in. Remembering where she had sought such refuge as a child, she sat up straighter and spoke with a sudden resolve. "Would you like to see them?"

"Who?"

"The Guardians. They were laid to rest here."

"Yes, I would like that very much."

Enna almost leapt to her feet, eager to have a clear direction, but as they emerged from the building a guard who had not been there when they entered drew to attention and blocked their path. "May I ask where you are going, Revered Sister?"

"Wherever I feel like," Enna snapped, pushing past him. "This is still my home."

The guard's hand raised as if he might reach for her, but it returned swiftly to his side as Tormjere stepped between them. Though Tormjere was not a large man, the guard still found himself looking up to meet the warning glare directed his way. Enna was annoyed enough that she almost wished the fool had actually grabbed her, just to see what Tormjere would have done to him. She silently prayed for Elurithlia's forgiveness almost immediately, for it was not a thought befitting one of Her faithful.

Dusk had settled over the city, and soft lights glowed in the branches above to provide just the right amount of illumination. She crossed the street towards the temple, but rather than take one of the tunnels which would return them to the cavernous Glade of Worship, she turned towards an almost invisible break in the trees surrounding it. The path she sought was narrow and marked by only a small pedestal of polished wood shaped with an image of the very warhammer that Shalindra now carried. It could have been Enna's imagination, but the column seemed to shimmer in awareness of their passing.

The evening breeze provided a soothing murmur as it rustled the canopy of leaves above them, and the light dimmed as they wound their way down a short hill. Enna's feet knew every root and irregularity, but those behind her did not and so she slowed her anxious steps. It had been so long.

The base of the trail widened into a secluded vale, and it was only then that Enna realized Tormjere was no longer with them. She resisted the urge to remove her boots and feel the carpet of soft grass between her toes as she had done so often as a child. She looked up past the treetops, to a sky lit by the moon and a multitude of stars.

Arranged around the perimeter stood a series of seven wooden statues, each a life-sized replica of an armored woman. Not a one bore any mark of carving, seeming to have grown into shape atop pedestals which had sprung from the ground beneath them.

Shalindra gazed at them in wonder. "It is a strange thing that I have never learned their names."

"You do not know them?" Enna asked in surprise. How could she have missed that? In all the years and all their conversations, the history of the Guardians had only come up in passing. The two of them had become so close, had helped each other through so many moments of weakness and trusted each other with doubts.

How had she failed Shalindra so badly?

"It never crossed my mind to ask. But standing here… I can feel them as if they were alive, and they call to me." Shalindra came to stand before the statue closest to their entrance, an ancient depiction of a woman in simple robes who cradled in her arms the hammer and armor worn by every other statue. "Who was she?"

"The first Guardian: Shalindralia."

Shalindra looked at her as if she had made a jest, but Enna held open her hands. "I thought you knew, and I assumed that you had taken your name in honor of hers. It is not uncommon."

"You are correct that Shalindra is not the name given to me at birth, but it was also not a name of my own choosing."

"Who then bestowed it upon you?"

Shalindra gave her an amused look that answered her question. Of course it was Tormjere.

"I need to learn to read elvish," Shalindra said, peering at the base of the statue, where the graceful script flowed like a vine grown across the scrollwork.

Enna had no need to look at the words—they were practically the first ones she had ever been taught.

When Her gifts follow the blood moon west
A Guardian shall ascend
To walk as two where only one may tread
And with the wisdom of the fallen
End that which should never have begun

"There is more to the prophecy than that, is there not?"

"Yes. Every Guardian has left us with their own piece of

wisdom, discovered as they attempted to fulfill their sacred duty." She indicated the next statue, whose effigy stood atop a base of mountains and forests. "Ellilanlia, who led our people to this land and named it Ildalyirilia."

"These names roll from your tongue like the melody of a harp, but my lips would struggle to make such sounds."

Enna smiled with understanding. "They are old names, from an older time. Even we grow weary of pronouncing some of them, and few outside the temples speak in such a manner. There have been debates about simplifying the language every so often, but tradition has always won in the end."

Shalindra considered this as she gazed at the statue. "What did she add to the prophecy?"

"She foretold that the Guardian would be able to raise the dead. Something for which I am eternally grateful."

"As am I," Shalindra agreed with a comforting smile.

Enna resisted the urge to rub her chest where the demon's claw had pierced her body on the battlefield outside Tiridon. How would her mother react, she wondered, if she were told how her daughter's life had been spared? Enna put the horrors of that day from her mind and continued to the next statue, which rose from a pedestal twisted and warped in unnatural ways.

"Ylvalia. She was rendered mad due to the influences of magic, but before her death, she foretold that the Guardian was destined to lose what was most precious to her. There is some debate about the exact meaning, as the wording could have referred to our people as a whole or simply a single person."

"So many things are precious to me. I can only pray that I will never be faced with such a loss, should I truly become a Guardian."

266

Enna moved to the next, where the woman stood triumphant above a winged serpent coiled tight around the base.

"Allatharial, who sacrificed herself to slay the vile dragon Valteroth. She declared that what must ultimately be given was 'all that was and all that will be.'"

Shalindra shivered. "What could that mean?"

"I am speaking in translations, first from the ancient tongue to modern elvish and then to the common speech that you understand. Some words do not have an equivalent in the other's vocabulary. Scholars interpret this to mean that our devotion to our goddess was incomplete. Not only must our Sisters devote themselves more completely, but our society as a whole must bend itself to this cause. It was after this that the churches of Elurithlia and Lithandris rose to prominence."

"Fascinating."

"It remains a touchy subject, as the realignment of our values caused a schism that split our race. Three hundred years later came Illathalirial, perhaps the most powerful Guardian there has ever been. She vanquished the withered hordes that had toppled one of the Three Great Empires. It was she who proclaimed that the Guardian would call to her a Valtilaniar, one who would defend her on her quest."

Shalindra seemed drawn to this representation, circling the statue as she studied the upstretched skeletal hands that sought to ensnare the woman above. She stared at it a long time before she spoke.

"'In all ways, he shall protect her,'" she quoted. "Her name is so similar to your own. Were you were named for her?"

"Yes. I was given my name when my mother first saw the

whiteness of my hair."

"I have always thought your hair to be beautiful. Is the color common among elves?"

"No." Enna hurried to the next statue, this one perched above a creature that looked all too familiar. "Next to ascend was Erithrial, who saved us from the demon Mentarashrhu but did not survive. Maetholmir was also lost. It was during this period that we achieved our knowledge of demons, though it remains limited. She claimed that the Guardian could succeed only with the wisdom of the fallen."

"When Kayala first showed me Shining Moon, she said she feared that she had placed me on a path filled with pain. From their stories, I can only believe that she was correct. And the last?"

Enna stood before the final statue, whose base was noticeably bare. "Alharania. She was convinced that Erithrial had been close to unravelling the true meaning of the prophecy. It is known that she ventured high into the Ironspike mountains, but she left no record as to her purpose. She was betrayed by her companions at the last, and though her body was returned our Mistress' gifts were lost."

"I wondered how weapon and armor became separated."

Enna hesitated, but the time for secrets was past. Shalindra deserved to know. "Shining Moon was found by humans and carried east. Her armor, forged from the same metal, was recovered years later and returned here. I should have told you these things before we came in search of it. I did not realize that my mother would attempt to reunite Her gifts so quickly and without setting aside old hatreds. I am sorry."

Shalindra placed a hand on her arm. "Such matters are easy to avoid when they are so painful to discuss. I do not believe that what you have conveyed would have changed any decision that has been made."

Enna swallowed the lump in her throat. "Your kindness is more than I deserve, but I thank you for it."

Shalindra's gaze encompassed the entire glade. "They are all elves."

"It has ever been this way."

"Until me. I have done as I have been asked, or at least in whatever way I was able. But when I look at who they were and hear what they have accomplished... how can I judge myself worthy to stand among them?"

"Whatever doubts you witness in yourself, Elurithlia has certainly seen strengths that you do not know exist. Listen to Her, believe in Her choice, for it is a good one."

Shalindra's smile was tinged with sadness. "I do not believe that your assessment is shared by many here."

"They do not know you."

"At times I wonder if I know myself. I feel as I did when Shining Moon first called to me: lost and uncertain." Her impossibly blue eyes bored into Enna. "I cannot help but think there are others who have been better prepared."

Enna looked down to see Shining Moon resting on Shalindra's open palms, and her breath caught in her throat.

"I do not know any of this history," Shalindra said. "I know nothing of my purpose beyond protecting Her armor. I offered to return this to Sister Kayala if she doubted that I should carry it. I would offer it now to one better suited for its purpose."

Was she serious? Was she actually willing to step away from

everything she was meant to be?

It was captivating the way the light shone from Shining Moon, dancing along the edges of every inscription in the silver metal. Enna longed to feel its touch again, as she had done for the briefest of moments just days after her life had been spared. She knew the power contained within. Were she to appear before her mother with Elurithlia's weapon in her hands, she would wear the Guardian's armor by the next full moon, and with it lead her people with the honor she had been told was hers from the day she was born.

Her hand shook as she reached towards it and wrapped Shalindra's fingers around the shaft. "There was a time I would have accepted your offer, certain that I would be fulfilling my destiny. But I have grown to know you too well over the years. You have been strong when I was not, you have inspired loyalty from those who should have been your enemy, and you have always carried Her weapon with the confidence and compassion it deserves. You have become my most cherished friend. Our Mistress has made Her choice, and you should never doubt that decision. You are the Guardian we need."

Shalindra's eyes were damp as she embraced Enna. "I could never have become what I am without you. But still I wonder, if I succeed, will I be laid beneath a statue here with them? What wisdom could I leave behind?"

There would be no higher honor in all the world, but Enna knew that such a simplistic explanation was not the answer Shalindra wished to hear.

"May I have a moment with them?" Shalindra asked as her gaze returned to the statues.

"You may have all the time you desire. They are your Sisters, and they have been waiting for you your whole life." Enna bowed her head. "I will await you outside."

"And tell Tormjere to stop worrying."

Enna blinked. "Of course." She would have an easier time converting her mother to Toush, but as Shalindra had asked, she would make the attempt.

Tormjere had placed himself conspicuously near the small pedestal that marked the path. A small crowd had gathered across the road, likely awaiting Shalindra's return, and Enna's reappearance drew murmurs of excitement.

"No harm will come to her here," Enna said to him.

"After that mess of an interrogation, I don't trust your mother." He inclined his head towards the crowd. "Or the ones sent to watch us."

Enna looked at the crowd once more, this time noting that a few of the onlookers were far too serious to be there for idle curiosity. "Neither do I. But my mother she remains, and as the Manalathlia, she has almost complete control of what happens."

"Is that why she wanted you to be the next Guardian?"

Enna could not even be surprised that he knew, and in many ways, she was thankful that both he and Shalindra now did. "Every parent has dreams for their children. I am not the first who was prepared for such a role, nor am I the first to fail."

Tormjere raised an eyebrow. "Do you call what you are a failure?"

"I am as yet unwilling to refer to it as success."

"Then we'll have to see what we can do to change that."

Chapter Twenty-Two

A Gathering Storm

News of Shining Moon's return seemed to have spread through the city, for a sizable gathering awaited Shalindra when she woke for morning prayers. She had expected that the normalcy of routine would allow for a more cordial day and dampen the passions that had affected her arrival, but the energy of the waiting crowd dashed such hopes.

"This is most unseemly," Olya grumbled as she peered through a window. "They have been like this since before midnight."

Shalindra was apologetic. "I had no intention of causing this type of disruption."

"Nonsense, my dear. This is not your doing."

"I can get us across the street easily enough," Tormjere said.

Olya laughed without humor and turned on him. "You'll do no such thing. You will walk a step behind her where you should, and none of your intimidating looks. She is among family and must act like it."

She beckoned several women to her, who jumped at her command and stood like soldiers at attention. "You and you will proceed Sister Shalindra. The pair of you, follow behind. Walk in Her light and represent Her virtue. Chin up and steady pace, as you should. They will move aside for you."

Olya smoothed Shalindra's robes one last time. "Now off you go. I'll not allow you to miss prayers on my account. Ennathalerial will know where you belong."

The women around her began to move as the door was opened, and Shalindra had little choice but to follow. Enna and Tormjere fell in behind her.

Shalindra adopted a look of confidence she did not feel but knew was important to project. No one in the crowd wished to see the apprehension that gnawed at her insides, or watch her hands shake and her knees wobble. They expected more of the woman who would be Guardian, and so she would be what she must.

As Olya had predicted, the crowd parted respectfully before them, and they crossed to the boundaries of the temple as easily as if the streets were empty. Shalindra's escort stepped to the side as they entered the cavernous Glade of Worship, as she had learned it was named, but Enna's whispered instructions pushed her onwards.

"Keep going around the left. You will be expected in the front."

Shalindra was mildly terrified to call such attention to herself. All the temples she had visited before held a few dozen Sisters at most, but there were thousands of elves within the circle of trees, and the space was not even half full. Standing on the rise at the far side were five of the Sisters Superior, one of whom was Elothlirial. Shalindra was thankful that Enna stepped ahead of her to guide the way, and prayed for the strength to not embarrass anyone today.

They circled to the front of the assemblage before turning

along the first row and continuing towards the center. Enna stopped, joining the first row at a point that Shalindra assumed was appropriate for their station, and Shalindra squeezed in beside her. An ancient woman—one of the Sisters Superior?—shifted to make room, smiling warmly as she did so.

Elothlirial took note of her arrival but gave no reaction. The ceremony commenced almost as soon as Shalindra had come to a stop, begun by a single note from one of the women above. One by one, the other women added their voices to the first, and when Elothlirial called out the final verse, the assembly replied in unison, then knelt as one. Shalindra could understand little of what was said, but her heart was uplifted as sunlight surged into the glade from every possible direction at once. The words the congregation continued to recite were foreign, so Shalindra honored Eluria with her own silent prayer.

There was a surprising lack of formality to the end of the ceremony. The voices of those who led rose and fell once more, and the brilliance of sunlight faded to its normal morning glow. She marveled at how it could have been accomplished.

"That was beautiful," she said as Elothlirial descended from the rise to meet them.

Elothlirial accepted the compliment politely. "Is it so different in your temples?"

"The feelings it invokes are the same, but they lack the grandeur of such a large congregation."

Elothlirial gave her a curious look and guided her away from the center of the clearing. "I spoke at length with our Mistress after you departed," Elothlirial said, "and I must offer my apologies. I fear that we were both unprepared for such a sudden outcome."

Shalindra remained wary of Elothlirial's intentions, but now was no time for rancor. "We faced many adversaries on our journey here, and it was a jarring adjustment to be so quickly among friends once more. I have been told that this is where my questions may be answered, and I am eager to learn more of my role in what is to come."

"As am I, but this discussion is ill suited to such a public forum. If I might invite your return to the Glade of Atonement. Just to talk," she added.

"I would be honored."

Tormjere, who had successfully remained with his back against a wall during the ceremony, moved to join them as they left the massive worship area behind.

Elothlirial chatted with her as they walked, idle conversation about her visit to the Guardians and her comfort at the dormitory, playing well her role as hostess of a distinguished visitor. Her attitude cooled as they entered the glade with the stone-edged pool once more.

"We are, of course, pleased beyond words at the return of Alta Suralia. Yet we have witnessed imposters and false prophets before. May we see it?"

Shalindra unhooked the warhammer and held it before her.

Elothlirial bent forward to study Shining Moon, and the wonder in her eyes was not for any sense of show. She slowly placed a hand above it and recited a prayer, causing it to grow warm in Shalindra's hands. When Elothlirial stepped back, each of the other clerics took their turn inspecting it. When they were finished, Shalindra returned it to her belt.

"There can be no thought of forgery. Well do we know the

consequences of the unworthy laying a hand on the sacred weapon of Elurithlia. But the worthy do not always ascend. We must ask: if you become our Guardian and don Her armor, what cause do you intend to commit yourself to?"

"I do not know what She intends for me yet, only that I was to protect Her gifts."

"Elurithlia made her will known to every Guardian that has come before you. Each ascended with purpose and clarity, certain of the task before them. You claim to have spoken to Her, the first person in centuries to have received the blessed communion of Alta Amalia. How closely did you listen? What has our Mistress asked of you?"

Shalindra's fingers drifted across her symbol. "Many things that I might have wished not to do. I was shown Ildalarial in flames and the last of our Sisters dying to preserve the armor which resides here."

"There are many who have attempted to bring about our ruin," another Sister said. "What was the cause of this cataclysm?"

"A demon."

Elothlirial appeared unimpressed. "Such is a tale that could have been spun by any minstrel with the most passing knowledge of our history, but it is human armies that now threaten us with extinction."

One of the other women started to speak, but Elothlirial continued: "We will not drape you in Elurithlia's might only to see them turned against us."

"I am not a conqueror, and I have no intention of seeing Her gifts, or any other weapon, used against your people."

"Are you certain? We are aware of your lineage. What will you choose when the bonds of family are at odds with your loyalty to Her?"

Shalindra's resolve wavered. "That is a choice I have already been forced to make."

"Have you?" Elothlirial pressed. "You arrive lacking purpose. You know little of what you ask for and even less about what you intend to do afterwards. These relics you speak of so casually took decades to recover after they were stolen."

"I have always endeavored to serve Eluria as She has commanded. I do not know what else I could have done to prove my devotion."

Elothlirial smiled like a spider whose web danced with a freshly caught meal. "The Guardian has always been a peacemaker before soldier, one who seeks to use might to protect rather than to take. Establish your worthiness by stopping these assaults upon our homeland, and it will prove beyond any doubt that you are Her chosen."

How convenient that Eluria's peace meets her own selfish needs so closely. I thought we were done playing games.

It seems we are not, but she has given me little option.

We could just take the armor. You know it's close by.

It was to prevent its forceful removal that I came here, not to become the thief who steals it.

"I shall do as you suggest," Shalindra said, "but not simply because you wish it. Such a peaceful resolution will benefit all who follow in Her light, human and elf alike, and in so doing I will not be forced to choose between family and faith."

Her statement rang true with her audience, as heads bobbed thoughtfully.

The older woman who had stood beside her at the morning prayer, gave Shalindra a nod of admiration as she spoke. "Manalathlia, I believe that such an endeavor would require a resolution from the Grand Calontier. Without their blessing, such a quest would be no more than a fool's errand, no matter what it achieved."

Elothlirial's self-assured smile wavered. "I will petition them, though when and what they will allow I cannot say."

Shalindra fixed her with a determined stare. "Haste may be in order. Should you wait too long and my vision come to pass, there may not be anyone left for me to save."

* * *

Shalindra was thankful that her words must have had their intended effect because a messenger brought word that she was expected at a meeting of the Calontier that same evening. It was a blessing that the meeting came so soon, as she had grown increasingly nervous waiting for news.

Olya arranged another escort, as throngs of people remained outside the dormitory, waiting for her to reappear. They pressed closer to her this time, many calling out her name or holding forth their hands, hoping to be touched.

Shalindra struggled to understand their adulations as she had not ascended, and might never do so. But they believed, no matter how she felt about it. She could never hope to respond to them all, and so she held out her hands and pressed them against as many as she could. It was a relief when they finally reached what had to be the chambers of the Grand Calontier.

Elothlirial was waiting for her when they arrived.

"All weapons are forbidden within, unless carried by a

Guardian ascended."

Shalindra handed Shining Moon to Tormjere, who accepted it once more with an unfriendly glare directed at Elothlirial.

Elothlirial ignored him. "The Grand Calontier has agreed to a special assembly this evening to debate the merits of this agreement you wish you achieve."

She waved Shalindra through the doorway. Enna jumped to follow, fast enough that she was past her mother before any objection could be raised, and the doors were closed behind the three women.

Nicely done. Her mother was trying to isolate you again.

It is a childish game that I have seen all too many times, but I will not allow it to defeat my purpose.

The room was a curious blend of forest and structure. Walls of stone and dark wood filled the gaps between the trunks of trees that ringed the space, supporting a soot-stained roof of living branches and sturdy beams. The smokey hint of long extinguished fires mixed with the perfumes of brightly colored flowers set in pots beneath every window. The preponderance of living wood muffled every sound and lent an intimacy to the timeless quality of the space.

Ten elves stood awaiting her. Five women wore the white robes of Eluria, three of whom Shalindra recognized as Sisters Superior from the temple. One of the councilors was clearly a military man, another a follower of Lithandris, and the remainder she took to be merchants or members of the nobility based on the manner of their dress.

Elothlirial took her place among them and brought the meeting to order. "Councilors, we have before us Sister Shalindra of Actondel, who wishes a resolution to our current conflict."

"Are you here to answer for your Kingdom's reckless provocations?" the militant elf challenged.

"What of their constant encroachment?" asked another.

"I am not here to answer for anyone or anything," Shalindra replied defensively. "I have been asked to broker a peace between our two nations, and so I shall."

One of the noble elves waved his hand dismissively. "Actondel's armies could turn around today and still we would be left with their towns and fields cut into our forests. They should be thrown from our lands, not bargained with."

"Peace requires participation by both parties or it will be doomed to failure," Shalindra countered. "And it cannot be achieved in a day."

Several of the elves nodded, even one of the Sisters. No stranger to politics, Shalindra had already considered what arguments she could bring to sway their opinions, but before she could continue they all began speaking at once.

"If she is to establish peace, let her do so. It does not require our involvement."

"She must work through our representative."

"Actondel has rebuffed our every attempt."

"But she is human and can carry our message more freely."

"We will never allow a human to negotiate on our behalf!" That from the militant-looking elf. "Not that it even matters. Actondel has slaughtered every emissary that has crossed the river."

"It costs less to chance another than to sit and wait," the follower of Lithandris argued. "They are coming the moment the river falls enough for them to make the crossing."

"We risk losing Alta Suralia," one of the clerics pointed out.

"The risk is not lessened if it remains here."

Elothlirial had remained silent throughout the discussion, seemingly willing to allow the others to argue. She undoubtably knew how the argument would play out and it was not a stretch to believe she had prepared some of the participants. Shalindra could have easily done the same with every member of her own council in Newlmir. The elves were growing louder in their protests, and Shalindra became bombarded with questions faster than she could answer them.

"Councilors, please!" Enna shouted, stepping forward. Their voices died swiftly as she commanded their attention. "While I can vouch for my Sister's willingness and ability to undertake such a task on our behalf, I understand only too well the pitfalls of leaving our fate in another's hands. If it pleases the Calontier, I will accompany Sister Shalindra and carry our offer on behalf of my people."

That was clearly not what Elothlirial had expected, and her shock was as apparent as the rest of the suddenly quiet assembly. She began to speak, but Shalindra preempted her with an impassioned declaration of her own.

"And I would gladly accept Ennathalerial's aid. We have each been blessed by Eluria, in our own ways, but our trust and kinship can be the example needed to give both parties faith in our mission."

"Elurithlia has indeed blessed them both," the older Sister said. "There can be no dispute of that."

Elothlirial seemed willing to dispute it anyway, but the old woman continued: "I move that we provide these women with the

281

same offering we have attempted to convey before and pray that they find success where others have known only failure."

"A vote has been called," Elothlirial said with an unhappy glance at the old cleric. One by one, seven hands were raised in agreement. Whether by vote or abstention, Elothlirial's was not one of them.

"Sister Ennathalerial, it is the will of the Grand Calontier that you be provided an agreement to deliver to Actondel. You will have the authority to negotiate the end of hostilities only and may not bargain past anything this council has agreed to and set forth."

"This will be our last attempt at peace," the soldier warned. "We will not sit idle and wait for our enemy to dictate every battle. Already the river subsides, and when the fords are revealed then nothing will stop this war."

* * *

"How could she have forced this upon you?" Enna demanded as she paced furiously in tight confines of the dormitory room. "No potential ascendant has ever been judged so harshly. Stopping a war is something you do *after* becoming Guardian, not before."

Shalindra drew a deep breath, looking too tired to debate the point. "Regardless, it is the task set before us, and it will benefit everyone equally. I am thankful that no one wished for Shining Moon to remain behind."

"I would have liked to see them try," Enna huffed. "Even my mother would not tempt Elurithlia's wrath so directly."

She looked at Tormjere, who usually had an opinion about such maneuverings, but he sat poking at the jeweled thing Honarch had given him. There was really nothing he could do about their predicament at this point, or at least nothing she would care for him to do, but there was the slightest hope that she could do something herself.

"I am going to speak with her," Enna said.

"Do you think it wise at this point?" Shalindra asked. "I do not wish to cause further strife within your family."

"Such differences have been there for longer than I have known you. It just took time for me to realize it."

Enna excused herself before they could talk her out of it. She was able to avoid the clumps of worshipers hoping to catch a glimpse of Shalindra, and crossed to the temple without incident. There was only one place that her mother would be at this hour. She had retreated to her own sanctuary, the Glade of Atonement, where she had attempted to judge Shalindra the day before.

Enna entered it with trepidation. As expected, her mother was there with three of her most senior Sisters. The four women turned in surprise as she entered, but, as always, it was her mother who spoke.

"I began to wonder if you would ever present yourself." With a motion, she dismissed the other women, who filed obediently from the glade.

"I am disappointed in you, daughter. It's been years, and still you've allowed this human woman to keep what does not belong to her."

"You think I have sat quietly all this time? I have safeguarded Alta Suralia, raised a temple devoted to Elurithlia's glory at the base of the Three Sisters, and helped pacify Maetholmir."

"Your destiny holds more than that of a simple missionary. The human church has abandoned most of our faith, clinging to only the basest form of our teachings."

"If they have drifted, we must accept some of the blame for withholding our knowledge."

"Take care, daughter. We have shared all that they are worthy of hearing."

"Who are we to judge their worthiness? Shalindra has so much strength. Were you to teach her as you did me, instead of sending her away, there would be no limit to what she might accomplish."

"It would seem my efforts on your behalf were squandered. You left us under the most noble of mandates, but you return as a servant to a thief."

"Eluria has made her choice, and it was the correct one," Enna said, fighting back her tears. "Shalindra has already fulfilled so many parts of the prophecy. She has raised the dead, called to her side—"

"He may call himself whatever he wishes. I fear nothing from your humans."

"You should, for you have placed yourself between Shalindra and what she deserves. I would sooner face a hundred demons than cross him."

"All men have their weaknesses."

Enna laughed. A sharp laugh. A human laugh. "You refuse to acknowledge the truth that stares you in the face. He would do anything—to anyone, at any cost—to protect her. As will I."

Elothlirial's jaw dropped open, but Enna left her no opportunity for a response.

"I will return with Shalindra in triumph or not at all. Goodbye, mother." She spun on her heel and left the glade behind, not caring if she ever saw it again.

Chapter Twenty-Three

An Unwelcome Road

Their time in Eitholmir had been short, remaining only long enough to receive the proposed peace agreement from the council, which was discreetly delivered two days later by a courier. The instructions that arrived with it had made clear that the contents of the document were not to be revealed or discussed with anyone in Ildalarial. The following day saw them travelling by boat once more, this time farther south to Sidirion. The town lay only thirty miles from the Kingdom stronghold of Adair, which stood over the merging of River Annyre with the Merallin River. Shalindra had been only too happy to depart, as the crowds had kept her a virtual prisoner in the dormitory.

Their arrival at the docks was greeted by an armed and armored squad of elves who, though not hostile, were openly suspicious. After a brief exchange they were ushered into a nearby building and presented to an elvish captain whose countenance was as every bit as stern as Birion's.

"Revered Sisters," the captain said. "Your presence here is a blessing, as always, but you risked much by arriving during the daylight."

"We were not told of the level of danger," Enna said, "but our business is urgent and we likely would not have delayed."

"I am unaware of any pressing needs in the city. Your Sisters here have done an admirable job in their duties."

"Our business takes us into Actondel."

The captain regarded the three of them before replying. "And may I know what this business is?"

"We are not at liberty to discuss it," Enna answered, placing a hand on the scroll case slung across her shoulder by a thin strap.

The manner of her refusal seemed to supply the captain with what he needed to understand their situation.

"Our enemy watches the bridge like hawks," he said. "Your crossing will be noticed, and they have been unkind to those they consider spies." He beckoned another soldier over. "Find Alindis and bring him here at once."

To Enna he said, "You are, of course, free to move about the city, but I would advise that you remain close and do not call further attention to yourselves. The Swan House should be able to accommodate you. Woodswarden Alindis will see to your crossing."

"Thank you," Enna said.

The Swan House was identified by a clearly visible depiction of the elegant bird which hung proudly above its door. The building gave every appearance of being an inn of some quality, even though it stood where the docks ended and the town began.

Unlike the subtle tension they had witnessed in the capital, Sidirion was a town preparing for war. What little Shalindra saw of the open, winding streets that the elves seemed to love had been blocked at strategic intersections. There were no battlements to be seen, but dense, thick walls of trees and stones formed an equally effective barrier around the city. There were sounds of happiness and laughter, and though the tunes they sang were merry, almost childish in their gaiety, the effort seemed an attempt at normalcy rather than entertainment.

Rather than an innkeep they were greeted at the door by a soldier, and told to take any empty room. Shalindra suppressed a sigh as they occupied the first with an open door. It was another prison of necessity, and no matter how much sense it made she was growing tired of hiding all day.

With a glance, Enna drew her attention to Tormjere's trembling hand. Shalindra was already aware, for she had felt the slow return of his hunger. He was making efforts to keep it in check, but there was little she could do about it now other than pray that the episodes that had plagued him in the valley remained a distant memory.

Enna unrolled the paper that contained the demands of the Grand Calontier, reminding her that they had larger issues to deal with now. Enna did not read far before she began to frown.

"What does it say?" Shalindra asked.

Enna could not keep the frustration from her voice. "The terms they request are not generous. I worry that even if we somehow manage to speak to your rulers, it will be rejected. I do not know how we are to succeed."

"Almost sounds like they don't want you to," Tormjere said. "Not getting wiped out isn't enough to ask for?"

Enna looked embarrassed. "We have reached accords before, but they have rarely been respected."

287

"The Edar Woods are just across the river, yes?" Shalindra asked. "I do recall an agreement about the area several years ago."

"River Merallindial was to be the original border. Then it moved to include everything within a hatchet's throw of the bank, and now Actondel claims everything east of River Annyre, right at the very doorstep of Eitholmir. I do not know how we can stop this thing," she said dejectedly.

Shalindra rose from her seat and looked out the window. "Only my father, the king, would be able to accept such an offering, though the Lordshouse would officially ratify it. That means we must reach Merallin and gain access to him."

"After the way you left last time…" Enna shook her head.

"We can figure out how once we're there," Tormjere said. "Merallin is a long way from here, and we can assume that elves are not welcome at the present. We'll need a disguise of some sort for Enna."

"Do not let him near your hair," Shalindra warned with a smile.

Tormjere did his best to look innocent. "I was just hoping for different clothes for both of you."

He was correct. Enna would be seen as the enemy, and risked capture as a spy at any time. Shalindra's own father had placed a bounty on her head, which she was certain someone would attempt to collect if they knew she had returned. They needed anonymity, but she was tired of pretending to be something other than what she was.

"I think not, this time," Shalindra said. "The world can deal with me as I am."

"That's fine for you," Tormjere pressed, "because there are

followers of Eluria throughout the Kingdom. So long as we avoid formal dinners, few people should recognize you after so long. But once we hit the Merallin River, we're unlikely to find many elves wandering about. Short of a hood, I can think of little that would work. Her hair will stand out as much as your warhammer, no matter what we do."

"We can wrap Shining Moon in cloth or a bedroll," she said, conceding the point.

"Or simply let Tormjere carry it," Enna suggested. "It might look less obvious."

Shalindra leaned back and closed her eyes in thought. Everything they said was sound, and something that should be considered. It was not the most fleshed-out plan she had ever begun, but no matter how vague or solid their ideas for reaching Merallin, she had no idea what she would do when she got there.

* * *

They crept towards the docks sometime after midnight. The moon was full, an auspicious omen, but thankfully its light was curtailed by the thick clouds. Shalindra wondered if the dreary rains would ever end this year, though she appreciated the shadows they provided tonight.

Alindis paused by the water with a final word of caution. "Once across the river, we will not be able to aid you in any way. This would be much safer were you to wait for a time when our enemy was less alert."

Shalindra agreed, but time was a luxury they no longer had. "Events move ahead without our consent, and there is little time to waste."

"Then stay as low in the boat as possible, and pray their sentries are all asleep."

Alindis and the other rower grunted as they angled upriver, paddling hard against the current. Shalindra felt if she compressed herself any further she might rupture the bottom of the boat, no matter how sturdy. Cold water splashed over the side and pooled about her legs, but she dared not risk repositioning herself, no matter how chilled it left her.

"Prepare," came Alindis' whispered warning.

Shalindra mouthed a silent prayer to Eluria. Someone tapped her on the back, and she leapt from the boat with Tormjere and Enna. Her feet struggled to find purchase on the slippery rocks, but she was thankful for Alindis' foresight, as the hard surface would hide any trace of their arrival.

The trio crouched still on the riverbank as the elves turned the boat towards the middle of the river without any acknowledgment of their parting. Almost immediately the soft sound of their oars was lost to the flow of water and the bellows of frogs.

Tormjere slowly straightened, staring into the darkened woods. Shalindra closed her eyes and sought his mind, feeling what he did as he searched the forest. It was like running her fingers across every tree, rock, and creature near them.

They were not alone.

She felt it the instant he did and was already moving when his piercing whisper carried to her ears.

"Run."

He leapt in front of them as bowstrings twanged in the darkness. From the river came a scream followed by a splash, but Shalindra did not slow, trusting in Tormjere's ability to find the way out of the darkened woods.

He brought their sprint to a sudden stop and motioned for silence.

Shalindra huddled with Enna behind a bush, clamping a hand over her own mouth to muffle the sounds of her breathing.

The snap of a twig gave away the position of their pursuers. Tormjere crouched with his knife in hand, waiting. She no longer needed his senses to know they were close. The forest grew still, and the heavy breathing she heard was not from Tormjere or Enna.

A rustling of branches as their pursuer poked the bushes with a spear, then moved slowly away.

Tormjere waited for a long time before motioning them to rise, and they crept in the opposite direction. Alternating periods of fleeing and hiding continued for most of the night, and by the time dawn began to brighten the sky she was exhausted.

Tormjere gave her a rueful look and at last broke their silence. "Why is it that we're always sneaking across your kingdom?"

Shalindra just shook her head as she sought familiar landmarks. "Where are we?"

"Somewhere east of the Annyre," Tormjere guessed. "Probably a day or so west of the Merallin River, and maybe two or three to Adair once we find the road."

Enna plopped down on a log. "This was not the beginning I had hoped for."

"Nor I," Shalindra said. "Let us eat and catch our breath, and then we will try to stop a war."

Chapter Twenty-Four

Friends and Foes

Adair was a large, multileveled city which had grown up the side of one of the countless rolling hills that rumpled the countryside, where a thick stream spilled into the Annyre river. The mass of structures was dominated by a squarish castle near the highest point, its walls bright with quicklime beneath peaked slate grey roofs. Stout battlements commanded a view over field and forest alike in every direction. The city below was given over to more common browns and greys surrounding islands of lighter tones where this mansion or that rose above the closely packed buildings.

It would have made for an idyllic setting on a more cheerful afternoon, but the clouds were a clumpy overcast that painted everything in a dull light and a gentle mist was falling in spite of the hints of blue that peeked through thin spots here and there. The hills around the city, which should have been green with pasture and farm, lay trampled and brown, dotted with tents and banners among which thousands of men moved like ants in a garden.

Tormjere's eyes swept the fields, counting. "I'd say close to twenty thousand here, which could mean as many as eight to twelve thousand more are already spread along the border."

"Many of the banners are from Ceringion houses," Shalindra noted. "Far more than our own."

Enna just shook her head. "Elurithlia protect us, my people will never survive that."

"We can only pray that we find some way to put an end to it," Shalindra said, though it was little comfort given that she had no idea how she would accomplish that.

She stiffened suddenly as a flash of green and gold caught her eye.

"What is it?" Enna asked.

"My brother Logian is here. His banner is a green field with a golden sword."

"Could he help us?"

"No. He is likely overjoyed at the prospect of testing himself in another battle. The Conclave would extend their hand to us before he would."

"It would take days to circumvent this," Tormjere said. "We'll find a place to stay for the night, then move on. Keep your cloaks up. At least the rain gives us a reason."

It was more than mile through the armed camp to the edge of town. Enna tucked close behind Shalindra and kept her head down, but her knuckles were white where they clenched her cloak. Thankfully, the weather kept everyone in their tents or huddled around their fires, and they were paid no more mind than any of the other travelers plodding up and down the busy road.

"Should we find someplace outside the walls?" Shalindra asked. As with most larger cities, what could be accurately described as a small village that had grown up outside the walls that marked the city proper.

"Even if we do, we'll still have to go through tomorrow." Tormjere glanced at the clouds. "We'll probably garner less attention now given the weather."

They continued up the road to the gate, where a line of people seeking entry had formed. Most of those ahead of them were allowed through after only a cursory inspection, but their progress seemed to slow the closer they drew to the gate.

By the time their turn came, Tormjere was beginning to wish they had elected to bypass the city, no matter how long it would have taken, but there was no way they could turn back now. Shalindra shuffled forward at an unassuming pace. He watched the guards' eyes crawling over her, but neither shifted from their bored posture. Tormjere was almost ready to relax when one of the guards dropped a gloved hand on Enna's shoulder.

"Where are you going, elf?" he challenged.

Enna tried to pull away, but his grip tightened. "I only wish to visit Eluria's temple," she stammered.

"I think you'll be visiting the dungeons."

"My good sir," Shalindra said as she stepped between them. "Need I remind you that Sisters of Eluria do not participate in armed conflict? Surely one in your position of responsibility is aware of this."

"She could be a spy," the man said defensively.

"She could sprout fairy wings and fly above this oversized fence as well, but I think that unlikely."

The guardsman blinked as he tried to imagine such a feat. "Well... what do you want in the city?"

Shalindra graced him with look that implied he had lost whatever sense he might have once possessed. "To get out of this rain like everyone else. Are you well?"

"I… yes. Begging your pardon, my lady, but…"

"Sister will do." She patted him on the shoulder. "I will pray for you this evening."

Without waiting for a response, she swept past him. Enna was as caught off guard as the soldiers, but a nudge from Tormjere sent her hurrying to catch up.

She giggled the moment they were out of sight of the gate. "You sounded like Sister Kayala."

That brought a smile to Shalindra's face, easing the lines of worry that had settled on her forehead. "I suppose I did."

Tormjere chuckled at the memory of the old cleric as well, but his merriment fled as he caught a flash of upswept blond hair in the crowd. He motioned them to a halt and peered through the mass of people. On the opposite side of the square, a halfling was watching the streets more carefully than his relaxed posture would indicate.

Weeby.

Here? Could he be looking for me again?

Let's find out. Wait here with Enna.

Be careful. I do not want to flee into the night again.

"Excuse me," Enna said. "Why are we standing here staring at the crowds?"

"I see someone that I should not," Tormjere said aloud. "Wait here."

He circled the market in an aimless fashion and approached the halfling from behind. "You look like you've lost something."

Weeby jerked his head around sharply in surprise. He grinned when he recognized Tormjere, but it came just slowly enough to seem forced. "And you turn up in the most interesting places. Nothing so dramatic for me this time, I am afraid. I'm just watching the people stroll by."

"There's enough of them alright, though I'm not sure if the rain or the army camped outside the walls is making them more miserable."

Weeby made a sour face as a squad of soldiers marched by. "They do tend to be an uptight lot, and they've taken the best food and the best women and all the money. But the rains this year are surely the vengeance of some unhappy god. I'm waiting for everything to move out so I can depart in peace."

"Why wait? The gates are open."

"It's rumored the elves might attack first," Weeby said. "I would hate to be caught along the road in front of a bunch of angry elves."

"Nothing a bit of magic couldn't save you from."

"If only I had a wizard to help me with that, as I've little talent for such things."

"You ever find your girl?"

Weeby shook his head. "Sadly, no, though I heard that she made her way to safety."

"Safety seems in short supply these days."

"That it does. And you've made a good point about waiting for the army. I've a few things to round up, but I think I'll chance the road north and trust the fates to keep me safe. Until next time."

The halfling sauntered off with a tip of his head.

"Weeby?" Tormjere called out.

The halfling paused and looked over his shoulder.

"You're a terrible liar."

Weeby laughed in genuine merriment. "And you're getting better. Next time I'll buy you that drink and we'll see who has the best story to tell."

Tormjere kept his eyes glued to the halfling until he had disappeared down a side street a few blocks away. He waited another moment before returning.

"I am not certain what that accomplished," Shalindra said as Tormjere rejoined them.

"He was waiting for someone, but not us. Or at least not here."

"You think it coincidence then?"

"The funny thing about coincidence is how often it reveals a hidden truth. But we should be gone before he can cause us any trouble."

Enna glanced about nervously. "I have no idea what either of you are talking about, but we should get moving before we bring trouble down on ourselves." Even tucked against the building with her hood up, she was still drawing unwelcome looks.

They set off again, heading away from the direction Weeby had chosen.

"Should we look for one of Eluria's temples?" Tormjere asked.

"There are several, if memory serves," Shalindra answered, "but I do not know where they might be, nor do I wish to wander longer than we must."

"Let's find an inn and get off the streets, then," Tormjere said. Though they could not see the sun through the clouds, the gloom of the afternoon was beginning to deepen.

Tormjere had never been to the city, but he kept them moving generally south. The streets they followed took them past statued common squares, markets, and mansions. There were areas where the streets grew narrow and the inhabitants less reputable, but the manor houses and markets that dominated the inland side of the city seemed to be doing their best to crowd them out.

It was not long before they located an inn of reasonable status that was situated near a series of modest houses. Tormjere spoke to the innkeep, and after handing over the required coins was directed up the stairs.

He latched the door once the trio was alone in the room.

"How much money do we have?" Shalindra asked.

Tormjere felt the weight of his coin pouch. "Enough to get to Merallin comfortably but not enough to do so quickly, or at least not by land. I'll check the docks and see if I can find us anything faster."

"I'll remain here," Enna said. "The more I am seen, the more likely it is to cause us problems. I witnessed only a handful of elves on the streets and none would even look at me, much less speak."

"I will wait as well," Shalindra said. "I doubt that there is anything I could accomplish save calling more attention to you."

Tormjere unhooked Shining Moon from his belt. Shalindra noticed the barest of tremors in his hand as he returned the weapon to her.

Are you...?

I'm fine. Don't worry about it.

Tormjere departed without another word, but the look Enna gave her said that she had seen it as well.

They set the latch on the door behind him and tried to make themselves comfortable.

Enna was the first to break the silence.

"If we are unable to stop this war, you must remain on the winning side and prevent the armor from being taken."

"You would wish me to raise arms against the elves?"

"I do not wish you to fight for either side, but Elurithlia is greater than any one people. That She has called you to service can only mean that there is a reason, and you must take your place as Her Guardian, no matter which side achieves victory."

She covered Enna's hands with her own. "I will do everything in my power to see that both sides may claim victory."

Enna smiled bravely, but her eyes were filled with worry.

As they waited away the evening, Shalindra occupied the time by trying to think of who she could speak to, anyone who might have any ability to stop the war. Logian was the only member of the family who could influence her father, and she had no idea who his advisors were now or if any would even care to speak to her after so long an absence. It would have to be her father, and the only person she might trust to get her there would be her mother or Kentrick.

It was well after dark when Tormjere returned, but neither woman had gone to sleep. He handed them small sacks filled with bread and fresh meats.

"What did you find?" Enna asked, accepting the food eagerly.

"The docks were as flooded with soldiers as everywhere else. Every available boat has either been bought or commandeered."

Shalindra winced, but not from the grittiness of the bread. She had known the answer as soon as he had, and had already come to the conclusion they all did. "Then tomorrow we walk."

* * *

Wake up, but remain silent.

Shalindra jolted awake, her eyes going to where Tormjere stood beside the door.

What is it?

Someone's coming through the door.

Should I wake Enna?

There's no time. Get ready.

The latch opened with the barest of clicks, and the door swung open soundlessly.

A shadowy figure rushed into the room, headed straight towards the bed where Enna still slept. Shalindra could see nothing about him save the glint of moonlight off a long dagger. Tormjere tackled the man, bending his arm painfully behind his back until the knife clattered to the floor.

Enna bolted upright in confusion. "What…"

Tormjere yanked the man to his feet by his hair. "Explain yourself."

The would-be assassin twisted away, leaving Tormjere holding only a handful of ripped out hair. Another blade appeared in the man's hand as he lunged.

Tormjere was faster, striking him hard enough to crack his skull. The assassin flopped dead to the floor.

Tormjere checked the hallway and found it empty, then returned and searched the body.

"Nothing," he said. "This wasn't a random robbery. He was going for Enna."

"Could someone know why I am here?"

"It's unlikely, but I don't want to hang around long enough to find out."

"I agree," Shalindra said, already gathering her things. "What of the body?"

Tormjere dragged it to the window, then poked his head outside and looked up and down the street. Seeing no one he heaved the body out the window.

"What?" he said in response to Enna's accusatory look. "We can't leave it to be found in our room."

It was a feeble effort at misdirection, but as they grabbed their belongings and hurried from the inn Shalindra could only pray that it would not somehow come back to haunt them.

Chapter Twenty-Five

Homecoming

Tormjere had always wanted to visit the capital of Merallin, but the childhood dreams he had shared with his brother Eljorn had involved much more celebratory circumstances.

It was an odd thought for Shalindra to have, but she was aware that it was not hers. The mental images that accompanied their strongest emotions tended to bleed into one another's consciousness, and was doing so with increasing frequency.

Enna walked beside her, lost in their own thoughts. She could not blame her for her silence. The suspicious looks she had drawn in the north had turned into hostile glares and muttered unpleasantries the farther south they travelled and Enna had to be terrified that she would be seized at any moment. Such hostility did not bode well for any meeting with the king, but Shalindra would have to find a way.

She turned her attentions back to the scene before them, taking note of what had changed and what remained the same. The river that flowed past the city was wide and swift, and higher than she could ever remember seeing it. Single-masted ships crewed by armed men in the King's colors patrolled the waters in greater numbers, while merchant vessels large and small moved in and out of the harbors. Colorful pennants fluttered from atop the many graceful spires of the quicklimed castle, which stood perched on a rocky slab of bedrock that rose some fifty feet above the water. Waves crashed on the rocks below, and sea birds called in the air. Beyond the walls of the city, the grass turned to sand along the shore, and the closest trees were miles away. It was on a gentle rise beneath one such tree that they paused to escape the heat.

"I never knew what so much water would look like," Tormjere said.

Shalindra's gaze shifted to ocean. "It is in constant motion, and always captivating. When we were children, we would play on the shore and draw shapes in the sand."

"That seems fun. Is the water cool?" he asked, wiping sweat from his forehead.

Shalindra smiled. "Not as cold as our mountain creeks but cool enough to feel good on your toes."

"At least you'd never go thirsty."

She laughed. "The ocean is salty—it tastes horrible."

"Wait," Enna interjected. "I know something you do not?"

Tormjere ignored the gibe and returned them to the task at hand. "How do you intend to find your mother?"

"Finding her will be less difficult than arranging an opportunity to speak with her. She dislikes being trapped inside the castle all day and makes regular trips through the city, or at least she used to, and we would often visit the docks. She always said it was so that she could learn more about the goods coming in, but I think she just wanted to look at the horizon."

"So we are to wait for her to come out of the castle and hope to follow her?"

"That would take too long. Agnes is Sister Superior of our temple here, and she often enters the castle to aid with injuries and see to the health of those inside. She was the one who first kindled my desire to join with Eluria. If anyone in the city can speak to my mother, it is her."

As a princess, she had been able to speak to anyone at any time. Now that luxury was denied to her, and after such a long absence she could think of no one else that might help them.

"Good morning!"

They all turned in surprise to see a young monk in the brown and yellow robes of Toush pulling a small handcart off the road and towards them. He huffed his way up the hill and stopped before them.

"It is wise to stand in the shade today. Are you going into the city?"

"That was our intent," Shalindra answered.

"Delightful! I thought I might never find you. I am Shiran." He bowed, sending his thick mop of tousled hair bouncing about.

"We are pleased to meet you," Shalindra said, "but I fear you have mistaken us for someone else."

Shiran glanced at Enna. "I will presume that neither of you have been here recently, if at all. Yes. You will definitely need my assistance." He clapped his hands eagerly and began rummaging in his cart.

"How do you know we need your help?" Shalindra asked.

"My path was shown to me. I was most pleased by this, as it means that I may soon continue to the next stage of my journey."

Shiran reappeared with a pair of nondescript gowns of common material and held them out to Shalindra and Enna. "These should do."

"Are you close to the red robes?" Tormjere asked. Shalindra understood it as an attempt at verifying the monk's intentions, but Shiran beamed at the question.

"You are familiar with our way! But not quite yet. There are six paths that must be walked to achieve true enlightenment, and multiple stages within each. How long each path takes varies with every journey."

"I always thought there should be another one once you've achieved the rest."

"Another path would be wonderful," Shiran agreed, "but six is challenge enough to fill a lifetime. Or several." He looked at the clothes still held in his hands. "The entrances into the city are heavily watched, and elves and clerics alike are often denied entry or detained, particularly those of your order."

Shalindra glanced at Tormjere, who simply shrugged. It would not be the first time the monks of Toush had helped them, and if what Shiran said was correct then they might indeed be forced to disguise who they were.

"How long have you been waiting?" Shalindra asked, accepting the clothing but not liking it one bit.

Shiran counted silently on his fingers before answering. "Two and a half years."

Enna looked at him incredulously. "You've been waiting here for that long?"

"Oh, not here the whole time. One's path can never be found by sitting still."

Shalindra wished that everyone would stop reminding her of how much time she had wasted in the valley, even if they did not mean to. "It may be that we need to hide who we are to enter the city, but simple robes will not conceal her race."

Shiran ran his fingers through Enna's hair, and the straight white strands darkened and curled into a thickness that easily hid her pointed ears.

"The effect will wear off in a few hours," Shiran said, noting her distressed look. "Now, I have something else for you."

He produced a woven basket filled with a variety of plants and foliage that looked to have been plucked from the forest floor, and handed it to Shalindra.

He next regarded Tormjere. "I was only shown the way for two people, but you can pass for any sell-sword easily enough. Might I suggest that you remain a few steps behind so it appears that we do not travel together? The guards will likely pay more attention to you than to us."

"You sound like you have done this before," Enna observed as she pulled the greyish dress over herself. It was much too long and bunched on the ground around her feet.

"In truth, I have simply been thinking about it for a long time. With the proper devotion of effort, one may become wise at anything." Shiran looked at her and tapped his chin. "Perhaps you should simply ride in the cart. If you slouch a bit, you could easily be mistaken for an older child."

Enna climbed into the cart and tucked her legs beneath her, attempting to look as small as possible. Shalindra was already sweating under the additional layer of clothing, and though she was willing to take a monk of Toush at his word she did not wish to waste time. "Let us be on our way, so that we can cease this mummery."

Shiran took hold of the cart and returned to the road as Tormjere drifted a few paces back. The walk was long and hot, but the monk refused every offer of help. The gate into the city was flanked by a pair of rounded stone towers, both taller than her castle in Newlmir. The green and gold banner of Actondel still waved above them. Shalindra could barely remember the days of riding a carriage through those gates, oblivious to the effort of covering the distance on foot. It was a different life that belonged to someone else.

She doubted they would be able to bluff their way in a second time, but as Shiran had predicted, the guards passed over them and devoted their attention to evaluating the weapons Tormjere carried. He did his best to avoid their gaze and look like someone amazed by the size and grandeur of the city, which was not difficult, given that he was.

They continued for several blocks before finding a shaded alley in which to regroup. Shalindra and Enna shed their commoners' robes, eager to be free of the extra layers in the heat of the day.

"Are you certain you do not need them?" Shiran asked.

"We should be fine from here," Shalindra said, enjoying the coolness provided by the sleeveless elvish robes once more.

"I hope that your path is now free of troubles, but should you ever find yourself in need, visit our monastery. It can be found back through that same gate, on the western edge of the King's forest."

"Is there anything we can do to repay you?" Shalindra asked.

"My path has already provided luxury." Shiran indicated the hand cart. "I can trade this for more food than I could carry, and I am certain there are others who need your attention more."

"Then know that you have our thanks."

Shiran smiled. "It is I who must thank you, as you have placed my feet once more upon my path. May you find success in yours as well."

Shiran took up his cart and pulled it away, whistling a merry tune as he went.

Enna shook her head. "There are few elves who follow Toush and so I have nothing to compare to, but was that normal?"

"The brotherhood is known for helping others in many ways," Shalindra responded, "and it is not the first time they have given us aid."

"And is their path of progression common knowledge as well?" Enna asked with a sideways glance at Tormjere.

"My brother's a monk," he answered.

Shalindra had almost forgotten that, but her own family was just as unknown to Tormjere and Enna as theirs were to her.

She looked around to get her bearings. "That tower is new, and it reminds me of Honarch's."

The spire jutting above the city had been positioned near the castle, and thought it was only slightly taller than the fortress, it cast an ominous shadow.

"Definitely a wizard's tower," Tormjere agreed. "There were lots of them in Tythir."

It seems the Imaretii are settling in.

They'll be embedded in other ways, like ticks on a dog.

You cannot know that.

One of them had become advisor to the king, if you recall. It's unlikely they've been content with only that.

You are correct, but I pray they have not caused further strife. At least our family banner has not been replaced by a Ceringion one.

"Where are we headed?" Enna asked. "I hope we are not going to stand here in silence all day."

"We should be able to stay at Eluria's temple," Shalindra said with a guilty glance at Tormjere as she began walking. "Sister Agnes knows me, and I trust her to keep us safe. I remember the way well enough to get there."

And we should stop speaking this way or she will think we are constantly daydreaming.

I'm not doing it on purpose.

Neither am I.

Shalindra had never walked from the gates to the temple. Actually, she had rarely walked anywhere within the city, instead riding in her mother's carriage surrounded by guards. It was not long before the white marble roof came into view, but she quickly became turned around, and paused to remember the way. "I think... through here."

The alley they entered was dirty and not somewhere she would have normally thought to visit, but it was cool and shaded and much less crowded. The street urchins huddled in the corners looked longingly at the silver medallions of Eluria that they carried, but Tormjere glared at them so fiercely that they lost interest. Shalindra was thankful when they emerged at the other end onto a familiar street.

"Yes, here we are," she said.

After two more turns they arrived at a side street which followed along the outer marble wall of the temple compound. Shalindra was heading towards the front entrance when a head popped out of a window above them.

"Sisters!" came a piercing whisper. They looked to see a middle-aged woman in the white of Eluria leaning out of a second-story window. "Over here, come quickly! Not through the front!"

Shalindra exchanged glances with Enna, and they turned towards a door beneath the woman. She disappeared from the window, and a moment later came the sound of a latch being thrown open. The door swung inwards.

"Inside, before you are seen!" the woman beckoned. "Why are you calling attention to yourselves?"

"We sought only to visit the temple," Shalindra said. "This is Sister Enna, of Ildalarial, and I am Sister Shalindra."

"Sister Constance," the woman replied. She began to say something else, then seemed to notice Shining Moon on Tormjere's belt. "Is it true?" Her hand went her mouth. "We heard rumors, but… the Guardian returned?" Her eyes went to Enna. "But why do you not carry it?"

Enna looked embarrassed. "Sister Shalindra is our Mistress' chosen."

Shalindra returned Shining Moon to her own belt, just to avoid further confusion.

Constance was clearly unsettled by all of it, but regained a measure of her composure and hurried onwards. "Please, follow me."

She led them through the building, which was largely given over to storage. The rooms were dark, and the halls echoed hollow with their steps.

"I do not understand the need for secrecy," Shalindra said. "What is happening?"

Constance grew more agitated than she already was. "These are dire times for Eluria's church and indeed for us all. There is talk that it is magic, not the gods, who are the way to prosperity. On top of that we have this war with the elves brewing, and anything related to them has come under scrutiny. Eluria has been branded an elvish goddess and not fit for humans. Many have turned to Amalthee or folk remedies for healing and avoid us now unless they are desperate."

Shalindra could not hide her shock. "You fear for your safety?"

"Some of our sisters have been accosted in the streets. There have been no attacks against the temple as yet, but..." She looked at Enna with concern, but said nothing else.

They entered the central shrine, where an aged woman knelt alone before the statue of Eluria. The woman rose at the sound of their hurried footsteps, but when she turned she was not the woman Shalindra remembered so fondly.

"Sister Superior," Constance said, "this is Sister Shalindra, who carries the Guardian's weapon!"

"Is it so?" the woman asked, her eyes alight with wonder.

"This is Shining Moon," Shalindra confirmed. "Forgive me, but where is Sister Agnes?"

"I am sorry, Sister, but she passed away last year. I am Sister Gale."

Shalindra put a hand to her face, struggling with the sudden sadness that washed over her. Agnes had been a wonderful woman, full of love for her goddess and with a gift for restorations that left those in her care with a healthier outlook on the world. And she had been the only link to her mother.

"I fear you have chosen a difficult time to return," Gale said, "for it is likely you will discover only unhappiness within these walls."

Shalindra swallowed her sorrows. "I shall always cherish my memories of her. But what has become of everyone who worshiped here?" The temple had once housed dozens of Eluria's followers and had seen a constant stream of visitors seeking aid.

"All but a handful of our Sisters have left, either by renouncing their faith or fleeing to safer places. It is only through the influence of a few wealthy benefactors that we have not been forced to close as well. If it should become known that we harbored an elf, we risk incurring the wizard's wrath. We could even lose Her temple itself."

Shalindra could not hide her shock. "Has it truly come to that?"

"The market temple was closed last year. The shrine near the Gold Gate remains, but its gardens are half the size they once were."

"Is that why you are here?" Constance blurted. "To help us?"

I should have been here, not hiding in the mountains.

The peace you'll achieve will aid them as well. You can't keep worrying about what you can't change.

Shalindra swallowed. "I believe so, though it may happen indirectly. But no one must know that I am here."

"Only the two of us are aware of your identity. It will certainly be kept in confidence, but you cannot remain here without notice by others who will be less accommodating."

"That became apparent as we talked," Shalindra said. "Is there an inn nearby where we would not attract too much suspicion?"

"Perhaps for a short time, but the king has agents everywhere, even in the more disreputable districts which I would never recommend. If safety is what you seek, I do not believe you will find it anywhere within the city right now. I am sorry, Sisters."

"I understand," Enna said. "I would rather leave and see Her temple endure than remain here and risk its ruin."

"I must attend to those seeking our aid right now, or they may leave of their own accord after helping themselves to our possessions. Sister Constance will see to your refreshment, but I beg you to stay only as long as you must."

"We will depart as soon as we have determined our direction," Shalindra said.

"May She guide you with Her light," Gale said, crestfallen. "I pray that when we next meet, I will be able to show you the honor you deserve."

Constance was so distraught that it seemed she might collapse, but she gathered her courage and led them to the kitchen.

On the verge of tears, she indicated the half-empty pantries. "Please, take anything you require. Our Sister Superior speaks the truth about our fate should you be found here, but it is unbearable for us to turn you away."

"It is not our first hardship," Shalindra said kindly. "Her light will see us all through these trials."

They refreshed themselves with clean water and fruits but did not linger, then made their way back to the side entrance. Tormjere plucked Shining Moon from Shalindra's belt and returned it to his own before they stepped outside.

The door closed behind them, but could not mask the sound of Constance's sobs.

"Where shall we go now?" Enna asked.

Shalindra had never imagined it would be this difficult to accomplish something so simple as finding a room in which to sleep. If she could not even do that, how could she possibly hope to stop a war?

"The monastery," Tormjere answered for her. "And you should both hide your symbols until we are there."

Enna did so, appalled at the necessity. "I begin to think that you must accomplish this attempt without me. You and Tormjere may travel easily enough without attracting attention, but my hair is already returning to its natural state, and I will be more hindrance than help."

Shalindra started to protest, but Enna cut her off.

"It is for the best. I can make my way there while you continue."

Tormjere shook his head. "There's no way we're splitting up until we have to. Shiran said it wasn't that far out of the city, and it will be easy enough for Shalindra and I to return without suspicion."

They both looked at her, the decision made. "I would have to agree, though I am loath to leave you behind."

As they made their way from the city in defeat Shalindra offered a silent prayer to Eluria to stave off her growing feeling of hopelessness.

* * *

The monastery of Toush, sequestered but a short distance inside the forest, was as easy to find as Shiran had claimed it would be.

A solitary monk waited at the gate. He was tall and strong, and despite the cleanliness of his appearance he had the look of one who spent his time away from civilization rather than in it. "Welcome, travelers," he greeted them pleasantly. "You may set aside your fears, for you will be safe here."

"Thank you," Shalindra said. She had time for no further pleasantries as the monk placed a cautionary finger to his lips.

"Come with me, please," was all he said.

Shalindra was surprised by his behavior, but followed as he led them away from what she assumed was the common building and towards a smaller one on the opposite side of the complex. As with the other monasteries they had visited the buildings here were geometrically aligned and sized in a manner that conveyed some deeper meaning. The floors of each were stacked like stones in a cairn, with each level smaller than the one beneath it. It was a quiet and contemplative place. Reaching one of the buildings, the monk slid the door open and ushered them inside.

"Please forgive the abruptness of my welcome," he said, once he had closed the door behind them. "I am Martyn."

"It is no trouble," Shalindra said, "though we require no special attention and wish only to avail ourselves of your common room for a few nights, if it is allowed."

"Our doors are open to all who need help along their path, yet it remains in your best interest as well as ours to keep such assistance from attracting the wrong types of attention."

"You've sheltered Sisters of Eluria before," Tormjere said.

Martyn sighed. "Far more of late than we would prefer. You are not the first of your order who has fled to the safety of our walls, and it is unlikely that you will be the last."

"Then I must thank you on behalf of every one of my Sisters, for what you have done."

"It is Toush above all who guides our actions, but we appreciate the sentiment. Does your path lead north or east?"

Shalindra shook her head. "Unfortunately, my business lies here in Merallin."

"Does it? I would have expected Brother Shiran to have found you first, then. He has been waiting for so long."

"We met him earlier this day. While he was most helpful our initial efforts inside the walls did not bear fruit. We were unprepared for the level of animosity Sister Enna was subjected to, and so we came here for help."

"I had hoped to remain here for a day or two," Enna added, "so that Sister Shalindra can attend to her business in peace."

"Ah." Martyn looked as if he would say more on the subject, then changed his mind. "You are welcome to guest with us as long as you need, as our hospitality does not follow the fickleness of common sentiment. If you intend to seek entry into the city once more, however, you would be well advised to change your attire."

"That we have already discovered," Shalindra said. "I do not wish to hide my faith, but as you suggest, it is indeed prudent."

He led her to a chest in the corner, which contained a variety of robes and gowns of various colors, all folded neatly. "Most of your Sisters have fled to Fallhaven or even Kirchmont. Regardless of their direction of travel, many have found themselves in the same predicament as you once on the road. I will leave you to decide your course. Food will be brought to you."

"We are grateful," Shalindra said.

The moment the door slid shut, Enna turned to her. "How are you to reach the king if we risk attack simply by walking around?"

"I will begin by changing clothes," Shalindra said, selecting a plain dress of pale blue from the chest. "After that I must determine the best way forward. I still believe that my mother will be the easiest way to him."

"Do you know of any other possible way?"

Shalindra's shoulders slumped. "No."

"We should probably wait until tomorrow, regardless," Tormjere said. "By the time we walk all the way back to the city it will be evening. As we can't stroll through the castle doors, even without Enna, there's little time left to accomplish anything today."

Shalindra did not want to sit idle with so much at stake. The skies were becoming more blue than grey, and the armies camped at Adair could begin moving at any time.

"It could be that a pause to settle your thoughts is the best thing," Enna said. "Would you want to wander the streets looking for somewhere to stay again?"

"No," she said, shaking her head. "No, you are both correct. We will stay here tonight, and perhaps Her wisdom will guide me to a suitable resolution."

"We know you can't go straight to her," Tormjere said, "but is there anyone else who can?"

"I can think of no one else with access to the castle."

"What about her trips outside? Is there anywhere she's likely to go?"

His question prompted a sudden thought. "Yes. I think I know of a way. My mother and I would visit shops throughout the city every three or four days, and I became quite familiar with those places we frequented the most. It might be possible to use one of them to bring her to us."

"What makes you think they would help you?" Enna asked.

"Most of them would not, but I can think of a handful who might be willing."

"It seems a stretch."

"It does, but as I can think of no other way it will have to do."

* * *

Shalindra frowned as she stared at the front of what should have been a candlemaker's shop, but the sign hanging above it now advertised the services of a seamstress.

I'm going to guess your mother does not come here to have her clothes fitted.

Milacole made the most exquisite candles. They were works of art to be collected rather than burned. His was one of my mother's favorite shops.

It was not even close to noon, and this was already their second failure. Was there anything from her past life that still existed?

We'll find someone.

"I know," she said aloud. They might have been the first words to leave her mouth since they had departed the monastery early that morning, though she and Tormjere had conversed almost constantly as she searched for someone who could get a message to her mother.

She put a hand against Eluria's symbol, still tucked inside her dress, and prayed that their next attempt would be successful. She did not wish to return to Enna empty-handed tonight.

She made her way towards the docks in as direct a manner as she could, eventually turning down a street where the establishments were orderly and well kept, with as much space given over to shops and merchants as to warehouses and more common buildings. The smells of saltwater and fish mingled with those of coffee and spices, and the clamor of the streets gave way to the sounds of the ocean.

Eluria must have heard her prayers, because the sign with the cake was still the same as it had always been.

A baker?

Altonsa deals with delicacies from the south, below the Ironspike mountains.

Shalindra inhaled deeply as she entered, savoring the rich aromas that filled her nose. The shop was unoccupied save for the now balding man behind the counter.

"Princess Kataria?" the man asked upon catching sight of her.

When she affirmed his assumption, he hurried around the counter and bowed. "My word, Your Highness, you've not graced my shop in years, but I'd know those beautiful blue eyes anywhere. How big you've gotten! You were a tiny thing when last I saw you."

"It is good to see you again as well, Master Altonsa."

Altonsa put a hand to his head. "I've a shipment of your favorites fresh delivered, and here I stand babbling like an old hen. Please, excuse me." He disappeared into the back of the shop and returned a moment later with a small box tied with a ribbon, which he placed on the counter and opened for her.

Shalindra eagerly took one of the dark confections and allowed it to melt in her mouth. The delightful sensation stirred memories of a time when all her troubles could be resolved by a simple treat.

Those taste good. What are they?

Truffles. They are made of chocolate from Cadonior. Ice is brought down from the mountains to keep them fresh aboard ship. Of everything I have lost, I think I miss these the most.

"These are wonderful, Master Altonsa, and they bring me more joy than you can know. Does my mother still visit you?"

"She does, my lady, on occasion." He twisted his fingers together nervously and began to say more, then stopped.

"You may speak plainly."

"Begging your pardon, my lady, it's not for folks like me to pry into these matters." He cast a nervous glance around his shop to ensure they were alone. "There was a reward offered to any who knew where you were. We'd heard rumors of some falling out between you and your family, long about the time of… the changes."

"Those rumors were true, unfortunately," she said, "but it is a situation that I intend to rectify. I need to speak with the queen but dare not approach the castle. Can you pass a message along to her?"

Altonsa again looked uncomfortable. "It would please me to no end to help you, of course, but such a message would pass through many hands on its way to her, and… Well, you understand the position that might leave me in, Your Highness."

"I do, and I certainly wish for nothing bad to come from my visit. Perhaps you could simply make her aware that her favorite sweets are here?"

His face brightened. "That I would be happy to do. I let Her Highness know of such things from time to time. Perchance she'd pay us a visit. With the recent piracy on the seas, we've not had them in a while. You are welcome to stay here, Your Highness. My home is yours."

"You are most gracious. I will remain in the back, so as not to distract from your business."

I'll wait outside, where I can watch the street.

Shalindra said a silent prayer as she retired to the back room, hoping that the delicacies would be enough to lure her mother out. Altonsa fussed over her briefly, but had to return to the front as more customers arrived. Shalindra wondered where his wife was, but after so much disheartening news she was too scared to inquire.

She remained unsettled as she waited. The last time she had seen her mother was the day she left with Sir Warron on their doomed journey to rendezvous with Steward Erbac nearly six years ago. She had never thought her goodbye would have lasted so long. What could have happened to her mother during those years? Was she sad to be apart from her daughter or appalled by her actions? What if she did not come?

Then we'll be back tomorrow, or we'll try something else.

And if she does not accept me? What then?

We'll find another way in, even if it's through the gates.

Despite his encouraging thoughts, she could tell that something was gnawing at Tormjere.

It is not the waiting that is bothering you. What is wrong?

I'm just hungry.

Should we be worried about that?

Not yet.

Customers came and went as the day dragged on. Altonsa poked his head in to let her know the message had been successfully delivered. Shalindra felt as if she should be doing something, but there was nothing that would make the time pass more quickly.

The sun was well past its zenith when Shalindra was jolted from her thoughts by the image of a carriage arriving.

She's here. Looks like your brother is with her.

321

Shalindra peeked from her hiding place to make sure no one other than Altonsa was there. She hurried into a corner of the shop, glancing nervously out the window as butterflies danced in her stomach.

Relax.

What are her guards doing?

Keeping an eye on me. I'm trying to look suspicious.

I doubt that is difficult.

Shalindra kept her back to the door and pretended to scan the shelves. One of the soldiers entered and looked around, then stepped back outside to watch the street. A moment later, her brother Kentrick escorted their mother into the shop.

They had both changed. Kentrick was taller and broader of shoulder. The cut of his tailored green doublet accented that shape, as did the dueling sword he wore.

Queen Eleanor Actondel's once dazzling blonde hair had faded to a sandy brown, and it was now worn up in an elaborate weave that must be the current fashion. Her dress was tight and stiff around her midsection and flared out in layered ruffles from her waist with enough cloth to cover two less important people. Her steel-blue eyes were as alive as ever, but she paid Shalindra no mind as she addressed Altonsa.

"Master Altonsa, it is good to see you again."

"I am delighted as well, Your Majesty," Altonsa said, bowing low. "You grace my humble shop with your presence, as always."

"You have always been my favorite," she teased, "especially when you've a new supply of my favorite chocolates on hand."

She smiles the same way you do.

Her mother's smile could brighten any room, but it seemed

somehow less than it had once been, as if she were searching for happiness rather than living it.

"They are fresh delivered just yesterday. I thought of you the moment they arrived and set some aside in the back, where it's cool and they wouldn't spoil. If you'll excuse me I will fetch them immediately." He scurried quickly into the storeroom.

Now was the time. Shalindra pushed aside the hollowness in her stomach. She approached slowly, heart pounding in her chest as she curtsied.

"Your Majesty," Shalindra said, her head down. She heard her mother's sudden intake of breath, and saw her stiffen as she gripped the nearby counter.

Shalindra raised her eyes apprehensively. Shock and sorrow warred with disbelief in her mother's face, and then she was clutching Shalindra close. "I thought you dead."

Shalindra let herself sink into that embrace, enjoying the warmth of her mother as the cares of the world slipped away, if only for a moment. When she pulled back, her eyes were damp.

"Kataria!" Kentrick exclaimed, hugging her as well.

"I am so sorry for what has happened," Shalindra said, "and that I never got a chance to tell you myself."

The queen straightened her dress and glanced at the door. "Kentrick told me of what transpired. I pleaded with your father to reverse his decision, but his mind was set."

"Begging Your Majesty's pardon," Altonsa said as he returned. "I could never say no to either of you. Your chocolates, as promised." He handed her a box tied with ribbon, then quickly retreated as far from them as possible.

"Where have you been," Kentrick asked, "and why did you

come back?"

"I am a Sister of Eluria now, as I always wished to be. What I have done would be too long to tell, but I mean to stop this war before it is too late, and for that I must speak to my father."

"That is incredibly dangerous," Eleanor said. "He has not forgiven you, nor have any of those who now have his ear."

"Regardless of anyone's feelings, I must. I cannot avoid such a conflict, nor can I bear to choose one side over the other."

"I do not even think it's possible at this point," Kentrick said with a dismissive wave of his hand. "We've amassed a huge force, bigger than any we have ever seen. We have to do something before..." He trailed off as Eleanor pointedly cleared her throat.

"I will figure out a way, Eluria willing. Only our enemies will benefit from such a conflict."

Her mother placed a cautionary hand on her arm. "Now more than ever, others wait for the slightest misstep, seeking to take what is ours. So many of the houses which once supported us have already fallen, and were you to accompany me, I do not believe you would reach Fabrian. There remains a price on your head."

"Is there a way for me to sneak in?" If the queen herself could not guarantee her safety...

Kentrick shook his head. "No longer. The ways you knew of are all sealed, and though there are probably others they are guarded in ways far more difficult to avoid."

"Then perhaps you could spirit me in, as a possible love interest?"

"I... Wait, what?" her brother stammered.

"You *are* interested in girls by now?"

Kentrick blushed. "A few."

"Then it is your princely prerogative to smuggle another back to the castle."

Kentrick's eyes flicked to his mother, then quickly looked at his feet.

A soldier's coming in.

Shalindra turned her back towards the door just before a member of the royal guard stepped into the shop. The queen waved him away. "Another moment, Jarrod. I am awaiting something from the back."

The soldier bowed respectfully and retreated outside once more.

"I will leave you two to each other then," the queen said with an amused shake of her head. "It would be best if I remain unaware of how my son is sneaking ladies into the castle. Remain in Kentrick's rooms once you are inside, and I will come for you after the evening meal." She embraced her daughter once more. "Be careful."

"I will."

The queen called Altonsa back to them, but her eyes remained on her daughter as she spoke. "If every visit to your shop offered such magnificent delights, I would be here every day. Thank you."

"You are too kind, Your Highness."

Eleanor went to the door and summoned a retainer. "Whatever price Master Altonsa asks for my goods, see that he is paid double."

The retainer bowed and did as commanded.

Shalindra walked outside with Kentrick, resisting the urge to look at Tormjere as her brother guided her away from the carriage.

I'll be close, but your mother's soldiers are still watching so I won't follow.

If I need you…

…I will know.

"We may continue," the queen announced as she was helped into the carriage. "Lord Kentrick will be returning to the keep at a later time."

One of the soldiers eyed Shalindra enviously, and gave Kentrick a knowing grin as the carriage pulled away.

Her brother stood awkwardly at her side, then cleared his throat. "Shall we walk?"

He set an unhurried pace as if they were simply enjoying the pleasant afternoon, but his furrowed brow revealed his worry.

"How have you…?"

"Are you still…?"

They began at the same time.

"You first," Kentrick insisted.

"How have you been?" she asked.

Kentrick looked away as he answered. "I have done as you asked when you… left. I have kept our mother safe."

The tightness in his voice revealed how difficult that must have been. Not for the first time, Shalindra wondered if she had made a horrible mistake by staying away for so long. "That could not have been easy."

"It was not. There have been many schemes and plots. They are succeeding with increased frequency of late, and while our family continues to hold the throne, it is a perilous seat."

"Logian?"

"Logian is… well, he has not changed. He sees this war with the elves as a way to reclaim our lost glory."

"What do you see it as?"

"A solution to the wrong problem, which is only going to be made more difficult by your return. What am I to do with you?"

He was attempting to lighten the mood, but the situation he painted was far more dire than she had expected. She wanted to see a smile on his face once more.

"I do not know, my lord," she answered coyly. "What do you normally do when wandering about with a fetching woman on your arm?"

Her brother's face turned as hot as an iron on the fire. "You're making this difficult. How am I supposed to take you to the castle unnoticed?"

"I am certain that you have ways," she said as she slipped her arm around his, causing him to fidget uncomfortably.

"Do not squirm. You are the one who is supposed to be taking advantage of me, not the other way around."

"You could always fluster any man when you wished, family member or not."

"I use my charms where I must." She giggled and batted her eyes at him. "Though if you turn any more red, you will be mistaken for a cooked lobster."

You're having way too much fun with this.

I know, but I am so happy to see my family once more.

"I missed you," Kentrick said, turning serious once more. "Nothing has been the same since that day."

Shalindra felt her smile droop. "As I have missed you. Would that things were different and the war had not forced us apart."

"Do you really believe you can stop what is coming?"

"I can only pray." She leaned her head against his shoulder. "Take me by the docks, so I can see the ships again."

Chapter Twenty-Six

What Was Lost

Shalindra paused at the top of the steps as Kentrick stuck his head through the door. After a quick check in both directions, he took her hand and pulled her from the servant's stairway and into the hall.

"Almost there," he said, though she did not need the reminder. It had been years, but she had walked the carpeted halls of the castle so many times she knew exactly where they were. The guards and household staff they had encountered had all made a point of not looking too closely at the woman the prince had brought into the castle, but there were other lords and ladies who would not remain so willfully oblivious.

Her brother paused to peek around the next corner.

"Prince Kentrick!"

He jumped and wheeled about, pushing her behind him. "Lord Redivers, how are you this evening?"

Redivers' green and gold tabard was richly trimmed and bore the emblem the royal guard. He approached with an efficiency of motion that reminded her of Birion, and eyed her distastefully.

"More focused on my priorities than you, apparently. His Majesty questioned why you were not present at dinner."

The mention of food reminded Shalindra that she had not eaten all day, but she was willing to skip every meal for a week if it would keep her safe. She snuggled closer behind her brother, as any guilty woman might, and kept her eyes on the floor.

"I was enjoying my walk around town and lost track of time," Kentrick said.

"If that's what you call it now. I would suggest that your plans for the evening not keep you from your sword drills in the morning, nor from your lessons with Master Ylnvan."

"I will be there," Kentrick said defensively.

Redivers gave him a doubtful look before continuing down the hall.

"Who is Ylnvan?" Shalindra asked as they headed in a different direction. "That name sounds familiar."

Kentrick looked as if he had swallowed a bug. "The court wizard who advises father now."

"You are studying magic?"

"Rulership, or at least, that is the pretext." Kentrick shook his head. "I think the Conclave hopes to indoctrinate me to their cause, whatever it may be."

There were no guards outside Kentrick's room—indeed, she had seen very few inside the keep at all—and they hurried inside.

Her brother leaned against a wall as he locked the door behind them. "That was far more stressful than I'd anticipated."

Shalindra collapsed into a chair, just as worn out.

"I probably should go put in an appearance," her brother said, "just to keep people from coming to look for me." He stepped in front of a mirror and smoothed his appearance. "I'll let mother know that you are here, and have food sent up."

"Thank you."

He hugged her. "I'm glad to see you again, no matter the reason."

"So am I," she said, hugging him back.

When he was gone, she looked about the empty room, then moved to the windows. Over the castle wall and beyond the tops of buildings lay the dark expanse of the ocean. She closed her eyes and sought Tormjere's mind.

I'm still here.

How far away?

Close to the castle, but the room cost almost everything I had.

I am certain that my brother will replenish our funds.

That depends on how tonight goes.

She turned away from the window.

Everything depends on it.

* * *

That same realization still echoed in her thoughts hours later as she followed her mother and Kentrick down the hallway that lead to her father's chambers. Paintings of former Actondel kings gazed down on her from either wall, as if passing judgement.

The castle was quiet and dark at this hour, and the two guards standing outside his room were the first people they had encountered. They looked at Shalindra suspiciously but snapped to attention as her mother opened the door and ushered them inside before any objection could be raised.

The chambers of King Fabrian the Second were spacious, reflecting the luxury of the monarch who controlled the Gold

Road. Plush seating dominated the open space, and the walls were draped in expensive silks. A desk that had been her grandfather's had been pushed back against a wall, for her father rarely worked from his room.

"Fabrian?" her mother called. "I have brought someone you need to see."

Her father entered the room from the balcony. His evening robe hung as loose around his thick midsection as the jowls now did around his chin. Though few would have considered her father an attractive man, the past few years had not been kind.

"You." Her father's voice was laced with disgust.

"Fabrian, you must listen to her," her mother pleaded.

Though the shock of seeing his daughter seemed to have rooted Fabrian's feet to the floor, his mouth held no such restriction. "I should have you locked in chains."

"I did not come here seeking conflict with you, father."

"Why else would you be here? To beg forgiveness? Or are you here to try and take my throne?"

"I do not wish to depose you. I am here to stop this senseless war."

It was such an audacious statement that her father stood momentarily dumbstruck. "What manner of fool have you become to think we would do your bidding? The elves have stood in our way for generations. They've betrayed entire towns. They've killed our people. They dance around the forest as if nothing in the world matters."

"Having been to Ildalarial, I would disagree with that assessment."

"Your assessment is irrelevant. I had hoped from your attire, impoverished though it is, you had given up on worshipping that elvish nonsense."

"I have not given up my faith." Shalindra untucked her symbol of Eluria from her dress. "And I cannot see what profit you hope to gain from another war. There is no resource they possess that we do not already have in abundance."

"And they have squandered it! They sit between us and untapped riches."

"They are different, and have different ideals, but they do not deserve to be destroyed."

"Why should you care what happens to them? Could it be that *you* have something to gain?"

Warmth came to Shalindra's cheeks.

"Ah, so there is something in this for you after all."

"I am here for a purpose," she replied. "Peace between our two kingdoms is a step towards that purpose."

"Your holy destiny again, is it?" he said with a disdainful wave of his hand.

"It is what I am meant to be."

"What you were meant to be was a bond between two houses, and you couldn't even accomplish that! Your marriage would have solidified my influence and gained allies in the middle of the kingdom, but you tossed that aside. You should have gone to your room that day and waited, as you were told to do. There were reasons. But instead you decided to turn your back on your family in front of half the court. I had few enough choices to save you before your little tirade. You left me with none after it."

Shalindra was speechless. More than once she had wondered why she had said the things she did, but she had never considered that there had been broader consequences. But she had been angry. Angry at his capitulation. Angry at being dismissed in such an off-handed manner. She knew the pressures of ruling far better now, and if there was any hope of averting the war, she needed to set things right between them.

"My outburst was unfortunate, but in the wake of all we had been through, could you blame me? The wizards you allied with tried to kill me, more than once. I watched their demons tear men to pieces, yet when I spoke of the carnage inflicted, you did not believe they were there."

"Of course the demons were there. Do you take me for a fool? They were seen by thousands of people. Men whose opinion I valued far more than yours brought word of what we faced. I could have expected you to act like the lady you were supposed to be, not some soldier in the field," he said, his voice rising. "I wanted you to make my rule easier, not impossibly difficult. I wanted you to not turn the Polonis against me. I wanted many things from you, daughter, and you've failed at them all."

Had she misread the situation so poorly that day? Kentrick glanced away rather than meet her eyes, but her mother's look confirmed the accusations.

"Yes, quite the surprise isn't it? You are the one most responsible for your own misery. Had you not acted like a spoiled child you would have remained a princess."

This was going nowhere. Her father held far too much animosity to consider anything in a rational manner. She needed to shift his attention to some common ground from which to begin regaining his trust.

"But why agree to our enemy's demands if you knew the truth?

If the wizards—"

"I was trying to salvage my kingdom!" Fabrian almost screamed. "And protect my family! While you were dancing through the woods singing songs to the moon like an elf, my kingdom was being destroyed piece by piece."

The door behind them flew open with a crash.

Wizard.

"Ylnvan," Fabrian said sternly to the robed man who swept into the room, "I have warned you before about entering my chambers unannounced."

"Forgive me, my lord," Ylnvan said smoothly with a bow deep enough to be proper but short enough to be mocking. "I became aware of your distress and…" He stopped abruptly as his eyes fell on Shalindra. In the heartbeat it took for him to ascertain the situation, his hand flicked out and pulsing energies shot towards her.

Eluria's symbol was already in her hand, and even so she barely reacted in time. The attack exploded against her shield, sending angry sparks spinning across the room.

"Stop!" Fabrian commanded. "I will have none of your foul magic in my bedchambers!"

"Yet foulness stands beside you!" Ylnvan circled warily. "What false platitudes has she whispered in your ear? Do you not remember what she cost you?"

"I do not need you to remind me of anything," Fabrian stated, though without conviction.

"Oh, but you do. Did you enjoy being made a fool of in front of your lords? How many turned against you that very day? Were it not for our gracious intervention, you might not even be here."

Fabrian's face was red, but he did not back down. "*I* will choose how to deal with her, not you."

Kentrick stepped forward, hand on his sword. "Our family's business is not your concern, wizard. Leave now."

"Defending your favorite sibling?" Ylnvan scoffed. "Or do you also seek the opportunity to advance your own station?"

"Guards!" Fabrian shouted. The men who had been standing outside entered the room. "Remove this man."

"There is no one left that will uphold your weakness." Ylnvan waved his hand and the door slammed itself shut. The guards drew weapons.

"This is *my* kingdom!" Fabrian roared, his fear lending energy to the declaration.

"*Was* your kingdom. You should be thankful we allowed you to remain here as a figurehead, but as I find you now in congress with the enemy your usefulness has expired." Magical energy pulsed on his fingertips. "Such a pity that I was unable to reach you before your treasonous daughter took her vengeance upon you, but fear not. Your death will be avenged. Kill them."

I need you.

Her mother screamed and ducked behind a divan as a blast of energy shot towards Fabrian. Shalindra turned it aside with her shield. Kentrick leaped forward, and steel clashed as he met the guard's attack.

Shalindra had no time to aid him. Ylnvan sent energy arcing towards her. It crackled impotently against her shield, obscuring her vision. Too late, she saw the wizard's hand whip out, lifting Kentrick with magic and sending him flying through the air to crash heavily against a wall.

Shalindra sent her shield surging forward, knocking one of the guards into the wizard. Ylnvan stumbled backwards but regained his feet before she could do anything more.

She needed to get to Kentrick.

The wizard sent another bolt of energy towards her as a distraction, and when the sparks cleared, she saw a purple-black mist swirling at his side, a few feet off the floor. She stood her ground, keeping herself between Ylnvan and her parents.

Tormjere tumbled from the mists, his sword striking the wizard a glancing blow. Ylnvan collapsed with a sharp cry, clutching his arm. Before he could recover, Tormjere scrambled up and slammed his fist into his jaw. The wizard flopped to the ground like a puppet whose strings had been cut.

The guards put their backs to each other and made a push towards the door, but it did little good as one and then the other died before the savagery of Tormjere's assault.

"What manner of wizardry is this!" Fabrian demanded, leveling a finger at Tormjere. "You! I recognize you from the last time I saw my daughter."

Tormjere ignored him and checked for a demon necklace around Ylnvan's neck, but came away empty handed. Shalindra recognized the wizard's condition even before Tormjere said it. "He's dead."

Shalindra raced with her mother to Kentrick, who sat up groggily.

"I'm fine," he said, waving off their attention. "Just knocked the wind out of me." He tried to stand, but gasped and made it no further than his knees.

Shalindra turned his face towards hers and dove into his eyes, seeking the source of his pain. Eluria's familiar warmth tingled down her arm at her whispered prayer, healing the damage to his body.

"Better?" she asked, helping her brother to his feet.

"That was... creepy," he said, rubbing his side. "But thank you."

"You get used to it," Tormjere said as he handed Shining Moon to Shalindra.

Shalindra took the weapon eagerly, happy to be reunited with it once more. "Father, mother, this is Tormjere. He is the Ranger who saw to my safety after Erbac's betrayal."

Eleanor was still in shock but recovered some of her poise. "I must thank you for your efforts on my daughter's behalf."

You are supposed to bow.

Tormjere dipped his head politely. "Thank you, Your Highness."

"What are we to do with all this?" Kentrick asked, indicating the bodies strewn about.

"Fabrian?" the queen asked.

The king looked around the room as if seeing it for the first time, and his shoulders slumped. "I am tired."

Shalindra placed a hand on his shoulder. "As are we all, father. We have spent too many years fighting ourselves, and it has gotten us nothing. Will you at least consider what the elves propose?"

Fabrian shook his head. "You ask me to leap into a pit of vipers after strangling the one at my neck."

"What harm in listening? That is all I ask of you."

"It's too late for words. Half the lords in our kingdom ride under Ceringion banners, and many of those are more loyal to the

Conclave than Gymerius. Westholm remains in chaos. I think they have three kings now; at one point there were five. We have no allies."

"What of the nations to the south?"

Kentrick answered. "The dwarves guard their mountains and care little for who they trade with. Namarin sits content to watch us kill each other, ready to move on the Gold Road the instant they feel they can take it."

"The elves distrust the Conclave as much as you, and they have suffered from the wizards' predations as well."

Her father looked at her as if she had lost her senses. "First you wish me to abort our invasion, and now you would have me ally with those we sought to conquer? That would cost me the support of those few I can still count on, which is not many."

"Even when they know of this?" she asked, pointing to Ylnvan's body. "We came to this city with an elf, one who carries Ildalarial's offer of peace. She is waiting for word that she will not be harmed, and she would be willing to speak to you, this night if you would allow it. Time is a luxury we do not have."

"What we feared has come to pass," Eleanor implored. "We knew it was only a matter of time before someone attempted to seize what is ours. You must do something drastic or our family will face the gruesome end Ylnvan promised us."

"Very well, but I will agree to nothing that advances any cause but our own."

"I'll get her," Tormjere said. "But I'll need to get north of the city as quickly as possible."

"I can see him to the gates," Kentrick said. "But what of you three? There are other wizards in the city and perhaps even the castle, and if our household guard cannot be trusted…"

"They cannot all have turned against us," Eleanor said, her words more a plea than a statement of fact.

"We could get to the stables," Kentrick said, "and take—"

"I will not flee my own castle," Fabrian said. "Wake Lords Anton and Redivers. They are loyal, and will know who else is, as well."

"And Eugeron," Eleanor added.

"Yes," the king agreed. "Speak to no one else. Escort them here, and instruct Redivers to bring a dozen of his most trusted men."

"Yes, father," Kentrick said. He moved towards the door, but Tormjere reached it first. After checking the corridor outside, he preceded the prince through the doorway.

Hurry back. I do not trust anyone.

Neither do I.

Chapter Twenty-Seven

An Offer Presented

Shalindra set the bar across the door after they had left, trying to imagine how the evening could go any more wrong. She closed and locked the doors onto the balcony as well, wistfully noting the last reds of sunset on the clouds over the ocean.

Her mother took a seat, still staring at the bodies. The rugs were soaked with blood, and the stench of death began to fill the room. Fabrian, never one to imbibe away from the table, poured himself a drink. When neither of her parents said anything about the dead men, Shalindra rolled the rugs over the bodies so that at least they would not have to look at them.

"I would have you know that I am sorry for the difficulties I may have caused you both," Shalindra said. "Though I do not regret my decisions, I do wish the outcome could have been different."

"Save your apologies for when the others arrive," Fabrian said in a weary but still untrusting voice. "I would have them hear it as well, so they may judge without the burden of family entanglements."

Her mother's eyes held more sympathy, but Shalindra sighed and resigned herself to waiting with them in silence. Her father was almost powerless to alter the current situation, and a king who felt powerless was just as likely to lash out as to respond favorably to offered help, no matter the source. There would be time for them all to come to terms with one another, but for now, she had to nurture the sliver of goodwill she had, regardless of how it had been attained. Peace was her purpose here tonight, not happiness.

They did not have to wait long before a sharp rap sounded at the door. Shalindra was on her feet even before they heard Kentrick's voice outside. She opened the door cautiously, her hand on Shining Moon.

"I have everyone," Kentrick said as he entered.

Redivers came right behind him, his eyes narrow as they swept back and forth. He had had the good sense to throw a gambeson on over his shirt, and his hand was tight on his sword as he circled the room, inspecting every nook and cranny in which someone could hide.

Next to enter was a thin, balding man with a grey beard who blinked sleep from his eyes and studied her. "Kataria? My dear, it has been too long. I do not know what foulness has occurred here, but it gives my heart joy to see you and your father together."

"I am pleased to see you as well, Master Eugeron," she replied, "though I am now named Shalindra."

She caught her father's frown out of the corner of her eye. It would have been better to bring that up while they were alone, but it was too late for such pleasantries.

The last to enter must have been Anton, a portly man with the eyes of a vulture, and whose face took on a calculating look as he spied the bodies on the floor.

"My lord," Redivers said to the king, though he kept one eye on Shalindra. "What has happened? We were told only that Master Ylnvan had betrayed you."

"Betrayed and then attempted to kill my entire family," Fabrian said, indicating the rugs.

Redivers pulled back one and then the other.

Kentrick pointed to the bodies of the soldiers. "These guards obeyed the wizard's commands. Kat— Shalindra and I managed to hold them off until her companion dealt with them."

"There is another swordsman in the castle?" Redivers asked sharply, covering the bodies once more.

"He's the one who left already," Kentrick said.

None of the men appeared to understand that explanation fully, though they were all fully awake now.

"If I may, Your Highness," Eugeron said. "Could we begin with how this all came to pass?"

Fabrian motioned at Shalindra. "She can tell you, and perhaps I will understand it better this time, as well."

Shalindra recounted her mission to bring Enna and the peace treaty to them, though she skipped any mention of her desire to become guardian or the monks who had helped.

"And you have brought an emissary from the elves with you?" Eugeron asked when she was finished.

"Yes. They have twice attempted to parley with you, but neither emissary returned."

"No elvish emissary has ever spoken to the king," Anton said smoothly. "Are you certain of this?"

"So I was told, and I do not believe those statements to be

false."

Look back towards the couches.

Shalindra did, though nothing occupied that part of the room. A swirl of purple-black mist manifested next to an elegantly embroidered divan. Redivers drew his sword, and the councilors and king scrambled back in fright as Tormjere dragged Enna from the mists.

Enna snatched her arm away from his and leveled a finger at him in warning. "Do not ever do that to me again." She stopped short at the sight of the bodies on the floor, then shot Shalindra a questioning look.

"My lords, may I present Ennathalerial, Sister of Eluria and envoy from Ildalarial."

Enna composed herself quickly as Tormjere drifted back to a wall. Shalindra almost chuckled at his ability to make himself invisible in formal settings.

Kentrick stepped forward to take Enna's hand as he bowed. "Kentrick Actondel, at your service."

Enna allowed him to kiss her hand, though Shalindra could tell she enjoyed that courtesy only slightly more than the method of her arrival. The other men introduced themselves as well, and Enna bowed politely in turn.

Fabrian motioned to Anton, who drew himself up and spoke formally. "His Most Royal Majesty King Fabrian the Second, Lord High Commander of the Fleet of Lansdown, Duke of Merallin, and Sovereign Lord and Defender of the Kingdom of Actondel, is pleased to receive the representative from our neighbors in Ildalarial."

Enna looked unsure of what to say. She seemed suddenly small, an elf surrounded by much larger men, and Shalindra moved to her side where a page or squire might have stood. "Ennathalerial, Sister of Elurithlia and daughter to Manalathlia Elothlirial, chief councilwoman of Ildalarial, is pleased to return your welcome and presents an offer of treaty with the Kingdom of Actondel."

The minimum of formalities satisfied, Fabrian waved to a nearby table. "It is late. Let us sit before I reconsider the merits of this negotiation."

Shalindra wished he would have chosen somewhere further from the bodies, covered or not. Anton turned his nose up, but no one disputed his command.

Enna produced the scroll her mother had penned. "I apologize for the choice of language, but the Calontier felt haste was in order. If I may translate? The Grand Calontier of Ildalarial, being—"

"You may skip the beginning," Fabrian said, his frown deepening. "I do not need to know the names of everyone involved."

"Of course, Your Majesty." Enna scanned down and began reading. "Recognizing that continued hostility between our nations is a detriment to all, Ildalarial desires that, in the interest of peace and security, all standing armies be withdrawn from the border for a period of no less than three years.

"Further, Actondel agrees to renounce its claims to the Edar Wood and reopen access to the Merallin River.

"In exchange, Ildalarial pledges to make no attempt to expand its borders beyond the Edar Wood nor beyond the agreed upon border to the north, up to and excluding the Aldantan mountains."

"That's all you offer?" Eugeron asked.

"Out of the question," Anton scoffed before she could answer.

"Those read like the demands of a conqueror."

"The prior accords said we would split the Edar Wood," Redivers stated. "Those trees are tall and strong, and needed for the masts of our ships."

"Those accords have not been followed," Enna countered. "Logging and hunting continues deep into our forests, and there are many uses for such ancient trees that do not require cutting them down."

"If I may," Shalindra interrupted, in no mood to let this conversation degrade as quickly as her earlier one. "Might I suggest that we do not attempt to solve every conflict between our peoples this evening, or we will surely remain in these seats until this time next year."

That drew a chuckle from Eugeron.

"I would also point out that, regardless of what was written, Ennathalerial was only given authority to negotiate a cessation of hostilities. To ask anything more will place her in an unwinnable situation."

"These matters needs must be addressed," Fabrian said sternly. "The issues are linked, and we cannot succumb to demands for resolving one without the other."

Anton leaned forward. "There is also the elvish encroachment near Merrywood to consider, and contention around the eel harvests. The list of disputes is long."

"I agree that it is," Enna said. "And I believe that my people are as willing as yours to coexist in peace. But given the war that looms between us and the attempt upon your life, I beg you to consider taking the first steps with us. This road cannot be travelled in a single day."

"There is wisdom in what you have said." Fabrian fidgeted with the hem of his shirt as he considered.

"Your Majesty, it may be that Ylnvan's actions have forced our hand," Eugeron said, indicating the wizard's body. "We will not be able to pass off his death as an accident, and if we are to believe his admission of treachery, we must also conclude that he was in league with others who mean to depose you. There are also the other considerations which may play into this."

Fabrian acknowledged the hidden meaning of those words, whatever they were, with a narrowing of his eyes. He rose and began to pace back and forth in silence, then stopped before a painting of his grandfather.

Does it always take him this long for something so simple?
Unfortunately.

"I need Logian here to evaluate this."

Eyes rolled behind the king's back. Shalindra began to speak, but Kentrick stopped her with a shake of his head and a pointed glance at Eugeron.

"Your Majesty," Eugeron said. "It would be impossible to recall him here without arousing suspicion, and even if we found a way, we risk additional consequences every day we delay."

"I am less reticent about the delay," Anton interjected, "for decisions of such magnitude should not be reached rashly. But Master Eugeron is accurate in pointing out the implications."

"You are correct," Fabrian declared as he turned to them with sudden resolve. "I will go to Prince Logian myself."

"My Lord," Anton protested. "Given the current situation…"

"Adair is not far. Nor is there anything untoward about a king touring his army in the field, and a king I still am. I'll not pen a message that can be misplaced or misread."

"I think all those in attendance tonight should accompany you," Eugeron said.

Redivers objected immediately. "We have close to five hundred men who wear the green and gold, but after tonight I don't trust half of them."

"Then half is what we will take," Fabrian said.

Leaving the untrustworthy ones to occupy his castle. I begin to see why the Ceringions won.

Shalindra bit her tongue, certain that anything she said would only exacerbate the problem. Enna and her offer of peace had been almost totally forgotten at this point, at least by her father.

"Your Majesty," Eugeron said. "It seems that we have a number of issues to discuss which are unrelated to Ildalarial's proposal. Might I suggest that we allow our distinguished guest to retire while we attend to business?"

"You are correct." Fabrian turned to Enna. "The hour is late, and we should not trouble you with our internal concerns. Prince Kentrick will see that rooms are prepared for you. Both of you," he added, making clear that Shalindra was also only a guest.

Kentrick shared a concerned look with her, but offered his arm to Enna and led them from the room. Tormjere pushed off the wall and joined them.

The castle's not secure, bodies are rotting on the floor, and we're being sent to bed?

It is difficult to sway him when he seizes upon an idea.

I'm not even going to pretend that staying here is a good idea.

Nor will I. For once, I will join you in not sleeping.

And I thought that getting here would be the hard part.

347

Shalindra sighed. It was only going to get harder.

* * *

Shalindra entered her father's study the next morning to find him seated at the head of a long table, discussing some matter with Eugeron.

"You wished to see me, father?"

Both men stood and Eugeron bowed to her. "Your Highness, it is a pleasure to see you in the daylight hours and in more relaxed circumstances. I must say that the white sets off your eyes perfectly."

Her mother had seen to it that new robes were sewn for her. How she had managed that while the entire castle was asleep was a mystery, but Shalindra had to admit that the finely woven material felt good against her skin, even if it had sleeves.

"I thank you for your kind appraisal," she answered with a smile of her own.

Eugeron bowed again to the king. "Your Majesty, if it pleases you, I will allow you to handle this matter privately."

Fabrian waved a hand in acknowledgement and Eugeron retreated from the room, but not before giving her a consoling smile that served only to increase her nervousness.

Her father stood indecisively until the silence between them stretched uncomfortably long. Finally, he beckoned her closer. "Please, sit."

This she did, perched on the edge of the chair and properly attentive as she had so many times as a girl.

"I am reinstating you as my daughter and as a Princess of House Actondel."

She swallowed against the unexpected lump in her throat.

"Thank you, father. I have always been your daughter, no matter the words that I spoke in anger."

Fabrian seemed almost not to have heard her. "I was warned against this decision by more than one of my advisors, and I myself was reluctant no matter what intentions you profess, as it could be interpreted as a further sign of weakness."

"It seems everything is, somehow."

"But your mother was adamant, and so it was done in no small part to appease her. Kentrick argued that this would also allow you to return more easily to Ildalarial with your friend. Towards that purpose, I have also named you as our envoy to the elves."

"Anything that would speed Enna's journey home is welcome news." Her father was clearly building up to something else.

Fabrian's face clouded. "Eugeron has some scheme of how we can spin this as a deliberate charade to protect you, but the shame you brought to our family will not be forgiven so easily within these walls."

"I did not expect that it would," Shalindra almost whispered, the brief glimmer of hope that he had given her now dashed against the rocks of reality.

"Whether we decide to delay this war or not, you are to remain in Ildalarial until you convince the elves to give up their ridiculous demands, and to do so without their damnable dancing about. I loathe everything about those moon-followers, and I care not for their fate. When this is finished, I will have my kingdom. Whether they still have theirs does not concern me."

"That is an unfortunate perspective, but as they hold a similar opinion of your realm, it is the best I can ask for."

"Good. Tomorrow we ride for—"

"As for your generous offer of an ambassadorship," Shalindra cut him off, "you will need to seek another for that position. I have responsibilities of my own to attend to. I will do nothing to undermine your rule, but I am no longer yours to command." She inclined her head politely as she stood to leave. "Your Majesty."

The guards drew to attention as she walked from the room, but she did not care. Whether they named her princess or peacemaker or traitor, she would not allow Ildalarial to fall.

Chapter Twenty-Eight

The Enemy Within

Shalindra nudged her horse closer to Enna's, interposing herself between her friend and the groomsman who had been glaring at her. The man dealt her an equally unpleasant look as he moved off. It seemed that no one here liked elves.

Her father walked uncomfortably towards his horse. He was already sweating beneath his ceremonial armor of polished silver plate edged in gold. A squire set a step beside his mount, and Fabrian pulled himself onto it with effort. He sat easily, if a bit stiffly, and signaled them forward with a kingly wave of his arm.

And now we can finally leave.

Shalindra shook her head, but agreed with the sentiment. She was eager to be on their way as well, and the need to wait for the entire retinue to assemble was maddening. Lords Eugeron and Anton were tucked into carriages not far behind her, along with at least a dozen minor functionaries. Lord Redivers she had spotted in the van, leading a company of lancers.

Adair was close enough that someone in a hurry could have walked the distance in a day, but the two hundred horse carried the weight of their armored riders, and the carriages were limited in speed even on the well-maintained road. It would take them at least two days of travel.

She sighed, resigning herself to days of boredom. And anxiety. Eugeron seemed genuinely interested in pursuing peace. Anton and Redivers seemed willing to tilt whichever way best served their own interests. She had the feeling that their support was tenuous at best, but at least it was possible. Her brother Logian could undo all of it. He would likely be more difficult to persuade than her father, no matter what facts were presented.

Three days ago we struggled to walk through the gates. You'll figure it out.

I pray you are correct.

The sun seemed, at long last, to be gaining the upper hand over the rain clouds that had clung stubbornly over them all year, and the soggy heat was made worse by the complete lack of shade along the road. The cheerfulness of a blue sky was a welcome sight but served as a reminder that neither army would remain bogged down much longer.

It was on the afternoon of the first day that a rider approached at a fast pace and drew alongside the king. The man had blond hair and was dressed as a woodsman, but Shalindra could not get a good enough look at him. He and her father conducted a brief exchange, then the rider bowed and moved to the side of the column to rest his horse.

By the time they caught up to the newcomer, Shalindra did indeed recognize him: the Ranger Loren, who had followed them when they fled from Halisford years ago. He caught sight of them as well and nudged his horse into line.

"Your Highness," Loren addressed her with a polite bow before sliding alongside Tormjere and giving him a quizzical look. "It's good to see that your fortunes are improving."

"Life has been interesting of late," Tormjere replied. "And I thought you didn't like me."

Loren grinned. "I was told not to like you, which is different."

"How have you been?"

"Busy, in more ways than I care to name. There have been many threats to the Kingdom since you disappeared. Speaking of which, as it seems that past transgressions are being forgiven, we could use someone like you."

"I've got a job, but thank you."

"I gathered as much, but had to ask." Loren leaned down to adjust his stirrup, and his voice dropped so that the nearby soldiers would not hear. "We were given little in the way of explanation for this sudden shift and even less time to prepare. While I'm relieved that no wizard rides at His Majesty's side, I would dearly love to know why, and I can only imagine that you have the answer."

"Ylnvan tried to depose the king, we killed him, and now we're going to stop the war and everyone will be happy."

Loren sat back in his saddle. "I will assume, based on your level of sarcasm, that you are already aware of just how far from happy this situation is. I hope it was not the princess who put this idea in the King's head to ride to Adair. Three quarters of the forces there are Ceringion, and there are several Conclave wizards."

Why must they be everywhere we wish to go?

"His decisions are his own, even the foolish ones."

Loren chuckled. "I forgot that being circumspect is not your strong suit, but that is answer enough for now. How much do you know about this war you mean to stop?"

"Untapped riches to be plundered, or something to that effect."

That was clearly not the response Loren had hoped for, and the Ranger studied him before speaking. "There are other reasons you should be made aware of, but this is not the place for such discussions. I would caution you to stay close to those you care for in the coming days." He shot a meaningful look towards Shalindra as he set heels to his horse and galloped away.

* * *

They reached the fields and farms surrounding Adair on the afternoon of the next day. Shalindra spied Loren waiting atop a shallow rise, and the column came to a stop as the King and Lord Redivers rode out to meet with him. Whatever transpired between the men, both Loren and Redivers appeared unsettled by it.

Shalindra was not included in the conversation, but as Fabrian and Redivers returned she moved her horse close enough to hear what was being said.

"My lord," Redivers was saying, "is that wise? We do not know the disposition of any of these forces. The city would be easier to secure."

"Nonsense," Fabrian said. "We shall be safe enough here in the shadow of the walls. Lord Gilinster has ever been loyal to the throne."

Shalindra glanced at the city, which was at least two miles away.

"Set my camp here," Fabrian said, "and inform Prince Logian of my arrival."

Redivers' worry was apparent, but he bowed his head and hurried away, barking orders.

Workers erected and then furnished a large pavilion, around which several smaller tents sprang up. The smallest was given to Enna, which she retired to almost immediately. Having little desire to remain with her father, Shalindra joined her. It was cramped and filled with a musty odor, but having her stand in the open would only invite trouble.

Tormjere poked his head in some hours later. "Your brother's coming."

Both women emerged as the troop of riders trotted up the hill. Shalindra was not surprised that he rode at the head of twenty men fully armored in mail—her brother had always been one to enjoy such displays of power.

Logian drew to a stop a short distance from where Fabrian awaited him and dismounted smoothly, tossing his reins to a waiting groomsman. He was a tall man, and handsome after a fashion, though neither trait had been inherited from their father. His hawkish features held not a hint of softness, and he carried himself with the confidence of one used to command, striding forward with a vigor her father had never possessed.

"Your Majesty," Logian said with the curtest of bows. "We were not informed of your arrival. Why do you make camp here? And where is Master Ylnvan?"

"I make camp here because it is a pleasant hill on which to do so," Fabrian said, "and we shall discuss the other matters over dinner."

Logian began to respond when he caught sight of Enna. "What is this?" he demanded angrily, reaching for his sword.

"She is no longer a threat," Fabrian said. "Situations have transpired that force me to reevaluate the wisdom of this campaign.

Greater problems exist."

"Greater than our enemy riding beside you? We sat in council last fall and agreed to Master Ylnvan's recommendations. Are we not to complete these plans?"

Fabrian's face clouded. "Ylnvan's treachery was revealed when he sought my life. The Conclave's hold on my kingdom will end."

So much for keeping it a secret.

Shalindra had seen the reactions around them as well. Everyone from soldiers to cooks and stewards stood within earshot.

"Where is your wizard?" the king demanded.

"Master Allisade is… I do not know."

"You are to apprehend him so that we may discover his awareness of these plots."

"We cannot do that," Logian protested vigorously. "Lord Donatuc would surely turn against us. Had I known your intentions in advance, such conflicts could have been avoided."

"Everything cannot be known in advance, but if it comes to conflict, I am here and we will hold the city easily."

"With what?" Logian scoffed. "A few horsemen?"

"Take care with your tone, Logian."

The prince took a deep breath, but his eyes burned with barely contained fury.

"Sire," Redivers interjected. "Would it not be wise to retire to your tent and listen to Prince Logian's evaluation?"

"They gave me no time, and so I will spare them none. Your wizard will answer for this attack by his colleague. Seize him and bring him before me this evening. I will occupy the command tent as it stands. Inform me when all is ready."

Fabrian dismissed them all with a wave of his hand and huffed his way up to his tent.

Logian looked around in disbelief, and his face hardened as his eyes fell on Shalindra. "So, it's true," he said with even less warmth than he had greeted the king. "You've returned."

Shalindra turned to face him. "Brother, it is—"

"Don't call me that." He took an angry step towards her. "Don't ever call me that again. You made the woeful decision to abandon your family. Do not make the bigger mistake of thinking that it will ever be forgiven."

She had long since given up on that concept. "Your forgiveness is not why I am here."

If Logian heard her, he gave no sign. "It was a slow death your selfish display sent us towards. Why not speak the truth and say you're just here to finish what you started?"

"It is to prevent our ruin that I have come. This war serves no purpose but to weaken us."

"Afraid your elf friends will lose, or are you worried your little colony will be next when we're finished with them?"

"They have offered a peace with us."

Logian somehow grew more infuriated than he already was. "I don't know what lies you told my father. His ineptitude cost us the last war. It won't happen again."

With that he stormed off after the king, followed closely by four of his men.

Shalindra looked at Tormjere in alarm.

Go. I'll find a safe place for Enna.

Shalindra caught up to her brother just as he reached the king's tent and stormed in through the open flaps. Fabrian sat with a cooling drink in hand.

"You are a fool if you think I will order an attack against those who have our trust," Logian said. "It will destroy everything."

Fabrian shot to his feet, his face red. "You dare? This is my land. I am the king!"

"Then start acting like one!" Logian shouted. "You cannot cast aside allies like some useless toy whenever it serves your fancy. Make a decision and stick to it for once."

"Logian," Shalindra cut in, "you do not know everything that has transpired."

"Do not pretend that you do. You can dance in the woods all you want; it won't win this war."

"We will not fight a war of the wizard's choosing," Fabrian said. "Now get out of this tent and do as I command!"

"I am not yours to order about."

"This is *my* kingdom!" Fabrian shouted once more.

"Not anymore."

Shalindra did not see the knife that flashed in Logian's hand until it was buried in her father's chest. The world hung suspended within that single heartbeat, as unprepared for such events as those who witnessed it. Her father's face was frozen in shock, his neck bent at an odd angle as he stared down at the blade he had presented to his son on his fourteenth birthday. Then he was falling, and Shalindra could not escape her paralysis in time to catch him.

The tent exploded into chaos.

There were shouts and curses as every hand produced a weapon. She lost sight of her father in the melee. The king's guard rushed in side-by-side with Logian's men, no one certain of who they should be fighting. Shalindra started towards her father, but

Tormjere was somehow there, yanking her back. Steel flashed past her face, and Tormjere threw himself at the man who had tried to end her life. She tripped over a box and fell to her knees. Amidst a forest of legs and feet, her father lay gasping for breath, his arm twitching feebly. She crawled towards him, oblivious to being kicked or trampled.

Reaching him, she pulled the knife from his chest. He spasmed, and a bloody froth issued from his mouth.

"Father!" she cried out, turning his face towards hers. Covering the wound with her hand, she plunged into his eyes, but encountered nothing but a confused jumble of emotions and pain that defied her ability to identify. The words of her prayer tumbled over themselves as she sought to repair what had been done to him, but his head lolled to the side.

Why can I not heal him?

Tormjere was shouting, but she could not hear anything beyond the ringing in her ears.

Eluria, please. He must live.

Suddenly, Enna was shoving her away. Her delicate fingers pressed against Fabrian's bloody shirt, and her plea came insistent and fast, the normally melodic elvish words an indecipherable blur of sound. Shalindra could only watch and pray that it was working.

With agonizing slowness the gouge in his chest began to close. Muscle and skin pulled themselves together, and Fabrian took a ragged breath.

Enna sat back on her heels and took a deep breath to steady herself before placing a hand on Shalindra's shoulder.

Shalindra tore her gaze from her father's pale face and looked numbly around the now silent tent. Blood was splattered across the living and the dead, and dripped down the walls. Two of Logian's men had been subdued, and the rest lay scattered about the floor. Outside the tent the sounds of combat swelled and then ceased abruptly.

Tormjere had Logian pinned on his knees, both arms twisted behind him. She noticed in a detached way that one of her brother's shoulders was dislocated.

"You should have let him die!" Logian spat, his eyes wide with pain. "You are more a coward than he ever was."

Redivers jerked Logian's head back and held a dagger against his throat. "Say that again, usurper."

Shalindra stood and placed a calming hand on Redivers' arm. He dropped his gaze without apology, but offered no protest as she took the knife from his hand.

"You will always be weak," Logian raged, "and our house will crumble to nothing. I am our only hope of salvation."

Shalindra was unsure if she should feel pity or revulsion for Logian, but either way she was trapped. Had her father felt this way when passing sentence on her? "You are not the first man I have been forced to pass judgement on," she said, "and it grieves me to declare you guilty of attempting to kill your king."

"Your judgement is as meaningless as your threats." Logian struggled but was helpless in Tormjere's grip. "You will all be dead soon, and I will have what is mine by right!"

"I think not. I am sorry, brother."

Shalindra looked at the knife in her hand, knowing what needed to be done but just as unwilling to order another to do it. Before she could complete the thought, Tormjere twisted Logian's head backwards, and her brother died with his rage frozen on his face.

Why?

You didn't need to be the one to do it.

Shalindra handed the knife back to Redivers, who accepted it without comment.

Her father twitched, and a small moan escaped his lips, breaking the silence that had settled over the tent. Enna beckoned to Tormjere, who righted a cot that had been disturbed and lifted the king onto it gently.

Redivers eyes burned with fury as he rounded on the captives. "Why did you attack the king?"

One of the men looked away fearfully, while the other sulked in silence.

Redivers drove the hilt of the knife into the stomach of the more unrepentant captive. "I'll tolerate no silence from you, traitor. You'd best loosen your tongue while you still have it. What was Logian's purpose?"

"To free our kingdom from that fool's stupidity."

Redivers struck him across the face. "No one decides to murder their father on a whim. What was he planning?"

The man spit blood at him. "Hang around awhile, and you'll find out."

Redivers reversed his grip on the knife. Shalindra raised a hand to stop him, but the words never left her mouth.

Don't. We need to know.

Redivers drove the knife through the man's throat before turning to the second captive, who started babbling before a question had been asked.

"Prince Logian and the wizard met yesterday when they

learned the King would come here. They planned to lure him into the city and force him to abdicate. That's all I know, my lord, I swear."

Redivers looked at him in disgust. "Take him outside and hang him from the nearest tree."

The condemned man pleaded for his life, but a hand was clamped over his mouth as he was dragged roughly from the tent. Redivers addressed Shalindra.

"Apologies for that display, Your Highness, but we have little time for pleasantries. Can His Majesty travel?" he asked Enna, who still knelt beside the king.

"A short distance perhaps," she answered. "The wound was deep and caused significant damage. Should he be jostled, we risk it reopening."

Fabrian's lips moved, but his eyes continued to stare at nothing.

A panicked soldier ran into the tent and stopped before Redivers. "Sir, we're being encircled."

Redivers rushed outside and returned moments later. "Logian's troop occupies the road to Merallin, and we've Ceringions flanking us to the east. Their camp stirs. They may be aware of what has happened. Your Highness, with the king wounded and your brother dead, by rights you now have command."

Shalindra shook her head. "These are your men, and Prince Kentrick is now Heir Apparent, not I."

Redivers spoke insistently. "That may be, Your Highness, but your brother is not here and we cannot wait. This hill is indefensible, and there is no hope for us to prevail against such superior numbers. With our retreat to Merallin cut off, we are left with no choice but to flee into the city and attempt to hold until reinforcements can be arranged."

"And if we cannot reach the city?"

"Then may the gods take pity on us."

Shalindra looked back to where her father lay unconscious on the ground, wishing she had been stronger when he needed her.

This is not my war.

Just because you keep saying it, doesn't make it true.

"See it done, Lord Redivers."

Redivers bowed his head, then hurried from the tent barking orders. "We ride now! Leave behind what you cannot carry!"

Panic swept through the camp, which had not yet settled from the ride, and a mad scramble began. The carriages had been parked and their horses staked out, and so a wagon was fetched and brought before the king's tent.

"I am sorry," Enna said as Shalindra's father was carried out and placed on a cushion of blankets in the back of the wagon.

Shalindra embraced her. "I can never thank you enough for saving my father's life. I could not focus, and I faltered when I was most needed."

"In this, you are like everyone else. There is always difficulty when restoration is mixed with personal feelings."

Personal attachment had never affected her before now, but it was something to deal with at a later time. She needed to get her father to safety.

"I will stay with him," Enna said, climbing into the wagon. Two soldiers took position with her, shields in hand.

Shalindra turned to find a horse, but Tormjere had already secured a pair. They pulled themselves up as Redivers came galloping back and wheeled his mount to a stop.

"We must go now."

The soldiers who were available formed up around them, and they set off down the hill at a steady trot, not waiting for the unready. Redivers was leading them straight down the muddy hill rather than turn for the road. She worried at the wagon becoming stuck, but for now the soft ground did as much to soften the ride as slow their progress.

They made it to the base of the hill, and the ground settled into a more level series of undulations. The road to their left gradually converged with the path of their flight, both routes drawing ever closer to the safety of the city gates.

From the army outside the city walls a company in colors she did not recognize began moving to cut them off even before it had fully formed up. Only the broad but shallow creek which ran right to the city provided any semblance of a barrier between them, but the hostile forces would reach the gate long before they did.

"First Company, remain on the wagon!" Redivers shouted. "Everyone else to the creek! Defensive wall north! For Actondel!"

Almost every soldier veered to her right and raced towards the creek, leaving only a handful with Redivers to protect the king.

Redivers looked behind them and swore. Shalindra risked a glance over her shoulder and saw Logian's troops charging down the road towards them. Unencumbered by a wagon, their horsemen would overtake them long before they could reach safety.

"Go!" Shalindra shouted to Redivers, putting heels to her own horse. Redivers did the same, and soon the wagon was bouncing along with them. She could only pray that her father would survive the ride.

It became a deadly game of time and distance. The wagon hurtled towards the city gates, drawing even with the battle raging at the creek. Actondel's outnumbered defenders fought to keep the way open for them, but their lines were already beginning to crumble. From behind, Logian's cavalry continued to gain.

"Henry!" Redivers shouted. "Our rear!"

The knight saluted, grim faced. At his signal, the last of their soldiers pulled to a stop and turned to block the road for as long as they could, desperately outnumbered.

Only Shalindra and Redivers now rode beside the wagon.

An arrow struck the ground in front of her, and then another lodged itself in the side of the wagon. More missiles began to fall around them, and the soldiers inside threw their bodies and shields over the king. Flashes of silvery blue flickered above as Enna lent her talents to the effort.

Shalindra spurred her horse closer to them, fighting against a rising panic. The gate was no more than a quarter mile away, but it could have been all the way back in Merallin.

Suddenly, she became aware that Tormjere was no longer beside her.

She cast about until spotting him. He had set his horse to a gallop, racing towards fighting at the creek.

You do not have to do this.

You won't make it if I don't.

Shalindra reigned in her horse, ignoring Redivers' frantic shouts to continue.

The Ceringions had forced their way across the creek, splitting the Kingdom defenders into two groups. Tormjere vaulted from his saddle as he reached the gap between them, slamming into the

Ceringions like a battering ram. Men were blasted to the ground, and Tormjere forced his way into the hole they left before the next rank could react, his sword lashing out in every direction.

The Ceringions reacted in a practiced manner, regrouping to deal with this new threat, but it did them no good. Driven by his inhuman strength, Tormjere cleaved his way through shield and flesh with equal ease.

Spears were thrust at him from every direction, but what he could not dodge glanced away in flashes of silver that pulsed around him.

Stay with your father. You don't have to help.

I will not allow you to sacrifice yourself for me.

I wasn't planning on dying.

You cannot defeat them all.

His sword cut through flesh and steel, and more Ceringions died.

I don't need to.

His next cut spun the hapless soldier before him around, almost gutting him like a fish. Tormjere gripped him by the belt and lifted him above the fray. He drew a deep breath, hastening the man's death by drawing the life from him. The soldier managed a shivering, wet scream as his body shriveled. Tormjere cast the corpse aside and reached for another man. The Ceringion ranks disintegrated as men sought desperately to escape his path.

Suddenly the way was open and he continued his charge up the hill. A second line formed beyond the first, closing ranks into a bristling wall of spears.

Tormjere thrust out a hand, causing a swirling void of purple-black smoke to appear just in front of them. Into it he dove, emerging from the other end behind the confused soldiers.

As the mist gate closed behind him, he grasped the tendrils of smoke from its edges and sent them racing like a giant claw through the rear of the tightly packed Ceringions. Dozens died, their bodies pierced by an assault for which they had no defense. The savagery of his attack left them panicked, and they fell over themselves in their attempt to flee.

Only the muddy grass of the hill now stood between Tormjere and his goal: the knot of commanders standing with a robed figure.

A man with a plumed helm was pointing at him and arguing with the wizard, who only shook his head.

Tormjere kept his eyes locked on the sorcerer and he advanced.

In a show of bravery, a knight in polished armor set himself in Tormjere's path. Tormjere struck him so hard that his sword travelled through the man's blade, shield, and armored body as if it were a block of cheese. Unslowed, he stalked up the hill towards wizard and commander.

The knight in the plumed helm drew his sword, then cast it to the ground in disgust. "We yield!" he shouted.

After a moment's hesitation, those around him echoed his motion.

Tormjere continued walking towards them.

They have surrendered. You must stop.

They still have something I need.

He did not halt until he stood toe to toe with the wizard. Hatred was replaced by fear in the wizard's eyes, and he held his hands up plaintively.

Tormjere fingered the demon necklace around the wizard's neck. "Summon it."

The wizard swallowed. "There is no cause."

Tormjere twisted the chain tighter around his throat. "That was not a request."

What are you doing?

The wizard reluctantly took the pendant in hand and mouthed the incantation, returning his hands to his side the moment it was done. A swirling portal appeared next to them, and an ape-like demon stepped through. It surveyed the field in eager anticipation, then froze when it saw Tormjere.

Tormjere yanked the necklace from around the wizard's neck and clenched it in his fist. Pulsing fire licked from between his fingers, followed by a shattering sound. Dark tendrils of mist shrieked as they escaped from between his fingers, but Tormjere drew them close and sent them streaking like javelins towards the demon. They passed through its thick body without slowing. The demon jerked, then collapsed to the ground.

Why did you do that?

I'm hungry.

Tormjere watched the reddish embers rise from the demon's corpse. He needed them to restore his strength and satiate the emptiness that gnawed at his stomach without end. Nothing else could satisfy it.

A flicker of blue caught his attention, and he shifted his focus from the demon before him, through the swath of destruction and trail of mangled bodies, to the bottom of the hill where Shalindra stood, her white robes rising like a beacon from the muck of the battlefield.

You do not need it.

What happens when we're surrounded by demons instead of men?

368

We do not know what will come to pass.

We're strong enough to kill every soldier on this field, but it's not enough.

What will be left of you when it is?

The embers stopped, hovering silently in the air before him, so close that he could taste the burn that would come as he absorbed them.

I do not need a demon at my side; I need you.

One by one, the embers began to fizzle out of existence. Tormjere's hand clenched into a fist. With a sigh, he released them to drift away, watching the flecks of red slowly burning away to nothing until only the blue of her eyes held his attention.

That is the bravest thing I have ever seen you do.

Or the stupidest. The line between the two is often blurred.

Tormjere wiped his blade on the demon's corpse and sheathed his sword. He was now alone on a hill, surrounded by thousands of men who were likely wondering if now was their chance to kill him. He tore a piece of the demon off and turned back to the commander and wizard.

"Gentlemen," he said as he took a bite of the dripping flesh. "Her Highness would like a word with you both."

Chapter Twenty-Nine

Decisions of Necessity

Shalindra stood on a second-story balcony, surrounded by potted flowers. Well-tended gardens filled the courtyard below, and a small fountain bubbled pleasantly in the middle. Guards in her father's green and gold were posted at every entrance to the compound, and patrolled in pairs inside the walls.

Her attention was not held by the gardens or fountain but kept drifting to the castle at the top of the city. Lord Gilinster, ruler of Adair and head of a family with deep ties to her own, had been taken hostage. It was unclear who was in control of the fortification, but whoever it might have been was not friendly to the Kingdom. She ran a hand over her face, wondering what she was going to do about it.

I could just knock the door down.

She turned an exasperated glare at Tormjere as he sat perched on the railing, but her retort was preempted as Enna joined them.

"Good morning," she said.

"You look as tired as she does," Tormjere replied.

"Your father sleeps again," Enna said to Shalindra, ignoring him.

Shalindra's brow furrowed. "I would have expected him to wake by now."

Enna hesitated before responding. "He lost much blood, and while he is in no immediate danger, he is not a strong man. I am concerned there may have been other damage."

Shalindra hung her head in guilt.

"It was not your fault," Enna admonished. "Restoration is always more complicated with those you care for."

"I have never had difficulty with either of you."

Enna looked to Tormjere for help.

"We aren't family," he pointed out. "No matter how much you like us."

Shalindra recognized it as a valid point, but it did little to dispel her doubts. "We may be of different bloodlines, but you are as much my family as any who share my heritage."

There had also been no issue when she had healed Kentrick. It made little sense. If there was anything, the past week had shown her just how much she had missed her family. Now one of them was dead by her own command, and another clung to life because of her failure to act quickly enough. All she wanted was to care for those who remained, but once again she found herself responsible for far more than her own fate.

"None of it's fair," Tormjere said. "But the past can't be changed."

"You are both correct, and I must not turn to self-doubt when my attention must be on breaking the Ceringion hold on the city."

"I will help you," Enna said.

Shalindra shook her head, but Enna cut off her refusal. "I know you wish to keep me safe, but your father is well tended now. I need to be where I can do the most good."

Shalindra caught the hint of an approving smile on Tormjere's face and held her hands up in surrender.

"You are certainly not bound to my father's side. But there is no telling how long this will take. It might be best for you to return to Ildalarial while we salvage what we can from this situation."

Enna shook her head. "Absolutely not. Were I to appear without you, my mother would heap the rewards upon me. This will be your victory."

Shalindra gazed out the window once more. "It feels a hollow one. This conflict we find ourselves in has been simmering for years, and the chaos that has been unleashed could spill over in any direction. Plus, we still have no peace treaty."

There was a soft knock on the door, and Redivers entered. His eyes flicked warily towards Tormjere, then he bowed to Shalindra. "Your Highness. How is the King?"

"He sleeps again."

Redivers seemed unsurprised by that answer and made efforts to keep his voice positive. "It is my fervent hope that he awakes soon."

"What is the state of our forces today?" Shalindra asked, praying that she could do more for them than she had for her father.

"Less than fifty of us made it to safety yesterday. Lord Anton is missing and presumed lost. We have been able to make contact with the garrison, and the city itself is largely under Kingdom control, save for the castle. The armies outside the walls seem to have divided themselves by allegiance, though we have no direct contact with any of them. Some skirmishing has taken place between them. Regardless of who declares for Actondel, there are far more Ceringion troops here than our own."

"What of my brother's men?"

"Logian's banner is absent from the field this morning."

Shalindra felt a stab of panic. Her mother would be completely unaware of what had happened, and would not realize the threat should they seek her out. "Where have they gone?"

"We do not know. They either snuck off during the night or struck their colors and melted into other units. Either way we should have the jump on them. The moment we were safe I found our Ranger and sent him to Merallin with a warning for the Queen and Prince Kentrick."

"Thank you," Shalindra said, breathing a sigh of relief. "And the castle here?"

"That is more difficult to ascertain. It seems that at least one of the towers may remain under Duke Gilinster's control. The only thing keeping this from turning into a bloodbath is having Lord Donatuc as our captive." Redivers' eyes went to Tormjere once more. "We are fortunate he was persuaded to surrender."

"And the wizard with him?"

"He was stripped of all personal effects and remains bound to a chair in the gatehouse. He is... displeased with such accommodations."

"He will continue to be so, though he is too dangerous to hold for long. Which of these threats do you suggest we deal with first?"

"Master Eugeron may have a solution to several. I had hoped His Majesty would be able to hear this proposal, but given his condition it will require your blessings in his place." He held up a hand to forestall her protests. "We would all prefer it if there was someone else, but I fear that if we wait even the two days it would take a fast rider to travel to Merallin and back with your brother's answer it may come too late. An army left idle will find its own battles to fight."

"Then I would hear this plan at once."

Redivers led Shalindra and Tormjere to the first floor and across to the opposite side of the compound, to a comfortable sitting room occupied by Eugeron and the now-disarmed Ceringion lord.

"Your Highness," Eugeron welcomed her.

"Gentlemen," she said courteously. "I understand that we have come to some agreement that will prevent further conflict?"

"We have. Lord Donatuc has graciously offered a sum of seven thousand gold coins of mixed denomination in return for the release of himself and the men under his command, to be accompanied by a pledge of mutual non-aggression."

"And where are you planning to go, Lord Donatuc?"

"I intend to return to my home in Spolito, Your Highness."

"I have been told that you were most eager to prosecute a war with the elves. Why the sudden change of heart?"

Donatuc inclined his head towards Tormjere. "I watched your man carve his way through a few hundred of my finest soldiers while the wizard that sold us on this conquest stood impotent at my side. I have had enough of this sorcery. It may have won you the day, but it will be your undoing in the end."

"Seven thousand is half what you should be offering," Redivers said.

"It is what I have at my disposal. I have six thousand men to march across your kingdom, which will take weeks. Should I fail to pay them during that time, discipline will slip and some may turn to marauding."

Redivers bristled at the threat, but Shalindra was far more interested in ridding themselves of their enemies than seeking financial gain.

"Seven thousand gold," she countered, "and you escort the wizard back with you. He will likely wish to make his report to the Conclave firsthand."

While he's still got his hands.

Sometimes it is best to not *chop your enemies to pieces.*

Donatuc looked less than pleased at the added duty, but he bowed. "I will agree to that."

"When will you depart?" Shalindra asked.

"We will break camp today and begin leaving on the morrow, if you will permit it."

Shalindra looked at Redivers, who nodded. "Very well. I thank you for your haste in this matter. I will leave the details of the payment to Master Eugeron."

She rose, and the men did the same, bowing as she left the room.

Shalindra made her way up the steps, but her legs felt heavy and she leaned on the railing far more than she should have.

You should sleep.

How can I? My father is not recovering. The lord of this city is a hostage in his own castle, and Enna is still here rather than in Ildalarial.

You disposed of the Ceringion forces easily enough. We can take the castle and be on our way.

You did more to end that battle than anyone else.

Both guards outside her room snapped to attention as she approached. She managed a half-hearted acknowledgement of their salute as she pushed through the door and collapsed heavily into a chair.

I do not want to wait here much longer. What if the elves do not get word in time?

I don't think they'll attack first.

And if they do?

You don't have to solve everything yourself.

She almost laughed aloud.

Did I not advise you of that same condition once?

Redivers came bursting into the room. "The castle is ours! Your Highness, the wizard holding Lord Gilinster has fled."

"To where?" Shalindra asked as Eugeron entered at a more stately pace behind him.

"We do not know," Redivers said. "With your permission, I will begin a search."

"Seek the help of the city watch. My father's safety remains paramount. Please also communicate our relief to Lord Gilinster."

"He will likely visit us as soon as he learns our location," Eugeron said, "and will insist that we shelter in the keep."

"A suggestion I would gladly follow, but only once we are certain it is safe." She paused. "Did Donatuc agree to leave too easily?"

Eugeron shook his head. "Perhaps more readily than normal, but not more than could be expected. I believe that his objection to the use of magic is real. You would have no way of knowing, but he fought against you at Tiridon."

Shalindra remembered only too well the horrors which the Conclave had released on that battlefield. Even the Ceringion army had felt its terrible effects, though unintentionally.

"Put another way," Redivers said, "he simply wants to remove himself from another battle over the Kingdom. He sees the mess this has become as easily as we do."

"That eases my mind. I have been so far removed from the intrigues of the court that I am blind to many of these nuances."

Eugeron cleared his throat. "On that topic, I believe that there are some things you should know before speaking to Lord Gilinster."

Redivers shot him a warning glance.

"Were the situation less dire I would not speak of it, but given recent events she must be told."

"Be told what?" Shalindra asked.

"Why your father agreed to war with the elves," Eugeron said.

"No one was to know," Redivers protested. "Princess or not."

"I think that her loyalty is no longer in question, and a false step now could cost us more than this city."

Redivers acquiesced. "It's on your head, but you are probably correct. If there's any hope of saving this house, she will be a part of it."

Shalindra shook her head. "I must agree with your caution. My father may have named me princess, but I am here only to secure peace between the Kingdom and Ildalarial. I should not be involved in the politics of the realm."

"On the contrary," Eugeron said. "You are in many ways the perfect choice. Your father restored you as a member of the royal family, yet you have neither the desire nor standing to assume his throne. At a time when members of your family are already suspect, you are uniquely suited to act on your father's behalf without appearing to do so out of self-interest."

"I have not been in the court in years. My brother would be better for whatever tasks must be accomplished."

"Kentrick will be our next king, and though it pains me to say it, his time may come sooner than any of us desire. But any action he takes now will be judged through the lens of Logian's betrayal. If one brother could plot against the king, then the other could just as easily do the same. If you wish to keep him above suspicion we need you in this role, at least until we can solidify control."

"The queen and Prince Kentrick are both aware of what Eugeron speaks," Redivers added, perhaps sensing her hesitation.

Eugeron directed her attention out the window, to the hills still covered with tents and men. "The Ceringions won the war, due in no small part to the assistance of the Conclave wizards. Even had you defeated their army at Tiridon, the Gold Road was all but lost. There were indications that not everything was going as they had planned, and that was likely why they offered a truce when they did. Ceringion lords were established in many of our fiefdoms, but your father had maintained political control, or so we had thought. Much of his support fled before the ink was dry on the treaty."

"A situation which I had some influence on."

"To a degree. It was an obvious wound atop many smaller ones, but the embarrassment of your leaving was far less than that of losing the war. So we set about rebuilding the realm. Our plan was to wear down the new Ceringion lords until such time as we could expel them from our borders. We forced them to deal with the goblin incursions and the pirate activity in the Rossian Sea, further sapping their strength."

"These were minor things," Redivers interrupted, "and they were taking far too long to be effective. In the end, we needed something bigger."

"The elves," Shalindra said.

Eugeron nodded. "We had a hostile army in our kingdom, and when Ylnvan advanced his plan for the conquest of Ildalarial, your father jumped at the opportunity it presented. If the elves and Ceringions killed each other, we could not only recover what had been taken, but also expand at the same time."

Shalindra had dabbled in the intrigues of court more than once, even at a young age, but only in ways that would affect her immediate comforts. She had never imagined this degree of plotting existed within her own kingdom. The offhanded manner in which an entire nation could have been wiped out was unsettling.

"Why are you telling me this?"

"Because with your father clinging to life and the wizards dead or on the run, there is no longer any purpose to a war with the elves. Were we to proceed, we may well end up fighting on two fronts, and it would mark our certain downfall."

Redivers agreed. "Not only that, but to strike an accord with Ildalarial could further throw our enemies within the kingdom off balance. Donatuc will honor his ransom, or at least closely enough to suit our needs. He'll likely pillage a town or two between here and the Small Sea, but by the time he reaches the border it will be late in the campaign season and he will not trouble us until next year."

"So you are saying...?"

Eugeron smiled. "I will ratify the treaty on behalf of the Lordshouse. His Majesty was likely to approve it anyway, if for no other reason than because we need the levies to return to their fields. Beyond that, we need only the signature of an Actondel."

Shalindra shook her head. "No one will accept my choice."

"But the legalities will be met," Eugeron said smoothly, "Lord Gilinster will follow His Majesty's decisions, whether he agrees with them or not, and no one is going to raise serious objections over the elves. If he is told that this peace was already agreed upon, he will complain, but he will support us."

"And if he discovers that it was not my father's idea?"

Eugeron sighed. "He will likely brand you a usurper and imprison all of us."

Shalindra returned to the window and watched the clouds as they marched across the sky. The treaty was exactly what she needed, and why she had come here to begin with. Only one piece was missing.

"What do you want from me?"

"I think we have asked more than enough of you already, Your Highness," Eugeron said.

She turned to face them. "You were willing to go to war with the elves in the hopes of grinding down the Ceringions. That such an outcome is no longer feasible I can accept. Yet now you are willing to make peace with them while doing almost nothing about the existing threat. Why?"

Eugeron hesitated, and glanced at Redivers.

"Go ahead and tell her," Redivers said.

"Because of Logian's betrayal," Eugeron said, his shoulders slumping. "Your brother was party to every one of our meetings, and knew of our plans. His actions yesterday would indicate that he intended to further his own designs and may well have been playing both sides against each other."

"Or that he was already in league with our enemies," Redivers added. "His were not the only forces attempting to kill us. Either way, we must assume that others are now aware of what we intended."

"And again I must ask what role you expect me to play."

Eugeron took a deep breath. "You are correct, in that there are two things we wish from you, and I hope you do not think unkindly of us for it. In the now, we must ensure Lord Gilinster's loyalty to Actondel, whether that be to your father or brother."

Shalindra shook her head. "You could have simply asked for that, and I would have agreed. And the second?"

"The war with Ildalarial was our last hope for regaining control of our kingdom. That plan began to unravel the moment Ylnvan died, and by the time we escaped Logian's attempted coup it was left in tatters. Actondel has no allies, Your Highness. If either Ceringion or the Conclave decide to move against us, we may well be sending you to Ildalarial begging for an alliance. Should that come to pass, you could be the bridge to them that we need."

"What he means," Redivers said, "is that by this time next year, Ildalarial may be your family's only hope for survival."

* * *

Lord Gilinster arrived at the mansion that evening, at the head of fifty armed men. Shalindra awaited him arrival in the same room where they had arranged the treaty with Donatuc. Thought the duke had been a frequent visitor to Merallin during her youth, his attentions had always been for her brothers, and she remembered him only distantly.

Redivers had taken the precaution of placing at least three men in every room and hallway, and she would not have been surprised to find another hiding in an armoire. She was certain that Tormjere was the only protection she would need, but Redivers had been insistent on the show of strength and she was too exhausted to protest. All she could think about was getting through this meeting and gaining the signed treaty. It was her fervent prayer that her father would regain consciousness so she would no longer have an obligation to do these things.

Enna is doing all she can.

I know, and it is a blessing to have her here, but once again I find myself making decisions that should rightfully be determined by others.

You're better at it than you realize. It's why they trust you.

They trust me because they have no choice.

Eugeron entered the room and announced the duke. Shalindra rose to greet him.

Lord Gilinster was a tall man with thinning grey hair, and his broad shoulders and stiff bearing gave the appearance of a retired soldier. His eyes took in the room with a single sweep that seemed to supply all the information he needed.

"Your Highness," he said stiffly.

"Lord Gilinster," she replied with the proper amount of courtesy. "We are relieved to see you unharmed. Is your family well?"

"They are, thank you. I was told the king did not accept my offer of protection because he could not be moved?"

"He was sorely wounded during the attempt on his life and has slept almost continuously since receiving his injury."

Gilinster kept his demeanor neutral, but his voice betrayed his suspicion. "This situation is far removed from the one we arrived at in counsel with His Majesty just a short time ago. Can you explain what happened here?"

"I will convey what has happened, but I do not know if it will explain anything. Ylnvan, the Conclave wizard who was assigned to my father, attempted to kill him two days ago when he learned that Ildalarial wished to pursue peace."

"The wizards grow more unreliable with every day," Gilinster said darkly.

"His Majesty had negotiated a treaty with the elves, and it was given to me to escort the elvish emissary home. We rode here with my father, as he desired to make the proclamation himself. When we arrived, we learned of the fighting and that you had been taken prisoner. Prince Logian..." Her words were blocked by a sudden lump in her throat.

Eugeron came to her aid. "The prince became angry at His Majesty's decision and attempted a coup, attacking his own father and leaving the king grievously wounded. Prince Logian was slain and his conspirators hung. The princess and Lord Redivers then prosecuted an attack to prevent the Ceringions from seizing the city or striking towards Merallin."

"That a wizard wished the king dead is credible, but for his prized son to attempt the same is not. Were these two men not here with you I would name you a traitor and have you executed before the sun sets."

Redivers bristled, but Shalindra raised a calming hand. "I made decisions out of necessity, not from any desire to rule Actondel. This is my father's kingdom, and I have other responsibilities.

Until he is recovered, you are wise to look to Lord Kentrick for guidance."

"It grows difficult to know who to trust. More than a few have accused you of being the one to murder your brother and father."

She should not have been surprised by that, but it hurt her all the same. "That is an unfortunate rumor, but a rumor it remains, and I shall allow my actions to counter it more effectively than any words I might speak. I will be leaving for Ildalarial as soon as I am able. My father will return to his throne, and it is he whom you should continue to support."

The duke looked unconvinced. "We shall see. I will maintain my city, and honor His Majesty's accords, but we must have direction soon—and stick with it. Decisions so easily undone are just as easily ignored."

With a perfunctory bow he left them.

You handled that well.

It did not feel that way.

Does it ever?

"What are we to do with the king?" Redivers asked, breaking the silence. "Can he be moved?"

"Yes," Shalindra answered. "The journey may be uncomfortable, but his wound is sufficiently healed that he will suffer no additional harm. Do we have enough men to protect him?"

"So long as the Ceringions honor their pledge."

Eugeron stroked his chin. "I agree that His Majesty should be returned home as soon as possible. A king in his own city is stronger than when he is in another's, no matter how loyal a vassal controls it."

"We had hoped you would return with us," Redivers said.

"As did I, but I must see Enna safely to Ildalarial with news of the peace. I will see you safely on the road to Merallin, but beyond that, I do not know what my future holds."

Chapter Thirty

A Promise Fulfilled

Shalindra's arrival in the capital of Eitholmir could not have been more different than her first visit. She had slipped in almost unnoticed then, but this time she rode surrounded by two dozen elvish warriors resplendent in shining armor of metal scales. The city had thrown open its doors in welcome, and throngs of elves came out to watch. Mothers presented their babies for blessings while minstrels danced down the streets in front of her. It was an exuberance that left Shalindra baffled and more than a little overwhelmed.

The entire Grand Calontier had turned out to greet her, arraying themselves in a semi-circle in front of the temple grounds. She slid from her horse, and Enna and Tormjere did the same.

Elothlirial raised a hand, and her voice carried above the hushed silence that settled over the street. "It gives all our people great joy to see your return, Sister Ascendant."

Shalindra caught Enna's surprise at her mother's behavior, but in so public a setting there could be no contests. "I am equally pleased to bring word that Actondel has agreed to peace between our nations."

This proclamation drew a rousing cheer from all who had heard.

Enna produced the case containing the signed document, but Elothlirial stopped her. "Not here. The Grand Calontier will review it later, in a more calm setting. Come. We will retire and make our plans."

They passed through the Glade of Worship and continued down the trail in the back, entering the Glade of Atonement where she had been initially tested. Four of the Sisters Superior awaited them, including the oldest who beamed as if Shalindra were her own daughter.

Shalindra desperately wanted to sit down somewhere after the long ride, but Elothlirial spoke with the authority of one who would be responsible for the success or failure of what would come.

"Your day has been long, but I would ask your forbearance for a few moments as we must prepare for the timing of the Ascension."

Shalindra indicated she should continue.

"The ritual must coincide with the full moon. That which comes closest to the summer solstice is considered the most auspicious. Five of your predecessors have ascended at that time. The winter solstice the least favorable, but the choice is yours alone."

"I have been waiting for years, yet I continue to feel an urgency I cannot ignore. I wish to proceed as soon as you are able."

Elothlirial looked at each of the other women in turn, and received nods of agreement.

"Then it shall occur upon the next full moon, Her second cycle of the year, in nine days' time. Given the short span of days before us, we must also select those who will participate. Three shall you have to lift you, as Elurithlia was given when she returned to the sky. I shall be the first, as such duties have always rested with the Manalathlia. Of the others, one will be of my choosing and one will be yours. Whom shall you request?"

"I would ask Ennathalerial."

Enna's green eyes sparkled with happiness. "I would be most honored to assist you."

Elothlirial turned to the woman closest to her, the same old woman who had spoken in support of Shalindra's mission. "Avrilia, who has served Elurithlia longer than any of us, will you stand with us as we grant her Ascension?"

The woman bowed. "There is no greater service in Her light."

"Each of the three shall in turn call three more to aid them, as it was in the beginning. This gives us twelve, one for each orbit of the moon in a year. Are there any others you would wish to include?"

Shalindra shook her head. "Were they able, I would ask Sisters Adira, Marie, and Kayala, but I fear that none are close enough. In this, I must defer to your judgement."

"That decision may wait until tomorrow. Last, you must name your choice of protector."

"That is perhaps the easiest decision I have ever had to make. Tormjere will continue in that role, for I would never have reached this pinnacle without him."

Assuming you wish to stay, of course.

I'm not going anywhere.

Elothlirial spread her arms to include the entire gathering.

"Then we are called to service in Her light. To this end, and in Her glory, we must prepare." She dismissed the other clerics, who filed from the clearing.

"Come," Elothlirial beckoned Shalindra.

They exited the glade, this time turning right down an intersecting path that wound its way deeper into the woods before reaching a series of small buildings.

"These are the residences of those of us whose lives are devoted to Her service," Elothlirial explained.

She came to a stop before an ancient cottage. Its walls were of stacked stone now covered in patches of moss, with wooden shingles covering the roof. There was neither fence nor gate to obstruct the narrow path that connected their current trail with the doorway. The building was such a part of the forest that it could have grown there.

Elothlirial opened the door. "This is yours, as it has been for every Guardian. The Velantriar will reside next to you. The strongest protections we can effect watch over us here, and there is no safer place in all the world."

Shalindra had to duck to enter. The interior was sparse, a single room containing only a bed, fireplace, and a writing table and chair. Eluria's symbol was etched into a circular stone set above the mantle. Small windows allowed light to enter. The floor was of more recent construction than the walls by centuries, yet it was smooth and warped with age. The linens were fresh, as was the firewood stacked on the hearth.

There was a calmness to the cottage, a cozy familiarity as it welcomed her with a warmth that penetrated her in ways no flame ever could. She bit her lip as she attempted to control the emotions surging through her. "Thank you."

"Your road has been long," Elothlirial said kindly. "Rest tonight. Tomorrow you will learn what it truly means to be a Guardian."

* * *

The days that followed were a whirlwind of preparations. Shalindra's schedule was managed from sunup to sundown, and occasionally after. She spent countless hours learning the rights and responsibilities expected of a Guardian. What history Enna had touched on before, Elothlirial now conveyed in the most intimate detail. Every question Shalindra asked was answered without reservation. She was instructed on how to pronounce the elvish language in a manner that was reasonably proper, at least enough to navigate the ceremony.

She was told that the city outside was festive and filled beyond capacity, but the enchantments surrounding the temple made it immune to the noise. Thousands had hastened to Eitholmir to witness her ascension, an event which had not taken place in almost two hundred years. Bells rang and singers added their voices to those of the birds that sang merrily in the canopy above. Shalindra had remained apart from it all, her every waking moment spent absorbing as much lore as she could.

At last, all was ready.

The final day before her Ascension was one of rest and atonement, a time in which Shalindra was blessedly left to her own devices. She chose to spend its entirety in the Glade of Guardians, surrounded by the only people who could truly understand what she was.

It was quiet.

She walked among them, and at other times she knelt or sat in the grass. Food was brought to her, though she ate sparingly. She spent hours studying every detail, seeking to learn the Guardian's stories through the grain and texture of the wood that depicted their heroics.

Yet always she was drawn back to Illathalirial, the powerful warrior who had defeated the wither hordes of legend. Most of the shriveled hands beneath her feet were attempting to grasp her and drag her down, but there were two, each cupping her heels, that could have just as easily been seeking the opposite effect. It was a curious thing, one of a million curiosities she wanted to have an answer for. And how does one defeat a horde? Would that each of them had left behind something more than a cryptic phrase to guide her.

Shalindra wondered if it would be a demon or a wizard who would share her statue one day, and, if so, which of them would be standing above the other.

* * *

Dusk had settled over the forests of Ildalarial, and soft lights hovering above each of the Guardians lent the statues an almost magical glow. Enna stood beneath Illathalirial, wondering at what might have been, and what was. She was neither sad nor bitter. Had she the ability, she would change nothing of what had happened. But still, she wondered if she had done all that she could have.

"Do you consider yourself a success now?"

The words could have been her own, but there was only one man who knew her well enough to put voice to her inner struggles. She turned to see Tormjere leaning against a tree, watching her.

"Did you come here to pose that question to me or to ask it of yourself?"

"Maybe a little of both," he answered as he joined her. "But I only have to live up to my own expectations, so the argument is easier."

Enna regarded the statue once more. "Shalindra is where she is meant to be, as am I. I rejoice in the part I have played, no matter how large or small it may have been, for it seems fate has chosen my role as surely as it chose yours."

"There's a fine line between being chosen and being used. I haven't done the things I've done for any prophecy or god, nor for any purpose save my promise to see her safe."

Enna saw the tremor in his hand and took it into hers, and this time he did not pull away. "And have you put your demons to rest?"

"I think I'm learning to live with them. It's not something that can be given up just yet."

"I long for the time when you will be freed of such requirements. Do you ever think of what might happen when this is over?"

"Will it ever be over? Do you believe she will be the final Guardian, the one who defeats whatever it is that needs defeating?"

"This cannot continue forever, can it? Every conflict has an end. Every battle a victor and a vanquished."

"I intend to see her on the winning side." His hand slipped from hers. "No matter the cost."

She stared into his eyes, dark pools of determination that drew her into their infinite depths. She wanted to plunge into them, sink into who and what he was and let the currents take her where they may. Instead, she allowed her arms to return to her side.

"No matter the cost."

Chapter Thirty-One

Ascension

Shalindra awoke to a morning that was clear and cool, rising as the sun was just beginning to color the sky. The hush of early morning surrounded her as she followed the narrow trail from her cottage to the immense Glade of Worship. The brightest stars still sparkled in the slowly brightening sky, their luster not yet obscured by the coming dawn. The moon was absent, though it would return in its full splendor late that afternoon. She would not see it again until it shone down upon her at the peak of the ceremony.

The glade was expected to be filled with thousands of the faithful who would await her presentation as their Guardian at the conclusion of the ritual. A pair of Sisters hurried past her, carrying bundles of who knew what that would be used either for the ceremony or the festivities that would follow. They bowed their heads to her but did not speak, as she remained within her time of contemplation and it would have been inconsiderate to trouble her with mundane conversation.

Shalindra circled the clearing and made her way onto the curving path that led down into the Glade of Guardians. It was so different from when she had first arrived. Interest in the Guardians had been kindled anew by the pronouncement of her ascendency, and the rarely visited glade had seen a constant stream of visitors, so many that it had been closed along with the rest of the temple forest two days ago. The particular roots and turns of the trail were familiar to her feet now, and she caught sight of the statues she sought almost before she realized she was there.

Tormjere, of course, was waiting for her.

"One of these days I will catch you asleep," she said disapprovingly as she drew close. "What is it that troubles you now? Are you haunted by the past or fearful of the future?"

He grinned. "Neither. I just couldn't sleep."

She gave him an amused frown but said nothing. His mind was free of the turbulence that had plagued him upon his return, but the changes that had been forced upon him could never be undone. Yet he remained as good a man as the one who had rescued her from her would-be kidnappers so long ago, and she trusted in him more than in herself. No matter how her course became altered, she would never allow that opinion to change.

"We won't ever be the same," he said softly. "And I think that is what bothers you the most."

He always knew exactly what she was thinking and what concerns she carried. It occurred to her that it had become so natural, such a part of who they were, that she took for granted how special a connection it was.

"I do feel a sense of unease, though whether it is a greater disquiet or simple nervousness I cannot say. I am not certain that I am ready for what is expected of me, though I no longer harbor doubts of my worth." Her gaze encompassed all the statues. "They all gave so much, in the end."

"Yours will be a happier story."

Her eyes sought his, taking comfort in their calm depths. "Were anyone else to say that to me, I would consider them foolish for trying to predict the future."

"It's not that hard to predict. There will be a ceremony with lots of words and prayers, and probably singing. After that will come a gathering where everyone will want to talk to you, and finally it will be assumed that you have answers to every question and a resolution to every problem."

She rolled her eyes, even as she stifled a laugh. She looked back at the statue of Illathalirial once more and wondered if she had experienced the same doubts and fears before her ascension. Had the elvish warrior hoped that her fate could be changed? That she would not be forced to sacrifice her life as had the others before her? Fatalism seemed an unlikely trait of any of these women, yet all had come to an unpleasant end.

"I fear that whatever lies ahead of us will be so much worse than what we have already faced." She swallowed a sudden lump in her throat. "Promise me that no matter what happens after this, whether it be happy or sad, you will not allow me to lose sight of who I am."

"Never."

She felt the approach of someone even as his eyes flicked towards the path.

Enna's coming.

Shalindra took a deep breath to steady herself, but it served only to fuel to the butterflies that danced in her stomach.

Give me strength, Eluria, so that I may be what you need me to be.

Enna entered the glade and bowed deeply to both of them, and when she straightened her face radiated a joy unlike anything Shalindra had never seen. "Are you ready, Sister Ascendant?"

"I am as prepared as I can ever be."

Perhaps hearing the trace of nervousness in that statement, Enna took Shalindra's hands in her own. "With all you have accomplished, there should be no doubts. Believe in yourself, as we believe in you."

Shalindra gave her hands a small squeeze of gratitude. "You have done so much for me, both of you. Though I will be the one standing upon a pedestal, this is in many ways more a culmination of your triumphs than mine. I can never repay your kindness, nor will I ever forget it."

Enna's eyes misted, and though it was improper she embraced Shalindra. She dabbed at her eyes as she withdrew, then motioned towards the path. "It is your time, Sister Ascendant."

Shalindra put a hand to Eluria's symbol. It *was* time, and she was ready. As she followed Enna down the path, she felt Tormjere's thoughts return to the statue of Illathalirial.

They passed back through the Glade of Worship, now filled with people preparing this or that for the ceremony. No one spoke to them, but everyone knew she was there and a hundred eyes followed her. Those closest to her bowed, which Shalindra returned with a smile and a nod. Everyone wanted her to be as eager and joyful as they were for this event, but no matter the face she presented, Shalindra's mind was focused on those things she must do today.

They took the same path at the back of the glade that would

lead to her house and the other clearings that served as meeting places, but this time they branched off in a new direction.

The trail leading to the Glade of Ascension was even more narrow and winding. Vines blooming with white flowers brushed against her shoulders on either side, their meandering stems interwoven into the thick foliage and steered by centuries of guidance from those who maintained them. Together the vines and hedges formed a high-walled corridor left open at the top. Sunlight sprinkled through the ancient trees whose leaves rustled in the gentle breeze. Small animals scurried to and fro, and birds chirped their songs to each other.

Though she had walked this way two days before, their arrival at the end of the path nevertheless took her by surprise. An archway of carved, rounded stones marked the entrance to a small, circular clearing. At its peak, the arch was inscribed with the symbol of the new moon.

Enna came to a stop before the arch and recited a prayer with words which flowed like wind in the branches. When she had finished, they stepped into the clearing, and a curtain of vines descended behind them to close the doorway.

There were three other exits from the space, each marked by a matching stone arch set into the lush green walls. All but the one to her right were now blocked by a curtain of vines.

The one directly in front of her, watched over by two elder Sisters, led directly into the Glade of Ascension. Viewed from above it would have matched the center circle of the symbol of Eluria that Shalindra wore, as the small space she stood in aligned with the top of the outer ring. She would pass through each of the two other outer glades throughout the day, returning to this same one near sunset after completing her circuit.

The words Enna spoke next were formal, and their pronunciation more lyrical than the elvish sounds Shalindra was familiar with, but beyond references to herself and Eluria, she understood none of it. Both clerics flanking the door bowed, and Enna turned and passed beneath the open archway to her right.

The Guardian's Ascension had officially begun.

Shalindra's heart beat fast as she again followed Enna. She was thankful that her friend was there to guide her, or her footsteps would have slowed of their own accord.

The curving green tunnel had a timeless quality about it, as if she was moving into the past more than the future. Her feet crossed twenty-eight stones that mirrored the dots on her symbol, one for each day in the lunar month. At its end was another inscribed arch, this one adorned with the waxing half-moon. Enna paused to complete another prayer, then stepped to the side so Shalindra could enter.

Shalindra felt a soft tingle of energy as she passed into the clearing. In the center of the grassy floor lay a natural pool whose outline unmistakably resembled that of a half-moon. A low haze of steam hung invitingly above the Pool of Chalalia, the only known hot spring in all of Ildalarial. Two Sisters, one old and one young, stood on the far side of the pool.

Enna turned to her and spoke the formal words: "Now is the time to leave everything behind, that you may become something more than what you once were."

The other two elves responded in unison, though in elvish.

Resting on a polished stump beside them was a simple wooden case as old as the forest around her. Enna lifted it reverently and held it open, revealing an interior lined with a dense, fine moss as soft as velvet. It was set with indentations perfectly sized for both Shining Moon and her symbol. Shalindra took the silver disc from around her neck and placed it in the case, then wound the chain neatly beside it. She unhooked Shining Moon from her belt and set it inside as well. Her fingers remained in contact with the handle, feeling a certain reluctance to be separated from the weapon that had grown to be as much a part of her as she was of it. Aside from when Tormjere had carried it, Shining Moon had not left her side since the day it was given to her. The hammer almost seemed to shiver, sharing the sentiment.

Enna gave her an understanding smile as Shalindra withdrew her fingers, and closed the lid while reciting the next words.

"Now is the time for you to cleanse your body as you prepare to cleanse your soul."

Shalindra disrobed. The air was cool but not uncomfortable against her skin, and she kept her movements deliberate and reverent as she entered the crystal-clear water. The rippled walls of the pool formed natural steps, becoming smoother as the bottom twisted into an ever-tightening funnel which disappeared into the depths of the earth.

The younger attending Sister assisted her as she bathed while the older prayed in a calming tone. Shalindra could feel the tingle of Eluria's presence as their prayers wrapped her in a cocoon warmer than the water.

At a gentle pressure on her shoulders, Shalindra stepped off the shelf and submerged fully. The walls of the pool were white and the water perfectly clear, and she felt almost as if she had floated to a different place. She closed her eyes, allowing the deep, rhythmic gurgling of the waters to sooth her.

When she emerged from the pool, she was wrapped in soft towels. Petals from a multitude of flowers were squeezed, yielding a series of gently fragrant oils that were rubbed into her hair.

After completely drying herself, she was dressed in white robes that fell to just below her knees. They were sleeveless in the elvish fashion she was now accustomed to and as smooth as the finest silks she had ever touched. Her feet were left bare, and she toyed with the grass between her toes.

Enna had waited in silence throughout the ritual, and now she smiled as she inclined her head towards the exit. This time it was to be Shalindra who led the way, as a Guardian must.

The stones on the floor here depicted the mountains of the Three Sisters, representing the bottom section of Eluria's symbol. The mental image of the majestic peaks she had gazed upon every day while in the valley was reassuring, and the thought of their strength and solidity added purpose to her stride.

An elf awaited them outside the next archway, which was topped by the symbol of the waning half-moon.

"Now is my time," Shalindra said. "I must contemplate all that I am to become."

"What proof do you bring?" the woman ritually challenged.

"Now is her time," Enna said in answer. "She has held Alta Suralia, communed with Elurithlia in Alta Amalia, and been judged worthy in Her light."

"As Elurithlia speaks, so we must listen," the elf intoned. Then she pulled aside the curtain, and Shalindra entered into the second glade, this one also covered in a carpet of fresh grass, but devoid of any adornment or furnishings.

Enna opened the case so that Shalindra could withdraw her symbol, then spoke in ritual once more. "You must spend the remainder of this day in uninterrupted meditation. Seek Her wisdom, know Her purpose, and take comfort in Her strength. When you are summoned, it will be time."

Enna closed the case containing Shining Moon, and her green eyes shone with fierce pride as she recited the oath required of any who watched over such relics. "With my life I will defend Her gifts, protect them from waste and ruin, and see them bestowed only to the one who is worthy." Then she added, "And I will answer your call and remain at your side, always, no matter what may come."

It was Shalindra's turn to cry now. She did not deserve such loyalty, but she treasured it above anything she had ever been given. She embraced Enna again, and they clung to each other for long moments until Enna withdrew. With a final smile of reassurance Enna left the glade, and Shalindra stood alone.

You're not alone.

And I never wish to be again. Could you have imagined, when we first met, that our lives would be anything like they have become?

No, but I don't regret a moment of it.

Neither do I.

This is probably the last quiet moment you will know for a while. Take this time as it was intended, but if you need me, I will be here.

Thank you.

Shalindra tried to settle herself, but her mind turned almost immediately to what would happen after the ceremony. Would she be welcomed amongst the elves, and find answers for her questions, or would she become lost in the trappings of ritual? Would Eluria speak to her more frequently, or more clearly? Where would she go? Certainly, she would not remain in Ildalarial forever. She had done enough waiting. Perhaps she should return to Newlmir next year and speak to Eluria on the mountain again.

Time passed as it would. Her questions faded to musings and then into dreams. At times she sat, and at others she paced slowly. Her concerns about the future faded, relegated to her subconscious for a time when they could be addressed. She listened to the sounds of the forest around her as the afternoon progressed to evening.

When the sun was sinking beneath the horizon, it was time.

They're coming to get you.

Shalindra stood and found that the butterflies had returned to her stomach.

Relax. All you'll have to do is stand there.

A young elf came to the glade and seemed surprised to find Shalindra waiting and ready. Without a word, she beckoned Shalindra to follow and led her into the final corridor.

The floor was composed of twelve massive stones that matched the braided rope on her symbol, one stone for each month in the lunar year. At its end, she returned to the glade of the new moon, where she had first entered that morning. This time, however, the clearing was not empty.

Elothlirial awaited her in the center. Flanking her on one side was Enna, beaming with pride and still cradling the case that held Shining Moon, and on the other was an elegantly carved stand on which hung the Guardian's armor. Crafted from the same silvery metal as Shining Moon, taken from the sky ages ago, it shone silver in the reflected light. Shalindra's step faltered and her breathing quickened as she approached, already feeling the weight of responsibility that would come from wearing it.

Elothlirial placed her hand on Shalindra's head and prayed, bestowing a final blessing upon her. Then she stepped aside so Shalindra could occupy her place.

Shalindra was first brought a comfortably padded vest of white with embroidered silver symbols and patterns at the edges. Next, the short coat of silver scales was lifted from the stand and lowered onto her shoulders, where it settled as easily as a tunic. It was surprisingly light and offered no resistance to her movements, despite the snugness. Just long enough to cover her hips, slits had been strategically placed so as not to hinder the motions of her legs.

Each piece of the armor that followed was accompanied by ritual words. Shalindra would have liked to know everything that was being said, but the tone and inflection of each prayer came one after another like different verses of the same song, and she found herself enjoying that even more.

The spaulders conformed to her shoulders as they were fastened around her arms, and the white and silver belt was buckled on next. Light-grey boots were slipped over her feet, the supple leather rising to cover her legs above the knee. Greaves were wrapped around her shins. Slender vambraces shielded her forearms, with the curved metal set atop leather bracers. Every peace had smoothly curving edges that made it appear as much a piece of art as protection in battle. Once complete, the entire suit of armor felt no heavier than a thick coat, and hugged her body as tightly as a court dress.

Enna stepped before her and opened the case containing Shining Moon.

Shalindra withdrew Eluria's sacred hammer and hung it from her right hip, where it had always resided, despite its use by her left hand. When she looked up she was taken aback by the reaction of those around her. Not even Elothlirial was unaffected.

"Come," she said, her voice heavy with unexpected emotion. "It is time for you to be our Guardian."

Elothlirial led the way beneath the arch inscribed with a full moon and into the Glade of Ascension. Shalindra trailed a step behind, with Enna and the other clerics filing in behind them. The clearing had seemed much larger when they had rehearsed several days ago, but today it was somehow smaller and more intimate.

To either side as she entered were the handful of Sisters who would observe the ceremony. To her right, where he always was, stood Tormjere. His clothes were clean and fresh but worn as casually as ever. As Valtilaniar, he would be formally announced at the end of the ceremony, and at that time become her protector in name, as he had always been in deed.

At the center of this glade was a large, nearly circular stone. It rose from the grass surrounding it to about knee height in the center, an irregular dome easily forty feet across. Markings had been etched into its surface: a series of circles and runes denoting where each participant would stand to channel the divine energies.

Shalindra stopped at its edge. Elothlirial stepped upon it and took her place in one of the smaller circles, then tilted her head towards the sky to judge the progression of the full moon. The ceremony had to be timed to ensure that the celestial body would be at its apex during the ascension.

Elothlirial raised her hand, and the already quiet gathering fell to a hushed silence. "Faithful of Elurithlia, behold. Now is the time of Ascension. Before us comes Shalindra, second of that name.

"Faith has guided our people since time unimaginable. Now,

in the four thousand four hundredth and sixty-fourth year of Her eternal dominion, we are gathered to bestow Elurithlia's blessing upon the one who is worthy. We have shielded her with armor."

"As She shields us from the darkness," the assembly chanted in unison.

"We have armed her with wisdom."

"As She guides us with justice," they answered.

"We have filled her with compassion."

"As Her love knows no bounds."

"So shall she ascend!" Elothlirial flung her arms open to Shalindra. "Who among us shall lend their strength to this purpose?"

Though the participants had been determined days before, it was not an entirely ceremonial question. During Shalindra's recent instruction, it had been revealed that the position was fraught with its own dangers. More than one of those assisting had died during prior ceremonies, and she prayed that such would not be the case today. Shalindra heard the soft footsteps behind her as those who had been chosen assembled at her back.

"I shall assist," came a voice.

"Avrilia, daughter of Ormalian," Eloth intoned.

Shalindra felt a soft touch against her back as the old elf walked past and took her assigned place.

"I shall assist," came Enna's voice.

"Ennathalerial, daughter of Elothlirial."

Another touch on her back, this one accompanied by a wink as Enna moved past her to assume her place within a circle. Nine more volunteers were recognized, each placing their hand symbolically on her back in a gesture of support.

Elothlirial turned to face her. "Now is the time. Shalindra of Actondel, Elurithlia has judged you worthy of ascension. Will you accept this charge and take up the mantle of Guardian, committing yourself to uphold Her values and glorify Her will?"

"I shall," she responded.

"And will you use these gifts to protect your Sisters and our people in Her name, and as She would, wielding them only for such purpose as She may choose?"

"I will always do what is best, in Her light," Shalindra affirmed.

"Take your place, Sister Ascendant."

Shalindra's eyes sought Tormjere's as she started forward, and the calmness she found there was the only thing that kept her knees from giving out. Reaching the center of the circle, she faced Elothlirial once more.

The nine outer clerics knelt on cue, followed by the three inner. Shalindra's emotions threatened to overwhelm her as she took a knee on the stone. Every woman who had worn Her armor and carried Her weapon had done the same, in this very spot. From the first of them more than four thousand years earlier, the woman whose name was so similar to her own, through to the last, whose purpose had never been fulfilled, each had done as she now did.

I pray that I am worthy of your legacies.

Shalindra turned her eyes heavenward as those around her began the ritualistic prayer. The full moon shone bright above, moments away from being in perfect alignment with the inscriptions upon the stone.

Their prayers layered protections that manifested as shimmering, faceted domes, encasing her one after another. The first served to prevent anyone from entering the circle. The next blocked sound, rendering the elves' own voices mute to Shalindra's ears. Another surrounded her with a curtain of hazy white fog that swirled gently, obscuring everything from her vision.

Shalindra was alone, isolated from the world and ready to meet Eluria as no one in living memory had. Time seemed to slow, until there was neither sound nor motion. Something familiar brushed against her mind, calling to her, and she cast her gaze to the heavens. Directly overhead, through a small circle in the fog surrounding her, was the moon. Shalindra felt their prayer end.

Precisely when it was supposed to.

Just as the full moon reached its zenith.

At the exact moment when she was ready.

Pinpricks of light began to fall about her like rain, each streaking down like a tiny star that tingled with warmth as it landed upon her. She closed her eyes, for she no longer needed them to see. She knew the detail of every thread and fiber of her robes, every curve and inlay in her armor, every note and tone of joy that lifted from the voices of those assembled around her, every motion and movement of the leaves in the trees that surrounded them.

The brightness of the moon grew until the purity of its light was all she could behold. The trees slipped away, then the people, and even the rock beneath her, and in that moment of unimaginable warmth and purity, she felt the touch of her goddess as she had before, and surrendered to Her embrace.

"Eluria, I am yours," she whispered.

Tormjere felt Shalindra's joy, if none of her fervor, from where he leaned against the branches of the wall encircling the glade. The hazy whiteness of the barriers that had been erected between them did not fully obscure his vision, and the column of light surrounding her sparkled off the scales of her armor, causing the air inside the protective dome to shimmer like a midday heat.

The elves had begun another prayer. Tormjere could understand their words no better than Shalindra, but the twelve priestesses were giving everything they had to the ceremony. Elothlirial's voice guided them, raising in pitch as it became more impassioned, and the other women lifted their voices to match. Her brow creased with the effort of it. Avrilia appeared equally challenged, but Enna's voice was strong and led them back to where they needed to be.

Tormjere continued watching, waiting for something to happen, but there was nothing to see. Out of idle curiosity he allowed his vision to shift as he did when seeking the energy of a dying demon, and the scene blossomed to life. Rather than shimmering light, he now saw flickering embers streaking towards her. A lattice of silvery tendrils served to funnel them into Shalindra, and they sparked as they were absorbed into her being. There was motion in those energies, a rhythm in the swirls and eddies as they descended. Yet, despite the power that he witnessed, the ceremony was both calm and deliberate, even loving. It was like the reverse of an act that he had performed countless times.

Except that he had consumed more from the demons he had killed than was being given to her.

The pitch of Elothlirial's voice deepened, which meant that the ceremony had passed its midpoint. But it was too soon, and it was a small gift indeed.

He had expected her to emerge from this ritual stronger than he could ever hope to become, an equal to the might of creatures that he knew existed. The realization that she would not brought a bitter taste to his mouth. She would continue to be woefully underprepared for whatever was to come—strong enough to try but weak enough to fail.

His fists clenched in frustration as he stared helplessly at the moon.

This will never be enough.

~ No, it will not ~

The words carried an all-consuming majesty that pierced his mind like icy daggers, and he winced even as they melted to a distressful warmth. He looked at Shalindra, certain that it was not her thought he had heard. That could only mean…

Mistress Eluria?

~ So I am named ~

Tormjere probably should have knelt or bowed or otherwise offered some form of respect, but his question formed before he could prevent it.

If you know this is not enough, why is it all she receives?

It was probably blasphemous to question a god, but he struggled to focus as Her words blotted out every sense that he possessed.

~ The Ascension is the greatest request they may make of me ~

Can't you just give her more?

He hoped that thought was as complimentary as possible.

~ Even for those whom you call gods, there are rules ~

That made little sense, but he was certainly not going to argue the point.

~ That which cannot be given, must be taken ~

His skin was beginning to prickle, as if it had been left in freezing water too long, and he was thankful he was leaning against a tree or he surely would have fallen by now.

- You know of a way -

Did he? His body shuddered as a memory was dragged from the depths in which he had buried it, and it played before him as if he were again there.

The glade disappeared. He stood now on a rocky crag, staring down across a desolate plain dominated by a thick, conical spire so tall that its pinnacle, if it even had one, was lost in the dark clouds that perpetually blanketed the skies. The circumference of its base would have taken days to navigate, and its craggy surface was unmarred by road or doorway. Around and upon that spire danced thousands—perhaps tens of thousands—of demons, their massive bodies as tiny as ants from his vantage point. There came a terrible rending sound, as if the sky itself was being torn open, and the world shook with the rage of a tormented god. Streaks of red hurtled through the clouds like meteors of flame. Into the assembled hordes they fell, to be fought over and killed for in an orgy of power and death. When it was finished, every participant, both willing and unwilling alike, emerged with scars, but those closest to the top, those who had captured the largest bounties, strode forth stronger than any creature had a right to become.

The vision blurred and was gone, and Tormjere was left all the worse for having remembered it.

You suggest the impossible. I have never known such power.

- You have never asked -

Tormjere's mind reeled, too stunned with the implications of that statement to respond. Had Eluria actually offered to give him the power needed, only so he could use that same gift to force from Her what Shalindra needed?

Why? I do not carry your symbol, and I have never worshiped you.

~ *Do you not?* ~

She seemed amused at his confusion.

Tormjere had never… His eyes went again to Shalindra.

~ *Every day, since the first* ~

He was sitting in his home valley, hoping that the blue-eyed girl would be safe from the spies that followed her father.

~ *You have watched over her like no other* ~

He stood with sword in hand in the streets of Jonrin, facing her would-be kidnappers.

~ *Shielded her from darkness* ~

He held tight to her hand as the river surged around them, refusing to let go.

~ *Guided her path* ~

He looked out from a mountain searching for her uncle amidst armies who clashed in the fields.

~ *And stopped at nothing to protect her* ~

He stood alone before Mataasrhu as the demon beckoned him into the mist gate.

~ *And all you have ever asked for was her safety* ~

I didn't know anyone was listening.

~ *We are always listening. Take your place beside her* ~

His head ached from the conversation, but he forced his body to remain where it was.

Will it hurt you?

~ *Would it matter to you if it did?* ~

She already knew the answer as surely as he did. Without a sound he left his appointed place, walking past the startled looks of the other clerics in the room.

As he set foot on the stone, Enna's worried eyes met his.

What are you doing?

He slowed his steps just enough to allow her an answer.

Walking my path.

Tormjere passed through their barriers without any resistance, leaving Enna and the other elves behind.

The stone beneath him was bathed in pure light, while a hazy fog wrapped around them on all sides, obscuring everything outside. Shalindra knelt within the inscription of the full moon, her head tilted to the sky and her eyes closed.

The most wonderful feeling of peace enveloped them both, a deep and abiding sensation of contentment that eased away every worry and care.

Time slowed to a crawl, yet he knew that it was a commodity that could not be wasted. He stepped behind Shalindra and rested his hands on her shoulders, not understanding why but knowing it was needed.

He studied the stream of Eluria's gift that flowed into her. They were tangible things, little glowing pieces that fell from above to be absorbed by Shalindra. The memory of the demon ritual still fresh in his mind, Tormjere realized that the same process was happening here, but more gently. Instead of taking, the ceremony was an elaborate request, a prayer for a specific gift. Eluria wasn't just giving power or knowledge, She was giving *herself.*

His thoughts were interrupted by the delicate caress of Shalindra's mind touching his.

I knew you would come, because I needed you. This is all so much, so fast.

You'll be fine, and you will use this gift as no other could.

413

And if I fail them, in spite of what I have been given?

He realized that she was aware of the shortcomings of this gift, and of the almost certain failure that lay somewhere ahead of her.

If you fail, it will be because this isn't enough.

Yet it is all that they can do. And, as always, we will do all that we can.

Tormjere felt a nudge in his mind, and he knew that time was short.

She must be told, or I won't do it.

Do what? Who are talking to?

You need to meet your goddess.

I am already speaking with her.

Not like this.

What could he be talking about?

~ Sister Ascendant ~

Shalindra gasped as Eluria's words poured through her body like a warm drink on a winter's day. She could not breathe, could not think of anything beyond the glory washing over her, and could only be thankful she was already on her knees. Tormjere's grip on her shoulder tightened, steadying her.

Mistress Eluria?

~ It is time to receive what you must, but for none of us will this be pleasant ~

Mistress, I have so many questions.

~ For our next meeting they must wait. Open yourself to him ~

I always have.

Tormjere slid into Shalindra's mind, seeking her connection to her goddess. Finding it, he made his request.

Eluria, allow me the strength to give her all that she deserves.

414

Power dwarfing anything Tormjere could have conceived was thrust upon him. It permeated him, burning its way into every extent of his body, and infusing him with such strength and purpose that he could have conquered armies and brought empires to heel without struggle. Like an ocean trapped in a bottle it demanded release, surging upwards of its own will, dragging Tormjere's consciousness with it. Up the streaming energies of Eluria's gifts they flew, past mountains and clouds and even sky. Somewhere in the darkness lit by infinite stars, they reached the junction between this world and the divine.

Through the barest of pinholes, Eluria's majesty trickled like a stream in drought. The power Tormjere channeled sought to force its way through, but it was denied. Recognizing the solution, he seized the edges of that gate, twisting at the very fabric that enforced limits on both night and day.

Fueled by Eluria's own power, Tormjere thrust himself through the opening. Ripping and shredding with almost carnal glee, he tore from her what could not be freely given, and like a river risen to flood, the gentle shower descending upon Shalindra turned to a raging torrent. Energy unimaginable fell unto the world, and he funneled it downwards to where it belonged.

Shalindra stiffened and let out a low moan. Her mortal form seemed to dissolve into nothingness, even as her consciousness expanded in ways impossible to name. Memories and feelings flooded into her, transforming her in strange and joyous ways.

She soared through the stars, travelled across ancient deserts to battle desiccated corpses brought to life, slew dragons, and brought order to a vast wilderness. The joys of a thousand childbirths threw her soul into ecstasy. Lore long forgotten came to her, but in pieces and fragments and strange groupings. There was a pattern to it, but she remained unaware of its predictability. Faraway lands, cosmic secrets, and places that had never seen a mortal's footsteps passed into her awareness.

Then, like a vessel filled to overflowing, her perceptions began to buckle. She grasped desperately for something tangible, but there was no reality from which she could escape, and her consciousness plummeted into the chaos of a world torn asunder.

Tormjere could feel her tumbling, lost to what was happening or why. He sought her mind, but it was in a thousand places at once. Cracks fractured the walls of reality around them.

It was too much.

He tried to free himself from power consuming him, to seal the gate and return to her or somehow slow its effects. But the power he channeled had a mind of its own and continued ravaging its prey regardless of his every attempt.

Shalindra's terror bombarded him suddenly from every direction. That blast of pain severed him from the power's control and sent him hurtling downwards. His eyes snapped open, and he was once more standing with his hands on her shoulders.

He had to get back to her.

He closed his eyes and forced his thoughts back to that place, seeking her mind, but it was as futile as grasping at clouds. Shalindra's body began to shake. He watched helplessly as embers of silvery power shot across his vision and disappeared into her. They needed to abort the ritual. Could no one see that it was wrong? He threw himself at the stream of Eluria's power, desperate to regain control before it drowned her with the very gifts that were meant to be her salvation. It resisted, forcing ever more… into her!

If it could not be breached or bent, could he follow it and reach her in the same way it did?

He conjured a memory of a flower he had seen earlier that day and thrust it into the stream. It stung like a thorn-prick as it left him, then shot downwards, a tiny flicker of red in a river of silver. He watched it until it landed inside her, illuminating Shalindra's mind like a beacon in the night. He made fleeting contact, but she disappeared again. Tormjere could no longer remember what he had just given her, but knew it had worked. He sent another memory into the stream, then another, tracking each sliver of redness steadily closer to her.

Eluria's helplessness washed over him.

- You must not. The cost is too great -

The calmness of his reply surprised even himself.

No. Not really.

Shalindra felt Tormjere's mind as it latched onto hers, supplying an anchor on which to focus within the incomprehensibility enveloping her. She clung to him, the only constant in a consciousness that was multiplying at an incomprehensible rate. Something pushed her towards him even as he pulled her closer, and the swirl of chaos receded briefly.

Eddies of what could only be described as raw energy whipped around her. She experienced the ultimate rapture as Eluria's mind touched hers, and suddenly she could comprehend fragments of what she was witnessing. With a new frame of reference, one no longer bound by mortal limits, Shalindra opened her eyes and began to think like a god.

She maintained her anchor to Tormjere as chaos sorted itself into order. Memories were arranged into complex, multi-dimensioned structures that began to align themselves in predictable ways, like a tapestry that had been burned full of holes but which could still be read. Her efforts were disrupted when a sharp pain sliced its way across the threads she was weaving.

What was that?

She sought the source of that feeling, for it was somehow far more familiar than the others. She discovered new images flowing into her, of demons and dark ceremonies. Of torment and agony. Of fighting in a barren landscape. Of things that were not of Eluria.

Why are you giving this to me?

You'll need... it.

I have more than I could have ever dreamed. You could simply have told me what I needed to know.

It... isn't the same. This way... is better.

He was holding something back, but she did not know what. Was he in pain? She reordered the layers of consciousness to make it less difficult to focus.

She sought the line that tethered her to him, seeing it as a red-tinged rope stretched tightly between their minds. But there was movement, a directional flow to that tenuous link by which she grounded herself. She examined it closely, allowing it to solidify into a series of images and scenes. In one, she saw a youthful Blackwolf as a puppy, and she smiled at his mischief. Then another of her brother sitting on his favorite rock in the creek.

But I do not have a brother with dark hair.

The image was gone before she could examine it, replaced by the burn of demonic flesh as she feasted on the dying creature. Different, more cosmically divine experiences sought to interpose themselves, but she forced her way past them. With some effort, she narrowed her thoughts to only those along the tether while storing the others for later. His memories seemed to follow the same pattern as those from her goddess yet felt subtly different, becoming her own as surely as if she had lived them herself.

She felt his hands contort on her shoulders. What was he doing that hurt him so much? Something was not right, but she could not even begin to identify it amidst the unfamiliarity of her own senses.

A memory of the demon ceremony was thrust before her from an unknown direction, and she watched, as he had been forced to relive it moments earlier. There did not seem to be any pain for the participants, beyond that which they inflicted on each other. She shuddered with the realization that he was taking parts of Eluria and giving them to her in the same way that the demons had, yet did so with Eluria's blessing. She cast her gaze up within the memory and saw the demon goddess, snarling in pain, fighting as each drop of power was torn from her body. She watched as the mightiest demons slaughtered thousands of lesser creatures to gain that power which fell from her torments.

If Tormjere's memories were mixed in now, then... Another scene flew past, of a young girl with long blonde hair and beautiful blue eyes running after a dog towards her, and...

Shalindra knew. She knew with horrible certainty what Tormjere was doing.

No, you must not!

The prophecy's right.

It is not—we can find another way. Not like this.

She felt his hands begin to tremble.

I did find a way to you.

No…no…no…

The memories of a lifetime that was not hers came pouring in faster. She sought to sever their connection, to push them away, but it was like fighting a waterfall.

You are meant to go where only one may walk.

No, no, please, no.

Shalindra clutched frantically at his hand, wanting it to stop. She tried to rise but could not. It was never supposed to be this way.

The final wall between them shattered, and his consciousness merged with hers like never before.

The burning pain of a million cuts swept over her, tearing a scream from her mouth that obliterated the fragile reality she had constructed. Cast helplessly into a swirling void of impossibility battling with insanity, her skin was peeled from her body only to regrow and be torn from her again as she tumbled down an infinite hill of razor-sharp blades, slicing her into endlessly smaller pieces.

Then a different pain, a physical pain, forced its way into her mind. She focused on it. It was a grip, a squeeze, a… hand on her shoulder. *His* hand on her shoulder!

She struggled to form an image of what a hand might look like, or her shoulder.

What was a shoulder?

Why was she standing in the ocean?

It is being torn from me.

Who is me?

A silvery shape of mist and light slid through the torrent of pain and chaos of her perceptions. But she was ephemeral and had no means to reach back.

Her shoulder!

She focused on that again. Arms attach to shoulders. She had little sense of what a shoulder might connect to, but she produced one anyway. A stream of black goo appeared and swirled around the shoulder. No, that was not an arm.

She searched helplessly for something called an arm.

Another appendage appeared, covered in hair—no, fur—and oddly angled. It dissolved to dust as the pain swept it away.

The thing coming towards her, reaching towards her—a hand! On an arm, and… her left arm shot forward and locked wrists with it. Its grip was weak, but energy pulsed through it.

Reality lurched.

She slammed down on the floor, cracking the marble tiles as if they were eggshells. She grabbed the edge of whatever was beside her and forced herself to her feet. Around her, in every direction, swirled the red torrent of his pain.

You… must…

Shalindra knew what she had to do. She knew how to do it. She allowed her perception to shift, and through her tears she saw the embers of him spinning away.

No.

Darkness exploded from her, casting aside the chaos, the pain, the floor she stood on, even her connection to Eluria. She forced everything away until nothing remained.

Nothing but embers of red floating in the infinite darkness.

All that I am, all that I will be…

Her soul screamed in agony as she drew them towards her, one by one.

I love you.

And then he was gone.

Epilogue

And it was that Eluria staggered against the side of the floating, marble-edged pool before losing her grip and collapsing heavily to the floor. Her eyes, completely black and dotted with stars, and with irises white in the shape of the full moon, lost focus as she fought desperately against the all-consuming pain that enveloped every part of her being. Dull and torn were her shimmering silver robes, a once magnificent garment which now fell haphazardly about her shriveled skin. Such was the illusion, the projected reality that she displayed, for even the gods needed a frame of reference to communicate.

Willingly, even eagerly, had she participated, yet her essence had been violated to an extent undreamed of. She hurt in ways that a god should never hurt, and her luster lay tarnished in ways few could have imagined. The others looked on with varying degrees of concern but offered not their assistance.

Such was not their way.

"So much was taken," came the delicate words of Amalthee, lady of wealth and wisdom. She brushed aside a ringlet of shimmering golden hair and wrote with a purposeful and graceful script upon the pages of a large tome held open in one arm.

It was Lithandris, slender and alert as a cat in the woods, who responded. "Yet so much more was given. For a mortal, I would never have thought such a thing possible."

Eluria summoned to herself a chair and struggled upon it, frail and weak, a mere shadow of her former self.

"So well were they chosen," observed Amalthee.

Remulus, Lord of Battles, loomed half again taller than the others as he rose scowling from his seat, and, in a booming voice that would make craven the bravest of men, flung his words like stones at an enemy. "This is not what had been agreed. Repercussions of the most dire nature shall emerge from this course of action, most especially given your current condition."

Eluria's sense of herself remained vague and distorted, but well aware was she of his implied meaning.

But it was Amalthee who replied with a calm accounting. "And yet now we have been presented with even greater advantage. Many and varied are the tasks which shall be made less exigent." And she thought for a moment, then continued her writing.

Hers was an attitude which angered Remulus, who stomped his foot and tossed his head so violently it shook fiery embers from his beard. "Will they? In all of time and across creation beyond measure, such as this has never been conceived! And for sound reasoning! The consequences—"

Eluria's brittle voice cut through his words and brought them all to silence. "I am most aware of the issues now arisen, particularly those with which I influence my own fate. That which cannot be undone is now done, and, therefore, adjustments shall we make."

The god of war scowled at her with a fury of such potency it could have laid waste to an empire, but his bitter retort was held fast behind clenched teeth.

Eluria drew herself upright, seeking to regain a flicker of her composure before she continued. "Each of us here has a part still to play in this. I have done... mine, as you must all continue to do yours."

Silent condonement was given by those around her, some more reluctantly than others, before each disappearing as they set themselves to their appointed tasks.

Lithandris held back, as was his wont. The misty white void that surrounded their gathering place eased closer to the pair, until at last they stood alone on a fragment floating in the nothing.

It was with no small curiosity that he asked of Eluria, "What did you take?"

This gave Eluria pause, for she had been apprehended and could no longer withhold her prize from him.

She stretched forth her left hand, slowly uncurling her fingers. Above her ravaged palm floated a small, bluish pearl that glowed and pulsed as fiery swirls of crimson streaked across its surface. It possessed at the same time both a manner of insignificance and an aura of vast determination.

Intently did Lithandris study this peculiarity. "Long have I wondered what that would resemble. It is a wonderous, if dangerous, thing."

"Could you have done it? Could any of us?"

Her questions amused Lithandris, who raised an eyebrow. "Of course not, for it is not in our nature." The god of the forest took fresh appraisal of her distressed state. "And its affect upon you appears… unsettling."

The orb floated towards Eluria's chest, passing into her with an unfamiliar sensation. Her breath came quickly as her lips parted, and the stars in her eyes flared with insurmountable resolve.

"No, not really."

Witness the thrilling conclusion to
the Guardian's Prophecy series!

GUARDIAN'S PROPHECY: BOOK FOUR

NEW MOON
RISING

Arriving Fall 2021

MEET THE AUTHOR

David A. Godwin was born in Tennessee, during a simpler era when daydreaming was still allowed. Though successful in a number of more practical pursuits, he prefers to spend his time exploring made-up worlds filled with magical creatures and endless possibilities, and is often observed in deep conversation with his imaginary friends.

VISIT THE AUTHOR AT

www.dagodwin.com

for
The Latest News
Upcoming Releases
Exclusive Content